Amber

of STEEPLECHASE

LOIS KULP

AMBER OF STEEPLECHASE
by Lois Kulp

Copyright © 2022
All rights reserved.

Library of Congress Control Number: 2022946584
International Standard Book Number: 978-1-60126-831-0

Masthof Press
219 Mill Road | Morgantown, PA 19543-9516
www.Masthof.com

MORE BOOKS

by Lois Kulp

Bittersweet Hollow

Dudley of Finney's Station

Heather

The Inn at the Mill

Lord of the Abbey

The Maid on Crow Hill

The Parson of Hunter Hall

The Village of Birches Ford

In memory of my brother

David

whose humor cheered our lives

and who died

too soon.

PROLOGUE

He stood by his horse, his hand on the saddle, his tall, slim body silhouetted by the setting sun. The young man was only vaguely aware of the brilliance of the red and golden sky that shouted of the work of an almighty God. However, the young man's thoughts were neither on God, nor the horse by his side. He merely gazed unblinkingly to the far horizon, his face grim. He was a handsome man with wide shoulders and firm chin. His dark hair lifted in the evening breeze and his blue eyes stared into space, seeing something his horse could not see. His heart was heavy with doubt and uncertainty and once he sighed heavily. After several minutes, he tore his eyes from the far horizon, and looking down at his shoe, kicked a stone out of his path. And then, having made his decision, he mounted his horse, flicked the reins and rode down the road at an easy trot.

After riding a mile or so into the twilight of the late summer evening, he arrived in a sleepy little town just as the clock on the town hall struck nine. He rode more slowly now, his eyes alert. After passing the mercantile, the candle shop, the bank and the post office, he arrived at the Dogcart Inn and here he reined in his horse and dismounted. With determined face, he tethered his horse. However, he did not enter the inn. Instead, he walked past the inn and turned down a path that soon led into the town park. It was a rather large park with a good-sized pond with many goldfish swimming happily in it. There were a few paths twisting among the many tall trees and flowering bushes throughout the park. After a while, he came to a wooden bench nestled in the shadows of the surrounding foliage, and here he took a seat. Yes, this should be a good spot. He would just sit and wait and if he saw nothing, he would go home again.

But he was uneasy. He let his mind review the events of the last couple weeks. Something was not right. There were subtle differences in her behavior. He felt like he had lost some connection to her that he had enjoyed earlier. One time recently, she started to speak and then stopped short as if nearly revealing something she did not mean for him to know. And just last evening, when he invited her to ride with him to see a carriage he was considering buying, she said she could not, and she was clearly uneasy when he pressed her for a reason. Finally, she just said she promised her cousin she would come for a visit. However, her eyes strayed from his face as she spoke, and he doubted it was the truth, He remembered his brother's words to him just a few days ago. He said he saw her in the park with someone else. It was very unsettling and he wanted to know the truth, however it may hurt. He would sit here and wait. Come what may.

He sat there for a half an hour. There was not much going on here. During the week the town went to bed early. Finally, one couple came toward him and his heartbeat quickened, but it was no one he knew. After another fifteen minutes, he got up and quietly walked through the park. There were gas lamps here and there but they did not give much light. The sky was now a deep blue and stars began twinkling above him.

He was nearly through the park when out of the evening shadows somewhere, he heard a giggle. He stopped short, the blood draining from his face. He knew that giggle well. He stood still a moment or two as realization, much like a heavy cloak settled around him. He had to digest this new reality. This blatant deceit. So it was true. He stared into the darkness and felt anger well up in him. *How did she dare do this to him?* He would never trust a woman again. He clenched his fists as he considered his actions. He wanted her to see him, but did not want to make a scene. He stood a moment or two, his chin firm, then continued walking past the bushes and around the bend in the path that now revealed his girlfriend in the arms of another man. They were unaware of him. He looked hard at the man but did not recognize him. He took a few more steps and when he was directly in front of them, he stopped.

And then she saw him.

Her reaction was immediate. She drew back in guilt and fear and even in the dim light of the gas lamp, he could see that the blood drained from her face. She uttered not a word. Neither did he. For a few long moments, he looked her in the eye. She sat stiff, not moving a muscle, the man next to her looking curiously from one to the other.

Then he slowly bent over, removed his shoe, blew the dust from it and put it back on. She would understand his action.

And without a word, he turned his back and walked out of the park.

CHAPTER 1

The carriage creaked alarmingly and we bounced a bit as the pair of black horses turned into the old Steeplechase cemetery and made their way up the path past the many weathered gravestones. Some were covered with moss, others stood at strange angles, having stood there for decades in the heavy snows, the lashing gales and blustery winters of Vermont. The new green leaves trying to open on the tall oaks were hanging low, dripping with the rain that fell steadily from laden skies. Just last week we enjoyed days of sunny, warm weather. This week was damp and cold. Maybe Mama would say it was the May storm, but it was a few weeks early for that. How I hated to hear her talk of the May storm when I was child, wanting to go barefoot in the green grass. But we had to wait till after the May storm before we could shed our shoes. And sure enough, toward the end of May, it nearly always came. A week of unpleasant, wet, cool weather.

May was a favorite month of mine, because that is when the lilacs bloomed along our house, wafting their fragrance into the living room, if the window was open. But today I was totally unaware of the beauty of springtime. My heart felt waterlogged, not from the rain, but from tears and grief. The carriage had stopped now and almost in a daze, I was helped from the undertaker's carriage. I waited as my father opened his huge black umbrella, holding it over both of us, and then I gripped his arm as we headed to the open grave. I realized for the first time that my papa was not the energetic doctor that I had known all my life. He had slowly aged without me noticing it. He was sixty on his last birthday. And now Mama's death had rocked him.

It had stunned all of us, but for Papa, half of him was ripped away. He was numb with grief and shock ever since she died so suddenly. Today his familiar cheery greeting was stilled with sorrow. His head was bowed with grief beneath the big, black umbrella over his head. I became aware that people he had served for many years stood already close to the gaping hole awaiting my mama's casket, paying their respects to their faithful physician at his wife's grave. As we stepped under the tarp that was stretched over the open grave, Papa closed the umbrella and I felt more exposed to the people. I wanted solitude, but at the same time was thankful for our many friends. Here they stood, faithfully standing by my father in his hour of grief, and they had only their umbrellas to shield them from the steady, soaking rain.

We stood back as my brothers Ray, Joe, and Floyd plus three brother-in-laws, carried Mama's coffin to the grave and set it down. When they walked away, I just stared at the coffin. This was the closest I would be to Mama for the last time on earth. Of course, I knew it was only her body that was in the casket, her spirit had taken sudden flight to her heavenly home. I had to wonder if God would allow her to see us standing at her grave. I somehow wanted her to see how many had come. How many people had loved her.

I wiped my eyes and blew my nose. Just days ago Mama was cooking and baking like always. She loved to cook. She loved to invite guests. She loved her family. And in the midst of life, in fact, in the midst of cooking supper for Papa, Ray and me, she was struck down with the burst aneurysm that took her life just minutes later. I wondered just what was going on in Papa's head as he stood by my side, staring at the casket in front of us. *What was he remembering? Was he reliving their courtship days? Or delivering their babies? How would he ever live without Mama?*

How would any of us?

I suddenly realized it had gotten quiet. Not that anyone was noisy, but the crowd was no longer making their way across the soggy cemetery to stand by the grave. They had arrived. The service in the church was over. This now, was the final goodbye. I had kept a brave face in the church, but now, with the very skies above me crying, a tear slid down my cheek. Someone started a hymn about heaven and the crowd joined in. The hymn was a comfort as long as I did not think too much about the words. If I did, there would be more tears escaping down my face and I would be too choked up to sing. My brother Ray, just two years younger than me, stood on the other side of Papa. He was a bit taller than Papa and slim. His straight brown hair was blowing in the wind and he, being the youngest of us all, would miss the mother that had probably spoiled him. Ray was a big tease, but today there was nothing of the tease in his eyes or manner.

My other siblings—there were seven of us in all—stood behind us with their spouses and young children. How Mama loved her grandchildren. She saw them all too seldom. They would miss her, too. Their Grandpa was often called away to a sick person in the midst of family gatherings, but Grandma was always there, cuddling them, feeding them cookies and just loving them.

Pastor Thomas was saying a few last words. A last verse of scripture. My mind wandered again. I had not been home much in the last two years. I was not far away, my cousin Sydney had joined his father in partnership in a large inn several miles from here in Flynn Falls, and had offered me a job. I had not been home very much since moving there. The town was larger than ours and I had met Jonas soon after starting to work there and he had been courting me for the last seven months. I should have come home oftener. But I could not change the past. There were surely going to be changes now. I sighed and looked around. I wished Jonas had come today. He said he had to work, but I think he did not want to come. He told me once that he hated funerals. So did I, but they were a part of life. And it would have been nice to have him by my side in my loss.

I bowed my head for the last prayer. I had missed everything Pastor Thomas had just said. Now I tried to concentrate on his words. At the end of the prayer, my grip on my father's arm tightened as the casket was lowered into the ground. Once it rested there, my sister Susan, who stood directly behind me, handed me a white rose. Mama loved flowers and especially roses. Papa was the one to suggest we all throw a rose into the grave to Mama. Papa had asked for a red rose for himself. Now Susan handed Papa his red rose, he looked at it a moment then he stepped forward, stood there silently for a short time, and then dropped his red rose into the open grave. He stood there quietly a few seconds more, and then stepped back. Then Ray and I stepped up and threw in our white roses. My other siblings followed suit—Ruby, Floyd, Joe, Susan and Connie.

The crowd stood silent, watching until all eight roses were thrown in on the casket.

The rain had let up a bit for the moment and for the first time I looked out over the many friends and acquaintances standing under the ancient oaks who had come to pay their respects. The umbrellas hid some faces but I saw my friend Mindy standing not far from me. Behind her was the sheriff, the banker, and the smithy, whose wife had borne ten children and Papa had delivered every one of them. My father was a fixture in our town and everyone knew him.

My eyes continued to scan the crowd and just before I turned to walk back to the carriage with Papa, I was arrested by the steady gaze of a pair of startlingly blue eyes. The man, a stranger to me, was standing under a dripping tree, holding a big black umbrella. We locked eyes just a few seconds and then I looked away. I wondered briefly who he was, but my father was turning away to follow the undertaker to the carriage once more and I followed him. It was time to return to the house. Many of our friends would be coming for refreshments.

When we got to the house there were already women from the church making coffee and tea and the dining room table was laden with cakes, fruit pies, lemon squares and an assortment of cookies that were brought by friends, family and church members. With the funeral behind me I could now enjoy visiting with siblings and nieces and nephews. I was closest to my sister Susan who had just married a year ago and was expecting her first child the beginning of October. However, there was also Ruby, the oldest of us all, whose husband was a farmer, working and living on the home farm of his in-laws. Then there was Connie, who was married to a dairy farmer, on the other side of Flynn Falls. Joe who had his own harness shop up towards Burlington and Floyd and his wife Alice who lived in Burlington and he worked in the hospital there. We saw each other too seldom and now our conversations were interrupted with well-meaning friends who wanted to show their love and concern.

About an hour later the house was cleared except for my siblings. We sat awhile but one by one my siblings also had to return home to the farm or business and goodbyes were said. Finally, it was just Susan and her husband.

"Amber, how can you stand it?" she asked me quietly.

"I barely can. And I hurt so badly for Papa. Who would have thought Mama would go so quickly? She wasn't even sick. I really can't believe she is gone. I keep thinking she is going to pop out of the kitchen any moment to say it is time for supper."

"I know. I feel the same way. And I so wanted her to see our baby," Susan said, tears running down her cheeks. "I am glad you are close by. But you no longer live here. What will Papa do?"

"I'll move back. I will be here for Papa."

"Thanks so much. That makes me feel better. He will be so lonely. I can't imagine him without Mama." She hugged me. "Now, Alan is waiting impatiently and I must run. Keep in touch."

When the door closed behind her, I turned to see Papa heading for his room.

"I'm taking a nap," he said shortly. "I'm worn out."

I felt something at my feet and looked down to see Muggins, our big gray striped tom cat looking at me.

"Oh Muggins, I forgot all about you. I barely saw you all day and you must be hungry. You are glad the people are gone again, aren't you? So am I, except for the family."

It felt good to do something normal on this abnormal day. I could hardly believe how empty the house felt with just one person missing. I took the cat out on the back porch to feed him, and to my surprise saw it was clearing to the west. I knew the rain had slackened, but now I saw some blue sky and sun peeking through the clouds. It lifted my spirits. Muggins fed, I went in for a light shawl and then I returned to the back porch and sat there in the late afternoon sunshine. I had a lot of thinking to do. Mama's death made a huge hole in our lives and there would be big changes to come. Our life as we knew it was past. It would never be the same again.

It wasn't long before Ray found his way out to the porch also. He sat down beside me, a last piece of pie in his hand.

"What will we do now with Mama gone?" he asked finally.

"I must talk to Papa, but I shall come back home. I can't let him here alone. I can easily be replaced at the inn. What are your plans? I hear you were working part time for a veterinarian. Didn't Papa need you to help him?"

"I've learned a lot from Papa and I shall leave in July for about six weeks of training in a recently opened medical school. I met this vet, Dr. Renwick, at the inn one evening and I asked him if I could watch him operate sometime. We hit it off good and I keep in touch with him and if I am free when he operates, I help him. In fact, if Papa does not need me, I work for the vet sometimes."

"But you want to follow in Papa's footsteps, not work with animals."

"Yes. I am sure about that."

A half hour later, Papa joined us.

"Any supper?"

"You're hungry already?"

"I need something besides sweets. I think I heard our neighbor say she brought us some beef stew for supper."

"She did. It just needs heating. I'll do it now. Shall I make some biscuits to eat with it?"

"Sounds good."

Papa always had a good appetite and I was glad he was hungry. No one had been hungry at lunchtime.

Supper was a rather quiet affair until a young boy knocked on the door to say his brother fell out of a tree and could the doctor come. Papa took his last bite of stew and biscuit and left. I think he was glad to do something normal. Something to fill the terrible vacuum in his life that was created by Mama's passing.

After supper I sat out on the front porch. The evening air was cool because the setting sun was on the other side of the house, but I wanted to be outdoors. I wrapped my shawl around me and sat on the glider. In spite of living in the middle of town, we were secluded here. Our large white house stood on the corner of North Street and Park Avenue. The park, better known as the village green and complete with a gazebo, was a block of land between our house and Main Street. Park Avenue was the narrow street in front of our house that went past the parsonage and the church and then made a sharp curve around the other end of the park and finally connected to Main Street. Although Steeplechase was big enough to be called a town, I still thought of it as a village. The Carriage Inn stood on the corner of Main and North Street and the block of buildings east of the inn were places of business. There was a covered boardwalk along Main Street on the north side that stretched across all the stores. The Steeplechase Town Hall stood on the corner of South Street and Main Street, across from the village green. The gazebo, standing in the middle of the green, was surrounded by tall oaks and shady maple trees and a few paths wound their way among the trees.

Ray soon joined me on the porch, as did Papa when he came back from his medical call. I think none of us could stand being in the house without the familiar sight of Mama. The walls just shouted her absence.

"What do we do with Mama gone?" asked Papa softly, taking a seat on a rocker that stood on the porch. I heard the strain in his voice.

"I'll move home," I said quickly. "I don't mind leaving the inn."

"You sure?" His eyes brightened.

"I'm sure. You need a housekeeper."

Papa was silent a few moments. "I may need you more in my office and to help me when Ray leaves. Mama did a lot for me that no one noticed. Helped me with the medicine supply, did bills and such and sometimes assisted if I needed her help. Maybe we should hire a housekeeper and you could help me with appointments and book work."

"Do we really need a housekeeper? I hate the thought of it."

"Yes, we do, even with you here. Maybe not every day. Maybe for a few days a week. The garden needs planting and someone to care for it. I think we will be surprised how much Mama did that we never noticed. We just took it for granted that it got done."

I had to think this through. It was bad enough with Mama gone, but to have a strange woman in the house sounded terrible.

"Do you have someone in mind for the housekeeper?"

Papa was silent a few minutes.

"Mrs. Harper comes to mind. She lives close by and as a widow, she could use the extra income. She barely had sufficient heat this past winter. And we know her. She would not be a stranger."

Mrs. Harper had been here helping with the refreshments just this afternoon. She was probably about Mama's age. I believed she would be a capable worker, but I did not really remember any of her food being anything special at our church gatherings. Could she cook? Mama was exceptional. She used many herbs and spices in her cooking and the meals were always interesting and tasty. To go to someone with lesser skills would be hard. Mrs. Harper was friendly enough, but I blinked back tears. With each change that Papa mentioned, my heart wrenched a bit more. I wanted to turn back the clock and have nothing to do with these terrible changes. But we could not hold onto the past. We could not hold onto Mama. Mama was gone.

"I didn't see Jonas today," said Papa, changing the subject.

"He wasn't at the funeral. He had to work."

Papa said nothing, but I felt bad. How often Jonas sat at our table eating my mother's cooking. I was disappointed that he had not wanted to be with us. It was, after all my mother. Had she lived, she would have possibly been his future mother-in-law. I wondered if he had even tried to get free for the funeral. Papa never said much about Jonas, but if he really liked someone, it showed.

An old man by the name of Bentley Queens who lived across from us on North Street came walking by. He was a kind old gentleman known for his soft voice and broad grin. When Bentley got to the gate, he turned in. This evening there was no smile on his face. He silently walked up on the porch, and held his hand out to Papa. They shook hands.

"I know what you are feeling," said Bentley softly. "I lost Emily five years ago. It seemed life could not go on without her." He paused. "Unfortunately, it does." He stopped and blinked back tears.

"I thought the sun would never come out again," he continued. "But it does. It just doesn't shine quite as brightly as before."

"Thank you," whispered Papa.

Bentley then nodded to Ray and me and then slowly made his way back home while we swallowed our tears.

Fifteen minutes later, I saw a young blonde man ride his horse into the avenue. Jonas had arrived. I was very glad to see him. He had come from Flynn Falls, which was several miles away to the south of us. I watched as he tethered his horse by the gate leading to our front door and then walked rather slowly up to us. He went immediately to Papa and extended his hand.

"I am sorry for your loss. I could not be at the funeral, we were too busy at work."

Papa just nodded. I had a feeling that Papa did not quite believe him. But I was glad to have Jonas here. It had been a rough day and I was happy for his company. He came then to me and sat down beside me.

"How are you?" he asked.

"I am glad the funeral is over. But…" I choked on tears. He reached over and laid his hand on mine. Papa soon left and Ray had already left before Jonas arrived.

"So you had a busy day?" I asked.

"Like always. Everyone needs furniture. But I'd rather be outside."

"Maybe you should be a farmer."

"No way. The farmers never get to leave their farms. There is always milking to be done and chickens to feed."

There was silence. I did not know what to say to him. I had just said goodbye to Mama and I could not easily pull myself from the day's events. However, when the silence got too long, I spoke.

"I missed you today."

When Jonas did not reply, I got a bit irritated, "Did you ask off?"

"I knew he needed me there. I didn't even bother to ask. But don't tell your father."

"Business is business," I said, not wanting to get into an argument. "I guess you should be glad you have work and that business is booming."

"What will your father do without your mother?"

"Learn to live without her as we all must. I shall move home."

"You will?"

"Yes. I can't leave him alone here without a cook."

"You will leave the inn?"

"Yes. They can easily get someone else."

"I won't see you often."

"That depends on you. You will definitely have to come farther to see me."

Silence reigned as Jonas thought of the change in his life.

"Jim and I are going fishing on Lake Champlain this weekend."

I said nothing. I seldom saw him on weekends. He loved to fish and he and his brother Jim spent many weekends fishing. I found myself somehow disappointed. Jonas did not ask anything else about the funeral and Mama was on my mind. I would have enjoyed talking about her. Remembering her good meals. Her cheery disposition. Her scolding Muggins when he would playfully grab her legs at an unexpected moment. But Jonas evidently did not feel at ease talking about her. The silence between us stretched out and I was actually relieved when he got up to go just twenty minutes later. He must have felt my mood and was uncomfortable with it.

The following month flew by as we adjusted to the upheaval in our lives. I moved home. Papa hired Mrs. Harper, who was happy to come on wash day, cleaning day and a day to bake. We settled on Monday, Wednesday and Friday. She lived two blocks beyond us on North Street and could walk to work. I helped Papa wherever he needed help. Sometimes I worked on bills and appointments. When Mrs. Harper was not there, I cooked and did the many other jobs around the house. That is, if Papa did not need me elsewhere. I was sent on errands. I put on a white coat and helped with the patient if necessary. I went to the drug store and bought supplies for Papa. My life was full. Sometimes I worked in the garden or baked bread, although Mrs. Harper usually spent Wednesday baking.

Life was not the same. It was not as pleasant with Mama gone. In fact, there was a big hole in our lives that no one could fill. And it screamed at us when we wanted so badly to have Mama there with us. But gradually we were adjusting. As old Bentley had said, the sun shines again, just not as brightly.

CHAPTER 2

Laura Harper was a motherly sort of person, probably around sixty and both kind and helpful. But I must admit, I did not like seeing her make herself at home in Mama's kitchen. I tried not to show it but I think I treated her a bit coolly. I think she realized what I was going through and did not seem to hold my lack of warmth against me. After the first week, it went better for me and I was friendlier.

One lovely June morning, I made breakfast since it was Mrs. Harper's day off. I made sausage and biscuits and fried eggs and was happy for the compliments from both Papa and Ray.

"Is this a day with Papa or are you with the vet today?" I asked my brother.

"With the vet. I am helping him with a surgery. Yesterday I helped him deliver twin calves at the MacGregor farm. The first one did not want to come out and he had to help it along. The second one came without a problem. It was quite the experience."

"Could we change the subject? I just lost my appetite." Sometimes my imagination was more vivid than I would have liked.

Ray chuckled. He was the only son of my father who would follow in his footsteps as a medical doctor.

"By the way," Ray continued, as he devoured his breakfast, "I think you need to tell Mrs. Harper some of Mama's cooking tricks. Her food is very bland."

"I hate to interfere. You can always add salt at the table."

"It is not just salt that is needed. Do you know how to make a beef roast like Mama?"

"I do."

"Make one for supper, will you? It seems like ages since we had a beef roast."

"I will if I get the chance to go to the butcher today."

Just as Ray was about to leave the house, he called to me.

"Get a big roast and I'll bring my boss along. I told him about Mama's Pennsylvania Dutch cooking."

"Okay. Will his wife come along?"

There was a brief hesitation. "I doubt it."

When the door slammed shut I wondered about Ray's comment. Why would a wife not come along? I sure hoped this was not a bad marriage. Ray seemed to think his boss was wonderful. But he never talked about the wife, but maybe she kept herself out of the business. Or maybe his business was the problem. Her husband probably smelled like a goat or pig most of the time and brought who knows what into the house on his shoes.

That evening, when I set the table, I thought I would rather be prepared for one too many than one not enough. So I set for five of us. It would do Papa good to have company again. He dealt with sickness all day and Mama was not here evenings to cheer him up with her domestic tales.

Supper was at six, and for a change, Papa was on time. Shortly before six, I heard the knocker and with one spoon stirring the gravy, I listened for the new voices. Actually, I listened for a female voice, but was disappointed. I would have enjoyed some female company. I had told Papa we would eat as soon as the company arrived because in this house, one never knew if one could finish the meal together without the interruption of a medical emergency. I took the steaming food to the dining room and was setting the large meat platter with the roast surrounded by carrots on the table, when the the men arrived in the room. I looked up to see a man of perhaps six feet with a head of heavy dark hair and a pair of very blue eyes.

"Dr. Renwick," said my brother, "this is my sister Amber. Amber, Dr. Renwick."

When Dr. Renwick soberly offered me his hand and took mine in his, I realized this was the man I had locked eyes with while standing at Mama's grave. He must have come to the funeral because Ray worked for him.

"Pleased to meet you," I said. "Your wife could not come with you?"

He gave me a blank look for a few seconds, his eyes studying me and then looked at Ray who was coughing into his hand. Dr. Renwick looked back at me, trying to hide a smile.

"I think there has been a miscommunication. There is no Mrs. Renwick."

"I just said I doubt if she will come," said my brother quickly, grinning mischievously.

I looked at Dr. Renwick who apparently had forgotten he was still holding my hand. I was embarrassed for my mistake and felt heat in my face looking into those blue eyes.

"I hope you don't feel obligated to pay my brother for his services," I said finally, freeing my hand.

There were chuckles from the three men in the room as I cleared away the extra place setting and returned to the table. By the time I was back at the table, the three were ready to be seated, letting me take my place at the opposite end from my father. Just before he sat down, Dr. Renwick, a nice looking gentleman probably not much older than I was, held the chair for me. Even Jonas rarely helped me sit at the table. My brother was quick to note Dr. Renwick's action.

"You don't need to help her, she is quite capable herself," he said, ever the tease.

"But she is a lady and she is not my sister," replied his boss quietly.

"It looks like you could learn more than medical skills from Dr. Renwick," said Papa with a grin. "It never hurts to be polite to a lady."

"My tomboy sister a lady?"

"Ray!" I objected.

"Weren't you still climbing trees last summer?"

"Only when Muggins was headed to that blue jay's nest."

"I thought you did not like the screaming blue jays," said Ray.

"I don't. I was scared the blue jay would injure Muggins."

There was another round of laughter and then, thankfully it was time to say the blessing on the meal. Papa prayed the blessing and the food was passed. There was a bit of quiet at the beginning of the meal as the food was dished out and then consumed by the hearty appetites of the three men. But then the conversation took off and never stopped during the whole meal. My place at the end of the table gave me a good opportunity to observe our guest without him noticing it. No matter who I looked at, I could see him in my peripheral vision. With the three men at the table all interested in the medical field, the talk tended to lean in that direction. However, my father was also meeting Dr. Renwick for the first time and had a lot of questions.

"You must be fairly new here in Steeplechase," said Papa.

"I moved here about seven months ago. I took over Dr. Toome's veterinary practice."

"Oh, I guess I should have known that. He had been my patient. But I did not have occasion to contact a veterinarian in the last eight months. Are you doing well?"

"I am."

"You are too young to have had too much experience," challenged Papa with a grin.

"Actually, I've been working with animals ever since eighth grade in school. Even before that. Any injured animal I saw, I tried to heal. I even attempted to help a skunk one time and got blasted for my efforts."

We all joined in the laughter.

"Where are you from?" asked Papa.

He mentioned a distant town.

"You have family?"

"Yes, my parents are both living. My father, like you, is a medical doctor. I am the oldest of their three sons."

"So, your father is also a doctor. And you have chosen animals over humans."

"It doesn't sound so good when you put it like that," he answered, grinning. "I did work with my father for a couple years. I learned a lot from him. I accompanied him on his rounds and when I begged to put stitches in, he gave me the chance. When my father saw my work, he let me do it without asking. But my love was working with animals and so I read all I could, worked with a veterinarian for a couple years and then came here to take over Dr. Toome's practice."

"Well, I am thankful that you allow Ray to help you," said Papa. "He is glad for the experience and it keeps him out of trouble. But the time will come when I hope he can replace me, rather than become a veterinarian. We need someone for the people here."

As Papa and Dr. Renwick talked, Ray gobbled up his food and I eventually went for the apple pie and coffee.

"Are you attending the town meeting tonight?" Papa asked Dr. Renwick.

"I am. For the first time."

Papa looked at his watch. "It is about time to go." He looked at me.

"Well, Amber, thank you for the good meal. Tasted just like Mama's roast and potatoes." He paused, then added in a softer voice, "I wish she would have been here to help eat it."

There was just a bit of a catch in Papa's voice and I blinked back sudden tears hearing it. There was a short pause while the three of us recovered from the pangs of her loss.

"Yeah, you can make a beef roast the next time our housekeeper has off again," said my brother finally.

While Papa went for his hat, Dr. Renwick turned to me, holding out his hand once more. He was quite the gentleman and I hoped some of it would rub off on Ray.

"That was the best meal I've eaten since my mother's Christmas dinner," he said, his blue eyes warm. "Thank you."

"I'm glad you liked it."

I cleaned up the dining room and the kitchen and fed the scraps to the cat. When I finally went out to sit on the front porch, I found myself thinking of our visitor. He was a fine man. He somehow had class. He carried himself well. He was taller than Papa or Ray and had thick wavy hair that fell a bit low on the neck, and his eyes were as blue as the heavens above our Vermont town.

My musings came to an end when a horse and rider came to a halt in front of the house. I was happy to see it was Jonas.

"Good evening, Jonas. This is a surprise."

He tethered his horse, named Horace, and came and sat with me on the glider.

"What is going on at the town hall?"

"Town meeting," I replied.

We could see the town hall from where we sat. There were some carriages, but the night was warm and most people walked to the meeting.

"How was your day?" I asked.

"It was okay, but I would rather be out fishing or hunting. I like the fresh air. I can't stand being inside all day long. What did you do all day?" he asked, taking my hand in his.

"I worked in the house. The housekeeper had off and I went shopping to the butcher and green grocer and made supper. We had a guest."

"Who was that?"

"A veterinarian."

"A vet? What is his name?"

"Dr. Renwick. He took over Dr. Toome's practice just out of town and Ray works part time for him."

"I brought my fishing line along. How about we go down South Street to the bridge and fish?"

"I don't know if I can find a fishing rod around here."

"I brought one for you, too."

Jonas collected the fishing equipment from his horse and we set out for the river. Crossing Main Street at the town hall, we were now on South Street, and it was not far to the river. A steep, short hill and a curve and we were there. We were now in shadows and it was almost cold by the water. We found a place away from the worst rocks and we talked and fished for an hour or so. Jonas lost his bait once and caught his line on a rock. When I lost my hook, we quit and headed back, no fish in tow. As we came struggling up the hill to the town hall, the meeting had just left out and the people were standing around outside chatting. I found myself looking for Papa and Dr. Renwick. I finally saw Papa chatting with the mayor and Dr. Renwick talking to a farmer from the area. I wondered if he had an animal that needed attention.

Arriving home, I offered Jonas the last piece of apple pie and an hour later he headed for home again. After he left, I went up to my room, Muggins padding up the stairs after me. I sat on the chair by the window and Muggins sat on the windowsill and observed the twinkling of the fireflies on the village green. I found myself musing about my relationship with Jonas. He was a very dashing, light haired young man. In fact, his hair was so blonde it was nearly white. He had light blue eyes and had a carefree, daring way about him. He was just perhaps six months younger than I and we had met at the inn where I had worked in Flynn Falls. I found him extremely handsome and felt very privileged to be courted by him. I wished sometimes that he would talk about marriage. Well, sometimes he did, but it was always in the distant future and spoken in a rather matter of fact manner. It left me somehow wanting. Reaching for more. But he would eventually settle down, I hoped.

My thoughts returned to Dr. Renwick. I wondered what his first name was. I wondered also why he was not married. Surely he had a girlfriend. He would have many girls falling for him. I had just walked away from the window when I heard a cat yowling outside. Muggins flung himself against the window, his nose pressed against the window screen. The screen was the kind one simply placed in the window and took out when it rained. He turned his green eyes to me, begging me to let him out. When I did nothing, Muggins growled and clawed at the screen.

"No, way, Muggins. I'm not letting you out to beat up, or get beat up by another cat."

But before I had finished talking, he had clawed the screen open, which fell out the window onto the roof. And before I could rescue the screen he had sprung to a tree branch and had disappeared to join the excitement of the night.

And it was my job to awkwardly hang out the window to get the screen off the roof and back into the window where it belonged.

CHAPTER 3

There was, in our village of Steeplechase, a band concert every Wednesday evening in the summertime. It was held on the village green and music lovers came early, spread their blankets and ate a picnic supper to the accompaniment of band music. Farmers, of course, could not come at that time of day, but those from town attended faithfully. I could have sat on the front porch and heard it clearly from there, but it was nice mingling with neighbors and friends on the village green. Papa did not really enjoy picnics. He would rather eat at the table and listen to the concert from the porch. Whereas I would make a sandwich of some sort and take a jar of tea made from our woolly mint that grew alongside of the house. Some families brought potato salad and cold fried chicken and ate a full meal as they listened to the band. Usually Jonas came—a bit late—but always happy for any food I had for him, and we would listen to the concert together. Ours was a very loose relationship, and I expected him to show up, but if he did not, I did not worry. He never said for certain that he would come.

On this particular June evening, I had just spread out my blanket, when I was joined by my friend Mindy.

"Mindy, why aren't you up in the gazebo playing with the band?"

She held up a finger. "I sliced my finger with a knife and bandaged fingers are no good on a flute."

"Well, have a seat. I always bring an extra sandwich just in case someone needs a bite. Do you like ham salad sandwiches?"

"I love them. I had no time to make a sandwich, but I did grab a couple doughnuts in the hopes of meeting up with you."

Mindy took a seat on my blanket and the band began playing. Although many people were sitting on their chairs or blankets, others simply strolled around talking to friends and acquaintances in the park while the band played.

"Isn't this a lovely evening for the concert?" Mindy said as she bit into her sandwich. "Last summer it rained partway through about half of the concerts. The band was protected under the roof of the gazebo, but it was disheartening week after week to see our listeners suddenly run in all directions, leaving us play to an empty park."

"I remember," I said. "By the end of the summer we knew enough to bring umbrellas. I, of course, could run to the porch and still hear the music. Here, have some tea."

"Do you expect Jonas this evening? Am I eating his sandwich?"

"I never know if he will show up. Our relationship doesn't really seem to go anywhere, but I enjoy his friendship."

"Carl isn't much better. Are girls more ready to settle down, do you think?"

"I don't know, but my grandma always said her boys didn't know what they really wanted until they were in their mid-twenties."

"Well, if that is true, I guess we need to wait a couple years for these boys to mature. Oh, there comes the handsome Hunter."

"Jonas? Already?" I looked in the direction she was looking but did not see him.

"Not Jonas, Hunter. Hunter Renwick."

"Hunter who?"

"The veterinarian. You don't know him? Oh, I guess you've been in Flynn Falls."

"His name is Hunter?"

"So I am told."

"How do you know him?"

"Mainly just from seeing him in town. All the women bring the latest gossip into the bakery and you remember I can see a lot of activity from my windows that look down on Main Street. And being the handsome bachelor that he is, I find it amusing how married women as well as the single women turn and watch him when he rides by on his horse."

I had to turn in order to look in the direction she was looking. Yes, there stood Dr. Renwick, talking to a young, slender woman who had brought her dog along to the park. Dr. Renwick was leaning down and petting the dog as they talked.

"You won't believe this, Mindy, but I cooked supper for him a few nights ago and did not know his first name."

"Dr. Renwick was at your house for supper? How do you rate?" She was obviously impressed.

"Ray works part time for him and Ray invited him for one of 'Mama's' beef roast dinners, but of course, I cooked it."

"How exciting. Did he talk to you?"

"Not really. Complimented me on the meal. He has beautiful blue eyes."

"He is beautiful all over, as far as I am concerned. I mentioned his looks in Carl's presence and he was not impressed. I must watch what I say about other men. But whenever Carl sees Julia White, he stops and talks to her and I know he finds her beautiful."

I could not easily see where Hunter was standing, since my back was to him.

"Is Dr. Renwick coming this way?"

She looked. "No, I think he just turned down another path. I have never seen him with a girl though. Actually, gossip says that a girl jilted him and he has never courted anyone since."

"Where did you hear that gossip? He only moved here in the last year."

"From my cousin, I think he used to live in her area."

"Interesting," I replied, remembering his steady gaze at the grave-side.

We were so busy talking that I barely heard the band music. Only when there was a lull in conversation, was I aware of the band. Our sandwiches were long gone as well as the cream-filled doughnuts from Mindy's parents' bakery on Main Street.

"Here comes Old Wolf," said Mindy in a near whisper. "He gives me the creeps."

Old Wolf was a familiar sight in our town. He was a man perhaps fifty years old who lived just outside of Steeplechase by the river. He lived with his aging parents and was born mentally ill and spent most of his time along the river behind his home. He liked to fish and probably just felt safer away from people. He was, unfortunately, the focus of teasing and abuse from children and teenagers. It was sad, because now he really was not a nice person to be around. He had proven a few times to be a real danger with his sudden fits of rage, which were probably the result of the verbal abuse from his tormentors. Some people thought he should be put away, but his parents wanted to keep him at home. Now he walked along, lost in his own world and it seemed no one bothered to greet him or say a kind word to him. I could not fault anyone else, because I myself was uncomfortable around him and did not look at him as he passed us. His last name was Wolf, and at this point of his life was referred to as "Old Wolf." Soon after he passed by, two young men from church walked past us, nodding their greetings. Groups of teenagers went by, talking and laughing and several of Papa's patients came by and talked a bit to me. And then, just as the concert was drawing to a close, Jonas arrived. Mindy went to Carl who was done playing and Jonas sat with me a while on the blanket.

"You missed the music," I said, greeting Jonas.

"I got to talking with the smithy who fixed my horse's shoe. He likes to hunt. He got a bear about three years ago up in the northeastern corner of the state."

We chatted a bit and then Jonas saw someone he wanted to talk to and was off again. As I was gathering up the blanket and remains of my picnic, I happened to glance across the park. Not far from me stood Dr. Renwick, talking with another man, both looking in my direction as they talked. When Dr. Renwick saw me looking in his direction, he nodded solemnly and then continued his conversation with the man.

A few minutes later Jonas and I headed to the house where I made Jonas a ham salad sandwich while he finished up the last of a lemon pie.

"I have an idea, Amber," he said when we were seated on the porch enjoying the dusk falling around us.

"I hope it is a good one."

"My ideas are always good. We are going to go on a hike."

"Oh? Where to? Up Mount Abe? I am not the best hiker, you know."

"Actually, I think it is on Mt. Roosevelt. There is a trail of sorts that one can find right close to the country store a few miles from Flynn Falls on Mountain Road. After a half a mile or so there is a fork to the right off the trail, which leads very soon to a nice-sized lake. We can go fishing there. I just talked to my friend Wally and he and his girl will come along. What do you think?"

"Sounds good. When do you want to go?"

"What about this Saturday?"

"Morning or afternoon?"

"Let's leave about two in the afternoon."

"Good, I'll pack food for a picnic."

"I'll pick you up at two o'clock sharp."

———

Saturday was clear and warm. A good day for fishing and hiking. Papa had no office hours on Saturdays, which gave him a bit more free time, especially now with Ray helping him, so we ate a leisurely breakfast together.

"So you are going hiking with Jonas?" Papa asked.

"Yes, and with his friend Wally and Wally's friend Jane."

"Where are you hiking?"

"Not far from Flynn Falls on Mount Roosevelt. There is a trail that leads to a lake where we can fish."

"Ah, I know that place. I was there at that lake once with your mother. A nice lake. A nice memory."

His voice grew soft with the memory and we sat in silence a bit, remembering Mama.

"Just stay together up there. You don't want to get separated."

"We'll be fine. There is a trail."

Jonas arrived promptly at two. I had made a lunch of fried chicken and potato salad and cold mint tea and a few apples and then we were off. We met Wally and his girl back in Flynn Falls and then each of the fellas took his own carriage.

Jonas was in a very good mood. He was definitely an outdoors person and he was already enjoying the day. He kept his horse at a good clip as we headed for the trail. Once on Mountain Road we were going up hill and he was a bit more gentle with the horse. When we arrived at the country store, Jonas went in to talk to the owner, whom he knew. With his permission we put the two horses in the small, fenced-in field next to the store so they could be free to roam.

And then we walked up the hill to the start of the trail and entered the woods.

It was the first time on this trail for all of us. I was immediately impressed by the silence of the woods. Tall trees all around us with sunlight filtering through the leaves and dancing on the path in front of us. We were now in a different world and always, when surrounded by nature minus the shouts of children and the rattle of carriage wheels on the dusty roads, I felt close to God. This would be a fun day and I was glad that Jonas suggested the hike.

Jonas led the way on the narrow trail, fishing rods in hand and whistling. I followed with the picnic basket. Wally and Jane followed me. I knew Wally but did not know his girlfriend. She was very quiet and did not speak unless spoken to. The trail was such easy access to the road that I supposed many people found their way sometime or other to the lake. I was surprised how hilly the trail was. It was not just an upward climb up the mountain, we were constantly going up and down. Perhaps ten steps upwards and then down again. Up and down, up and down, but always more steps up than down. But I loved it. I loved the vastness of the woods, the canopy of trees above us and above all the absence of noise. It was like we were alone on the mountain. I barely heard a bird. Our voices nearly got lost in the woods. Jane, a short, thin girl with big eyes, said not a word as we walked and I discovered she was frightened now in the mountains. She spooked easily and every so often, Jonas or Wally would pretend they saw a wild animal and Jane was nearly frightened out of her wits. But she finally relaxed a bit and with much laughter, we finally arrived at the fork in the trail. Jonas promptly took the path to the right, and in a short time we had arrived at the promised lake. It was larger than I expected here on the mountain. While the boys scouted around the lake, looking for the perfect place to fish, I prepared our picnic. This was Jane's first experience on a hike and I saw her constantly looking into the surrounding area as if fearful of a wild animal. I discovered she was just eighteen but Wally was Jonas' age.

"Do you live in Flynn Falls?" I asked.

"Yes, but my family just moved from New York City about a month ago, so I feel really new here."

"You will love Vermont," I assured her. "At least if you like the out of doors. It is just wonderful here in the autumn when the sugar maples are turning their brilliant red orange. Of course, we wait longer for spring up here and we have the terrible month of mud season."

"Mud season? What is that?"

"The month of April. The ground is frozen all winter and when it begins to thaw, all the roads become very muddy and the wagon wheels get stuck and it is a wretched time for the horses pulling the carriages. At the very worst spots they put up signs warning about the 'frost heaves.'"

"That sounds scary, too."

"April is long past and there is no mud now."

"Are there wild animals on this mountain?"

"Yes, I suppose there are, but we make enough noise they will not get close to us. They are probably as scared of us as we are of them. New York City is probably more dangerous than anything on this mountain."

Jonas and Wally returned from checking out the lake and soon we were enjoying our picnic. I always find it amazing how hungry one gets being out in the open air. My food was not only eaten, it was devoured. Not a scrap left. Tea was also gone. And soon after eating, Jonas and I were fishing at one part of the lake and Wally and Jane not too far from us. We fished for an hour or so. Jonas pulled one in but it was too small, so he threw it back. I was not such an experienced fisherman and got only nibbles and when Jonas said I should tug the line a bit when I felt a nibble, I did, but then I no longer even had a nibble. Wally and Jane were more interested in each other than fishing and were not catching anything. We eventually decided to give up on fishing and just sit by the lake and talk. Jonas was a big talker and there was nothing he liked better than to brag about his fishing and hunting expeditions—mostly exaggerated. I found that Wally could do his share of tall tales also. It was in the middle of one of Jonas' stories that we clearly heard some sizable animal not so very far from us. The boys were instantly on their feet while I cowered, too scared to move. We heard no more in the next minute or so, but Jonas was determined to see what this creature was.

"Come on, Wally," he said softly, "let's see what it is."

He was already on his way through the trees. Then he stopped, turning back to me.

"Amber, watch the stuff," he said

And with that the two were gone. Just as they began to be swallowed up in the trees, Jane jumped up. I was shocked how scared she looked. She was nearly in a panic. I began to tell her there was really nothing to be scared about when she gave a quick look around the lake and then headed after the boys.

"I'm scared here alone without the guys. I'm going, too."

And she was off and running. I watched her disappear in the trees and looked around me. How could it be that one minute I was sitting beside a lake with three friends and sixty seconds later, I was completely alone? I could not even hear them anymore. How quickly the sound of their footsteps was absorbed in the quietness of the mountain. Well, they wouldn't be gone long. Not with the scared Jane. I just sat there awhile in silence, absorbing my surroundings. After perhaps fifteen minutes and not hearing their return, I looked around. Close to me were four fishing rods, a tin box that contained bait, my picnic basket and a jar of water that Jane had brought along. Suddenly, I felt very, very alone. Was the wild creature coming for water? And would it circumvent the others and return? It was dead quiet. When I first entered the forest I had liked the silence. Now I wished for some sound. I couldn't even hear any birds. I strained my ears for Jonas' voice. But it seemed to me that the mountain had simply swallowed them up. I found myself looking cautiously around the lake almost afraid I might see a bear or even a wild cat of some kind. The lake would be their source of water. I remembered from school that there was the bobcat and also the Canada lynx in Vermont. Then I chided myself for being fearful. They would be back soon, so I would just gather the stuff together and when they returned, we would be ready to head out.

That done, I just stood a while beside the lake. Every so often I would hear some slight sound. My body would tense up and I hoped it was my returning friends. But no one came. The minutes ticked by. I remembered my father's admonition to stay together. And here I was all alone. I hoped that Jane caught up to the boys. What if she was wandering around on the mountain alone?

I gradually began to be angry with Jonas. I knew Papa was not very impressed with him. He never said much, but I could tell. Jonas bragged too much and never seemed to pay much attention to me. Not like other fellas treated their girls. But he was the most handsome fellow I knew and I considered it a privilege that he had chosen me as his girlfriend.

I don't know how long I sat there. I could not believe that the others had not returned. Had they completely forgotten about me? Were they so enjoying their hunt that they thought I was with them, just trailing behind?

I began praying for my safety and the safety of the others. They somehow must have lost their way. Certainly no wild animal would attack three people. I looked up to the sky and remembered a verse in the Bible. "I will lift up mine eyes unto the hills from whence cometh my help." But when I looked up, I saw only the sky above the lake. Surrounding the lake were the dark trees. I found myself begging God to bring the others back soon.

And then I saw a strange thing. I noticed two birds flying toward each other from opposite ends of the lake. One came from behind me and the other was coming toward me. Neither bird veered to the left or to the right. Curious, I watched as they came closer and closer to each other. It seemed odd to me that they stayed on track, never turning in another direction. Finally, just before they met, I saw one, obviously a bit higher than the other, drop something that the other bird caught in its beak. And both continued on their way—now flying away from each other. It must have been a mother and her young one, although they both looked the same size to me. But the mother was caring for its young. I remembered the Bible verse about God knowing when a sparrow falls. I wondered if God let me observe the birds to assure me that He was caring for me also. I took courage from that.

I was getting increasingly anxious. How much time had passed? An hour? Two hours? I was seeing nothing and hearing nothing. How could they get so lost? Or had one of them come to harm? Poor Jane. She was probably in a panic. I could tell that the sun was going down. It was June and the days were the longest of the year. But I remembered how dark it had seemed to me when we entered the woods and that was when the sun was high in the sky. The green leaves of the trees made a dark shade on the mountain. Outside it would not be so dark. Even here by the lake it was not dark, but in the woods around me, I could tell that light was fading. The sky above me stayed light and gave me courage, but the light was not coming down into the woods anymore. It surely was not yet dark, but the sun was getting lower in the sky and I was in shadow now here at the lake. *Why didn't the others return? How could they get so lost?* I tried not to panic. The more I thought about it, the more I knew I had to take action soon. I could not wait much longer. The light continued to get dimmer and it was time to get practical. I called out Jonas' name, but it scared me. I did not call a second time. Maybe I should have continued to call, but I did not want any animal to know where I was. I would have to find my way out of here alone. At least I had the trail. But there was no way I could carry a picnic basket, bait box and four fishing rods out. I looked around and saw a large rock. I would hide the rods and bait box behind the rock to be collected later. I did not want other hikers to find them and take them. With a last look at the darkening sky I began moving the things to the rock. I was frightened now. I had to get out of here.

There must be clouds in the west that were helping to dim the sun because it seemed to get darker more quickly now. I hoped it would not rain. I took a last look around. Did animals come for water at the end of the day? I should have left long ago. With the rods and box safely out of sight for anyone coming to the lake, and picnic basket on my arm, I made my way to the trail. It was much darker away from the open sky above the lake, as I had expected, and I had to look closely for the trail but my eyes soon adjusted. I soon arrived at the fork in the trail and I quickly turned to the left and hurried along my way, eager now to be out of here. On the way in, we had been talking and laughing and the boys had been teasing Jane about animals and the path had not seemed long. Now it seemed to take much longer. I looked only at the trail, which went up and down, up and down. At least I was facing the west on my way out and so the light was in front of me.

I was hurrying down one of the many little hills on the trail when I moved a bit to the left to miss a rock sticking up in the path and my picnic basket hit a tree and nearly knocked me off my feet. I stumbled to the opposite side of the path and bumped into a tree, nearly falling, and only stayed upright by forcing my foot to hold my weight until I righted myself. As a result, I wrenched the front of my foot. I stood just a minute until the worst pain was past, then tried walking. I was forced to move a lot slower. I did not let myself think what would have happened if I had fallen and broken a bone. The thought was too frightening.

After perhaps twenty minutes, I was at the road. I breathed a sigh of relief and sent a thank you heavenward. I was out. And I was glad to see a lot more daylight than I had seen in the woods. I limped my way down the road to the country store. It was closed, but I went to the side door, which led to the owner's living quarters and knocked. A woman came to the door.

"Oh, you hikers are back late," she greeted me, looking for the others.

I quickly explained to her my plight. I told her I would try to take Jonas' carriage and would ask someone to come for the other one as soon as I was in Flynn Falls.

"We must send someone out to find them," she replied, clearly concerned. "And you look like you are limping. Did you hurt yourself?"

"I hurt my foot coming back."

"I'll get my husband to take you to your friend's parents in Flynn Falls and he can perhaps bring someone back to get the horses and carriages."

I agreed to this and about twenty minutes later we arrived at Jonas' parents' home. I limped to the door and knocked. Jonas' father came to the door.

"You are rather late," he said. "Where is Jonas?"

I repeated my story to him. They were greatly concerned.

"The store keeper brought me here and he can take you and someone else back for the horses and carriages."

"Come in," he said, "and I will go for help. I will get someone from Wally's family to come along with me. Nora," he said to his wife, "give Amber some supper and check her foot. I'll stop and talk to the police also."

And so Nora clucked around me, giving me a glass of milk as she reheated ham and beans she had cooked for supper. It tasted good although I thought of the three who probably had neither food nor drink for their supper. Nora put ice on my foot, which was a bit swollen. She was quite worried about her son, but was relieved that they were most likely all together and kept saying they would find their way back. It was not long before the parents of Wally and also Jane arrived. Jane's parents were very concerned. They had not really wanted her to go and now she was lost out on the mountain. The mother was nearly hysterical and was free with her blame when she heard how Jonas had taken off to see what kind of animal was making the noise. Jonas' parents had his uncle and aunt there from Steeplechase and Nora suggested that I might want to go home with them.

"I can't go home until I know the others are safe," I said. "They will soon be found, but I must talk to them. Maybe your sister and husband would be kind enough to stop and tell my father that I am here so he does not worry."

This they agreed to do, and I put my foot up and tried to relax. And the wait continued.

CHAPTER 4

D r. Fredrick McDurfee was relaxing on the front porch of his home when Dr. Hunter Renwick rode slowly by on his horse.

"Good evening, Dr. Renwick," the good doctor called.

"Good evening to you, Dr. McDurfee," he replied, stopping his horse.

"Come on in and keep me company. I'm lonesome tonight."

Dr. Renwick tethered his horse and joined him on the porch.

"You are missing your wife," he said softly.

"Yes, I am, but I am also missing Amber. She went on a hike today with her boyfriend and another couple and they are not back yet. Left at two this afternoon already. Now it is nearly dark. I am a bit irritated at Jonas for keeping her out so long. Amber's Mama used to do the worrying. Now it is up to me. Jonas is not as responsible as I'd like," he grumbled.

"And Ray is gone also?"

"I think he found himself a girlfriend. He was a bit vague as to his whereabouts this evening."

The doctor paused just a bit. "And what about your girlfriend?"

Dr. Renwick smiled. "I do not have the pleasure of having one."

"What? Then it is no one's fault but your own! You would be an asset to any household."

"Thank you, sir, for your kind remarks."

"And I would like to call you by your first name if you have one."

Dr. Renwick chuckled. "I do have one. It's Hunter."

"And I am Fredrick." They shook hands, sealing the changed relationship.

A carriage was pulling into Park Avenue and conversation ceased as they watched its approach. It stopped right in front of the house. The man handed the reins to his wife and stepped down from the carriage and walked up to the men.

"Doctor McDurfee?" he asked.

"I am he," answered the doctor, getting to his feet, concern on his face.

"I come with a message from your daughter Amber. She is at the home of Jonas Williams and there seems to have been a problem on their outing and she is back, but the others are still somewhere out on the mountain."

"What? Why was she not with the others?"

"I do not know, but I think it is good she was not with the others since she is the only one who has arrived home."

"Is she hurt? Why did she not come with you?"

"She did hurt her foot and although we offered her a ride home, she was quite determined to stay until the other three hikers got back. But she wanted you to know that she is safe."

"Thank you very much, but I shall go after her right now. Who knows when they will find the others."

As the carriage drove away, the doctor turned to go into the house when there was a shout from the park. He turned and saw a boy running across the village green toward the house. He waited until the person arrived. It was a young man, known to the doctor, who lived with his parents down on South Street.

"Doctor McDurfee, we need you to come. My father is very sick."

"What happened?"

"Nothing, he just fell over in pain."

The doctor looked at Hunter. "When it rains, it pours. I shall have to let Amber in Flynn Falls."

He turned to go to the house. Hunter hesitated just a second or two.

"Would you like me to fetch her?"

The doctor looked back at him. "You would?"

"I will be glad to go for her. I shall just go home and hitch Ruggles to my carriage."

"I would be most grateful. The Williams live in the red brick house directly across from the Flynn Falls Inn."

"I think I know the house."

Hunter turned and began walking out to his horse.

"And Hunter."

"Yes?"

"Make her come home. She is stubborn. Use force if you have to," he added with a grin.

Hunter smiled just a bit and then mounted Ruggles and headed home for the carriage.

———

It was ten o'clock and I was weary with apprehension. How would they ever find Jonas and the others on the mountain in the dark? I was tired of the near hysterics of Jane's mother. No wonder Jane was so scared. She got it from her mother. Furthermore, I was tired of making excuses for Jonas who had run off and abandoned me. The police had been here to question me and a search party of sorts was sent out, but they did not promise much beyond waiting till daylight and hoping they had found their way back by then. It seemed this happened every so often that someone got lost on the mountain, but they usually turned up again by morning.

I was relieved to hear the knocker, ever hopeful, although Jonas would not have knocked. But perhaps someone had news. Mr. Williams, who had been chatting with Wally's father, got up quickly and went out in the hall to answer the door. No one spoke in the room, all ears straining to hear who had come. The voice sounded familiar but I could not place it. It almost sounded like Dr. Renwick, but he would not be here. And then the door opened and Mr. Williams looked at me.

"Someone for you, Amber," he said, stepping back as a very sober Dr. Renwick stepped into the room. After glancing around the room, and nodding to the others, his eyes met mine and he made his way slowly to me. Stopping in front of me he spoke in low tones.

"Your father sent me to bring you home."

I was shocked. Why would he send this man to pick me up? I'm afraid I looked at him rather blankly.

"Why did he not come?" I asked warily, wondering what the Williamses thought of this handsome stranger coming in the dark of night to pick me up.

"He just left on a sick call. And I happened to be there."

I sat there, not knowing what to do. I really wanted to stay till the others were found. They might be hurt. Although I was cross with Jonas, I wanted badly to know what happened. I did not want to leave without talking to them. Maybe I would even stay overnight if they invited me. I looked up at Dr. Renwick, not making a move to stand up.

"I sent word with someone from Steeplechase that I would stay here till the others show up."

"He knows that but he gave me instructions to bring you home." Dr. Renwick was not smiling.

I made no move. I felt guilty leaving, knowing my friends were out on the dark mountain.

"I come at your father's express wish," Dr. Renwick repeated, holding my gaze. He hesitated just a moment and then added quietly, "He said I should use force if necessary."

That was clearly a warning to get up and follow. There was something about those sober blue eyes looking so intensely at me that caused me to blush. Although he had spoken in a very low tone, I was sure everyone in the room had heard every word and I was very embarrassed over the fact that I blushed for this man and hoped the Williamses did not notice. It sounded like Papa was determined I come home and although I was old enough to make my own decisions, I knew I had to obey Papa. I looked away from those steady, sober eyes and got up, forgetting for the moment about my foot and I instantly cringed in pain.

"You are hurt," said my rescuer, taking hold of my arm.

"Not bad. I just forgot. I wrenched my foot on the mountain."

"Which foot?"

"The left foot."

"Then I shall stand to your left and you can take hold of my arm."

I did as he said, not looking at anyone else in the room, which remained quiet, all eyes, I am sure, on this stranger. I limped a bit as I walked to the door and when I got to Jonas' parents, I stopped. This needed an explanation.

"Thank you so much for everything you did for me. My father wishes me home and has sent Dr. Renwick to bring me since he had to leave on a sick call."

"We understand," said Mr. Williams, talking a good look at Dr. Renwick. "We will let you know when the others are found."

We then stepped out of the house and walked to the carriage. I was tired and my foot hurt and I am afraid I leaned rather heavily and now gratefully on Dr. Renwick's arm.

"Step up with your good foot and I will assist you," he said as we arrived at the carriage.

I did so and he put his hands on my waist and lifted me so that I barely used either foot. It was not long until he was sitting by my side and with a flick of the reins, we were heading up the moonlit road to Steeplechase.

At first there was no talking. There was something very formal about Dr. Renwick. He was not the kind of person around whom I could relax. I felt like we both sat rather stiffly in the silence and for the life of me, I could not think of anything to say to him. Finally he spoke.

"May I ask how you got separated from the others?"

"We were just talking around the lake when we heard some heavy sound in the woods not too far away. It had to be an animal. Jonas instantly called to Wally and off they went to see what it was."

Silence.

"And without a word he was gone?"

"Well, he said I should watch the fishing equipment."

Once again there was silence and I felt I had said something wrong.

"And the other girl?"

"Jane? She is a city girl and was simply petrified of the woods to begin with and when Wally was just about out of sight, she took off after him. I guess she felt safer with him than with me."

"What time was this?"

"I don't know. I really don't know, but I must have sat there for hours. Literally hours. When it got too dark, I knew I had to get out of there. So I hid the equipment and followed the trail back. It was even darker in the woods, away from the lake, and it seemed twice as far on the way out."

"And you got hurt."

"Not bad. It could have been worse. I was almost running because the woods was quite dark already and I wanted to get out of there as quickly as possible and my picnic basket hit a tree and threw me off balance and well, I got hold of a tree for support and kept from falling by sheer determination, but by keeping my weight on the front of my foot at a dumb angle, it got sprained."

There was silence for several minutes and the only sound was the clopping of the horse and the squeaking of the carriage in the warm night air. There was a bright moon rising in the east and myriads of stars above us. We passed a house where I could see by the dim light of the oil lamp in the window, a cat on the windowsill. I could not tell if it was on the outside looking in, or on the inside looking out. After several miles, we made the turn toward Steeplechase.

"Tell me about your friend," said Dr. Renwick.

"Jonas?"

"Yes, your father called him your boyfriend."

"What do you want to know?"

I looked up at him, but he did not look at me. He looked straight ahead although he must have noticed the movement of my head.

"How long has he been courting you?"

I hesitated at his choice of words. I suddenly realized that it did not quite feel like courting. We did not have serious discussions. We had fun together. Jonas always had some plan for fun or fishing. Mostly fishing.

"About seven months."

No comment. I wondered what he was thinking. I wondered if Papa could have made some remark about Jonas to Dr. Renwick. For some reason, I felt like I had to defend him.

"Jonas did not plan for this day to turn out as it did."

Hunter did not answer immediately and when he did speak he ignored what I had said in Jonas' behalf.

"What does your friend do for a living?"

"He works in a furniture factory. But he does not like it."

As soon as I said it, I regretted it.

"What does he like to do?"

I thought Dr. Renwick put extra emphasis on the word like.

"That is easy. He is an outdoors person and loves to fish and hunt. He also has a boat. We went out fishing on Lake Champlain one time."

The horse's clopping was the only sound for a half a minute.

"What do you enjoy?"

"Me?"

"Yes, you."

It seemed like a strange question. We were talking about Jonas. I felt somehow that he was telling me something.

"I don't care that he likes hunting and fishing," I said defensively.

There was a slight hesitation.

"That is not what I asked you," Dr. Renwick said softly.

"I enjoy people and my cat and chatting with my friends, especially Mindy. I enjoy cooking and baking."

"And fishing?"

I hesitated. "Yes, I enjoy fishing." But I had hesitated first.

"Sometimes," he said.

"Yes, sometimes."

"What are the qualities you like best about Jonas?"

I remained silent. How did he come up with all these questions? There was a part of me that was enjoying this deep discussion with Dr. Renwick. I had never had such a serious discussion with Jonas. At the same time, I felt like it was not only Jonas that was coming up on the short stick. I was, too. I remembered what Mindy had heard about this man. He did not have a good opinion of women after his disappointment with a girl. It was not only Jonas that he disapproved of, he seemed to be finding me shallow as well. In fact, I felt a bit shallow as we talked. But I was proud to be Jonas' girlfriend. Or at least had been up to now.

"I enjoy Jonas as he is," I said suddenly, defensively once more.

Dr. Renwick looked straight ahead saying nothing. But in the silence I felt his disapproval. The truth of the matter was that I did not know what good qualities would count for Dr. Renwick. I really did not know what to say and I felt young and immature. And looking at Jonas through Dr. Renwick's eyes, Jonas looked shallow to me also. Or at least immature.

"Why can't you answer my question?" asked my interrogator.

"I can," I said even more defensively. "Jonas is always full of life, always doing something. He is good looking and...."

I stopped. I had not said enough on one hand and too much was understood by my listener.

He must think me very young and foolish. In my embarrassment, I lashed out at him.

"You don't have a good impression of women do you?"

I shocked him by my question. He turned and looked at me.

"Why do you say that?"

"Well," I said, hesitating because I had shocked myself as well. But he had asked personal questions of me and I was now fighting back. "I think you must have had a bad experience with a girl."

I stopped short. I was tired and feeling disapproved of and the words had just slipped out. There was a short silence.

"Would you mind repeating that?"

I was silent. That was a wretched slip of the tongue. He would know that I had listened to gossip about him.

"Miss McDurfee?"

"I am sorry. I should not have said that. One hears gossip."

"What, exactly, did the gossips say?" There was a slight edge to his voice.

"I was told you don't trust women. That you don't court anyone because of a bad experience."

There were a few moments silence once more.

"I suppose the source was reliable?" he asked when I remained silent.

"You yourself would know if it was true. You alone know the truth."

"But you would not know if it were true."

"No," I said, and then on the spur of the moment added, "is it true?"

Dr. Renwick had turned his head away from me but now he gave me a long, silent look before he spoke. My face felt hot.

"I have good reasons for my opinions."

After this talk with me, I was sure he had not changed his opinion of women, rather, I had surely reinforced it. He could well think it of me. I thought of his questions about Jonas. I suddenly felt that Jonas and I were both badly wanting. And I had no clue how to defend myself.

"So you admit it?" I asked, still on the defensive.

He did not answer.

I sat in silence, embarrassed and feeling that he must have a terrible opinion of me.

To my relief, I noticed we were turning in on Park Avenue. As we approached the house, I could see Papa, barely discernible in the darkness, waiting for us on the front porch. Seeing the carriage, he got up and slowly walked out to meet us. He watched silently as Dr. Renwick got out of the carriage and carefully assisted me as I stepped down.

"I owe you, Hunter," said Papa. "You need to come for supper one day next week. We'll get in touch."

"Glad to be of help. How was your patient?"

"Dead of an apparent heart attack before I got there," Papa answered with a sigh.

Poor Papa. He always blamed himself when he lost a patient. I felt Dr. Renwick's eyes on me and I somewhat reluctantly held out my hand to him. I felt very young and exposed, after our talk. *What must he think of me?* I felt like I had not said a decent thing to him all evening.

"Thank you for bringing me home, Dr. Renwick."

He took my hand and kept it as he gave me a sober look.

"Don't sell yourself short, Amber," he said softly.

And then he turned, got in his carriage and without another word left us. It was the first time he called me by my name and I did not know why, but it pleased me. He had asked questions that were none of his business, but there was something about him I liked. Perhaps it was substance.

Papa, seeing my limp, offered his arm.

"So you got hurt?"

"Not bad."

I gave him a quick rendition of my near fall and once in the house, Papa asked a few questions and probed my foot. It hurt but he assured me nothing was broken. It was midnight and time for bed.

"You are exhausted," said Papa. "We will talk in the morning."

I climbed the stairs, leaning heavily on the railing, my head whirling with the events of the day. I wearily undressed, praying for the three who were lost on the mountain and collapsed in bed, my thoughts switching at the last moment to the conversation with Dr. Renwick. Just what did he mean by selling myself short?

CHAPTER 5

Sunday morning I awoke to bright sunshine. It would be a warm day. I immediately thought of Jonas and prayed that the hikers were found. Now, in the light of day, I found myself not so worried about them. I got out of bed and gingerly stepped on my foot. The night's rest had done wonders for it. I barely felt any pain. Since Laura would not be here today, I made my way downstairs to make breakfast. Papa was already in the kitchen having coffee. Ray had yet to show his face but by the time breakfast was ready, he stumbled in.

"When did you get home last night, Ray?" asked Papa.

"I went to a birthday party on Pipers Hill. It got late."

"Who had the birthday?"

"Marty Spinner."

"Tobias Spinner's daughter?"

"Yeah."

"Never heard you mention her before."

"Only met her last week. Dr. Renwick and I were at the Spinners' farm to see a sick cow."

"Anyone besides you at the party?" asked Papa with a grin.

"There were about sixteen of us and we had a bonfire and the night just sort of got away from us. It was fun."

"You didn't encounter any lost hikers, did you?"

Ray looked at me.

"No."

"The other three got lost," I said.

"What? How long were they lost and why were you not with them?"

So I told the story. Papa was hearing details for the first time also. Somehow this morning with the bright sunlight I had hopes they were all home again. But I was eager for some word of them.

Because the church was just two doors down from us on Park Avenue, we left the house just minutes before the service began. Now, as we made our way off the front porch, a carriage drove up to the house and stopped.

"Jonas! I am so glad to see you! Whatever happened?"

Jonas swung down from the carriage and tethered his horse, looking so well and happy that I wondered for just a few seconds if it was all a trick they played on me.

"How are you?" I asked.

"I am fine. We all are."

"When did you get home?"

"About an hour after sunrise."

"Tell me the story."

"He will tell us all after the worship service," said Papa in a firm voice, his eyes on Jonas. "I think we need to find our pews and thank God that everyone is safe."

Jonas gave Papa a surprised look. Papa had given no word of greeting. And now Papa was laying down the law and if Jonas knew what was good for him, he would come to church with us, although he was not exactly dressed for it. He rather meekly walked beside me into the church.

The service was about to begin. Papa always sat close to the back because sometimes he was called out for a sick person. Now as we followed Papa into a pew about four rows from the back I gave a quick glance at the pews behind us, to find a pair of blue eyes looking into mine. Dr. Renwick. I had to wonder what his thoughts were at this moment.

After the service we all walked over to the house and into the parlor.

"Now Jonas," said Papa, "let us hear what happened."

"Well," he began with a quick look at me, "when I heard this animal in the trees, I wanted to see what it was. It sounded big. So Wally and I took off to see it."

"And Amber was told to hold the fort in the meantime?"

"Yeah, well, I thought we would be back soon. But Jane, she is scared of her own shadow and did not want to lose sight of Wally, so she came running after us. We probably followed the animal sounds ten or fifteen minutes, and were not too far from the trail, I don't think, when we saw a moose. A big one. It was not all that close to us, but Jane freaked out. I mean she went crazy and ran as if chased by a dragon. She just took off and there was no stopping her. She did not follow a trail, she was just in a panic to get away. Then Wally took off after her and I finally went after Wally, so we would not get separated. By the time we caught up to Jane, she had fallen and hurt herself and was nearly hysterical. We could not do anything but let her rest a while as Wally tried to calm her. When we finally could try to get back to the lake, we had no idea where we were and had to move slowly because Jane was hurting. But we could not find the trail and finally realized we were hopelessly lost.

So we went toward the light and it was uphill for a while but eventually we were going down the mountain. It took a long, long time because we were not on a trail and walking was difficult."

Jonas, shook his head, almost in disgust and then continued his tale.

"We just could not get to the bottom of the mountain. We walked for hours and had finally decided we must sleep on the mountain when I saw a glimmer of light. We headed for that light. It took a long time but we finally got to a little cabin. As we approached the door, the light went out. They were going to bed. We knocked at the door. They did not want to open it. Finally Jane talked to them and they opened the door. It was an old couple. Harris, I think the name was. They gave us sandwiches and coffee and let Jane sleep in a little storage room and Wally and I slept in the living room on the floor."

Jonas looked at Papa.

"And then?" I asked.

"This morning the old man took us back to the country store, but the carriages were no longer there. So he took us to my house. We came down on the wrong side of the mountain so we had a rather long ride home."

None of us said anything. Jonas looked at me.

"Did you bring the rods and other things?"

"I could not carry them out. I hid them behind a rock so no one would steal them."

"You don't have them?" His face darkened a bit and I glanced at Papa, whose face was getting red.

"I will give you instructions exactly where they are. You will find them easily."

"You mean I have to go back again?"

"If you want your fishing rods."

"When can we go?"

"I will not go along. I hurt my foot and I have no wish to go back there again for a long time."

"What happened to your foot?"

"I almost fell when trying to get out of the woods before dark after waiting hours for you all, and in trying not to fall, I sprained my foot."

"But it is alright now?"

"Almost."

Jonas gave me a long, curious look. I was not talking to him as I usually did. Somehow I was seeing him in a bit different light today.

"Where do I find my rods?"

"Along the narrow part of the lake that we came to first. I hid them behind the big rock at that end of the lake. You will easily find them."

"Who picked you up last evening at our house?"

I wondered if his father or mother wondered about my escort.

"A friend of Papa's."

Papa looked like a thundercloud and I was very relieved when the door shut on Jonas a few minutes later. Jonas was not invited for dinner, although I do not think he would have stayed if asked. Then Papa turned to me a gave me a long look.

"Is that what you want in a husband?" he asked me and walked out of the room. I got up and made dinner.

Ray kept us entertained at dinnertime, but in the afternoon I sat for a long time on the porch. My weekend had been an eye opener. Jonas had looks, was very entertaining and, let's face it, was very self centered. He really was not good husband material. But I did not want him to think I was quitting him just because he left me alone on the mountain to find my way home alone. He had not meant to do that. Maybe I would wait a week or so before I called it quits.

Monday morning arrived with a thunder shower. But rather than cooling things down, it seemed to add to the humidity. After breakfast, Ray was sent out to check on some patients and Laura arrived for the day to cook and do the laundry. I was free to help Papa. After an hour at his desk, I was called to the office. A little girl named Polly was the patient with a boil on her leg. She was terribly frightened and the mother could barely control her when Papa wanted to examine the boil. I did not blame her. I am sure it hurt. I chatted with the little girl and promised her a lollipop, if she would hold still. Then I helped her mother hold her down while Papa worked on the boil. I was quite exhausted by the time I handed Polly the promised sweet. After a light lunch, I headed to the bank and took care of Papa's finances. Then to the post office and apothecary for medicinal supplies for Papa.

When I stepped out once more onto the hot sidewalk. I glanced across the street to the bakery that Mindy's parents owned. Mindy had only recently moved to an apartment above the shop and I had yet to see it. I decided I would take time now to see her apartment. We had a lot of catching up to do. I waited for a team of horses pulling a wagon of hay down the dusty street and then walked across to the bakery. The boardwalk along the stores was covered with a tin roof, which made it very nice in rainy or snowy weather. Even now, it gave shade from the hot sun.

"Hello, Amber," called Mindy's mother on seeing me. "How are you?"

"Fine. I am looking for Mindy."

"She is finished for the day and is up in her apartment. Go on up."

"Thank you, I think I shall."

I went out of the shop and entered the door that led from the street to the upstairs. It was a long flight of stairs and I somewhat wearily counted them as I went up. Thirty steps! Who wanted to climb thirty steps every time one went home? At the top of the stairs was an open space from which one could go down a back stairs to the back of the stores. But I turned to the right, entering a wide hall and knocked on the first door. I soon heard footsteps and the door swung open.

"Amber! I was hoping it was you! I saw you come out of the bank. Come see my very own apartment!"

Mindy's space consisted of a living room and small dining room all in one, plus a kitchen and bedroom and a small washroom. The ceilings were high and so were the windows that looked out onto Main Street.

"Oh, this is lovely! How I envy you! How did you ever convince your folks to let you have it?"

"They said it really wasn't proper, me being here by myself, but I am twenty-one and I told them if they did not make it to the bakery some day, I would be right here. Sometimes in the snow they did not get here early enough. And since their renter recently got married, it was available."

"Wow! You can keep track of everyone from here," I replied, walking over to one of the two windows that offered an unobstructed view of the busy street below.

"I can—and I do. It is very interesting. Except the roof over the boardwalk is somewhat restrictive for directly below the windows. And I almost don't even have to put a coat on to go to work in the winter!"

"I envy your privacy."

"How is everything at your house? Is the housekeeper working out?"

"She is, really. And she is a sweet woman, but I don't think cooking is her passion, like it was Mama's. She cooks probably like most other women, but we are accustomed to Mama's cooking and Ray is always after me to cook like Mama on Laura's days off."

As I talked, we were both idly watching the activity on the street below us. I saw the stagecoach leaving the inn. I saw a variety of carriages and wagons, and farmers bringing their fresh vegetables to the grocer just up the street. The window was open to let in the air and as we talked I saw a familiar carriage coming down the street.

"Oh, here comes Dr. Renwick," said Mindy. "I often see him heading up to Pipers Hill. He probably serves the farmers up there."

As she talked, Hunter slowly came down the street. He looked very handsome on his horse and I could understand anyone who stopped and watched him ride by. One of us must have moved at the window and it caught his attention. He looked up and I had no time to look away. Our eyes met and held for a second or two. He nodded without a smile and somehow I felt uncomfortable, hoping he did not think we were watching for him. After our ride home on Saturday night, I felt he knew too much about me. As of yet, Mindy knew nothing of my hiking experience.

"That reminds me," I said, "Papa told Ray this morning to invite Hunter for supper tomorrow evening again, so I need to ask Ray what to cook. Ray has his favorites and may want something special for the occasion."

"Dr. Renwick is coming for supper again? And what is the occasion?"

"You mean why is he coming?"

"Yes."

"That is a long story. Do you have time?"

"I always have time for a story."

Mindy went to her kitchen and brought us each a glass of iced tea with ice chips in to cool us off. She also offered me an iced cupcake from the bakery. We took seats by the window, for my sake, and as we drank our tea, I gave her a detailed account of the weekend's adventures. For some reason, I left out some of the serious questions that Dr. Renwick had asked me on the way home.

"Wow. So you were riding around with the formidable Dr. Renwick late at night while Jonas was lost on the mountain. Was Jonas jealous when he found out how you got home?"

"I doubt it. He does not seem the jealous type. In fact, maybe he doesn't care enough to be jealous."

"Oh?" Mindy gave me a long look.

"Our relationship is not going anywhere. What about you and Carl?"

"We are not moving very fast, but I still have hopes something will develop."

I stood. "I must get home. Papa will think I got lost. See you at the band concert on Wednesday."

I was no sooner home, than I got a visitor. Peggy, the minister's wife, came over. The parsonage was next door and all my life we were free to just run into each other's houses when we needed something.

"What have you run out of, Peggy?" I asked with a smile when she knocked and came in the door. Sometimes it was bread, a cup of sugar or some vanilla flavoring she needed.

"People!" she announced.

"People? Are you losing church members?"

"No," she laughed. "But I am in dire straits for someone to stand at the church table on the fourth of July. No one is free. It seems everyone is either in the parade, the Outhouse Race, selling food or who knows what and no one wants to do the church table. And Julia Cooper, who is always eager to help, is sick."

"I'm free," I said. "I'll do it."

"I've always loved you, Amber. Just never forget that and now I love you even a bit more."

We laughed together. Peggy was, she claimed, thirty-nine but it seemed she was that age a long time. In fact, she was most likely closer to forty-nine. She was a very positive person and was good for her husband who was perhaps ten years older than she was and took life very seriously and was sometimes it seemed, overly concerned about his parish.

"Are the prices on?"

"Not yet. Can you help with that?"

"I can."

"Come over to the church basement Thursday evening and we will do it together. Is that good for you?"

"It is."

Independence Day was a huge event for the town of Steeple-chase. It was always celebrated with a parade that went down Main Street, up North Street and around a few other streets. Nearly everyone in the village was somehow involved. There would be many craft tables set up on the village green, the band would be playing, there would be food sold, and some people would have their own private "flea market." Besides this, the church had a sale. That table sold anything the church members wanted to donate, and the money that was collected went to the church to pay the coal for the winter. The table could have jams, jellies, pillows, needlework, used items—you name it—it could be on that table.

And so I had a job for the day. I was not sorry. It would be a fun thing and one met so many people. I had convinced myself that I was done with Jonas, however telling him would be hard and it would be good to be busy and get my thoughts on other things.

"What do you want me to make for supper, Ray?" I asked at breakfast on Tuesday morning.

"Mama's chicken pot pie," he answered promptly.

"Do you think Hunter will like that?"

"Yes. I already told him about it."

"Does he cook for himself?"

"Not much. I think he eats sandwiches at noon."

"Does he have a housekeeper?"

"He has some girl that comes in and cleans once a week and does his laundry, too. I think he usually eats at the inn evenings."

And so it was, that I went to the butcher and bought a chicken and went home and made my homemade noodles. I was glad that the heat was giving us a break. The day was almost cool, which made cooking easier.

I had mixed emotions about the supper. There was something about Hunter that I liked, but another part of me wanted to stay my distance. He was too keen in his gazes. His looks were contemplative and I worried about what he was thinking. With what I heard of his opinion of women, I always felt he was looking for a fault. And I knew I had them. I felt sure that he thought of me as a very shallow person and I resented that. I told myself I did not care what he thought, but obviously I did care. Who wanted to be regarded as a shallow person? Besides, he definitely thought Jonas was shallow. What had he said that night upon leaving? Something about me not selling myself short.

I had to think of other things or I would be a nervous wreck at the supper table. And I remembered that when he saw me at Mindy's window he had nodded but I had not returned his greeting at all, but instead stood as if frozen as I watched him ride out of sight. Whatever must he think of me? Surely he thought I had no manners at all. I wished suddenly that he had not been invited, but this was Papa's way of thanking him for fetching me from Flynn Falls.

I cooked the chicken and Muggins was happy for the skin and the meat I gave him bit by bit as I boned the chicken.

"You are getting too fat, Muggins. Any cat your age should let up on food."

But Muggins was happily licking his chops and giving his face and paws a thorough washing after all that fat, and completely ignored me. The cat was a part of our family for years and Mama and I had thoroughly spoiled him.

The pot was cooking, the pies were in the oven and I had the veggies ready to heat. I would go out and sit under the tree a bit and mentally prepare myself for Dr. Hunter Renwick.

CHAPTER 6

Supper was at six thirty and shortly before supper I slid the two apple pies out of the oven. We could eat them hot, or at least warm. I made a lettuce salad from our garden lettuce and heated the corn Mama had canned last summer.

As it turned out, both Papa and Dr. Renwick were a bit late. Both because of emergency care of humans and animals. But by seven we were ready to eat. As the men came to the table, I gave a quick look at our guest. His eyes always startled me.

"Good evening, Dr. Renwick," I said.

Before he could answer, Papa interrupted.

"I think we know each other well enough to dispense with the formalities, do we not, Hunter?"

"I agree," replied Hunter. Then he looked at me and paused just a second.

"Good evening, Amber."

If he had not paused and turned those very meaningful blue eyes on me before he spoke, I would not have blushed. But I felt the blush coming and quickly spoke so no one would notice.

"Please take seats."

Once more, Hunter helped me sit and Papa said the blessing on the meal.

"Hunter, have you ever eaten chicken pot pie?" asked Papa as we filled our plates.

"Not yet, but it smells wonderful."

"My wife was from Pennsylvania and so she fed us her Pennsylvania Dutch recipes. I am glad she taught my daughters how to make them. And how is your cooking?"

Hunter chuckled. "I am afraid I am not making any headway in that area, but then, I can't say I have really tried. I confess I am quite satisfied to make a sandwich at noon and I fairly often eat at the inn in the evening. Being in a public place helps my business."

"Yes, I suppose it does," answered Papa. "Of course, one day you will have a wife to do your cooking for you."

Hunter did not reply and we ate just a short while in silence.

"Did Mrs. Kenny come for her cat?" asked Ray.

"She did and before she left she told me the whole story again. Thanks to her I arrived here late."

Ray laughed. "I guess when you don't have a child you make your pet your child. But the way she coos and talks to that little Susie cat, I never heard the likes." He looked suddenly at me. "Of course Amber comes close to it. You should hear her greet the cat in the morning."

"Don't you fuss over me talking to Muggins," I said quickly, afraid of what Ray might say about me now. "Muggins needs all the love he can get with you around to tease him," I added, aware of Hunter's gaze. "What happened to Mrs. Kenny's cat?"

"A dog tried to take a bite out of it."

"How terrible. If a dog came after Muggins when I was around it would be the dog needing a veterinarian."

"You sound quite violent," commented Hunter, trying not to smile. "I would hate to get into a fight with you."

"Just don't touch my cat," I said, smiling.

"Is that a threat?" asked Hunter, his eyes challenging me.

"Believe me, it is," said Ray.

Papa chuckled and the rest of us followed suit.

"So it is hands off on Muggins," said Hunter, still looking at me with a slight grin.

"Not really. I am sure you are very kind to animals, with your line of work. However, Ray here is another story altogether."

There was a bit of a lull in the conversation.

"So the other hikers got back safely?" our guest asked me, changing the subject abruptly.

"They did," I replied, giving a quick summery of their rescue.

"So 'all's well that ends well,'" said Hunter, leaning back in his chair now, observing me.

"Sort of," I said, or rather mumbled. I was glad when he asked no more.

After dessert the men went to the front porch and before I was finished doing the clean up, Hunter had been found by a distressed farmer and had to leave. Before he left, he came into the kitchen.

"Thank you for another wonderful meal."

"You are welcome and if you are interested, I have an extra pie you may take along."

His eyes widened. "Really?"

"Really. I am trying to use up the old apples because we will soon have ripe apples on our tree. And I doubt you bake pies."

"So it is not just pity for my circumstances?"

I laughed. "Do you need pity?"

"I accept your gift with a grateful heart," he said, grinning and bowing ever so slightly.

And then he was gone and I was left smiling in the kitchen.

Wednesday dawned with a bright sun. This was Laura's baking day and she promised to help me later to can green beans, but I needed to pick them first. I put on my sun bonnet and worked in the garden that was planted behind the house and which bordered Papa's office. The hot sun beat down on me and it was not long until I was too warm. Muggins followed me and found a shady spot between the rows of beans and flopped down to sleep. As I looked over the garden I saw a part of it that badly needed to be weeded. Instead of picking beans, I began weeding. As I worked, I heard voices over at the parsonage. Looking over, I saw Pastor Thomas over in his backyard, sitting with a young man I had never seen before. Fifteen minutes later I looked up to see the two of them coming over to the garden.

"Good morning, Amber," called Pastor Thomas.

"Good morning, Pastor, excuse my dirty hands."

"I want you to meet my nephew who will be living with us for some time."

The young man with him had straight brown hair, was of medium height and had warm, brown eyes.

"His name is Waldo Buckum," continued the pastor. "Waldo, this is Amber McDurfee."

I smiled but did not offer my dirty hand.

"Pleased to meet you and what brings you to Steeplechase?" I asked.

"My parents just returned to South America in mission work and I am temporarily living with my uncle and aunt."

"Welcome to our village," I said. "I hope your time here will be enjoyable."

"Thanks. Do you need help weeding?"

I looked at this young man. He seemed sincere. Maybe he needed something to do.

"I will always accept help in the garden. It is not my favorite job."

"Looks like you have green beans to pick also."

"That is what I came out to do, but I could not stand the sight of the weeds."

"Let me help. I am at loose ends just now and need something to do. My uncle has things to do that I cannot help with this morning."

For the next two hours, Waldo helped me in the garden. We talked mostly of vegetables and gardening, but I did discover he was at a crossroads in his life. He had thought he wanted to be a medical doctor, but changed his mind. He was now interested in the ministry. He would observe his uncle and help where he could for a month or two and then decide if that is what he wanted to do.

"I've spent a lot of time praying about it and am hoping the Lord shows me the way."

"I'm sure He will," I said as he left.

But I felt guilty after he left. I wasn't at all sure that God would tell him. It seemed God was not so eager to show me the way. I felt at very loose ends. Sure, Papa was glad for my help, but I think he was a bit worried that I was not involved in a solid courtship by now. And Jonas was not his idea of a husband for me. Prayer. Did it really work?

I got to the band concert just a bit late. I had eaten supper at home because Laura had tried one of Mama's recipes and I felt I should eat with the others. Actually, her meal was very good and I complimented her on it. She seemed quite happy to use Mama's recipes but Mama, of course, did not write all her added seasonings down. She just knew what would taste good.

By the time I got to the concert, the band was already playing and I saw Mindy was once more up in the gazebo with the other band members, playing her flute. To my surprise, Jonas came within minutes of my own arrival.

"Hi Jonas, you got here early this evening."

"Hi," he said, sitting down beside me. "What, no food?"

He looked so disappointed I had to laugh.

"I ate at home. If you are hungry, you may go to the house and eat the leftovers."

He looked at the house and then his eyes went to the shops on Main Street.

"I think I'll get a sandwich at the inn and bring it back."

He left me again and I sat back and enjoyed the music and chatted with people who passed my blanket. It would be hard for me to tell Jonas that I wanted our relationship to end. But now that I was convinced that it must happen, it made no sense to continue.

When Jonas returned, one of his friends came by and remained with us until the concert came to an end. By then he and his friend had a fishing trip planned for Saturday. As the village green slowly cleared of people, Jonas seemed in no hurry to leave, so we remained there.

"I'm going fishing with John on Saturday, but I'll come by Sunday," he said as he finally got to his feet.

I looked around the park Only a few people remained strolling around the green. I was irritated by his fishing with his friend. I realized that I was, and probably had always been, second fiddle to Jonas' love of fishing. I took a deep breath.

"Jonas, we need to talk," I said.

He must have heard the seriousness in my voice and sat down again, looking at me curiously.

"What about?"

"About us."

"Us?"

"Yes. I think it is time to call it quits."

"What do you mean?" I could see the shock on his face.

"I feel like I always take second place to fishing in your life. We have been seeing each other for seven or eight months and I think we ...have run our course."

"Is this because of the hike?"

"No, you certainly did not plan to get lost on the mountain. But at the same time, it was an eye opener for me. I don't think we really need each other and I am not inviting you to visit me on Sunday."

Jonas looked at me a long time.

"So this is it? Can I do something so this does not happen?"

"What can you do? You love fishing. It is your first love and perhaps always will be. No, I hope we can remain friends, but I don't believe we will ever be anything more."

He stood and looked across the park in deep thought. Then back at me. I heard a rumble of thunder in the distance.

"So, I guess I'll go. I'm sorry."

He suddenly looked forlorn. I had never seen this expression on his face. He was always so sure of himself and all was right in his world. I suddenly felt choked up and I blinked back tears. However, I knew this was the right thing to do.

"I'm sorry, too," I said.

He had left his horse tethered at the front of our house. We walked across the green in complete silence to his horse. I saw Papa was on the porch. I stood and watched as Jonas mounted his horse and with a last glance at me, rode off into the rumbling thunder. I did not want to talk to Papa or to anyone else. I did not look toward the porch. I turned and walked away from the house. My head was bowed and as I walked, I had very mixed feelings. I was happy and sad at the same time. I was relieved that I had made the break, but sad that I had hurt my friend. I walked to the end of the avenue and down Main to North Street. I suddenly realized I had tears on my cheeks. As I made the turn to North Street, a carriage turned from Main also onto North Street. I looked up briefly and met the gaze of Hunter Renwick. It was nearly dark, but I saw his face by the light of the gas lamp that stood on the corner. I saw him nod in recognition.

Then the rain hit and I ran home through the wind, letting the rain wash away my tears and it felt good. I felt washed clean.

CHAPTER 7

$\mathcal{I}$ndependence Day dawned with a hot sun and a lot of activity on the village green. I rose from my bed and walked to the window. I had a good view of the park although some parts were hidden by trees. Already craft stands were being set up. People would be coming to the park early. It was time I got out there myself. I was excited about my day. I dressed hurriedly and went down to make breakfast.

An hour later I was out on the green. I watched as Waldo and his uncle brought the table for the church items out on the green and I put one of Mama's tablecloths on it. Then they brought a wagon of sorts with boxes holding the many items for my table. It took me a good hour to set it up. At the same time lots of other tables were being set up. There were tables with all sorts of crafts. Some were full of scarves and hats that were either knitted or crocheted. A few artists had their artwork either on tables or set up on the lawn. A man was filling balloons with helium and someone else was displaying home crafted wooden toys. Some tables were simply full of items people wanted to get rid of—old tools, kitchen ware, old dishes. My table was jams, jellies, hand crafted pot holders and pillows. Some embroidery items and even sunbonnets and aprons were made and donated by ladies of the church for this table. Before I finished setting up, people were already coming by to see what was being offered for sale.

Just then a former school chum of Ray's came running up to me. "Amber, is Ray around?"

"Yes, but I am not sure where."

"If you see him, tell him we need him in the Outhouse Race. Jack broke his arm."

"Oh dear, did he break his arm practicing the race?"

"No, he fell out of a tree yesterday. Oh, there I see Ray."

And he was off. I knew that Ray and some of his friends had won the race one year, but Ray had not been in the race for the last couple years. Now, with him having had no practice, I doubted they could win.

The Outhouse Race was well known in our community. It was a team event and the name of the team was appropriate to the type of race it was. Need I say more? The name was painted on the side of the outhouse. The team would build an outhouse using the lightest wood so it would be easier to push. And there were wheels on the bottom. Inside the outhouse was a seat for the lightest of the boys to sit on. During the race, this outhouse had to be pushed clear around the village green on Park Avenue without the person on the seat falling off.

At nine o'clock the green was crowded with people and the parade began. There was music by the town band in which Mindy and Carl took part. There were various wagons with children or groups of fiddlers playing music. The village school marched by and a team of horses pulled the village fire pump. The woman who owned the candy shop rode on a carriage pulled by her pony and threw candy to the children, which was received with squeals of joy. The businessmen of the village walked down the street, advertising their wares. Close to the end of the parade, I was amused and surprised to see Dr. Hunter Renwick walking down the middle of the street, his "doctor" bag in one hand and a big dog of questionable breed on a leash in the other. The village vet was offering his services. I wondered if it was his own dog. He was, in some respects a rather reserved person and I was surprised he did this. He did not see me, but I saw him nodding to people he knew.

Immediately after the parade, came the annual Outhouse Race. This was the highlight of the day. Now there was great excitement as school boys, mostly teenagers and other young adults lined up for the race. All loose stones of any size were carefully swept away earlier so there would be smoother sailing for the five outhouses, which now stood in a row. It looked like close quarters for the racers. It was, of course, only youth who participated. Each outhouse had one person inside sitting down and two pushing. No one was at the booths just now, as we all wanted to watch the race. There was a moment of suspense as we waited for the signal. And then a shout and they were off. The outhouses careened wildly up North Street to Park Avenue, sometimes nearly hitting each other. As they rounded the corner to come in Park Avenue and past our house, one runner slid, falling to the road and was nearly run over by another outhouse. But quick as a whip he was up and running again. I was surprised to see Ray's group in second place as they flew past our house and the parsonage. However, something went wrong in front of the church and their outhouse swung nearly into the grass and they were now the last in the race. However, the first outhouse went around the next corner too fast and flipped over and another outhouse slammed into it. No one appeared hurt, but now one outhouse was out of the race and the other one had a hard time catching up. By this time the other three teams were out on Main Street and racing for the finish. Now everyone was yelling, including me. Finally one outhouse made it safely across the line, Ray's group close on their heels and the team that had crashed came limping in a bit later. I heard the mayor jokingly call out to the victors that they should take a victory run around the park, but they had all collapsed on the grass and were trying to catch their breaths.

I hurried back to my booth. Peggy soon joined me. Because of the nice weather, business was good. It seemed the whole village was out to celebrate. Lots of people came by and many bought jam, jelly, or some crocheted item. I looked across the park and saw Mindy selling sweets from the bakery. I would check that out a bit later.

While Peggy was busy chatting with a lady from our church about a ladies' tea, Waldo came by.

"Good morning, Waldo, can I sell you some jam?"

He laughed. "Not today and no pillows either."

"Did you watch the race?"

"I did," he said, his warm brown eyes sparkling. "It was the only race of its kind I've ever seen."

"It is an annual event," I replied, "and a lot of work goes into it. And it is always fun. Usually there is some kind of accident, but so far no one has been seriously hurt."

"I think my uncle said your brother was in it."

"He was, as a last-minute substitute due to another person getting hurt. A few years back Ray was on the winning team, so I guess they thought him a good choice. But he had no practice running for today's event. However, due to the crash, they did make second."

A woman with two children came and after admiring the pillows, chose one. As I took her money, Waldo wandered off again. Jonas was usually here on this day. Flynn Falls did not have an outhouse race, and he always came to see it. I looked around cautiously, but did not see him.

An old woman came to the booth. She always looked cross. I knew her as Miss Frank.

"What's in them there jars?" she asked, her face wrinkled in what I knew was a perpetual frown.

"Jam. Homemade jams."

"What for kind?"

She was holding one jar up and squinting badly, trying to read the label.

"That one is gooseberry."

She nearly threw the jar down. "Gooseberry? That ain't good. Too sour. My mother always made me eat gooseberry pie and I hated it. What is this one?"

I took the jar from her to read the label.

"Blackberry."

Another woman came to check out the jams. Miss Frank paused to look at her.

"Don't get that one," she said, pointing at the gooseberry jam, "it ain't good. Too sour."

The woman, a stranger to me, glanced at me with a bit of a smile. She picked up the jar and read the label.

"I like gooseberry jam," she said softly, "and I haven't had it for a long time. I'll take it."

Miss Frank looked at the woman in amazement.

"You like that sour jam?"

"I do. Not every day, but sometimes."

Miss Frank mumbled something under her breath and ambled on, cane stomping the lawn, not buying any jam.

I found myself hoping that Hunter would come by. Although I never felt quite comfortable around him, he intrigued me. I found our conversations challenging and I wanted to know more about him. However, I saw no sign of him. When there was a bit of a lull, I asked Peggy to stay while I ran down to Mindy for some sweets. When I got to her booth, she was, as I knew she would be, very busy, but I got in line.

"Amber, what can I get you?"

"Please tell me you still have a mini cherry tart."

"Here it is and one of the last. I'll be sold out by noon. I saw the race. I did not know Ray would be in it."

"He did not either until shortly before the race. He replaced someone who broke his arm yesterday."

I went back to the booth and Peggy left, promising to relieve me at noon. My busiest time was probably past and I could manage on my own. Next to my booth was an artist selling watercolors. He had a tarp over his paintings, just in case of rain. Beyond him was a man selling old glassware. Other booths were of various wood crafts, paper crafts and someone was selling caramel popcorn. It was just about noon when Jonas and Wally came past. Jonas looked straight ahead, while Wally smiled at me. I wondered if Jane was still involved with Wally or if her parents had not allowed her to continue that relationship. I was hurt that Jonas would not talk to me. I had hurt him, or at least his pride had been hurt. His actions just reminded me that he had some growing up to do. With his good looks, he could easily get another girl, I had no doubt. Probably he was never turned down before. My thoughts returned to Hunter. His pride must have been hurt, too, to have given up completely on women. A man's ego must be a very fragile thing, I decided.

A couple girls that I had gone to school with came by pushing baby carriages. A part of me envied them. They were settled. They had a husband and were starting families. I felt more like a bird flying hither and thither, looking for a nest.

I saw Bentley heading my way. He walked slower these days although he was never a man to move very quickly. He had worked in the bank all his life and now I would see him sometimes puttering around his garden.

He grinned his famous grin as he stopped by my booth.

"Hello Bentley. I did not see you in the outhouse race."

He chuckled. "They did not want me."

He looked at my wares a bit.

"Where is the boyfriend?"

"It is over."

He just looked at me a moment. "The men must be blind these days."

I just smiled. I would not tell him it was my fault.

"One of them will catch you yet."

"I hope it is the right one."

"It will be. How is Papa?"

"He is keeping busy."

"That is good." He paused. "His work will be a good thing for him. It is the end of the day that is hard. When he comes in the house to talk with your Mama and hold her hand...."

He had me blinking back tears. Then he quietly ambled off again. I was glad for Bentley. He had always been a friend of the family. After his wife died, he had sometimes come and sat in the kitchen to chat with Mama while she cooked or baked. He knew by experience the loneliness that Papa was going through.

At noon Peggy came and took my place while I went for lunch. Since I was so close to home I went home for lunch, making myself a sandwich, which I enjoyed with a glass of milk and made the same for Papa. Ray would find something in the park.

"Sell anything?" I asked Peggy when I returned to the booth.

"Not a thing," said Peggy. "Everyone was having lunch. But you sold quite a bit."

"I did, but I think it always sells best in the morning."

Shortly after Peggy left again, Old Wolf came by and actually looked a bit at our table. I doubt that he ever bought anything. I did not know if he even could buy on his own. His face needed a shave and he really did not look very clean. I always thought I should say something to him but did not know what to say. I did not even know his first name.

"Did you see the outhouse race?" I asked him finally.

But Old Wolf just looked at me and then walked away. As I watched him disappear down the pathway, I saw a couple boys coming toward him. Just as they got to him, the one boy put out his foot to trip him. He did not quite manage it, but Old Wolf knew they meant him harm and my breath caught when I saw the look he turned to the departing, laughing boys.

And then I saw Hunter coming in my direction. I automatically brushed my hair from my face and my heart immediately beat a bit faster. I looked at my wares. There was nothing to interest him. The only jam left was gooseberry, which I did not like myself and I could not recommend it to him. And the other items were more for women. But when he came by, he stopped. He still had his dog with him.

He gave me a long look before he spoke. That was enough to rattle me.

"How are the sales going?"

"Not bad but I am tired of it now. I'm trying to get rid of my gooseberry jam. Do you need any?"

He chuckled. "That is one jam I can do without."

"Is this your dog? I didn't know you had a dog."

"I just inherited him from a client. Don't ask me what breed he is. A mutt of some kind."

I went to the dog and petted him. He immediately rolled over on his back.

"He is big enough and shaggy. What is his name?"

"Beanbags."

"Beanbags? Surely not!"

"Beanbags."

"What a terrible name. I am surprised he is still living with such a name."

Hunter laughed. "I thought of changing his name, but I think he has at least ten years behind him and I hate to confuse him at this late date."

"Hello, Dr. Renwick! So nice to see you again."

I looked up to see a very elegant woman leading her small dog on a leash. I did not think she was from our village. She had eyes only for Hunter.

"Good afternoon, Miss Gordon. I see you are giving Sadie a bit of exercise."

"She loves to go walking. But what is this monster with you? Will he hurt Sadie?"

"This is Beanbags," said Hunter, "and he is a real teddy bear."

"Oh, hello Beanbags," said the woman, who was not really hearing the pitiful name for the dog. She was too busy smiling and batting her eyelashes at Hunter. I found I was disgusted that she stole Hunter from my little chat with him. Although he made me uncomfortable, I enjoyed talking with him. I took another look at Miss Gordon smiling beguilingly at him and for just a fleeting moment I considered throwing the glass of gooseberry jam in her direction, but did not think it would serve my purpose.

They, still chatting, walked away and I was left fuming at my little gooseberry stand. And then Waldo arrived.

"How's it going, Amber?"

"Good. I've sold most of the items. When the table is no longer so full, people don't stop to look. How about buying a glass of gooseberry jam?"

Waldo laughed. "Gooseberries and I have never been very friendly."

I was glad for someone to talk to and Waldo seemed to be looking for conversation.

"I can only offer you the grass to sit on, but I am a bit bored right now and would like company."

"You have it," he said, sitting on the grass. "When does this end?"

"Usually around three, which means another hour here."

I looked where Hunter and the woman were still talking. I hoped he would come back this way and see Waldo talking with me. I wasn't sure why.

"Any fireworks this evening?"

"Yes, around nine thirty. They set them off in the open field just at the edge of town. The whole town comes out for it. Where did you grow up? Did you have fireworks and a parade?"

"I was born in Vermont but I spent most of my growing-up years in Honduras where my parents were and still are, missionaries."

Over the next half hour I only asked a few questions. Waldo loved talking about his time in Honduras and he had many stories to tell.

"So you did not go back with your folks."

"I must find my own way and I am not finding it very fast. My parents have great faith in prayer as the way to find out God's will. But I don't seem to find that God gives very direct answers. Do you believe in prayer?"

He surprised me with his question.

"Yes, of course," I said, probably too quickly.

No one had ever asked me that before. It was assumed I did since I was a baptized Christian. Then I thought of my frantic prayers for my mother when I had been horrified to see her lying on the kitchen floor in her own blood. But, it seemed, God had turned a deaf ear. As a child I had prayed for the whole month before Christmas for a doll house like a school mate had. I had been invited to her birthday party a month or so before and she had received the doll house from her wealthy parents. I prayed earnestly the whole month of December. I never got it. My parents, knowing what I wanted and knowing it was too expensive, asked my uncle to make one for me. I am sure my parents saw the disappointment on my face on Christmas morning, when I viewed the very simple doll house. I did not say anything, but I felt God had let me down.

"But I must not be praying right," I continued. "I don't often get what I pray for." I looked at Waldo. "Goodness, I never said that out loud before."

Just then it thundered very loud and I jumped, thinking I was about to be punished for my lack of faith.

"Hey," said Waldo, "I think we are going to get rained on."

I had been so caught up in Waldo's stories that neither of us noticed the storm moving in. Within minutes we could hear the rain coming in the trees. Together we pulled the empty boxes out from under the table and put the remaining items in the boxes. Other people had bigger problems. Those with artwork or books or anything that could be damaged by wind and rain were really scrambling. We shoved my boxes under the table and Waldo and I ran in different directions, helping others get their crafts or whatever under cover.

Finally, not seeing Waldo anymore, I ran across the park and into the house. I was dripping wet and did not think I had a dry spot on my body. That was the end of the celebration for me, except for the fireworks in the evening.

I cooked supper for Papa and Ray and about quarter after nine Ray and I headed to the open field where the fireworks would be set off. It never did clear off but at least it was not raining. Ray soon left me and I mingled and talked with friends and acquaintances as we all headed for the open field. Once there, I looked around for Mindy, but I could not find her. The crowd was too large and it was too dark. I wished I had made plans to go with her because it seemed I had now wandered into a group of people I did not know. Suddenly I heard a voice I did know. Jonas. He was standing not far from me with a girl. As I was trying to see if I knew her, he turned toward me. I saw him look to see who I was with and then turned away again. It felt funny not saying hello. I was sorry we were not free to be just friends.

And then the show in the night sky began. I just loved the wonderful explosions of color and light raining down on us and between the noise of the fireworks and the oohs and ahs of the crowd, I forgot all else, although it would have been more fun with a friend. The show, I knew, would not be very long and I was still keeping my eyes open for Mindy. I began moving about between explosions and finally my search was rewarded. She was standing with Carl and we talked a few minutes and all too soon the show was over. As the last display lit up the sky there was sharp lightning and a roll of thunder. The wind picked up and the first drops of the approaching storm began to fall. I had already been soaked once today and did not really wish to get soaked a second time. The crowd quickly dispersed and as I hurried off the field to Main Street, a man stepped close to me and I suddenly felt his hand on my lower back.

"I'll see you home," said Hunter.

"Thank you," I said, rattled by his sudden appearance and the touch of his hand. "You at least had the presence of mind to bring your carriage. I should have thought to bring an umbrella. I was soaked once already today."

He made no reply and in seconds we were by the road where his horse, Ruggles, was tethered.

There was no carriage. I gave Hunter a quick look. He looked down at me with a twinkle in his eye.

"It appears that the carriage dissolved in the rain."

He mounted and held out his hand. I hesitated. Could I do this?

"Give me your hand."

With buckets of water falling over me, I did as he said and in short order I was behind Hunter on his horse.

"Put your arms around me and lock your fingers together!" he shouted above the thunder.

This took a bit of courage, but the pouring rain gave me no option. I encircled him with my arms and locked my fingers.

"Hold tight!" he called as another streak of lightning lit up the sky and the thunder rolled.

And I did. The rain was coming down in torrents and we were off. I automatically leaned my head against Hunter's back to keep my face protected. And suddenly, I was enjoying my ride. This was fun. Whoever would have thought my evening would end like this? I was finding the ride with Hunter was a lot more exciting than the fireworks. But alas, it could not last forever. When we got to the house he grabbed my arm as I slid to the ground.

"Thanks!" I shouted above the storm, but he was already gone with the wind.

CHAPTER 8

The following day Ray took the train to New York City where he would attend a six-week course on the latest findings in the medical field. I was sorry to see him leave. It was bad enough with Mama gone and now Ray was gone, too. I had to think back to the days when all my siblings were still home. How different it was now. Instead of a house full of shouting children, just Papa and I rattled around in the big house at night.

The first week or two I worked hard in the garden and Laura, who I was learning to know and like more and more, helped me do some much needed housecleaning. But the July sun was hot and it was sometimes so muggy I just did not want to move. I saw little of Mindy who had taken on more responsibility in the bakery and even Waldo, who had been around so much, came only evenings and sat on the porch with us. On concert evenings, I would look for Hunter, but he did not show up. Even Muggins barely moved these days and when he did move, he seemed not to quite know where he was going. There was a swimming hole in the river that flowed along the road from Pipers Hill and one desperately hot afternoon Mindy and I went there in an effort to cool off. It worked. The water was cold in the mountain stream and although we did little swimming, we stood in the water and watched some young boys dive off a big rock into the deepest part of the swimming hole.

The last week in July on a hot afternoon, I happened to meet Mindy in town as I was coming back from the post office. She suggested we go into the inn and have a cold drink. She said her apartment was too hot and she wanted to chat. The dimness of the inn made it at least feel cooler than out on the blazing street and we found a small table right at the window where we could watch people go by. The inn was a two-story dark frame building. It had an upper as well as a lower porch for the guests to sit out and observe the activity on Main Street while waiting for the stagecoach, but this was not a busy time of day for that.

"What is new with you?" I asked, once we were seated and waiting for our cold drinks.

"As far as Carl is concerned, I have a feeling things are going in the wrong direction. I really like him, but I saw him talking with Julia White the other day from my window. He was down the street a way—somewhere around the shoe store—and they stood there too long as far as I am concerned."

"Oh dear. Does he ever talk about her?"

"No, but he never talks about our future either."

We sat in silence a few moments, sipping our drinks.

"By the way," Mindy continued, "guess who has just been put on town council?"

"I have no idea."

"Dr. Hunter Renwick."

"Really? How did he get on council so fast?"

"Besides being liked by all the females in town, the mayor must like him as well."

"But although the females like him, he sure knows how to keep his distance, doesn't he?"

"He must have been hurt badly. I think the mayor has a party for the members of the council annually. Maybe he will take you to that. You seem to have more contact with him than any other female that I know," said Mindy.

"That is just because he is friends with Ray. And Papa. When is the party?"

"I forget. I just know there is one sometime in the summer."

"Hmm. Do you think he will need a partner for the party?"

"I don't think there is another single man on council. My guess is that he, if he is smart at all, will ask a girl to go with him. Maybe you should offer your services."

"Me?"

"Don't tell me you don't like him."

"I am no good at flirting and I could never suggest to him that he take me," I paused. "Even though I did go horseback riding with him one night."

"You what?"

I had to laugh out loud at Mindy. I looked around and noticed a few people watching us. They appeared bored, possibly waiting for the stage to arrive and were probably listening in on our conversation.

"What are you not telling me?"

Mindy was wide eyed and nearly in my face.

"It was after the fireworks. I did not know he was there. Then when the storm hit, I ran for Main Street and suddenly he was running beside me, his hand on my back, telling me he would take me home. I thought he had his carriage, but it was just his horse. But he helped me up on Ruggles and I hung on for dear life and all too soon we were at home."

"That is all?"

"That is all. I enjoyed it. But don't expect anything to come of it. As I said, he is friends with my brother and my father enjoys chatting with him also. I am just part of the family."

"Would you go out with him if he asked?"

"Of course, but although he is always polite and the perfect gentleman, I feel like he has an arm out to keep me at a distance. He obviously does not want to get involved. Now with Muggins it is a completely different story. Muggins likes him and will go to him and even jump on his lap for a few minutes and then he scratches Muggins under his chin and around his ears and the cat nearly goes cross eyed with pleasure."

"So, you know what to do," said Mindy with a twinkle in her eyes, "sit on his lap."

The picture this brought up in our minds set us both laughing rather wildly.

"Well, I should be going," said Mindy some time later, glancing out the window. "Oh, is that the handsome Dr. Renwick going into the post office?"

I tried to look, but someone was coming in the door of the inn and blocked my view. However, I did see Old Wolf was walking by. He was just passing the inn, carrying something in a paper bag. His eyes were on the sidewalk in front of him and not far behind him were two young boys, their eyes on Old Wolf. One of the boys held a long stick that looked like it came from a weeping willow tree, and every so often the boy would poke him with the stick. I could not hear what they said, but it was not kind, that I am sure.

"What is it that makes children pick on those who are less fortunate?" I asked as I saw Old Wolf turn and glare at the boys.

"The only thing I can think of is that everyone else bosses the children and here they see someone they can torment," answered Mindy. "But they better watch out. Once in a while he gets angry and then he becomes dangerous. And I don't blame him."

I was so busy watching the boys that I barely heard her. The boys stopped taunting Old Wolf just long enough to run up on the porch of the inn probably to look in the window where we sat. But as they ran up to the window, I saw Old Wolf take a bottle from his bag and as he lifted his arm, I realized the boys were in danger. I knocked on the window to warn the boys and in that instant, Old Wolf threw the bottle. It hit the window hard. Right where I sat. I barely know what happened in the next minutes. I remember smelling vinegar, but I was also aware of pain and of something running down my face and arm. There was a large hole in the window and I heard people screaming. One of those screaming was Mindy. She had blood running down her face, too, and then the innkeeper got between us and everyone was looking out the broken window and door. There was a scuffle going on outside. But I was not interested in the scuffle. I was hurting and bleeding. I had gotten a direct hit.

"Hey, this woman needs a doctor," I heard a man say close to me.

I was the daughter of the doctor and I was not far from home. I tried to ignore the burning pain of the cuts as I rather blindly made my way past the people who had gathered at the window and walked unsteadily to the rear of the inn. When I got out the back door, I walked as fast as possible across the parking lot and past the livery. It seemed to take a long time and I wondered if I was going to make it. I felt the blood running down my face and my arm hurt badly where the bottle had hit me.

The sun seemed too bright for my eyes and I almost ran into a carriage parked outside the livery. I was hurting badly. Because of the blood running down my face, I could barely see where I was going. I just wanted to get home to Papa. *How could it seem so far to get home?* I feared I would faint. I had to keep moving although I wanted badly to sit down on the grass along the sidewalk. I had maybe a half a block to go when I heard someone run up behind me. In that moment all I could think of was Old Wolf's angry face. I cringed and turned in fear. But it was not Old Wolf. It was Hunter. I felt myself sway a bit in my relief.

"I've got you," he said, putting a strong arm around me. "Lean on me."

I was more than glad to lean on him. I was scared I would collapse and wanted to get home on my own two feet. We slowly, oh so slowly, crossed the street to my house and then made our way back to Papa's office. I did not feel good at all. In fact, I felt worse all the time. I kept hoping I would not faint, and my cuts, which seemed to be many, hurt and burned from the vinegar. I know Hunter was saying encouraging words to me, but I could not concentrate. I just wanted Papa. I remember Hunter saying we were almost there and then I felt myself slumping and I don't remember how Hunter got me to my father's office. But it seemed just as we approached the office door, we met Papa coming out with his bag.

"Amber! What happened?"

I was so glad to be home and in Papa's care that I paid no attention to what Hunter told Papa and I don't rightly remember how it happened, but I suddenly found myself on the table in Papa's surgery.

"Stay here, Hunter," I heard Papa say. "I may need you. Can you help me? I just got a message from Mrs. Boyle's husband that she is in labor and I need to leave. Her babies come quickly."

"If I can be of any assistance, I will help."

"I want to see how bad the cuts are."

Papa made quick work of looking me over.

"Hunter, go get Laura. She should be in the house."

Hunter left and was back shortly with Laura who gasped upon seeing me, her hand across her mouth.

"Most of the cuts are not too deep, just bleed easily from the glass," said Papa, who had put gauze on all my cuts. "Just this one below the elbow is deep. That needs stitches. Hunter, you helped your father in his practice?"

"I did," said Hunter solemnly.

"I am sure you have stitched animals. Have you ever stitched a human? I think you said one time that you did."

"That is correct. A few times."

"I would like you to take care of Amber, Hunter. Will you do it? I cannot send you to Mrs. Boyle. She would not appreciate a vet attending her at the birth of her baby. But you could take care of Amber. This cut on her lower arm definitely needs stitches. Will you do it for me?"

When I heard Papa asking Hunter to stitch me up, I came out of my daze. This could not be. I looked at Hunter who must have seen the fear in my eyes.

"I shall, if she will allow me to."

"She will allow it," said my father shortly, giving me no choice in the matter. In fact, he never even glanced at me.

"Papa," I whispered, "I feel awful. It hurts so badly."

"We will get you fixed up in no time," said Papa, finally looking at me. "Hunter knows what he is doing. Laura, take this cloth and get the worst of the blood off of her."

Papa then turned to Hunter and as Laura was wiping the blood and vinegar from my body, I heard Papa giving Hunter instructions. I could hardly believe that Papa was going to leave me and allow a veterinarian to stitch me up. And all this talk of stitches scared me to bits. I had never had them and I did not want them now.

"Maybe I don't need stitches," I said to Papa between clenched teeth.

"Amber," Papa leaned closer, looking me in the eyes. "There is no doubt in my mind that Hunter will do a fine job. But now we need to stop the bleeding. Let me show him where to find supplies and I must be off or Mrs. Boyle will have the baby before I get there. Keep pressure on this gauze, Amber. We need to stop this bleeding."

Papa turned to Laura. "Get these bloody clothes off of her and put a gown on her. They are in the closet over here," he said, pointing. "I shall smell like a pickle when I get to Mrs. Boyle."

Papa gave me one last look and saw the pain I was in.

"And Laura, get her some brandy. It is in the cabinet by the door. It will take the edge off the pain."

Papa then gave a few instructions to Hunter and without another word was out the door. And me? I was left to the ministrations of a housekeeper and a veterinarian. My brain reeled. *How could Papa do this to me?* Hunter immediately took over. I was dully surprised how at ease he seemed in the situation. I heard him say something to Laura and then he walked out of the room.

Suddenly Laura was by my side with the brandy and a small glass. She poured some into the glass.

"Can you lift your head enough to drink this?"

Every cut was screaming, but I somehow managed it with her help. The brandy tasted terrible and I coughed and choked a bit on it.

"Close the door," I said, when she began removing my dress.

"Dr. Renwick, do not come in this room until I give you permission," she called, not closing the door.

"I hear you."

It took a lot of energy on my part until the dress was off of me and replaced with a gown. I was glad to lie down again. I felt faint from the effort and closed my eyes for a bit. My cuts hurt and the vinegar stung. However, I was thinking about the stitches Hunter was going to give me. When I heard Laura leave the room with my bloody dress, I opened my eyes again. On a small table next to me stood the bottle of brandy. I wanted more of it. I hated the taste of it, but I wanted the pain dulled as much as possible. The little bit I had swallowed had not done enough. I needed more. But how to get it? My good arm was on the wrong side of me and I felt half sick from pain already. However, Hunter would be returning soon and this was my chance. I somehow, painfully, forced myself up far enough into a sitting position so I could reach the bottle of brandy. With shaky hands and a hurting, bloody arm, I lifted it quickly to my lips and took a few gulps right from the bottle, nearly choking on the alcohol. The bottle began to slip from my fingers and it was only with supreme effort that I managed not to drop it and to get it safely back on the table. I had barely settled back, exhausted from the effort, when Hunter returned.

"What is this gauze doing on the floor? It must stay on your arm to stop the bleeding."

He took more gauze and pressed it against my arm.

"Can you hold it?"

I did not answer, but with my good arm, I tried to hold it tight against my wound. I was sure the gauze had fallen to the floor in my efforts to get the brandy.

Hunter was wearing one of Papa's white coats and I felt very exposed, lying on the table in the middle of the room with a gown on. Then his eyes fell on the brandy.

"Oh, here is the brandy. Shall I pour you some or don't you need it?"

I hesitated, thinking of the stitches. He had no clue that I had not only been offered some by Laura, but had also helped myself to more.

"I would like some," I replied, feeling guilty. It really was taking the edge off the pain and maybe if I drank enough I wouldn't feel the stitches at all.

He poured some in a small glass and he put his arm around my back to give me support. Any other time I would have been thrilled to have his arm around me. Now I was very ill at ease to say nothing of the burn of the cuts. I drank once more. I had never had brandy before and hoped I had not had too much.

A short time later, Laura was on my left and Hunter on my right. Laura followed Hunter's instructions about cleaning my wounds while he tried to stop the bleeding on the worst cuts. I found that I was feeling better and was so glad I had taken a few swallows of the brandy. Once Laura had the worst of the blood off of me, Hunter told her to press her hand on the bandage on the worst cut to stop the bleeding while he bandaged the smaller cuts. One cut was on my face. Not a deep cut, but bleeding. He wiped my face with some liquid to clean it. With those blue eyes so close to my face, I closed my eyes. It gave me a sense of privacy, which I badly needed.

Hunter then continued to work silently on the numerous cuts on my arms. Now I opened my eyes again. I wanted to see him. A few times I saw him glance at me. Laura stayed close by my side and tried chatting with me but I was mostly non-responsive. I was more aware of the handsome man gently caring for my cuts. Sometimes I would draw back if it hurt too much.

"Sorry, Amber, if I hurt you. I am used to working on animals that are asleep. Feel free to tell me if it hurts too much."

"Could I have a bit more brandy?"

Hunter looked surprised that I asked for it.

"You sure you need it?"

"Yes. I would rather drink the stuff than feel the stitches."

He somewhat reluctantly let Laura pour me another swallow or two. They had no clue what I had already consumed. Once again he supported me as I drank the brandy. Now I was beginning to enjoy his touch. Back on the table, Hunter continued working on my wounds, putting a salve on and bandaging them. The longer he worked, the better I felt. After a while, I rather enjoyed his nearness.

He finally was ready to work on the deepest cut. He removed the temporary bandage and took a good look at it. He cleaned it and put a powder on it. As he worked, I relaxed. So much so that I was quite happy that he was the one tending to me and that he was so very close to me. I now looked right into his eyes as he worked on my arm and I had a sudden urge to tell this man just what I was thinking.

"You know, Hunter, you have the most beautiful eyes of any man I know."

He looked at me a bit startled.

I laughed. "Didn't anyone ever tell you that before? They are so stunningly blue, so..."

"Laura," said Hunter, who was about to put in the first of the stitches, "take that bottle of brandy back to where you got it."

I giggled. I was just so relaxed and content. As he prepared the needle and thread, I spoke again. "I had a couple swallows when your back was turned."

Once again, Hunter stopped short and gave me a long, sober look. Then he looked at Laura. She was looking at Hunter with big eyes and was trying not to smile.

"Someone is not going to have a good day tomorrow," she said.

Hunter gave me a long look, the needle in his hands. I smiled broadly.

"You are incredibly handsome. I'd love..."

Hunter's finger came down on my lips with some pressure.

"Amber," he said in a sterner voice than I had ever heard from him, "I am about to stitch your arm and I don't want one word from you until I am finished. Is that clear?"

Hunter had never used that tone of voice with me and for just an instant I was hurt by it. But it was only a fleeting moment. I was too happy to care but I tried to gain his sympathy.

"Are you angry with me?" I gave him a very fake, sad look. I almost thought he would smile. But he ignored my question.

"Did you hear me?" he repeated very sternly, his blue eyes close to mine and not a smile on his handsome face. "Not one word."

I nodded. He sounded almost angry, although Laura was holding her hand over her mouth and her eyes were merry.

"Laura," said Hunter, "maybe you need to hold her arm down while I stitch. I do not want her moving it."

Laura maneuvered her way to where she could hold down my arm and for the next few minutes it was completely quiet. I felt the stitches but did not cry out. Neither did I talk. Hunter had talked very sternly and I did not want him angry with me.

When he was finished, Hunter gave his work a critical eye and then asked how I felt.

"Wonderful," I answered, with such enthusiasm that I am sure I heard a snort from Laura. "I never had such a handsome doctor. Just Papa. But now I will always ask for you."

I saw Hunter clench his jaw as if to keep from smiling, and his eyes danced as he exchanged another look with Laura. I was so glad to make him happy.

"I shall leave you now," said Hunter. "I hope your wounds heal well."

He abruptly turned and I saw him no more, but I quickly called after him, "You are my knight in shining armor!"

Laura was smiling as she helped me off the table and back into the house, but she did not talk. She even walked with me to my room where she gave me a housecoat to wear in place of the gown.

"There now," she said after I was settled on the bed. "Now you take a good rest and I'll make you some chicken soup for supper."

CHAPTER 9

I fell asleep and did not waken until after supper. In that time, Laura had gone home and Papa had returned. I did not see him but I heard him chatting with someone on the porch. I was hungry and I made my way downstairs, trying to get my head together. I hurt all over if I moved, but otherwise it was not too bad. I was too groggy to think straight, but I was so hungry it felt like my stomach was hanging crooked. I found the chicken soup and it was barely warm anymore, but I was too hungry to heat it. There were two biscuits on the counter and I picked them up and found the butter plate and then sat at the kitchen table to eat. I was famished. When had I eaten last? Breakfast was the only meal I remembered. I had a lemonade at the inn....

My thoughts got clearer. Old Wolf had thrown a bottle of vinegar at the inn. No, at the boys, but it had hit the window—and then me. My thoughts skimmed over the walk home to Papa's office. Somewhere along the way, someone had joined me. And then I was on the table in Papa's office and Papa had to leave and Hunter had put the stitches in me. Hunter. Hunter. I stopped chewing, the biscuit suddenly dry in my mouth. I tried to piece my afternoon together but it became really strange. Papa had given Hunter the job of taking care of my wounds while Papa went to deliver a baby. Yes, Hunter had put stitches in my arm. And we had talked. At least I had talked. I remembered his finger on my lips. *Why had he done that? What had I said to him?* Surely not what I was thinking now. I must have just thought it. Please God, let it have been just my thoughts, not my spoken words.

The door slammed and Papa came into the kitchen.

"Ahh, you woke up. How are you?"

"I am okay, I think," I said quickly, hoping he could not read my thoughts. "Was the baby born?"

"Almost before I got there. She has them easier than most women. How did Hunter do as a doctor?"

I hesitated. This was not a subject that I wanted to discuss with anyone, much less Papa. "Okay I guess."

"You are not sure?" Papa stopped what he was doing and gave me a hard look.

"Well he stitched me up and...." I found I did not want to think too much about Hunter stitching me up. "I forget. I'm still groggy from sleep."

"I see he has your arm bandaged well so I will wait until tomorrow to check those stitches. How many did he give you?"

"I...really don't know."

"You didn't ask? Or count as he did them?"

"No."

"I hope you did not embarrass me by hollering or crying out," teased Papa.

"Of course not," I answered, but somehow I was not feeling very good about the afternoon. I was pretty sure I had neither cried nor hollered. But as far as embarrassing Papa? I did not want to think too hard in that direction.

"I'm glad you did not get any glass in your eyes," continued Papa. "That one cut on your face is too close to the eye for comfort. But it could have been worse. I'm told the sheriff took Old Wolf home, but I expect he will be put in an asylum. Too bad."

I was wide awake by the time I finished eating, and ordinarily I would have gone out on the porch, but just in case Hunter came by, I stayed in the house. I did not want to see him. In fact, if I let my thoughts take root in my brain, I was pretty sure I never wanted to see him again.

Muggins scratched on the back door and I let him in and fed him. I hurt when I moved around so I went back to my room and sat by the window. Muggins came and sat at the window also. My thoughts went to Hunter, but I brushed them away. I did not want to think of him just now. I felt sorry for Old Wolf. I could still see his wild eyes as he threw that bottle. Now they would lock him away and it was not even his fault. He had been teased by those young boys.

My thoughts were interrupted. I saw Mindy walking up to the house. When she got close enough, I called down to her.

"Come on up, Mindy. I am staying in my room tonight."

When Mindy came into the room I saw a small cut on her face. I had only thought of myself. Others were maybe hurt also.

"Mindy, you got hurt, too."

"Nothing like you. I did not realize you were so hurt. You must have been directly in the path of the bottle that Old Wolf threw. It flew right over the boys' heads and they did not get hurt at all."

"I think the bottle itself must have hit me, as well as all that strong vinegar. I keep thinking I still smell it. And so much glass."

"I am so sorry I did not notice how badly you were hurt. I was busy watching the commotion outside. The sheriff was soon there and they took Old Wolf away. But wow! How many cuts do you have? You have bandages all over and you look pale. Do you feel okay?"

"Not really. My whole body hurts when I move. I almost feel like I have a bit of fever. I feel chilly. I slept for hours after I got my cuts taken care of."

"How did you get away without me seeing you?"

"I went out the back door."

"All alone? It is a wonder you did not faint by the way. Hunter came in soon after you left. I told him you were hurt but I did not know where you were."

I was wondering how much to tell Mindy. I really did not want to talk about the experience. There was too much I wanted to forget.

But she was my closest friend and I had to talk to someone. I could only imagine how she would react to my story.

"What are you not telling me?" she asked, seeing me hesitate.

"Actually," I said, "Hunter saw me and helped me get home."

"Hunter? He must have gone looking for you after I talked to him."

"I guess," I said slowly, having mixed emotions as to the rescue. "Can you keep a secret?"

"Of course." Mindy's eyes were shining with expectation.

"Just as we got home, Papa was leaving for a birthing. He knew that Hunter had some medical experience and after asking him a few questions, he left Hunter and our housekeeper, Laura, in charge of me and he went for the birthing."

"Hunter Renwick doctored you up?" Mindy almost choked as she said it.

"Shh! He even gave me stitches."

"You let a vet give you stitches?" She was horrified and amused at the same time.

"He was qualified. I was not the first one he sewed up."

"No, he sews up pigs, cows, horses, dogs and who knows what else. Maybe pet skunks."

I laughed perhaps for the first time since the accident, but it did not last long. It hurt my face.

"He sewed up people before. His father was a doctor and he was thinking of becoming one also, then chose to be a veterinarian instead."

Mindy just sat and looked at me for awhile. Then she burst out laughing.

"This is the story of the year. The princely bachelor who holds women at arm's length, cleans you up and gives you stitches. Now tell me the whole story in every detail. Was anyone else with you?"

"If only that was all there was to it."

Mindy's mouth was hanging open, her eyes wide.

"Laura is the one who cleaned me up and got me into a gown."

"You were in a gown? The kind where they are open in the back?"

"It was just my dress that Laura took off of me," I said a bit defensively. "And I was lying on my back. My dress was all bloody and smelled of vinegar. I must have smelled like a pickle barrel."

"What a tale," said Mindy just shaking her head in wonder at me. "Actually, I'm jealous."

"You were just horrified that a vet gave me stitches."

"I know. But I would let Hunter do anything to me. Well, within reason. What was it like? I'd have swooned. Did you holler 'ouch' when he put in the stitches?"

"No."

"You were brave?"

"No, Mindy, I was more foolish than I have ever been."

"What is that suppose to mean?"

"I won't tell you tonight. I must sleep on it. I hope I am getting reality mixed up with my dreams."

"Now you have me curious. Did Hunter propose to you?"

"No," I said sadly, "but for all I know, I might have proposed to him."

The next morning I woke early. I felt better. If I had a fever the night before, it was gone now. I just continued to lie in my bed and once again went over the sorry details of my love affair with the bottle of brandy. And its aftermath. I could not claim my memories were all a dream. I feared they were stark reality. I just knew that I did not want to see Hunter Renwick for a very long time. I could not face him after the things I said. Finally, after literally writhing with my memories, I got out of bed. Maybe coffee would help take the memories away. When I got to the kitchen about ten minutes later, Papa was making coffee.

"Amber, how are you feeling this morning?"

"Better. I think I had a slight fever last evening, but I feel better this morning."

"Let me see your arm where Hunter stitched you up. I hope my trust was not misdirected."

I sat down and let him open the bandage. He then took a quick look at the stitches.

"Six of them," he said. "They look good. Don't tell anyone I allowed a veterinarian to stitch you up. I would lose my practice. I missed Ray yesterday. I'll be glad when he returns. As for Hunter, I am indebted to him. I am going up that way this morning to check on Mrs. Boyle and I shall stop and invite him to supper some evening this week."

"Oh, not yet," I said quickly. "Let me recuperate first."

I said it too quickly and Papa looked at me curiously. I had been too vague yesterday when he asked how it had gone. Papa grunted something to himself but let the matter drop.

"I'm afraid Old Wolf will have to leave his parents' home. Too bad, but he really isn't safe here anymore."

"It was not his fault. Two boys were tormenting him."

"You can tell that to the authorities, but I don't think it will help. The townspeople do not feel safe with him."

"It still seems unfair."

"Life is often unfair," said Papa, looking out the window with a faraway look in his eyes and I wondered if he was thinking of Mama.

He soon went to his office. It was my day without Laura and I would have liked to talk to her. I was really warming to her. She was not my mama in any sense, but she was a good housekeeper, was learning to cook more like Mama and she always had a sympathetic ear. But now there was lots to do. I would not work in the garden today. Not with all my cuts. Anyway, it was looking like rain and I needed to do things for Papa in his office. Besides that, I had to make lunch and supper and with my sore arm, everything would take longer.

"And please God, don't let Papa invite Hunter for supper," I prayed under my breath.

Mindy must have been very busy, because she never showed all day, which was fine with me because I wanted to talk to Laura before I gave any sordid details to Mindy in regards to the brandy bottle. Maybe, just maybe, it was not as bad as I remembered. Maybe I was remembering it worse than it was.

At noon, Papa showed me the newspaper. There was an article about the incident. Old Wolf was at home only until a suitable institution was found for him.

———————

Laura arrived early the next day. It was her baking day. Bread, cake, pies. Whatever was needed. Papa was out making visits in the morning for a couple hours and I used that time to chat with Laura.

"How are you, Amber?" she asked once we were alone in the kitchen. I thought she looked a bit long at me when she asked.

"My wounds are healing," I said. Then, after a brief hesitation, I added, "But I have bad memories of the day and I hope you can dispel them."

She was kneading her bread and did not look at me. "What kind of memories?"

"I think you know."

She smiled. Then she giggled. Then she hooted laughing, holding her belly with her hands covered with flour.

"Oh, Laura, please tell me it wasn't as bad as I think," I said, horrified and amused at the same time at her laughter.

"I don't rightly know how bad you think it was," she said finally. "It was a very interesting afternoon. You just said things you normally would not have said. But Hunter and I both know that you were... not yourself."

"Oh, Laura," I moaned as I sat down and put my head flat down on the table, squashing my nose flat against it. "Tell me what I said. And please tell me it is not as bad as I remember."

"I'll just say you gave him a few very nice compliments. You said nothing 'out of line,' if you know what I mean, and I think you learned now that 'more' is not always better. At least not with brandy. It backfired on you rather badly."

"I can't ever face Hunter again."

"Yes, you can. He knows it was the brandy. You boosted his ego in a way you normally would not have. He even stopped you at one point, which was very admirable of him. A lesser person would have egged you on."

"He thinks I am a wanton woman with no morals."

"That he does not. Don't make it worse than it was."

I sat and tried to accept her words but in the end groaned out loud.

"Hunter of all people," I said. "Any other person I could probably laugh it off. But Hunter?"

"Why do you say that?"

"Well, he can look so solemn and is such a gentleman and....I don't know, but I wish it would have been anyone else but him."

"Even Waldo?"

"Even Waldo. Although he probably would have started preaching at me. I just hope Papa never hears what I said to Hunter. And Mama would just turn inside out if she knew."

"You just forget it. You have learned a lesson and you will be smarter for it."

———————

The day Papa took out my stitches is the day he informed me that Hunter was coming for supper. He had met him in town and felt indebted to him.

"Give him a good meal and a good dessert. And we will have him again in the not-too-distant future. He did me a good deed and I know he won't accept money."

In the meantime, I had told my whole sorry tale to an astonished Mindy. I went over to her apartment so no one would overhear my tale. But most of all she found it hilarious. I got no sympathy from her. Now I had to face Hunter. At least there were a few days gone by now for him to forget.

Mindy herself was not in good shape. It was all over with Carl. He wanted his freedom and she reluctantly gave it to him. She was cheered up though with my sorry tale and I left her in better spirits than I found her.

Cooking was the easy part of the day. I baked a ham, made green beans from our garden and put a big casserole of scalloped potatoes in the oven. I sliced our first tomatoes from the garden as well and served pickled beets that were canned from the previous summer. For dessert I made a chocolate cake and we would have black raspberries that we were given from a patient of Papa's. I would serve them with cream.

But I did not know how I would face the man.

I agonized all day about it. Ray was not at home and I would certainly be expected to be an active part of the conversation. I did not want to look into those blue eyes. I did not want to see Hunter reading my thoughts and thinking of what I had said to him.

Late afternoon, I went outside to throw some garbage at the back of the garden when I saw Waldo over at the parsonage.

"Hi, Waldo!" I called. "I see you are back again."

Waldo had told me he would be gone a week or two and now he came over to me.

"I heard some news about you. How are you?"

I could see him glancing at my arm that still had scars and a few scabs on it. The place where the stitches came out was easily seen, too, if one looked for it.

"I am fine. I have recovered well," I replied. And then I had an idea. "Waldo, we are having a guest for supper. Can you join us?"

"Unfortunately no. I am leaving in a few minutes with my uncle and aunt and we will be gone for supper and won't be back until around seven."

"Oh, too bad."

But I was thinking that we would not eat before six and maybe even later.

"Well, come on over for dessert when you get back. Tell us about your trip."

"Sounds good. I'll be there."

I felt a bit guilty and did not know what Papa would think. Maybe I would not tell him. Just let Waldo show up.

Supper was served at six fifteen. Papa was sitting on the porch when Hunter arrived. I did not hurry but by six twenty I could hold off no longer. I went to the door, said a very brief hello to Hunter—barely meeting his eyes—and announced that supper was ready. I was nervous and worked hard at acting calm. At the table, Hunter held the chair for me. I sat at the end of the table with Hunter sitting with no one across from him. I would save that for Waldo.

We bowed our heads and Papa thanked God for the food and also for Hunter and for what he had done for us the day of my injury. I held my breath, not happy about his bringing the subject up already in his prayer.

As soon as we were done praying, Papa looked at me.

"Amber, show Hunter your arm." Turning to Hunter, he said, "I removed the stitches this morning. Good work. I think there will be no scar at all."

As Hunter turned to me, I dutifully held out my arm and I looked at my arm, rather than at Hunter as he looked at it.

"Good," he said. "I'm glad you are satisfied."

I immediately started passing the food but it was just a bit awkward because I was sitting at the end.

"Amber, why aren't you sitting across from Hunter? We could pass the dishes better that way," said Papa.

"Oh, I told Waldo to come for dessert, so I left that place open."

Papa looked a bit confused. But Hunter immediately began a conversation with Papa that gave me the opportunity to simply listen. Now I felt guilty. Hunter was no dumb bunny and I think he knew exactly why I was sitting where I was and also why Waldo was coming. I had meant for them to think that Waldo just happened to drop in, but now I had been forced to give an explanation for the sitting arrangement. However there was nothing I could do about it. I tried to be a good hostess in spite of everything. The fact that Papa said nothing of the brandy flop, told Hunter that Papa knew nothing of it. And Hunter, being the gentleman that he was, acted like all was well.

"The meal is wonderful," he said, taking another piece of ham when I offered it. I gave him a quick glance and thanked him.

I already had dessert on the table when Waldo arrived. I went to the door when I heard the knocker and then showed him his place at the table. The two men knew each other from church and there was friendly discussion during the dessert. Waldo had been to conference in Pennsylvania and was telling us about it while Hunter and Papa and I listened. Finally the meal was over. Hunter and Papa went out on the porch and Waldo helped me clean up the kitchen. I enjoyed talking to Waldo. I liked him more every time I saw him. He was a dedicated Christian and I had a feeling he would give his life in some Christian service.

After the clean up in the kitchen, Waldo asked if I would go for a walk with him. I was glad to get away from the house. We went out the back door and walked around the block. Partway around, Waldo got serious.

"Amber, I really enjoy being with you and I would like to know you better. I would like to spend more time with you. I realize my future is very hazy just now, but...well, I am here right now. Would you let me court you?"

This came as a surprise. A big surprise. Before I knew it, I had agreed.

We talked a long time that evening. Or rather, Waldo talked. He wanted to go back to South or Central America somewhere in mission work. He felt God was calling him into the ministry. And he, though he did not say it directly, was looking for a wife to accompany him. I was excited. Maybe this was it for me. What more could I ask for? Waldo was nice looking, was a sincere Christian, knew what he wanted to do for his life's work and was now interested in me.

CHAPTER 10

August arrived and I now had a new focus in my life. I was spending time with Waldo daily. Now I was not just enjoying talking to him, I was trying to decide if I really should be dating this man that I was sure would not be spending the rest of his life in Vermont. At least not in Steeplechase, which was the only home I knew. I was aware that Waldo was in correspondence with a few organizations regarding missions at home and abroad. I did not feel such a calling, but then, the woman always went where her husband was called. It seemed the woman did not need that special calling. One simply stood by the husband. At least this was my observation.

I was not seeing Hunter and that was fine with me. I was still very embarrassed by my shameless words to him when he was stitching my arm. I spent my days canning beans, making applesauce and helping Papa. My focus was primarily on Waldo—on our courtship. On this particular Saturday, I worked on Papa's books and made a casserole for lunch. It had been raining since daybreak so I could not work in the garden.

Around three o'clock I put on my light raincoat, picked up my umbrella and headed to the library. I did not get much reading done, but when I got the chance, I wanted to have a book available. In spite of the rain, it was good to get outdoors. It was a steady but gentle summer rain and I enjoyed my walk. The library was just a couple blocks north of us and not very large. It was mostly one big room and when I entered, there were a few other people looking for books as well. I browsed through the fiction section and pulled out a couple books and sat down at the one table available to take time to look through them before I made my choice. To my delight, I was soon joined at the table by Mindy and for the next half hour we chatted softly. When she left again, I was the only person there anymore, but I quickly scanned through the books that I had chosen. Hearing the door, I glanced up and found myself looking into a pair of intense blue eyes. I automatically caught my breath. Those eyes always did a number on me. I immediately gathered my books and pushed back my chair in my attempt to stand when Hunter took two steps toward me.

"Stay sitting, Amber."

"I really must..."

I stood up, but Hunter came up to me and placed his hand on my shoulder, his eyes fixed on mine.

"Sit."

I sat. Hunter, who seemed to know just what he wanted, walked to a far corner of the library, picked up a book and then came and sat down across from me. He said nothing at first, he just gave me a long look, which eventually got too long for me and I looked away.

"Amber, we need to talk."

I said nothing although I knew what this was about. Just then the librarian stood up from her desk and looked in our direction.

"The library closes in five minutes."

"I shall see you home," said Hunter, standing up once more. "I have my carriage."

We went to the desk to check out our books. He let me go first. I was very nervous as I stood there knowing he was directly behind me. *What was he thinking?* When it was his turn, I turned toward the door, but something held me back. My raincoat had a belt and I had not buckled it. Now I found one end of it was in Hunter's pocket—where his hand was also. I was trying to figure out how that had happened when Hunter turned—a satisfied grin on his face—and followed me to the door. By the time we were in his carriage, he no longer had my belt in his pocket. However, when I met his glance once we were in the carriage, I could not hold back my smile.

"You really don't trust women, do you?" I asked.

"Where did you get that idea?"

It was a slip of the tongue. I said nothing.

"Just because I did not trust you at that moment, does not say I do not trust women in general."

I did not reply. He gave me a questioning look, as he flicked the reins. The carriage was directed toward my house, but he drove past Park Avenue and turned right on Main Street. It seemed we were taking the long way home.

"What makes you think I do not trust women?" he asked, nailing me with a look as we rode out of the village.

"One hears things."

"What is it that makes girls so susceptible to gossip?"

I looked away from his intense gaze and did not respond. I knew from Ray that Hunter was close friends with a young farmer up in Pipers Hill.

"Do you ever discuss girls with your friends?"

"That is different from spreading gossip."

I was curious about his past. I wished he would tell me why the rumor got out. And I really liked it that we were discussing him rather than me.

"So the gossips were wrong about you?"

He did not reply and I said no more. We were now out in the countryside and coming by the cemetery. He drove in and I could not but help remember the last time I had been here. Also under dripping trees. He drove through the gate, but immediately turned left and stopped there under the old, gnarled oak trees. Then he turned to me.

"Sorry. This may not have been the best place to stop. Should I go somewhere else?"

"You said you were taking me home."

"I shall. But first it is imperative that we have a little talk." He let the reins hang loose. "You don't seem to be able to face me ever since your injury."

He paused and waited for a reaction from me. I said nothing, wanting to forget the whole incident.

"And your silence is a confirmation that it is true," he continued. "You are letting your embarrassing moment come between us. I want to talk to you about that incident."

"Please, no," I said, looking away from him. "I just want to forget it."

He ignored my plea.

"Just how much brandy did you help yourself to?"

I took a deep breath. "I really don't know. I just know I was hurting badly and I thought it would dull the pain. And I was scared of the stitches."

I gave Hunter a quick glance. He was smiling and shaking his head.

"Are there any alcoholics in your family?"

"No!" I said emphatically. "Of course not. In fact, brandy is the only alcohol in the house."

"Did you like it?"

"Not at all. It was the first alcohol I ever had. You heard me cough and sputter, but I wanted to dull the pain."

He sat a moment, thinking.

"Had you eaten any lunch that day?"

I had to think. It had been a busy day and Papa had not come back from a patient. I had things to do and simply drank a bit of milk, thinking I would eat when Papa came back. But that had not happened. I remembered how famished I was later that evening.

"No," I replied. "I somehow missed lunch."

"That would explain some of it," said Hunter, looking into the distance.

There was only the silence of the rain on the carriage roof and occasional song of a bird.

"As to the compliments you gave me..."

"Oh, please, spare me!" I hid my face in my hands and a soft chuckle escaped him.

"Amber, this is what stands between us and I just want you to know I tried to get you to stop talking. Do you remember? I knew you would not say these things to me normally."

"Just forget them!" I said, still not looking at him.

He chuckled again. "I'd rather not forget them. Does your father know about the brandy?"

"No, and Laura did not tell him either, I don't think."

"Look at me, Amber."

He did not talk until I finally faced him.

"I just want you to know that I hold nothing against you for your words under the influence of brandy. In fact, I like compliments. But for your sake, forget them. I would like to think of you as my friend and when you try not to look at me, I feel like I lost a friend."

"I'm sorry," I said finally, touched by his kind words and apparent sincerity. "I do appreciate what you did for me that day."

"Thank you. So, we have it out in the open. Are we friends again?"

I looked at him, took a deep breath and smiled. "Of course."

Hunter flicked the reins and the carriage moved. Once out on the road he turned once more to me.

"As a friend, may I ask if Waldo is courting you?"

"Yes, he is."

There was a pause and I remembered another carriage ride with Hunter when he asked about a boyfriend.

"What are his plans for future work?"

"I am sure he will go into some full-time Christian service."

"Where?"

"God alone knows. Somewhere in South or Central America. He is praying about it."

"Do you pray about your future?"

I had not expected this question. I felt sure that Hunter meant in regards to going with Waldo into the unknown. I was rather scared to think about the future but I had prayed in regards to Waldo a few times. I enjoyed Waldo and held him in high esteem for his dedication to his Lord. I felt privileged that he was interested in me.

"I do, sometimes," I said slowly. But my hesitation had said more than I would have liked to admit. There followed a pause.

"Do you pray about your future?" I asked Hunter, partly to get the attention off of me.

He paused so long that I thought he might not answer. "Not as often as I should."

"Why not?"

"I don't really know. Perhaps I don't really think it helps." He looked at me. "That sounds like blasphemy to you doesn't it?"

"Maybe, but had you asked me the question, and if I were honest, my answer would have been the same. Do you think God cares about those things?"

"Yes," said Hunter immediately. "I believe He cares more than we think. But though I believe it in my head, I don't quite believe it in my heart, or something like that. Otherwise I would pray about it more often."

We had been sitting in front of my house for a few minutes. We were so engrossed in talking that I hadn't realized just when we had arrived.

"Oh, I must go in. It must be suppertime."

I looked at my watch and then I looked at Hunter. He was observing me quietly with a pensive look on his handsome face.

"It was..." I stopped. This was the talk I had dreaded. I smiled and finished with some chagrin. "It was nice talking to you."

Hunter smiled as if he knew just what I was thinking and I felt myself blush at his look.

"I'm glad we talked. Enjoy your evening."

CHAPTER 11

It was a Tuesday evening and Dr. McDurfee had just finished his supper. Amber was already over in the park, having her weekly picnic with Waldo while listening to the band music. It would be a good time for a visit with his neighbor. The doctor checked the front porch of the parsonage. No one. He went to the back of the house. Ah! Pastor Thomas was sitting out under the maple tree. The doctor headed his way and partway there, Pastor Thomas called a greeting to him.

"Good evening, neighbor! How do I rate a visit with you? Do I look ill?"

Dr. McDurfee laughed. "You look great. If all the residents of Steeplechase were as healthy as you I would need to change my vocation."

He took the chair by Pastor Thomas.

"But something tells me you came for a reason," said the pastor.

"Yes," said the doctor, making himself comfortable. He paused. "I've come for information regarding your nephew. I hope you don't mind my curiosity but he seems to be courting my daughter."

"So I've heard. And I don't blame you for asking. What do you want to know?"

"He is your brother's child?"

"Yes. Rupert and his wife Mary have four children and Waldo is the youngest."

"And the family has been in the mission field most of Waldo's life?"

"That is right. He was born here but spent most of his life in Honduras. Four years ago they came back. Waldo was seventeen at that time and he was going through a rough time in his life. He was ready to find his own way and his parents realized their son needed them. Engrossed in their work they had not noticed his needs, his rebellion. They decided to postpone their return to the mission field until he found his way. Waldo did not really want his folks to stay home, but they did. He got a job in town at a carriage shop. He did not really enjoy his job, but he stuck to it. Then he fell in love with a girl from town that his parents disapproved of. She had no time for the church, but neither did Waldo at this time. Roughly two years passed. A lot of prayers were lifted on Waldo's behalf. One thing Waldo really enjoyed was camping. There was a group of young men from the church that he was now only rarely attending, going camping. He was invited to go along. That camping trip was the turning point in his life. He makes friends easily and bonded with one of the boys that was camping with him. One day the group was boating out on Lake Champlain and a storm came up and the boat capsized. Waldo was drowning and this friend saved him. That evening they had a good talk around the campfire and Waldo gave his life to the Lord."

Pastor Thomas took a deep breath.

"It was certainly an answer to prayer. Waldo himself now wants to go into Christian service. His life is changed and he is eager to get on with it. First he thought of work in the medical field, but now he feels God is calling him into the ministry. He gave up the girlfriend and is looking for someone to join him in the mission field. He was raised in Central America and has little understanding for the huge transition it is for someone else. He has a lot to learn yet about waiting on the Lord. I hope Amber will be able to help him wait before he goes on without the Lord's guidance."

The doctor sat quiet a long time.

"I hope so, too," he said quietly. He did not add that he was not sure she could help Waldo in that area of his life.

They chatted then of other things and when the music from the concert on the green came to an end the doctor stood up and offered his hand to the pastor.

"I appreciate your honesty. I'll be praying."

———————

It was at noon three days later that Papa announced that he had invited Hunter home for supper that night. I looked up at him in surprise.

"I still owe him a meal for the work he did on you," he said taking a big bite of his sandwich. "Besides that, I miss Ray. Hunter gives me a male to chat with."

"This is not my day to cook, so why don't we invite Laura for supper, too, and we can make it together?"

Papa paused. "Why not? She works all day here and then goes home to cook for herself in an empty house. Invite her."

Laura was pleased with the invitation and together we made fried chicken, warm potato salad and had sliced tomatoes and pickled yellow beans. For dessert we made a sour cherry pie.

As we were working on the meal, I happened to look out the window and saw Muggins walking rather strangely across the lawn. He turned to the back porch and bumped right into the railing post. It was so strange that I went out to him.

"Are you drunk, Muggins? You walked right into the post."

Muggins came over to me and rubbed, I thought a bit awkwardly against my legs.

"You are getting old, Muggins. You must watch better where you are going."

When I came back into the house, Muggins came also and once in the kitchen I forgot about him.

Supper was at six thirty. It was just the four of us and I did not think Papa would want Laura sitting at the end where Mama used to sit, so I had Hunter and Papa at the ends and Laura and I sat across from each other.

"Mrs. Harper," said Papa after saying grace and we had begun to eat, "the reason Hunter is here this evening is because of his filling in for me when Amber was cut so badly. And you helped also, and I want to show my appreciation for what you did."

"Oh, I was just glad I was here to help. She looked terrible."

"Actually," continued Papa, putting some black raspberry jam on his bread, "I never heard much about the incident. Amber has been pretty quiet about it. I thought she might lay into me for letting an animal doctor take care of her," he added with a twinkle in his eyes.

Laura smiled and did not respond. I busied myself eating my potato salad and did not look at Hunter. It was still embarrassing to me although some of the pain of it lessened since our talk. Getting no reply, Papa turned to Hunter.

"I hope she did not cause you any trouble."

I gave Hunter a quick glance, afraid of what he might say. He looked at me, a hint of a grin on his face and his blue eyes saying too much. But he did not respond to Papa.

"Does anyone need bread? I'm not sure if it was passed," I said.

"It was around," said Papa, with just a bit of impatience, "but I get the feeling I am missing something here. I thought I would get a bit of information tonight regarding the incident and I am getting no more information than I did with Amber."

All was quiet except for forks hitting the dinner plates.

"You were hurting pretty badly, Amber. I hope someone gave you some brandy."

"I did," said Laura and Hunter simultaneously.

Laura and Hunter looked at each other in surprise. I concentrated on my piece of fried chicken.

Papa stopped chewing and looked at them.

"It looks like you both gave brandy and did not know the other had given it."

"Oh, I almost forgot," said Laura, "she asked for more."

"So you got two shots of brandy?" asked Papa, surprise on his face.

I could not respond without lying. I merely shrugged and no one else said anything.

"I find this conversation rather odd," said Papa now to anyone listening. He put down his fork and sat back in his chair. "There is a twinkle in both Hunter's and Mrs. Harper's eyes and Amber is eating chicken like she never had it before and may never get to eat it again. I am thinking it was the brandy she never had before and I am wondering why she is not complaining about the taste of it."

Papa was beginning to enjoy the conversation even if he was mostly talking to himself. He sensed there was a story and he wanted to know what it was. He was a dog sniffing for a bone.

"Potato salad, anyone?" I asked.

"Amber," said Papa. "We have food on our plates. Just put that potato salad down. It is becoming quite clear to me that you are trying to cover something up."

"All went well, Papa. And the stitches were well done," I said in a last attempt to cover my disgrace. However, Papa was not fooled.

"Did you like the brandy?"

I hesitated. "It tasted terrible." I did not look at either Hunter or Laura.

"But you asked for more?"

"I was scared of the stitches."

"Then why is everyone trying not to laugh?"

Hunter and Mrs. Harper both chuckled at this point. They could chuckle. I could not. Despite the forced talk I had with Hunter, reviewing the incident was anything but pleasant.

Now Papa centered his eyes on me.

"Just how much brandy did you have, Amber?"

I felt like everyone held their breaths.

"Amber?" he repeated.

"I really don't know, Papa," I said softly.

"You don't know?" Papa's voice went up a notch as he looked at Hunter and then at Mrs. Harper.

"Were you in the room with Amber the whole time, Mrs. Harper?"

"I was with her the whole time...well, except for running quickly for the brandy and later for fresh water and I had to get rid of the bloody dress."

"Mrs. Harper, you are not telling the whole story," said Papa. It was interesting to me that Laura blushed.

"It is not in my place to talk," she replied.

"Hunter?"

"If there is anything to be told, it should be your daughter who tells it."

Papa's curiosity was peaked. He pushed his dinner plate even farther away from him.

"There is no question that there is something to be told, but there seems to be a conspiracy to keep it quiet."

I looked quickly at Hunter who was looking at me, keeping a straight face but I found myself blushing when I looked into his eyes.

"Amber," said Hunter, "I think you need to come clean or your father will think something worse than what it was."

"I can't imagine what that could be," I said, knowing I had to say something to appease Papa.

"I am waiting," said Papa, looking at me and not even making a pretense of eating.

"Could we serve dessert?"

"Dessert will wait until I have heard the whole story," said Papa firmly. But he looked eager for a story and did not look so stern. "How can it possibly be that you do not know how much brandy you drank?"

I looked at my empty plate, and idly moved my fork back and forth on it. "Laura fetched the brandy and gave me a small glass of it.

She set the bottle on a small stand next to the table because she had to clean me up."

"And then?"

"Oh, Papa, I don't know exactly how it was anymore, but at some point Hunter came in and seeing the brandy setting there, offered me a glass." I paused. "I took it because I was hurting badly and I felt almost sick."

"That is two glasses. And then?" prompted Papa.

"Then Hunter walked over to the cabinet to get something and although I could hardly do it, I reached for the bottle with my good arm and...had some more."

"Straight from the bottle?"

I nodded and I could see Laura holding the back of her hand across her face to cover her smile and Hunter was clenching his jaw to keep from smiling. But his eyes were merry and I think a bit shocked by what I said.

"And after all that, you requested yet another glass from Hunter who had no clue what you had already had?" Papa's face was a study.

"That was just before the stitches," I said quickly. "I was scared of the stitches."

By this time Laura, Hunter and I were all laughing, and Papa finally gave in and joined us. Then he got serious.

"Amber, you perhaps never knew this, but I had an uncle who was an alcoholic."

"Papa, don't worry. I don't even like the stuff. It tasted terrible. I just liked what it did to me. It dulled the pain."

"Amber, Amber," said Papa with a sigh and leaning toward me. "That is exactly the reason alcoholics drink. They have pain and want to dull the pain. Not for the physical pain always, but for the emotional pain. The pain of loss, rejection, guilt, or sin in their lives. That could one day be you. Promise me you will never do such a thing again."

"I promise," I said quickly. Too quickly for Papa.

"That is easy for you to say right now. Your tummy is full and you have a house to live in, and friends and family around you. But if that were taken away?" He let that sink in for just a moment. "And now tell me the rest of the story."

I looked at Papa in consternation.

"The rest of what story?"

"The rest of the Amber and brandy story. There is a reason for the smiles and laughter around this table tonight."

Papa looked at Hunter. "I hope she did not damage my reputation."

"She was not talking about you," Hunter said chuckling and Laura began laughing again.

Papa looked from me to Hunter. I did not dare look at Hunter. Papa must have seen my red face.

"I suppose she gave you a few compliments?" asked Papa finally of Hunter.

"A few."

"And you accepted them?"

"I tried my best to stop her."

Papa looked again at my red face.

"I did not mean them Papa. But I was so happy."

Everyone burst out laughing and Papa called for dessert.

I did not allow Laura to help with the clean up, so she left right after the meal. Papa and Hunter went out on the porch to talk. Later, I went out to offer mint tea with ice chips to keep it cold and then I stayed on the porch, expecting that Waldo would probably stop by.

"Amber, what is with this cat?" asked Papa. "He bumps into things. You haven't been giving him brandy have you?"

Papa's humor was lost on me. I looked at Muggins who was now sitting at Hunter's feet.

"I saw him bump into something this afternoon," I replied, my heart in my throat.

I looked at Hunter and I am sure he saw the fear in my eyes. Without a word he lifted the cat in his arms. Muggins liked Hunter and put up no resistance. I sat in quiet fear as Hunter looked at Muggin's eyes.

"I thought he just was careless," I said, watching Hunter quietly looking into Muggins' eyes.

"What do you think it is? Do you think he is going blind?"

He hesitated, then said softly, "I think it more probable that he has a brain tumor."

"Oh no! Not Muggins." I felt moisture in my eyes just thinking of it. There was a painful pause. I could not think of losing Muggins. "He is much too young for that," I added.

"Amber, if I remember right, this cat was a birthday gift to you on your tenth birthday or thereabouts. And what are you now? Nearly twenty-five."

But I barely heard what Papa said. I was already mourning my cat.

"Can you help him, Hunter?" I begged, knowing I was asking in vain.

"I can put him out of his misery," Hunter said softly, pity in his eyes.

"Not yet. I can't give him up yet. Not Muggins, too."

I could not bear the thought. First Mama and now Muggins. It was too much. Maybe the cat would get better. Perhaps Hunter was wrong.

After Hunter left, I picked up my cat and went up to my room with him. I needed to be alone. I had to hold my furry friend close. I could not bear the thought of losing him.

CHAPTER 12

About a half hour later, I heard Waldo's voice out the window. I left Muggins in my room and went out on the porch with Waldo. I was glad to see him. I needed to think of something other than Muggins.

By now Waldo and I had some lengthy talks behind us. He was so committed to working for the Lord in the foreign field that I was getting caught up in his excitement. Although he did not come right out and say it, I could tell he envisioned us working together there. I began giving the whole prospect some serious thought. If I compared him to Jonas, there was no comparison. Jonas thought only of fishing. I was merely a friend. Now Waldo was thinking much more seriously. He wanted to go into the mission field, and seemed to think I should go with him. It was important, he told me recently, that he go as a married man—that the mission board preferred that. Perhaps it was so that the single man would not get too lonely and start looking for a wife from among the pagans. More than once Waldo had told me I was beautiful and I had glowed in the light of his warm brown eyes. He also assured me that I would be an asset on any mission field, since I grew up in a doctor's family. This was heady stuff for me. It sounded good and right. At the same time, I felt guilty that I was not nearly as excited as he about the mission field. But I was excited about the adventure. I had lived in Vermont all my life. It would be fun to learn a whole new culture. I wondered how long it took to learn a language.

Now, tonight, as we talked, I gave Waldo a scrutinizing look. He was a nice looking young man. He was friendly and enthusiastic. He was a year or two younger than I was, but that did not matter. He was slightly taller than I and he was a gentleman. He did not have the stature and princely bearing of Hunter, but why was I even thinking of Hunter? He was not my beau. Someone had burned Hunter badly and he was not about to get burned the second time. I turned my attention to Waldo. He was excited.

"Guess what, Amber, I heard back from the Missions Office. There is a possibility of an opening for me in Honduras. They are thinking of opening a clinic in a rural area about fifty miles from where my parents are living. That would be perfect. I was once in that area. It is not far from the ocean. You would love it."

I said nothing. This was becoming more and more real. And it was becoming a bit scary. I really liked Waldo, but he was about to embark on a mission far from home. I had never, ever even thought of this as a possibility for me. Now he was looking at me with his warm brown eyes. I was reminded of a puppy begging, hoping.

"I know this is much too soon, but I want you to consider going to the mission field with me."

I just looked at Waldo. *Just what was he saying?*

"Will there be other single girls working there?" I asked.

"I would like to go as a married man," he said, watching me closely.

"I don't quite know what you are saying, Waldo."

"I don't quite know how to say this, because it is so sudden. But I do want to go if they will take me and I really care for you. I believe I love you. I just want you to think about it. Think seriously about it. Very seriously."

"Waldo, they do not speak English in Honduras. You know Spanish. I do not. Not one word. I would be frightfully lonesome."

"No, you would not. You would learn Spanish at a language school. My parents went without knowing any Spanish and they learned it at a language school somewhere or other. I don't know where since I was not around then yet. I learned both languages at the same time from my parents. You are smart. You would learn it in no time."

It was at this point that Papa came out on the porch. He greeted Waldo and began asking him how he was doing. Waldo immediately began giving him the exciting news that he would most probably be going to Honduras. I don't quite remember all the conversation, but it struck me a bit odd that Papa came out there when he knew that Waldo was there. And especially since we were obviously having a serious talk. A very serious talk. Usually, Papa was aware of us needing our space and gave it. However, tonight I welcomed his coming. I was getting very confused and needed some space to think. Papa joined our conversation and stayed out until Waldo said he needed to go home and write a letter to the mission board. Just as he left, he turned again to me.

"Promise me you will think hard about what I said," he said softly as he said goodnight.

"I promise."

I thought maybe Papa would say something. Had he overheard us talking? I had the distinct feeling he had come out to interrupt our conversation. But he said nothing. He just picked up his newspaper and started reading.

I went up into my room and there my thoughts quickly returned to Muggins, who turned his head toward me and meowed. This was not quite normal for him. I took him in my arms and held him and could not stop the tears that ran down my face. Muggins and I were through a lot together. He could not, did not dare to be seriously sick.

Later, as I lay in bed no sleep in sight, I thought about what Waldo had said. In essence he was asking me to seriously think about marrying him—and probably in a very short time. It scared me. On the other hand, I believed he would be a very fine husband. True, I did not know him for long, but he had a good upbringing and his heart belonged to God. My arguments turned round and round in my brain and finally, exhausted from thinking, my thoughts blurred and I somehow got Waldo's warm brown eyes mixed up with Hunter's blue eyes.

———————————

I woke the next morning with a headache. My night had not been very restful. I had awakened often and always my thoughts went to Waldo. And Honduras. Or to Muggins. My heart was heavy. At five o'clock, Muggins meowed. He did not come to me. He stayed on his blanket by the window.

This was not like Muggins and it broke my heart. I could not stand his suffering.

I got up soon after six and dressed. I took Muggins to the garden where he promptly did his business. I carried him back in and fed him, but he barely ate. By the time I had made breakfast for Papa, I was fighting tears. Muggins was sick. Very sick. Papa, seeing my tears, encouraged me to put him to sleep. Hard as it was, I knew it was what I should do. So it was decided. Papa had to check on a patient at nine o'clock. He would drop me and Muggins off at Hunter's office on the way.

Shortly before nine, with tears in my eyes, I took Muggins in my arms and then handed him to Papa 'til I got seated beside him in the carriage. The ride to Hunter's was so very, very short. Papa let me off at the end of the lane.

"Do you want me to come along?" he asked.

"No, Papa. I can do this. And I'll walk home."

Hunter's office was next to the stable, out behind his house. I walked slowly to the office, but saw a sign on the door that said he was not in at the time. I had counted on Hunter being home. Now what would I do? It was so hard deciding to bring Muggins here but I could not imagine carrying him home again. I looked at the house and thought I saw some movement at the kitchen window. I walked up to the back door and knocked. A young woman came to the door. I knew he had a woman that did his cleaning and laundry and I suspected she had watched me from the kitchen window.

"Yes?" she said when she came to the door.

She was a woman perhaps in her mid twenties. She was very thin and had, I thought, sad eyes.

"I am looking for Dr. Renwick."

"I am sorry, but he was called out." She looked at the clock hanging somewhere in the kitchen. "But he thought he would be back by now. Would you like to come in and wait for him?"

I did not feel like talking to anyone. I preferred being outdoors. I looked around and saw a bench outside the office door.

"If he will not be long in coming, I would prefer to wait outside," I replied.

"You have a nice big cat. Is it ill?"

I just nodded. It was hard to talk about Muggins.

"You just sit there in the shade. He will be back soon."

I had not sat there ten minutes when I saw his carriage come in the lane. I suddenly did not want to face him and I just put my chin down in Muggins' fur and waited for him to come to me. He tethered his horse and when his footsteps stopped close to me, I looked up. Hunter was just looking at me with a very somber expression.

"So you brought him," he said.

I stood, but I could not talk. I handed Muggins to Hunter and stood back, fighting tears.

"Go in my office," he said.

I opened the door and he followed with Muggins in his arms. Muggins was very placid and did not seem to care what was happening to him.

"Am I to put him to sleep?" Hunter asked softly.

I could not speak. I took a deep breath and then nodded.

Hunter just looked at me a moment. I put up a hand to Muggins, to pet him one last time, then I turned away.

"I'll be back shortly," said Hunter. Then he went into another room and closed the door.

I can do this, I told myself. It is just a cat. It is not like when Mama went. I tried to think of what I needed to do in the garden and what I needed to shop for, but all I could see was the beautiful furry face of my Muggins. He was not healthy anymore and could not see and bumped into things. He is better off, I told myself. But my heart felt like someone was squeezing it with giant hands.

Hunter was not gone long. Perhaps five or ten minutes later, I heard the door open. I was standing, looking out the window. I took a deep breath and turned.

Hunter closed the door behind him and stopped. When I looked into his eyes and his empty arms, I knew my Muggins was no more. A quick rush of emotion hit me and I turned and hid my face in my hands. I tried to take a breath but I was hurting so badly it came out in sobs. And then Hunter was standing by my side, his arm around my shoulders. He held me firmly until I got control of myself.

"Sorry," I said, sniffing, "it is just a cat...."

"No," said Hunter in a firm, but soft voice. "It is Muggins."

He understood and it was somehow very comforting to me.

"I liked the old tiger myself," he added, and I thought his voice a bit husky.

"I forgot my purse. I have no money along."

"You owe me one meal for putting him to sleep and one for burying him. Or do you want to take him back with you?"

"I did not think that far," I said, wiping my eyes.

"Come with me. I would like to show you something."

I followed Hunter out the door and behind the building. Some distance from his office was a fenced-off plot.

"This is where Dr. Toome buried pets for people who wished it. So far there are three dogs, two cats, and one pony. I'm glad I did not have to bury the pony. They all have a small marker on the grave. I can bury Muggins here, if you so wish."

He looked at me and waited. Muggins did not belong in a graveyard. But it was reality, not my wish.

"I think I would like that," I said, wiping new tears from my eyes.

"Good. I will take care of that immediately and you can make the marker and when you have it ready, you can bring it back and place it on the grave sometime."

"You really don't want any money?"

"Not from you. I want two meals." I had to smile at the look he was giving me.

"Thank you. You are very kind."

I saw the twinkle come into his eyes.

"Just kind today?"

"No, not really."

He grinned and I could not hold back a smile.

"You will get the meals."

I turned then and walked home, a smile on my lips. Maybe that was Hunter's intention with his dig about the compliment. I was relieved that Muggins suffered no more. I was thankful for a thoughtful veterinarian...and friend.

And for the moment I forgot about Waldo.

CHAPTER 13

*I*t was the last week in August. Although we had a few very humid days, the summer had been good. Hot, but with a fair amount of showers. There was an abundance of tomatoes in our garden to can and a farmer just south of us paid his medical bill in the form of sweet corn. I was thrilled. But he gave us fifty ears and I had to can some of it. I was so busy that I was almost overwhelmed with work. I was so glad for Laura. She chipped in with whatever needed doing. Today, with the laundry washed and dried, she readily helped me with the sweet corn.

Of course, even working hard at canning, my thoughts were always with Waldo and his questions and hopes for me. How I prayed. Did praying really help? I thought of my conversation with Hunter about prayer. It seemed I was getting no answers.

"Laura," I said suddenly, needing help in my quest, "does God answer your prayers?"

She looked at the corn she was husking for a few seconds.

"God hears my prayers, I have no doubt. But does He give me what I want? Sometimes. Sometimes not. At those times I find it good to remember that God wants us to make our requests known to Him because He wants our fellowship. He already knows our needs. But prayer is not us trying to talk God into giving us what we want. It is laying the problem before Him and asking for His help and for His will to be done."

I thought about that for a while. It was a new thought for me.

"But what if He does not answer immediately and we need to have the answer right away?"

Laura smiled as she took the silk off an ear of corn.

"God never seems in a hurry to me. I am the one in a hurry. And you, perhaps. But God has time to work out His plan. Time is in His hands. If the plan is not clear to you, then I do not believe God would want you to jump ahead of His answer. Waiting is always the hardest."

That had comforted me somehow.

It was also time for Ray to return home. I was glad. He would be here to help Papa. And if he did not have enough to do, he could do the billing and paperwork. I could find other things to do. I would also ask him to make the marker for Muggins' grave. He was rather handy with woodworking and Papa had set aside a small part of the stable for such work. Besides all the physical work, my brain was working overtime.

After the work was finished and supper was cleared away, I was glad to sit out on the porch and relax. Laura had gone home and Papa had been called out on a sick call. The evenings were pretty cool already with the sun setting earlier. The last band concert was already past. Where had the summer gone?

It was not long before Waldo came over. He came over every evening and this evening he was really geared up about Honduras. His eyes were bright.

"Amber! How are you? I was out making calls with my uncle today. I was just thinking how different the pastoral calls are here in comparison with the mission field. In Honduras most of the calls include some medical need and there is much poverty. But it is so wonderful to be able to help where help is so needed."

I don't think he realized that he had not given me time to answer him. He was so excited and at peace about his calling. It was not long before he was looking for a response from me. I can't say he actually proposed and asked me to be his wife, but he made it clear that he wanted me to go to Honduras with him—as a married couple. It seemed to me that something was missing. I liked Waldo and enjoyed being with him. But what was love? I did not know if I was in love with him. Yes, he had told me he thought he was in love with me, but that seemed vague also. If I did not accept his offer, was I throwing my chance away of a marriage with a very fine person? He was a committed Christian and joyfully wanting to serve the Lord. I held him in high esteem for his fervor.

Now he looked at me with his gentle smile and warm brown eyes.

"I expect to hear from the office any day now. Have you made your decision?"

I saw the hope in his eyes. I was torn. Did I love him...or perhaps hold him in enough esteem to make a happy marriage? And what about a move to Honduras? I knew only what Waldo told me. I knew only a few Spanish words that he had taught me. There was a certain excitement about moving to another country. It was indeed an adventure I had not expected to have. My mind was a whirl. Who knows, maybe God took Muggins to help me make the move. Before I could answer, I was aware of a horse stopping in front of the house. I looked up. Hunter got off his horse and tethered it. Then he came slowly up to the porch.

"Good evening, Hunter."

"Good evening, Amber." He nodded to Waldo and then looked back at me.

"Is your father at home?"

"He was called out after supper just over on Main Street. He just walked over there. I expect he will be home shortly."

Hunter's eyes went from me to Waldo, in a moment of silence.

"I was wondering when Ray is coming home."

"Tomorrow."

"Great, I miss him."

It seemed Hunter just looked at me for a long moment and I remembered how good it felt when his arm was around me in his office while I wept over my cat. He always managed to stir emotions in me that no other could do. I found myself nearly blushing from his look right now.

"In that case I shall leave again," said Hunter, turning back to his horse.

I was reluctant to ask him to join us because of the seriousness of our discussion.

"Wait," I said, "I believe I see Papa just coming across the street right now. Come up and join us. Papa is always glad to chat with you."

Hunter did come up on the porch and in no time flat Papa was there, too. It gave me a break from Waldo's questions, but Waldo was not defeated.

"Could we go for a walk?" he asked softly.

"Of course." I could hardly refuse him.

We headed across the park and I was sure Papa's and Hunter's eyes followed us. Waldo talked the whole way across the green and finding the gazebo unoccupied, we went up into it and found seats. Once there, Waldo lost no time returning to the subject at hand.

"Amber, I want to marry you. You know that, don't you?"

I hesitated. "I think I do know that, but I am not sure I am in love. Are you sure?"

"I know I love you. You are a perfect fit for me and for the work."

I am afraid I just looked at him, miserable that I could not readily give an answer.

"Are you in love with someone else?" he asked.

"Of course not. Who would I be in love with?"

"What about Dr. Renwick?"

I thought again of Hunter's arm around me. I thought of some of our talks. But Hunter never gave me any reason to think he wanted to marry me.

"Hunter? He is not interested in marriage. He does not trust women." For some reason I felt my face heat up.

"Did he tell you that?"

"No, but I've heard gossip and he does not court anyone."

For the next hour we discussed the pros and cons of my joining the team in Honduras. We went in circles.

"This does not sound good of me, Waldo, but I can barely stand the thought of leaving my family and friends here in Vermont. You are so dedicated, so sure. You are not going to a strange land. It is more your home almost than America. I am looking at a country that is completely strange to me. I will not be able to speak good Spanish for a long time. And I know already that I shall be terribly, terribly homesick."

Waldo reached over to me and took my hand. His brown eyes smiled at me.

"I love you, Amber. I will be there with you. And God will give you a love for the people and the work. You can go to language school and then I will help you with the language and we will be happy together. I know it. Please go with me."

We were now sitting in the gazebo and across the park, I could see Hunter mounting his horse. I wished I were on the porch with Papa instead of here with Waldo. What should I say?

I looked into Waldo's trusting eyes. He had been very kind to me with all my hesitations. I could not keep him hanging forever.

"Waldo, give me one more night. I promise you I will give you an answer tomorrow morning."

"Please, let it be a yes," said Waldo, squeezing my hand.

We made our way across the park. And then he went his way and I went mine. I had promised, but the weight of the promise had my head bowed and tears on the surface as I entered the house.

Papa was just coming from the kitchen with a glass of water. He paused when he saw me.

"Amber, come to the living room. I want to talk to you."

I followed obediently. I am sure he saw my moods over the last days. I was sure what this was about. Now Papa sat on the sofa and patted the place beside him.

When I was seated, he just looked at me a while.

"You are unhappy."

I blinked back more tears. "I am so confused." My voice trembled.

"Tell me about it."

I discovered that I was glad to spill out my woes. I desperately needed some help and I should have gone to Papa before this. Papa was a wise man.

"Waldo is a dedicated man, Papa," I said at the end, "but it is a big decision and I don't know how I feel for sure."

"Amber," said Papa, "God is not in a hurry for your answer. Waldo is, but not God. There is no need for a final answer now. If you are to go to the mission field with Waldo, God will work it out. It would be wrong for you to go before you are at peace about your answer. It is only Waldo who cannot wait. It is wrong for him to try to force an answer at this time. Just relax. Trust God. God knows your heart. If you have no peace about going, I doubt that God is calling you there."

"But it is such a good, noble calling. I feel guilty for even hesitating."

"It is a noble calling. But it is not for everyone. God has a plan for your life and in due time, He will make it plain. It seems God has called Waldo. But I do not think that means that He has called you."

I felt some of the weight lifting from my shoulders.

"Has he proposed marriage?" asked Papa.

"Not exactly the way I think of a marriage proposal. But he does want to marry me so that we can go in missions together."

"You did not promise to marry him?"

I looked at Papa, a bit surprised at his direct question.

"No. Not yet." I thought Papa looked relieved.

"Could it be that his marriage proposal is dependent on whether you go with him or not?"

I had to think about that a bit. Yes, it seemed it was and my eyes opened a bit with the knowledge.

"I believe so."

"Is that kind of proposal all right with you?"

"I don't know. I did not see it quite like that. But if he is determined to go to Honduras, then of course he would not marry me if I would not go with him."

"What is Waldo's hurry?"

"He expects to hear from the mission board any day."

"You cannot just up and go to another country. There must be a passport, possibly injections against disease. Papers to fill out."

"Probably he just wants me to go with him to the headquarters in Pennsylvania...with the promise to go."

"Do you believe that God is big enough to get you to Honduras or wherever He may want you, without a pressured answer to Waldo right now?"

I was silent. It made such sense when Papa put it like that.

"Yes," I said slowly, "but I told him to give me one more night and I would give him his answer tomorrow morning. He has been wanting my consent to go with him for days already."

Papa just looked at me for a few seconds.

"Do you have your answer now?"

"No," I said, miserably.

"Can you wait for God's peace about it before you give Waldo his answer?"

I took a deep breath. "I promised an answer by tomorrow morning."

There followed a silence. Finally Papa spoke softly. "I wish Mama were here. I am no good at this."

I had been fighting tears all evening and now I could no longer hold them. I cried for Papa who was missing Mama. I cried for me and my need of her advice. I cried for the hole she left in our home.

Papa had his arm around me and I did not realize Papa was crying, too, until I heard him blowing his nose into one of his big white handkerchiefs. It made quite a noise and somehow brought our crying to an end.

"Amber."

I looked at Papa. I had never seen him so serious.

"I want you to make me a promise." He paused and I waited. "I know you are not a child anymore and that you have a right to your own decisions. However, I feel Waldo is pressuring you and this decision is not one to make lightly. If you want to go to the mission field, I will support you. I will be proud to have you serve God where you feel He is wanting you to serve. However, you faced some big changes this year and I would like you to promise me that you will not give Waldo a final answer until one year from now. You must be led by your own heart—by God's voice—not Waldo's."

"A year? A whole year? I promised Waldo an answer by tomorrow morning!"

"Waldo is not the one you ultimately have to answer to. Your calling must be from God."

Papa was not giving in. He held my gaze. What would Waldo think? Would he give up on me? Did I want him to give up on me? But oh, the relief, if I could wait.

Papa was not backing down.

"I promise, Papa."

I would like to say I slept good that night. But I did not. What Papa said made sense, but the other side of the coin was that I had promised Waldo an answer. I felt a certain obligation to that promise. I was taught to keep my promises. And I had kept him waiting for a long time already. At least it seemed that way to him. And I had such a high respect for Waldo. His heart was the Lord's. He thought only of serving God on the foreign field. And I? I was hesitant. Did I not love God enough? I thought of the sacrifice of those leaving family and home and all things familiar to go to a land where they spoke a language they did not understand and who knows what kind of strange food they had to eat. At one point I lit a candle to see what time it was. Two twenty. And I had not slept. I finally came to a conclusion. I would tell Waldo my tentative answer was a yes, but the final answer had to wait a year. Papa's orders. He had to accept that. I could not fight him and Papa. I was exhausted. I blew out the candle and fell into a fitful sleep plagued by dreams of an angry Waldo and a sad Papa.

At six o'clock I woke to the sound of Waldo's voice. I thought I must be dreaming. Did he come for my answer so early? Then I realized the sound came through the screen in the window. He was outside. I got out of bed just in time to see Waldo throw a bag into a carriage and then jump in himself and off went the carriage down the avenue. Why was Waldo up so early? And where was he going? Why the bag? The confusion in my brain seemed to increase. Nothing made sense anymore. When would he be back? He was waiting for my answer. It was so important to him. Or did he give up on me?

I knew I would have no peace until I talked to Waldo, but he obviously was not home right now so at seven I got up and made breakfast for Papa and myself although I barely got anything down. Papa was silent and I had nothing to say. I thought perhaps Waldo would come over for my answer during breakfast. Surely wherever he went, he would be back by now. But when he did not come by eight o'clock, I could no longer stand the weight of my decision. I had to get it over with. I walked over to the parsonage. I went to the front door and knocked. Pastor Thomas answered.

"Good morning, Amber! I was expecting you. Come into the parlor."

"I am looking for Waldo," I said, wondering why I was being called into the parlor.

"So I understand. Please take a seat."

I was about to say I would not be there that long when I saw Pastor Thomas was waiting for me to sit. I wondered at that as I took my seat.

"Is Waldo here?" I asked.

Pastor Thomas took his time in answering.

"Actually, no. He left at six o'clock this morning for Pennsylvania."

"What?"

Pastor Thomas took a deep breath and took his time in answering.

"It seems an unopened letter to him from the mission's office was misplaced possibly two days ago already. I always bring the mail into my office and look through it there. I believe it slid off the desk when I was not looking and just as I was ready to retire last evening, I happened to see it between my desk and the bookcase. I saw it was the letter that Waldo was so anxiously awaiting. I took it to him immediately. He was very happy to receive it and when he read it and realized it was here a couple days already he was more than anxious to respond without delay."

The pastor paused and looked at me a moment before resuming.

"Waldo is usually in a hurry. He wants things to happen now. Not later. He decided to take the early train this morning to the mission headquarters in Pennsylvania. He took everything he had here and he wrote a letter that I am to give to you."

Now Pastor Thomas reached over to a table standing at the end of the sofa and handed a letter to me. "I am sure this comes as a surprise to you and I hope there will be a good explanation for his actions in the letter."

I was in shock, but partly relieved. I could barely fathom, after all his wanting an answer from me, that Waldo would leave without a personal word with me.

"I took him to Flynn Falls this morning for the early train. I'm sorry."

I stood up and found my legs feeling shaky.

"I admit I am in a bit of shock, Pastor Thomas, but I am sure there will be a reasonable explanation in the letter. Thank you for your time."

I left quickly. I was in more of a shock than what I wanted to admit. I had considered marrying Waldo and moving to a far country with him. Now he took off without so much as a goodbye. When I got to the house, I stayed on the porch to read the letter. It read as follows:

My dear Amber,

    My uncle will explain to you about my sudden departure. Due to the letter being lost for a couple days, I did not dare wait. I will be in Pennsylvania for a week. Maybe longer. Please send me your answer today. I will keep you informed, but have no time to write more now.

    Hopefully yours,
        Waldo

Included in the letter was the Pennsylvania address where I should send the letter. I don't know how long I sat on the front porch, staring unseeing over the village green. Waldo was gone. Gone without a word. I had to somehow get that into my brain. I had to come to terms with the fact that Waldo, who could not wait for my answer to a life-changing question, could, when I had finally promised an answer in the morning, up and leave me with my answer unknown. There was a part of me that was disturbed about his actions. It seemed so wrong. Another part of me breathed easier. The pressure was definitely off. That felt good.

I finally stood up and went into the house. Some time later, Papa came looking for me. He needed me to help calm a little girl who had broken her leg and her mother was beside herself, which did not help the situation. By the time I had calmed the little girl, he found some other office work for me. Then it was time to make lunch and plan supper. Today Ray would come home. I made a tuna and macaroni salad and sliced tomatoes for lunch. After eating in silence for a few moments, Papa looked at me.

"May I know what happened this morning?"

"If you want to know how I answered Waldo, he does not yet know my answer."

"How so?"

I told Papa the story of my morning. At the end he waited for more. He wanted to know my reaction. My decision.

"And now?"

"I shall send him a letter right after lunch." I paused, realizing I would not give the answer I had been planning to give. "I shall decline his offer and wish him well," I concluded. I was surprised to find myself fighting tears.

"I think you will not be disappointed, Amber. Are you at peace?"

"Over my decision, yes. But I am a bit miffed that he left without saying goodbye. It somehow hurts."

"Maybe he did not know this was goodbye," said Papa graciously.

"I guess you are right," I conceded.

That afternoon Ray arrived home. I was very glad to welcome him and a new topic of conversation after the thoughts of the morning and of the last days. Strange, but it seemed my brother was a bit more mature after just six weeks. It was probably the longest he had been away from family and he was getting into his career as a medical doctor. He had learned a lot and our supper that evening was a wonderful time of him sharing his stories of his time in New York. Finally he looked around the kitchen and then at me.

"Where is that wild cat of yours, Amber? I'm missing him."

"I am, too," I replied. "He is in cat heaven."

"Really? Old Muggins is gone?"

I was glad to see my brother looked sad at the news.

"Hunter believes he had a brain tumor. He is now in a special animal cemetery behind Hunter's office and I need you to make a nice marker for his grave."

For once Ray made no nasty remarks about poor Muggins. There was a brief silence as he consumed a large piece of apple pie.

"Is Walter or was it Waldo still hanging around you?"

"He recently left for Pennsylvania to get ready for the mission field."

I said no more. He would hear it from Papa or me later. I remembered that he barely knew Waldo. He had just arrived here shortly before Ray left. The rest of the meal was strictly medical talk. After dessert the two men went out on the porch to discuss what Ray had learned. Papa was always eager to hear anything new in the medical field.

CHAPTER 14

The following day was my birthday. We never did anything big for birthdays except for a birthday cake. Perhaps a small gift. I had almost forgotten my birthday was coming up with all that had happened. Papa remembered, as did Ray, and they congratulated me on my five and twenty years at the breakfast table and Papa suggested that Laura stay for supper.

The day passed quickly. Ray was eager to get to work with Papa. He spent the morning with him and after lunch he went for a quick visit to Hunter. He was eager to talk to him also. In the middle of the afternoon there was a carriage accident on Main Street and two bloodied men were brought into the office and Papa was glad Ray was there to assist him.

Laura and I were busy with supper. She did not bake a cake, but she made a lemon pie and a beef roast was placed in the oven for the evening meal.

Shortly before supper, Papa called me into the office to take care of some medical supplies he had received and by the time I was finished, the table was set and we were ready to eat. I took a quick glance at the table. Laura had made it a bit festive with a small bunch of colorful zinnias in the center. I just realized she had set for too many when the knocker sounded. I went to the door to find Mindy standing there with a birthday cake nicely decorated for me. She had been invited without my knowledge. By the time we had taken the cake to the kitchen I heard the knocker again.

"Oh, dear, who is coming now, just when we are ready to eat," I wondered aloud. No one went to the door, so I went. And met a pair of very blue eyes.

"Happy birthday, Amber."

How could I possibly blush just when he said those three words to me? He was holding a small unwrapped box.

"Please come in," I said. "I did not know you were invited."

"I am collecting on your bill," he said smiling.

Once in the door, he immediately handed me the box. There was not even a lid on it. I looked into the box and caught my breath. Looking at me with round blue eyes, was a small black kitten with a white bib and white paws. I fell in love with the kitten on sight.

"Oh, she is so cute!"

"He," said Hunter.

I forgot everything and everybody as I picked up the kitten, held it close to my neck and threw the box aside. The kitten immediately crawled out of my hand and up on my shoulder where he began nibbling on my ear lobe. I giggled at the tickle. I was so enthralled about the kitten that Papa had to call us to the table, which was now loaded with dishes of steaming food.

"What do I do with the kitten?" I asked.

"Put him back in the box," said Hunter. "He can't get out."

"Thank you so much."

"It is good to see you smile again," he replied.

It was a happy time at the meal. Ray and Hunter were exchanging stories and Mindy was eyeing up Hunter. It was the first time that she was really with him. I realized now why Laura had been so generous with all the food and vegetables. She knew we were feeding six rather than four.

"Shouldn't Waldo be here?" Mindy asked softly.

It seemed everyone at the table got quiet. It was probably just a lull in the conversation, but I cringed.

"He is off to missions," I said softly to her, but audible to anyone at the table. She gave me a shocked look. "I'll tell you later."

Laura at that point announced dessert and I got up and helped clear the dirty dishes from the table. Before she came back with the cake, which had my age displayed on the top, I quickly gave the kitten a little bowl of milk in his box. He quickly, happily lapped it up.

"Wow, Amber, you are a quarter of a century old. How does that feel?" asked Ray when I successfully had blown out all the candles.

"You will know soon enough, Ray. Your maturity will then, hopefully be complete."

"Ouch," said Hunter as the others laughed.

The pie was brought in as well as the ice cream that Ray had made in the basement that afternoon when I thought he was with Papa.

"So what are you going to name the kitten?" asked Papa, taking a bite of cake.

"I will have to think about it."

"Wait! I have a name. I met a cat in New York. His name was Murf," said Ray.

"Murf? I never heard the name before."

I looked to my right where I had placed the box so I could see into it. The little furry face was looking up at me.

"Are you a Murf?" I asked.

To my amazement the cat mewed at me.

"What did he say?" asked Hunter with a grin.

"He said I am."

So Murf it was.

It was a nice birthday and a happy evening. I told Laura I would do the clean up. She refused. She said it was her gift to me. Later, when she could have gone home, she joined us on the porch. I held Murf most of the time, but he was a busy kitten and sometimes needed to go back in his box.

The men were on one side of the porch talking medical interests and I told Mindy and Laura the latest on Waldo. We talked then of other things and when the party broke up, Hunter offered Laura a ride home, which she accepted. Before they left, he came over to me.

"I wish you many happy years, Amber."

"Thank you. And thank you so much for Murf. I just love him!"

"I know you do," he said slowly, looking handsome as always. "I'm almost jealous of the kitten."

I blushed and changed the subject.

"So my cat bill is half paid."

He gave me a questioning look. "Oh, yes. You don't like debts do you? I wasn't keeping track. That reminds me, I have a basket of tomatoes and a basket of apples in my carriage. It was my payment for services rendered and I really don't know what to with them. Will you take them? I know I am giving you more work."

Laura, standing by, heard him and said, "Maybe your housekeeper would have time to can them for you."

"I don't think so. She works for me only one day a week and if my memory serves me correctly, she is at other places on the other days."

"Probably taking care of other men who are needing a wife rather than a housekeeper," said Laura, with a glint in her eye. Hunter made no comment.

"I have an idea," Laura continued. "Let Amber and me can them for you. Then you can eat tomato soup and applesauce for your lunches."

He looked at her a moment. Then at me.

"That is a good idea, Laura. Ray is home now and I will have more time. We will do it together."

"Do you have any jars?" Laura asked Hunter.

"I'm not sure, I must look in the basement. I know a lot of things were left in the basement. I don't often go down there, I'm afraid."

"If you don't, I have extra," said Laura. "It would be nice if we could do it at your place."

"I would like that," said Hunter.

"So take those baskets home again," said Laura. She looked at me. "Can we work at them tomorrow?"

"We can."

"That will put me in your debt," said Hunter looking at us.

"I'd love that," I said quickly, barely knowing why I said it.

Hunter gave me a long, speculative look and I looked away first.

———

By nine o'clock the next morning, Laura and I were busy working on the basket of tomatoes in Hunter's kitchen. I found out that Hunter took Laura along to his house the night before and she looked at what he had in the house for canning. There were plenty of jars in the basement. I was very interested in seeing just what his house looked like. It was a two-story white frame house like ours, but not quite as big. It had an upper porch that looked to the south. It had a nice sized kitchen with a pump, which brought water inside and both a dining room and living room. The house was obviously needing a woman's touch. I longed to put a colorful bouquet of flowers on the table and a few bright pillows in the living room. The house needed plants and the cupboards were needing some order. Hunter himself was gone for most of the morning, but it happened to be the day his housekeeper was there. She arrived about the same time we did and was probably shocked to see us come into the house.

After introductions, Laura explained our visit. "We are here to can for Dr. Renwick. I hope we will not be in your way."

"Oh, I was wondering why you were here. No, that is fine. I will work on laundry first and I will clean the kitchen last."

Laura had set the required big dishpans and bowls out on the table the night before already and soon she was washing jars and I was working on the tomatoes. We made a good team and the morning passed quickly. I had taken sliced beef sandwiches and pickled beets along for lunch and had made enough for Hunter also, should he come. Instead, it was Minna who joined us for lunch.

"You brought your cat here recently," she said as we ate.

"Yes, it was a sad day for me. Now I just got a new kitten. I hope he is not getting into trouble at home. They have so much energy when they are kittens, I remember Muggins when he was little and I was just glad when he would collapse for a nap."

"Are you from the Stork family from Westville?" asked Laura of Minna.

"No, I was an Albright and I married a Stork."

"Oh," said Laura, "I did not realize you were married."

"I was married," said Minna. "Abie died in a fire in Flynn Falls."

"The pants factory fire?" I asked.

"Yes," said Minna a bit reluctantly. "The pants factory fire."

"I am so sorry," I said. "How long had you been married?"

"About a year and a half."

"That must have been a terrible shock."

She did not comment and I said no more. I did not know what to say. It had to be a huge loss for her. Just before we finished our sandwiches, she spoke again.

"I was so distressed that I lost our baby."

"Oh, I am so sorry!" I said, horrified for what she must have gone through. I could see she was fighting tears and I reached over and took her hand. She grasped mine hard.

"I knew the Stork family," said Laura, "and I believe I vaguely remember Abie."

After lunch, Minna went outside to bring in the dry wash and we finished canning tomatoes and applesauce. Hunter had not shown himself at all and I could only presume he knew he would not be welcome in the kitchen. We were finished by two o'clock and we left the jars sitting on the counter. They looked nice and I was happy that we did them for Hunter, although it was his own fault he did not have a wife to can for him.

When I got home I found a letter waiting for me from Waldo. I had mixed feelings about his leaving and was curious how he would explain himself. I knew now that I would not be going with him but I was still hurting that after saying I would give an answer the next day, he was in such a hurry to leave he left before I could give it.

Murf was more than happy to see me and I spent fifteen minutes with him before I checked the ice box for food for supper. I then took the letter to my room to read in private. I was hot from canning and slipped out of my dress and sat on the bed, pillow behind my back and opened the letter, while Murf chased his tail on the bed.

My dear Amber,

I am sure you were surprised by my sudden departure, but when I realized the letter from the missions office had come two days earlier, I felt I had to act immediately in order to assure them of my interest. I have now talked to the board and they have definitely accepted me as a part of a small team that will be going to the new mission in Honduras. I am very excited. I have told the board about you and we are waiting for your answer. Please write to me at the address that you will find on the back of this envelope. Please come and join our team. I miss you already.

Hopefully yours,

Waldo

I found myself getting frustrated. Did he have to write that he missed me already? Waldo had told them about me? I suddenly found my insides churning once more. Was he that sure of my answer after all my hesitations? For just a moment I doubted myself once more. Or was he just not really in tune with me? Did he never really hear me? I reread the letter. He said he missed me. I really doubted he had time to miss me. I found no reason in the letter to believe he missed me. There was no word of love. He missed me like one misses his supper.

Nothing more. So he wanted a letter. I would write him a letter. I had to put this behind me. I was not in love with Waldo, but basically he was a fine man. I still admired him. He maybe needed to mature in some areas. So did I. Maybe he needed to know how to woo a woman. I sincerely hoped he would find a good wife to serve with him in Honduras.

I spent a half hour on the letter. I did not want to hurt him, but I had to write plainly. I would not be going with him to Honduras. But I did wish him joy and blessing in his work. I could wish that with a full heart. I wrote the letter, signed it and sealed it. After supper, I walked to the post office to mail the letter. I wanted the whole business behind me. I wanted Waldo to get the letter before he would come back for me!

Walking back from the post office, I entered the village green and finding the gazebo empty, climbed the few steps and sat down. In spite of my feelings about the mission, I would miss my talks with Waldo. I felt a certain emptiness within me in spite of the relief of having made my decision. I had seriously thought maybe Waldo with the warm brown eyes was my partner for life. He certainly wanted me with him. It was nice to be wanted. And I had entertained the thought. And now it was all down the river. And I was alone. I felt somehow empty. I mentally reviewed my losses of the past summer. Mama, Jonas, Muggins and now Waldo. I admit to succumbing to a bit of a pity party and I let the tears run down my face as I watched the lamplighter light the lamps in the park and along Main Street. Did God even care? Did he know how empty I felt? How did one pray so that one got answers? Just how did prayer work? Had I not asked for God's guidance?

I was so lost in thought that I did not hear any footsteps until Hunter stepped up into the gazebo. I looked up in surprise and something on his face made me remember the tears on my own. I brushed them off with a hand motion.

"Am I intruding?" he asked quietly, looking closely at me. As always, his presence affected me. He made me happy and nervous at the same time.

"Not at all. Please sit down."

He sat down beside me and we sat in silence a moment or two. His masculine presence now was uppermost in my mind, my other thoughts had flown.

"I came to thank you for the applesauce and canned tomatoes. I appreciate the work you and Laura put into it," he said finally in a low voice.

"You are welcome," I said, glad for something to discuss. "We had fun doing it. I hope it tastes good to you on a cold winter's night when it is too snowy to go to the inn for supper."

He chuckled as he stretched out his long legs in front of him.

"Do you even know how to make tomato soup?" I asked.

There was such a funny look on Hunter's face that I smiled broadly.

"I guess you have my answer," he said, looking sheepish, "but it can't be too hard."

"It isn't, but there is just one trick," I said. "Just heat the tomatoes to boiling and then add just a pinch of baking soda. It will immediately fizz. Then pour in the milk. Otherwise it will curdle."

"What is curdle?"

I smiled again.

"What is the smile about?"

"It's fun when a person of your knowledge asks simple questions. It gives me pleasure."

"Well, then I am glad to give you pleasure," he said. "Now tell me about curdle."

"Just try making the soup once without the baking soda and you will know. It will still be edible but won't look as nice."

He looked at me and shook his head just a bit.

"I think I could be much amused watching you make your first soup."

"Maybe I should invite you to watch."

I laughed lightly. He continued to look at me. A long look.

"At least I seem to have cheered you up."

I paused, nervous at his scrutiny. "That you did. By the way, how did you get Minna as housekeeper?"

He thought a moment. "They had a dog, she and her mother. And the dog was ill and they had no money so, aware that I was a bachelor and living alone, Minna offered to work for me to pay the bill. In the meantime, knowing of her plight, I kept her on one day a week for laundry and cleaning. I think she has a full week of cleaning for people now. She seems like a nice, honest worker."

"When you talk of her plight, I presume you mean the death of her husband and child."

"A child, too?"

"She was expecting a child."

"And lost it?"

"Seems so. She lost it due to stress."

We sat awhile in the dusk of the evening. The town was quiet. I remembered our talk on prayer.

"Have you learned anything new about prayer?" I asked. "I am not doing so well."

Hunter looked at me in surprise then looked off into the distance.

"I have learned to say 'thy kingdom come, thy will be done on earth as it is in heaven.'"

"That is such a familiar phrase."

"Perhaps too familiar. We don't think about what we are saying oftentimes when we 'repeat' the Lord's prayer. Do I want God's will or, in the end is it really my will I want?"

"I am not sure God even hears me."

Hunter chuckled again. "Do you consider that He perhaps does hear you and is saying no?"

"But what is the use of praying if I don't get what I want?"

Hunter chuckled again. "You stun me with your honesty. And I think God must be smiling. I hope I can be as honest in my prayers. Are you praying to get what you want or what God wants?"

I did not answer and we sat again in silence.

"Keep talking to Him, Amber. I had a wonderful grandfather who would talk about the Lord to me. I am not so much giving you my wisdom, but rather what my grandfather said to me without me even asking questions. I think he was maybe reminding himself of these nuggets of truth that he passed on to me. But I remember him saying God wants us to talk to Him. He wants us to be free to tell Him anything. But then grandpa said I must take time to listen, too. It is a learning experience. But He does not give you answers like you expect. Not usually. But I believe in your quest for answers, you will learn to know Him so well, that you can truly pray for His will to be done." He paused. "I have experienced His answers when looking back at a later date. God does not give direct answers. I find that He lets us search and we grow with the searching. The journey is important and we learn from mistakes. Hopefully."

It was getting cool in the gazebo and the sun was low. I was hugging myself to keep warm.

"Let me walk you home," said Hunter. "It is getting chilly."

We walked across the park, a comfortable silence between us. I stood by as Hunter mounted Ruggles, who had been tethered at our house. Just before leaving, Hunter looked down at me from his horse.

"Don't worry about praying with the right words or style, Amber. Just talk to Him. God sees your heart."

I nodded.

And then he rode away into the night and I stood and watched him disappear in the darkness.

When I said my prayers that night, I thought of how I had prayed for help regarding my Waldo decision. And I realized that God had indeed heard my prayer. Through circumstances, God had indeed given me the help I needed. I knew that Waldo was not the man for me. I knew that through Waldo's actions and my father's council, God had indeed answered my prayers.

CHAPTER 15

School had begun in Steeplechase and with it came an outbreak of measles. Ray and Papa were kept busy running around town and country, caring for the sick children. At the same time, Ray was trying to finish the marker for Muggins' grave. Finally one morning he told me he had it finished and wanted to know when we could go and have the "ceremonial" placing of it. I had not planned on a ceremony, but Ray had worked hard on the marker and so I gave in.

We went early the next morning. Papa stayed home, but Ray took me in his carriage.

"Where is the marker?" I asked on the way.

"In the back."

He was so secretive about it, I was a bit curious. He had never talked nice of Muggins, but I knew he liked him. Arriving at Hunter's place, Ray drove to the office and parked. As he did so, Hunter came out of the house.

"We just came to place the marker," I called to him. "We have no sick pet for you. Thankfully."

He smiled and walked up to us.

"May I join you for the ceremony?"

"It won't be a ceremony. But Ray won't show me the marker until he puts it on the grave."

Hunter grinned. Ray was often at Hunter's place and perhaps knew more about the marker than I did.

"Let me show you where I buried him," said Hunter, as Ray pulled out a wooden marker from under the carriage seat. I looked at it but there was a cloth covering the marker itself. We followed Hunter to the spot. I was glad I had Murf. It took the edge off the hurt now as I saw where my good friend Muggins was buried. I stood in silence as Ray worked the marker into the ground. Then he stood back to let me see it.

Ray had more artistic talent than I had and he had made the marker itself into a sitting cat. On the body of the cat were these words:

Muggins McDurfee
Dead
after 15 years of
terrorizing
both the
mice and men
of
Steeplechase

We all laughed. It was funny, but there was good reason for the words he wrote. In his younger years, Muggins had caught many, many mice. He did not always eat them, but he would lay them at the back door. And unfortunately, sometimes at the office door to Papa's practice, which was not exactly what a patient wants to see when going to the doctor. But worse yet, there was a tree that grew along the path to the office door with a tree branch that hung low over the path. It was a thick branch and to cut it off would have spoiled the look of the tree. So we let it on. But more than once Muggins had lain there in wait for an unsuspecting victim—male or female wearing a hat—and at the right time, with one good swipe of his furry paw, would take the hat right off the head of the patient walking beneath him and send it sailing into space.

"Thank you, Ray for your artwork. You really did like him for all your complaining about him."

"I tolerated him," said Ray, refusing to admit he liked the cat.

Hunter returned to his office when he saw a client arriving and Ray and I climbed into the carriage.

"You know, Ray, I owe Hunter another meal in exchange for him burying Muggins."

"Shall I go in and ask him to come for supper?" he asked.

"Tomorrow night. On Saturday. Then I will be cooking."

He was not gone long. But Hunter could not come. He had plans that he could not change. I was a bit surprised. He did not come across as a person with much going on besides his work.

Murf was waiting for me when I got home. I was glad to see him and when I picked him up, he rewarded me with loud purring.

The following day I received a letter from my sister Susan who was expecting her first baby in October. She asked if it were possible that I come and spend a couple weeks with her over the time of her confinement. I talked it over with Papa and Laura and it was decided that Laura would come every day while I was gone and I was free to go. I knew I could not get in the post office anymore that day, but I wanted to get my answer to Susan as soon as possible and so after supper I wrote my letter, assuring her of my coming. I then walked to the post office where I could drop it in the box. As I turned to go back home, I nearly bumped into Minna, who was coming with some mail of her own.

"Amber," she said, "I was hoping to see you."

"Aren't you out late today?"

"Yes, and I can't be gone too long, I have a mile to walk after I pass Dr. Renwick's house. But, do you have time to talk?"

"Of course, come, we can sit in the gazebo on the green," I answered, wondering what she had to talk to me about. We walked without talking and when we were seated in the gazebo, I looked at her, waiting for her to begin. She seemed now to hesitate.

"I have a big favor to ask," she began, "but first I want you to hear my story." She looked at me with pleading eyes. "I could feel your sympathy the other day when I told you about Abie dying in the fire."

"It was a terrible thing to have happened," I said. Again she hesitated.

"I have a friend from school days, whose name is Bertie. She kept in touch with me and we became very close. She was not married, but just two months ago, she married a man who lives in the northeastern part of Vermont, close to Brighton. I was invited to come to the wedding. At first I did not want to go. Money is scarce. But my mother, with whom I now live, encouraged me to go. Just for a break. A bit of vacation to get my mind on other things. And so I took the train to a town called Wildcat that is close to Brighton and my friend picked me up there. The wedding was held the following day. Eventually the couple left for a brief honeymoon and I was taken back to the town of Wildcat to wait for my train. The town was not large and the train station was on Main Street. As I sat there waiting for the train, I watched the people walk by on the other side of the street."

Minna stopped and looked at me. She cleared her throat and swallowed.

"And that is when I saw him."

"Saw who?" I asked, thinking I missed something.

"Abie."

"Abie? I thought..."

I stopped talking. Minna was just looking at me. A chill went up my spine. I felt like the hair on the back of my neck stood up. I sat, not speaking for a moment. This woman, I told myself, was dealing with a great amount of grief. She lost her husband and then her child.

I chose my words carefully. "Do you think it is possible that you wanted it to be him so badly that you thought it was him?"

"It was Abie. The man walked just like Abie. He looked like Abie." She said it with conviction without raising her voice.

"But Abie died in the fire." Somehow the words made my mouth feel dry.

"But his body was never found."

This was new to me. I just looked at her, silent.

"Abie and I got married very young. We met at a town festival. In six months we were married." She paused. "It was too soon. We were much too young and he made very little money."

When I said nothing, she continued.

"But we loved each other, and although money was scarce, we were happy. After a while he sometimes hung out with friends at night. I told myself that he was young and probably missed his friends. When we were married almost a year, I discovered I was expecting a baby. I was so happy. I thought now he will stay home with me. But he was not happy about the baby. He wanted...." She drew in a shaky breath. "He wanted me to get rid of it."

Minna paused. I looked at her wide-eyed, trying to digest what she was saying.

"I was horrified. Such a thing never came into question as far as I was concerned. We argued a long time about it and then one day he gave me the address of some woman who would take care of the pregnancy, but I threw the paper into the stove. After that it seemed he stayed away more and more.

"When I was about three months pregnant, the pants factory burned down. I was overwhelmed when I was told Abie died in the fire. I loved Abie and I believe he still loved me although he was upset about the coming baby. I think he just did not think we could afford a child. He had lost some work due to an injury and I had some illness that kept me going to the doctor for six months. It was a terrible financial struggle." She drew a deep breath. "It has been very hard for me that the body was not found. In spite of the fact that he died in the fire, it would have been nice to have had the body for burial."

"Did they find nothing at all of his clothes or body?"

"They found a belt that I know was his and a shoe that looked like his. The shoe was partly burned, but the belt was not burned at all."

"That is strange," I said. "How could the belt not have burned if he...." I said no more. It was not a happy subject to discuss. It must have been a terrible thing to have happened.

"Yes, it is curious," she said, knowing what I meant to say.

"Did anyone else die in the fire?"

"One other man. They found his body."

We ate in silence a few moments. I was trying to figure this out.

"Are you sure the belt was his?"

"Yes. I had given it to him as a gift."

Minna was just staring out across the green, seeing nothing but certainly trying to comprehend the mystery of the belt that had survived the fire.

"And the other shoe?"

"Nothing left of it."

"Strange," I said, still thinking of the belt. "Did he sometimes take his belt off at work?"

"He never took his belt off until we went to bed."

We sat in silence a few moments.

"It was very hard for me that the body was not found," she said. "There should have been something left of him. No one could understand that there was no body."

"But there were his shoes," I reminded her.

"Yes."

"How did the fire start?"

"There was an explosion in the building. I don't know where he was at the time of the explosion. Maybe he was closest to it. But of course, everyone would run to see if they could help." She stopped talking and the silence grew long.

"You had a funeral?"

"Although we had no body to bury, we had a memorial service at the church. We put up a marker in the church cemetery."

The sun had disappeared and a slight breeze was blowing my hair into my eyes. I thought Minna had finished her story when she turned once more to me.

"And three weeks later I lost the baby. My little girl."

Minna fought tears and my heart went out to her. When I saw a tear slide down her cheek, I put my arm around her. I did not know what to say. I could not convince her otherwise, I was sure. She wanted to believe it was Abie that she had seen.

"I have since written to my friend," she continued "and told her I was sure I saw him. I asked her to watch out for him because she knows him also. But in her return letter, she said they were moving farther away now to work on her father-in-law's dairy farm. However, she told me of an agricultural fair that will be held in Wildcat, which is not far from Brighton, on the third Saturday of this month. An annual fair that many people from surrounding towns attend also."

I suddenly remembered that she came to ask a favor of me.

"And you want to go," I said softly.

"Yes, and I want you to go with me."

I caught my breath. She certainly did not expect me to get involved in this?

"Pardon?"

"Please go with me," she said, looking at me with pleading eyes. "I must go and I do not want to go alone."

"You want me to go with you to this festival, to see if you can find this man that looks like your husband?" I refused to say to look for her husband.

"Yes. I like you. You do not tell me I am crazy. I do not want to go alone. Will you come with me?"

I sat back on the bench and suddenly realized it was nearly dark. And Minna had to walk probably a mile and a half to get home. In the distance I heard a roll of thunder.

"Minna, you must get home. Come with me and I will ask Papa if I can take you home in the carriage."

She got up with me and we walked to the house where I found Papa in the living room.

"Papa, this is Minna. She is housekeeper to Hunter. Could I use the carriage to take her home? She lives about a mile beyond Hunter."

Papa looked at Minna.

"Mrs. Stork?"

"Yes," she said. And I realized that Papa was probably her doctor when she lost the baby.

"Go ahead," said Papa, "but I heard thunder. Get going."

We left immediately. All the time, I was wondering what I should say to Minna. I felt very sorry for her. But it would be such a wild goose chase.

"Is the festival more than a day? Would we need to stay overnight?" I asked as we headed up North Street.

"It is only one day, but it goes into the night. We must stay overnight."

We were just passing Hunter's house and I was silent, I glanced in as we passed. His house set back from the road a bit. I was surprised to see by the glow in the open doorway, two people standing in the near darkness. Hunter was recognizable. But who was the woman who stood close to him? It somehow gave me a jolt. This could not be a client with an animal. This was personal. My heart for some strange reason seemed to drop to my feet, which was ridiculous. I had no claim on Hunter Renwick. He was a friend of my brother, a friend of my father and yes, a friend to me. That was all. He did not trust women. But what about the one on his front porch? I suddenly realized Minna was talking.

"The festival is in two weeks. I have some money saved. I will pay your way. I just want someone with me."

"Minna, I must think about this. Give me time to think and I will get back to you. But if I do come with you, I will pay my own way. Otherwise the answer is no. But let me sleep on it and I will get in touch."

"I will be in town again to shop in two days," Minna answered. "I always come with a neighbor. I will stop by then."

"You must tell me when we get to your house," I said. "I do not know where you live."

"Just ahead on the right. Where the elm tree stands by the road."

We pulled in the lane and we agreed on a time to meet and with hearty thanks, she stepped out of the carriage and ran to the house.

There was a flash of lightning and a crack of thunder. The horse whinnied and I headed home. As I passed Hunter's house, a carriage was just coming out the lane. The porch was all in darkness.

CHAPTER 16

The next day Mindy came to see me on a short break from the bakery.

"Amber," she said, huffing from walking so quickly. "I must get back to the bakery right away, but I heard some gossip that will interest you. There is a barbecue at the mayor's house this evening for the council members and I have it on good authority that Hunter will be there with a girl. I have a plan. Come to my apartment this afternoon. Can you come? And make no plans for this evening."

"Hunter is taking a girl?"

"So I am told. I'll give you details later."

It was Saturday. I was on to cook and I still had mending to do, plus some applesauce to make. But if I hurried....

"What time?"

"Better come at three when I get done work. Or three thirty. Is that possible?"

"I'll make it possible."

In a flash she was gone again and I was left with a heart that seemed to have settled somewhere around my toes. Hunter, the man who did not trust women, would be with a woman at the celebration this evening. I went about my work, realizing that I was very disappointed. Why did he not ask me? I would have gone with him. With joy. And who was that woman on his porch last evening? I knew somehow that it must be the same woman. My only hope was in the plans Mindy had. Somehow, I believed she planned to find out more about this party.

At twenty after three I ran up the many steps to Mindy's apartment. I knocked and I heard her call and say I should walk in. I did so. And there I faced a Mindy with sparkling eyes.

"You and I are going to spy on Dr. Hunter Renwick this evening," she said.

"Hold it. Tell me again what this is all about."

"Mrs. Wilkes and Mrs. Juniper were talking in the bakery this morning. I did not hear the whole conversation, but it was about a party at the mayor's house this evening at six. An outside barbecue, I think she said, for those on the town council. And you know Hunter is now on town council and does not have a wife. Well, this Mrs. Wilkes, she lives somewhere between here and Pipers Hill and she evidently helps do the food for the mayor's parties." Mindy paused for breath. "She was in getting some doughnuts and other tarts and sweets for the party. I do not how they got on the subject of Hunter, but Mrs. Juniper said she knew about the party because Hunter was taking Lucille."

"Who is Lucille?" I asked, my heart in my throat. I already did not like even the sound of the girl's name.

"I don't know. Mrs. Juniper has a couple married daughters, but none that I know of that is still single."

I was silent a while. I was hurt, but I could not admit it. I was drawn to Hunter. And I thought sometimes he liked me even if he did not trust women. He always paid attention to me. And we had just had that wonderful discussion in the gazebo where he told me something of his grandpa.

"I would love to see the woman," I said. "I would like to see the two of them together. See if something is going on with them."

"I knew you would," said Mindy. "You like him more than you are willing to admit and I am trying my best to think up a way for us to spy on them."

"However could we spy on them?"

"I happen to have a spinster aunt who lives in the house next to the mayor. She is a fun aunt. She is in her forties and lives alone with an assortment of animals. Actually, she and Hunter would probably get along good. She has a few cats, one black goat, one sheep, and one horse. At least that was the assortment of animals the last time I was there. I don't think she has the cow anymore and the goose she had for Christmas dinner. I am thinking we could go to visit her right now. She is the type who, if we tell her what we are up to, she would help us."

"This sounds very scary," I said. "How do we do this? Hunter is not exactly the type of person that I would want to know I was spying on him."

I was not sure anymore if I really wanted to see Hunter with a woman. I was feeling worse the longer I thought about it. I don't think I even realized how much I liked Hunter. He was an interesting person. I liked his personality. I admit, the fact that he was cautious about women, appealed to me. I guess I thought I did not have to worry about anyone else. How could I be so foolish?

"First," said Mindy, "we need to talk to my aunt, so let's head over there."

It was not more than perhaps a half a mile walk to her Aunt Maggie's. Once we were out of the village, the river was on our right perhaps a hundred feet from the road. There was just one house on that side of the road and that is where the Wolf family lived. Not far from the edge of the village, there was a lane that forked off to the left and ran parallel to the road, but went up a hill and up there was where the mayor lived and close by, her aunt's house. When Mindy knocked at the door there was no response, so we walked around the house down the drive that led to the stable and found her aunt working in the garden.

"Is that you, Mindy?" she called when she saw us. "Oh dear, you brought a guest and I look like a tramp."

"Aunt Maggie, this is my friend Amber McDurfee."

"I know who she is. Her father is my doctor, although I try my best to have nothing to do with him," she laughed.

"Pleased to meet you," I said, "and I have seen you but did not know you were Mindy's aunt."

"So what brings two lovely girls to my house? Will you have a glass of mint tea?"

"Sure," said Mindy. "May Amber and I walk around your backyard while you get it?"

"Go ahead. But the flowers are past their peak and if you go in the animal pen, watch out for the goat. Just don't turn your back on him."

"Thanks for the warning."

Maggie went into the house and we ambled around the yard with eyes toward the neighboring house. There was a slatted fence separating the properties for a portion of the backyard where rambler roses and other flowers were growing. However, there was a path from the back door of Mindy's aunt's house to the back door of the mayor's. They seemed to be good friends. We walked back beyond the slatted fence. There were some bushes here and a sour cherry tree or two, but finally we came to a shed for the carriage and connected to it was a stable for the various animals that Mindy's aunt kept. There was a door from the stable that opened into the open field for the animals as well as one that opened to the drive. The open field included a small pond and a few old apple trees.

We turned back, eyes to the neighbor's property. There was activity there. I saw lanterns strung up and a couple tables set up close together. There were chairs being carried out of the house and the mayor's wife was just coming out the door with what looked like tablecloths in her hands.

When we were called back to the house to have our glass of tea, Mindy hesitantly told her aunt the real reason for the visit.

"Maggie, we need information about this evening's party at the mayor's house."

"What kind of information? It is the annual picnic for the town council. They have it every year. Just an evening of good eating and socializing. I was never there, but I see a lot. And sometimes I get some leftover food," she answered with a wink at me.

"Are you home tonight?"

"Of course. Where would I go? And when all this is happening at the neighbor's house, I can't afford to leave. I might miss something."

"We would like to come and do some spying on the party."

"Spying? That sounds interesting. Who do you want to spy on?"

"You must keep this to yourself," said Mindy with a glance at me.

"I'm safe. I'll spy with you if you need help."

"One of the council is a single man who just never dates and we are told he will be here this evening with a woman."

"Ahh!" said Maggie, brightening considerably, her bright eyes flicking from Mindy to me. "And who is interested in this young man?"

"We just want a bit of fun. We want to see who this bachelor finally asked out."

"I don't suppose he has a name?"

"He is a veterinarian and his name is Dr. Hunter Renwick."

"Oh, I know who he is. Nice chap. And good looking to boot. He was here for Bel one time."

"Bel?" I asked.

"Short for Belshazzar, the goat. He gets in scrapes all the time. Got cut bad on a tin can. Needed stitches. How do you intend to spy and how can I help?"

For the next hour we planned. In the end it was decided that I would dress like a man and Mindy would wear a hat to conceal her face and we would be a couple, visiting Maggie. The light would be dim outside and the light from the lanterns would not reach us, but just to play safe, we would disguise ourselves. That meant I would have to borrow a pair of pants from Ray without him knowing it. He certainly, of all people, could not know of this foolishness we were planning. Maggie was having a lot of fun helping us plan.

"But if it is barely light anymore, what will be our reason to be outside?" I asked.

"Well, first of all, the guests at my neighbor's will not be looking over here. They have no reason to. But we will walk openly out to the pen to see the animals. I will feed them or find something to do out there."

"Maybe we can see from the house windows?" I said, getting a bit scared. I certainly could not chance Hunter recognizing me dressed as a man.

"You can try, but they will be too far away. Even outside you may not really see what you wish. Bring your clothes and we'll dress you up here and see what happens. It also depends where they sit. But the food table is mostly on this side of the lawn and the tables where they sit are farther to the other side."

After supper that evening, I hurriedly cleaned up and then informed Papa that I was going over to Mindy's and did not know when I would be back. I found an old pair of Ray's pants, put them under my arm and headed off to our adventure.

Mindy was eagerly waiting me and we set off immediately. By the time Mindy and I got to the fork in the road, I suddenly realized we had to go past the mayor's house to get to Maggie's house. I had not thought of that before. However, all the carriages were out along the lane and I quickly recognized Ruggles, but I did not talk to him as we walked cautiously behind them and when we were no longer behind them, there were bushes and trees. But our precautions were really unnecessary because the guests were out back. We could smell some grilled meat and I was once more disappointed that Hunter had not asked me. Did he trust this Lucille more than me?

Maggie was waiting for us when we arrived. She was easy to like. She was slim, full of energy and had her brown, rather fuzzy hair loosely twisted and fastened on the back of her head with a pencil. Her eyes sparkled as she greeted us.

"We better get moving," she said to me. "The guests have been here a good hour already. Did you bring your brother's pants?"

"I did and I tried them on at home to make sure I could get into them."

"You can just go over here in the parlor to change. I pulled the shades."

That done, she handed me a hat. It really was not a man's hat but would pass for one in the darkness.

"And what about Mindy?" I asked. "Hunter knows her also and knows she is a friend of mine."

"I have an old hat for her and she can use my cane. Just bend over a bit," Maggie said. "Just in case someone looks over, but they won't, I am sure."

Just then there was a knock on the back door and at the same time the door opened and a voice called.

"Maggie?"

Maggie shoved us into the parlor and went into the kitchen. It was the mayor's wife. We listened with hearts pounding at the close encounter.

"Maggie, I am so embarrassed, but I don't have enough ice chips. Do you have any I could have?"

"Of course," said Maggie. "Actually, I have a quarter of an ice block in sawdust in the cellar and you can have the whole thing. The ice man comes again tomorrow. Go on back to your party and I will chip it and bring it over."

"You are such a wonderful neighbor. Thank you."

And she was gone.

"Just let me chip this ice for the party and then we'll head out," said Maggie to us.

While Maggie chipped ice, Mindy and I tried looking out windows. Upstairs and down. It just was not good enough to see anything of Hunter and his friend.

Finally, Maggie took the ice over to the party and when she returned, it was time for us to spy on Hunter.

I adjusted my pants and put on my hat. Mindy wore a light coat of Maggie's just to conceal herself and used a cane, bending over a bit as she walked. It was not completely dark outside, but the light was brighter at the neighbor's with the lanterns, so I felt pretty safe. However, my heart was pounding when Maggie opened the back door with a squeak and led the way out on the stoop and then down the few steps to the lawn.

Actually, going out the door and down the steps was our best chance of being seen. We were up higher here than on the lawn. I pulled my hat down a bit farther and hissed to Mindy to bend over a bit more. I wanted badly to look over to the party but would wait until we had either a slatted fence or a bush to look through. I could hear the chatter of the guests and nearly stumbled when I heard Hunter's voice. That made my heart stop for a second and I automatically looked over, keeping my head down, but I must have also turned in that direction because Mindy, bent over and holding on to my arm, stumbled over my foot and when I tried to help her, my hat fell off. Rather than be exposed to those at the party, I fell to my knees to put it back on and Mindy dropped to hers also and then we got the uncontrollable giggles. There were zinnias still blooming along the fence, and I just hoped we were hidden. The guests were at least fifteen feet, maybe even twenty feet from us and it was dark. Well, sort of dark. It seemed the mayor had lanterns and torches at every corner of the lawn.

Maggie, seeing us on the ground, came back to see what was wrong and we quickly got up and followed her, but Mindy forgot to bend over.

"Bend over!" I hissed as quietly as I could and still get the message across. I took a quick glance over the fence as we walked, not knowing if I would have such a chance this close again. I quickly picked out Hunter who was at a table, facing us. He was looking at the woman beside him who had to be Lucille and he looked very happy. Too happy for my sake. The food table was close to the fence and I got a good enough look at it to wish very much that I had been invited. There was grilled meat, potato salad, cabbage salad and deviled eggs and pasta dishes and pickles. My mouth was watering and I was feeling angry at Hunter. And although no one was getting food at it at the time being, I was very nervous about someone suddenly coming to it and seeing us.

We continued walking on back to the stable where Maggie proceeded to feed the animals. Maybe she did not even feed them. Maybe she just pretended. At any rate, it was so dark here, that I finally felt safe. We walked behind the bushes and tried to look through them. Everyone was just too far away. Although they did have lantern light on their faces, I could not get a good look at Lucille. I was dismayed however, that Hunter and Lucille seemed to have so much to say to each other, they barely took time to talk to anyone else, or so it seemed to me. They both looked like they were enjoying themselves way too much for my opinion and I began to wonder if he had this girlfriend for a long time and we were just kept in secret about it. I wondered if Ray knew something of the girl. I felt almost a bit nauseous at the thought. I found out though, that as my eyes got accustomed to the darkness, I could see better. I could not get past the fact that Hunter and Lucille were so at ease with each other, and I wondered again just how long this was going on. I felt sick. What I could see of her was a bit disheartening. She was attractive. I had hoped she was ugly with at least a hook nose or was cross-eyed.

After observing those at the table for maybe fifteen minutes, they began to get up and move around. Some went to another table to pick up a dessert. Hunter finally got up and went to the dessert table but came back to Lucille, evidently not sure what he should bring her. It seemed she was not interested in dessert but wanted a second helping of something on the main table. For this, they had to come closer to us and I could easily see Hunter's face. He was dressed handsomely. The two were laughing together and although she was doing most of the talking, he would add something and then they would laugh. She had, I thought a rather shrill laugh. Lucille was probably his age.

She was slim and willowy and had a huge smile, and if I have to say it myself, she was stunningly pretty. I was feeling sicker all the time. I think I could have stood up and shouted and Hunter would not have seen me. He had eyes only for the woman at his side.

And then Maggie was back with us. "Are you able to see anything?" she asked quietly.

"Enough. He is having too good a time," said Mindy with a sympathetic glance at me. I think she saw my disappointment.

"Maybe it is a relative. You said he doesn't date."

"It can't be a relative because Lucille's aunt was excited that he asked her."

"Do you want to continue to spy?" asked Maggie who now had a lit lantern in her hand.

"I don't think so. We spied successfully and I think we must be happy with that. Or unhappy," Mindy added with a glance at me.

"Come," said Maggie, "meet my animals."

She opened the gate and we made our way into the pen. She had a lamb born in the spring. It was black and I found it very lovable. Belshazzar the goat, was not to be seen, but I saw two yellow cats and her mare, Daisy. I was sorry not to see the goat, as I found them to be comical, but my main interest was back across the fence at the neighbors. As Maggie went back toward the gate I thought I saw something behind us in the field. Hoping it was Belshazzar, I stopped to look, but saw nothing more. In the meantime Maggie opened the gate, and she must have dropped something because she stooped down to pick it up and just then something black and white flew past me and butted Maggie face down into the field.

I cried out in horror, and at the same time I saw the naughty goat go speeding through the gate.

"The goat got out!" I said too loudly as I watched in relief as Maggie dragged herself to her feet.

"I declare, I am going to have that goat for Sunday dinner," she said, apparently not hurt. "That is the third time he has done that to me and I am getting a sore bottom. Where is that rascal? Did you say he got out?"

"I saw him go," I said.

I had no sooner spoken when a commotion broke out at the party next door. There was no question, it had to be Belshazzar.

"Oh no!" Maggie said in horror and took off after her ornery goat. We began following and suddenly realized we could not.

"Stay here, Mindy, or we will be seen."

"They already heard you yell."

"Did I yell?" My horror increased.

"Someone did. I think it was you. At any rate we better lay low."

We stood and listened as we tried to see what was happening. There were shouts and laughter over the fence in place of the quietness at the meal. At least they were getting some entertainment. We heard different voices giving warning as to where the goat was headed now and it sounded to me like the mayor's fine party was now in general chaos. I wanted badly to see what Hunter and his date were doing in the melee. We looked through the bushes that Bel had run through, and it looked like people were running everywhere and shouting. Finally, after maybe five or ten minutes there was a shout and then quiet. Maggie seemed to have gotten her Belshazzar. We waited in anticipation when suddenly I heard Hunter's voice approaching.

"Mindy! Hide! Hunter is bringing Bel back!"

The only direction we could run without being seen was into the stable. We ducked in there and waited with baited breath.

"You sure knew how to catch this goat but I'm afraid you got dirty in the process," Maggie was saying.

"No problem," said Hunter with a chuckle. "I've had a bit of experience catching animals in my profession. Now where do you want him?"

"Just put him in the field and I will close the gate. He caught me unawares and booted me in one direction and he went in the other— to the party."

Hunter chuckled and there was a part of me that wanted to keep Hunter here on this side of the fence and away from Lucille.

"I heard you yell and before we could see who needed help, the goat came flying into the mayor's lawn."

"That wasn't me that yelled, I didn't have time to yell." There followed a silence and Maggie must have realized what she said. "My niece was with me. She probably went in the house now."

"You sure you don't want Bel in the stable?"

I nearly gasped out loud and hurried to the other side of the horse to hide, aligning my legs with the mare's so Hunter could not see me.

"No, if the gate is closed, he'll be fine," said Maggie. "And thank you so much."

"Glad to be of help," said Hunter.

I heard his footsteps receding and I secretly hoped he smelled like a goat when he went back to the mysterious Lucille.

Our mission accomplished, we could go back into the house. As we headed in, I saw both Hunter and Lucille were at the food table. There was no way I could go past them now. Had I really yelled? And if so, Maggie said it was not her. Did he catch that? Of course he had no reason to be suspicious. He and Lucille finally went back to the table and I took that opportunity to hurry into the house. There, amid much relieved laughter, we got back into our regular clothes, thanked Maggie and headed home. We did not know how long the party would last and I certainly did not want Hunter seeing me leave Maggie's house—or see us along that road. The road was dark and I was glad when we were back on Main Street.

"It isn't that late," said Mindy. "Come in. I have some cream puffs from the bakery and I'll make us some coffee. Seeing all that good food made me hungry."

I followed her up the long stairs and soon we were reviewing every detail of our adventure and laughing a bit hysterically while enjoying the cream puffs.

"How do we find out more about Lucille?" I asked.

"Don't know. We should have told Maggie to ask her neighbor about the party. Maybe she could find something out."

When the clock struck eleven, I rose to go.

"Here, don't forget Ray's pants," said Mindy. "He might be looking for them."

"Not tonight. These are work pants for the garden and such."

With the pants under my arm, I headed back home, wondering if Hunter was home yet. Probably not. I wondered where Lucille's aunt lived. The streets were deserted. Just as I was about to cross North Street to our house a carriage came from Main Street. I waited for it to pass and was surprised when it stopped. And I held my breath when I saw it was Hunter. He said nothing for a moment, just looked at me. As for me, my mouth went dry and I was too shocked to even say hello.

"Aren't you out a bit late this evening?" he finally asked.

I was so glad to see him alone in the carriage, that I relaxed with joy. At least he was not having a long evening with Lucille.

"I could say the same for you. Were you out courting?"

I really don't know where that came from. As soon as the idea presented itself to me, I said it and just that soon I regretted it. I thought Hunter looked at me a long time.

"I was at a picnic at the mayor's house," he said, ignoring my question.

I was a bit miffed that he did not answer my question but did not dare to ask it again. In the meantime, Hunter was looking at what I was holding.

"What are you doing with a pair of men's pants on a Saturday evening?"

I looked at the pants and to my dismay, a leg was hanging down, and easily seen by the light of the street lamp.

"I..." I could not think of anything to say and hoped a carriage would come along so he would have to go.

"Or did the church sewing circle meet this evening?" he probed, but I could see the gleam in his eye as he asked.

"No," I finally stuttered as I frantically tried to think of another subject to talk about. If I thought Hunter gave me a long look before this, he now gave me an even longer look.

"Miss McDurfee, you are rather mysterious this evening," he said as his keen eyes sought mine and while I stood painfully mute, looking into his amused eyes. "I find you walking alone late at night on the dark streets of our village carrying a pair of pants that must either belong to your father or brother and you can give me no explanation."

"You seem very inquisitive this evening, Dr. Renwick," I said, determined not to look guilty. "You can't know everything. I was over at a friend's house."

"That does not answer my question, regarding the pants," he said, trying not to smile.

When I remained mute, he sobered.

"I advise you to get in the house and to bed. I don't think your Papa would want you walking the streets alone this late at night."

And with the flick of the reins he was off.

It took me a while to sleep when I finally got to bed. I ran the whole evening through my brain once more. Could Hunter have any idea where I was? Why did he have such a thing about the pants? Well, it was a bit strange for me carrying a pair of pants around on a Saturday night. My one consolation was that in spite of his evening with this woman Lucille, he had stopped to talk to me. I was embarrassed about the pants, but he had not seen me in the pants, so our secret was safe. I wondered what he was thinking about as he got ready for bed.

CHAPTER 17

Monday afternoon while I was pulling beets and carrots from the garden, Mindy stopped in.

"I have information," she said quietly to me with a glance at Laura, who was taking wash off the line.

"Oh, let's go out on the porch. I'll get us something to drink."

Once there, with glasses of tea in our hands, I waited for her information. It had to be about Lucille.

"Lucille's aunt was in the shop and since no one else was in at the time, I asked about Lucille."

"Just like that?"

"Not quite like that. I asked about the party that was at the mayor's. I said I had heard her talk about it. She immediately talked of Lucille, who went with Hunter. She was so thrilled that he asked her, so I asked about Lucille. She is a widow of two years. Has no children and lives, thankfully, some distance away."

"How does Hunter know her?"

"They went to the same school, wherever that was. And they were good friends and got into a lot of trouble together."

"She must have been the one to get into trouble. He doesn't quite seem that type," I replied.

"Well, he is a grown man now. But I do believe she is a live wire, from what she said."

"So if she is from far away, why was she here?"

"She came for a wedding that took place in Flynn Falls on Saturday morning. And according to her aunt, she looked up Hunter on

Friday night hoping he could come to her aunt's place on Saturday night for supper."

"She seems a bit pushy," I said, hoping I did not sound jealous.

"Because he had plans, he said she could come as his partner."

I was somewhat relieved. He had not sought her out. On the other hand, he could have asked me to go to the party with him.

"You would make a good detective," I said, grateful for the information.

"Well, you are the one really interested in him, so I could be more casual about asking questions. Anyway, she loves to talk and would have kept on except a customer came in."

"So she did not mention the goat at the party?"

"No. I guess she ran out of time. But at some point she did say she wished her niece would move here. She said there are no decent men available in her community."

A short time later, waving goodbye to Mindy I found myself praying.

"Dear God, please don't let Lucille move here!"

That evening at suppertime, we were interrupted by a knock at the back door. I answered the knock and the man, a stranger to me, said he brought a man who needed a doctor immediately. I quickly told Papa who left the table and headed to his office.

"Ray," Papa said, "I might need help to bring the patient in, maybe you should come, too."

I looked over the table to see what I should put back on the stove. Ray left the table and went out the back door. About five minutes later Ray returned as I was taking a bowl from a cupboard.

"It's Hunter, Amber."

"Hunter?" I nearly dropped the bowl I was holding. "What happened to him?"

"He got a bad kick from a cow. It did not break his leg, but he has a painful flesh wound on his leg and, I am sure, a badly bruised bone. And infection could easily set in."

"Who was the man?"

"I presume the farmer whose cow kicked him. I don't know his name."

When I heard Ray say pain, I thought immediately of the brandy bottle.

"Give him some brandy," I said. "He will need it."

When Ray left, I stood a long time at the stove, wondering just what was going on over in the office. Hunter was fortunate not to have a broken leg, but a cut from a cow's hoof sounded extremely dirty to me. Papa would give that a good cleaning. The farmer had to go back to his farm and sometime later, Ray took Hunter home. By that time I had made a quick soup from some of the stew I had made for supper and I sent it along for Hunter.

Later, when Papa returned, he said Hunter had to stay off that leg completely for two days and that he would go to change the bandage each day to make sure there was no infection. As for the soup I sent along, Papa doubted he would eat anything today anymore. He thought Hunter probably had too much pain to enjoy food.

"Did you give him brandy?" I asked.

"Yes," said Papa giving me a meaningful glance. "But not as much as you used. Ray told him you said he needed brandy and he grunted something in response but was in too much pain to repeat it."

"Did you give him stitches?"

"Eight."

Papa ate his supper and Ray returned after an hour or so.

"Hunter needs a housekeeper," said Ray when he returned. "How is he going to stay in bed the next two days?"

"Maybe this will make him realize he needs a wife," said Papa. "In the meantime, we can see that he gets food."

"I think Minna is there tomorrow," I said. "So she can take care of him tomorrow."

"And when I go see him in the morning, I'll tell him we will bring him food the next day," said Papa.

September was proving an eventful month. The outbreak of measles among the schoolchildren had not let up and there were so many sick children, the school had been closed for the last four days. Besides that, we were having so much rain the farmers had some trouble getting crops in and now there was talk of a storm that they called a hurricane in the Atlantic coming up along the east coast, which would possibly bring even more rain.

On Wednesday morning Laura came in the door dripping from the rain and when I told her Papa wanted us to supply Hunter's food that day, she made an extra loaf of bread and an apple pie for him. Papa went to change his dressing in the morning and said Hunter would not need a noon meal but he needed supper. I worked on a pot of root vegetables cooked with ham and potatoes. Somewhere around five o'clock, I asked Ray if he would deliver the food to Hunter. He was just on his way to another patient, probably another case of measles, but he said he could drop me and the food off there and I could walk back. I had to think this through a bit. I was very ill at ease visiting Hunter in his house alone, simply because of my own feelings for him. I liked him a lot. And he had just taken Lucille to the party and I felt rejected. Well, he did stop to talk to me after the party and that was another embarrassment. That dumb pants leg! At the same time, the temptation to see him was too strong. Papa was not home from his rounds and I had a pot of food keeping warm on the stove for us later.

"Are you coming?" asked Ray a bit impatiently. "And don't forget your umbrella."

"Yes. Here, help me carry the food."

Ten minutes later, Ray let me off at Hunter's back door. I carried the pot of hot food to the back porch and returned for the bread and pie. Ray then drove away and with my heart pounding, I knocked. I heard nothing. Was he in bed upstairs? I wished I had asked. When there was no reply, I gingerly opened the door and stuck my head in.

"Anybody home?"

"Come in."

He was not upstairs. The voice was too close. I walked in the door and carried the hot food to the kitchen table. Then I went out for the pie and the bread. When all was in, I took a deep breath and walked gingerly into what seemed to be the living room. There I found Hunter, sitting on the sofa, fully clothed from the waist up, but wearing a pair of loose pants with the leg rolled up for easy access for changing the bandage on his injury. My eyes took all this in with one quick glance and then I met the blue eyes under a heavy head of hair that was slightly messed up. I am sure he looked much better than he had in Papa's surgery, but it still was a bit of a shock to see him so vulnerable. I had thought if he was feeling bad I would be more relaxed. But his blue eyes, as alert as a fox, were fixed on me with an appraising look.

"So I have a visitor," he said. "Take a seat."

"You do not have a visitor," I responded. "You have meal service."

"I stand corrected."

"How are you?"

"I am better than yesterday."

"Was yesterday very bad?"

"I had a lot of pain."

"I am sorry," I said, and I was. "Are you hungry?"

"I am famished. Whatever you brought smells wonderful."

He made me very self conscious, his blue eyes studying me as we conversed.

"Do you have a tray?"

"In the kitchen. But the food can wait. Sit down a bit and visit. Or is someone waiting for you?"

"No, no one is waiting." I felt my answers were rather stilted, but he made me nervous and I was very aware that we were alone.

"Who brought you?"

"Ray dropped me off. It seems there is a measles outbreak. He and Papa are being kept busy. I shall walk home."

"Good. If you promise to stay while I eat, you may bring me my supper. Or did you plan to eat with me? I'll share."

"No, my own supper awaits me at home," I said as I returned to the kitchen for his pork chops, potatoes and vegetables. There were dirty dishes on the counter and seeing a basin, I took hot water from the stove reservoir, put in a bit of soap and put the dirty dishes in before getting his food on a plate for him. When I had given it to him, I went back and sliced the loaf of bread, found some butter in the cupboard, and took him a buttered slice.

"And there is a whole apple pie for you that Laura baked. She also made the bread for you."

"Please thank her."

"I'll do that."

"And now please take a seat."

When I hesitated. He stopped eating, looking at me in such a way as to say why are you not obeying me? I sat on a chair not far from him.

"Tell me about your injury. How did it happen?"

"The farmer has a cow with mastitis and she was hurting and I was not as careful as I should have been, so she gave me a vicious kick that knocked me down with a deep cut on my leg from her dirty hoof." He paused, his keen eyes on me. "I should have known better than to trust a female."

I know my eyes widened at his remark and I saw his eyes were sparkling as he waited for my reaction.

"Dr. Renwick," I huffed. "I am totally offended at your remark. Today two women cooked and baked for you over a hot oven. One came through the rain to deliver the food and you now tell me females are not to be trusted. I am tempted to take the pie and go home."

"I stand corrected once more," he chuckled. "And please do not steal the pie. I couldn't help myself. I was sure I would get a feisty reaction for that remark and I got it. In truth, I am humbly grateful for the wonderful supper as well as the splendid company while eating it. I couldn't have asked for better."

"You now sound like you were into the brandy," I said, not knowing what to do with the compliment. At the same time I was reminding myself of Lucille.

He chuckled and gave me a searching look. "I am surprised you brought up the brandy subject."

"You shocked me with your compliment. I didn't know what I was saying."

He chuckled again. "It feels good to laugh. I did no laughing these two days."

Seeing he was done with his meal, I went out into the kitchen to bring him his pie. While there, I found a container for the leftover supper and cleaned up what needed cleaning. Back in the living room, I gave him his pie.

"What about coffee?"

"I drank enough coffee today. I don't need any."

"Is there something that needs to be done that you would like me to do for you before I leave?"

He looked steadily at me a moment.

"Something within reason," I added. He chuckled.

"It sounds like you were already doing some clean up."

"I can't stand dirty dishes standing around. They are soaking now and I will wash them before I leave."

"Thank you. I can't think of anything else right now." He gave me the plate, which I took to the kitchen where I finished washing and drying his dishes before returning to the living room.

"Laura is at home tomorrow and said I should tell you she will make a vegetable soup for you and bring it at noon."

"I hope to be up tomorrow after your father gives me the okay. But I will be glad for the soup."

"Then I think I shall go."

"You seem eager to leave."

"Papa awaits his supper."

Hunter gave me a contemplative look.

"Come here, Amber."

I just looked at him. I was standing only a couple feet from him now. There was something about his words that gave me pause.

"Come here," he repeated as he held out his hand. "I want to thank you for the meal and the visit."

I stepped closer to him and rather gingerly placed my hand in his. I hoped I would not blush with my hand in his, wondering why the formality of shaking hands. Besides that, I thought he had already thanked me.

"I am very grateful for what you and Laura did for me. Thank you."

"We were glad to do it," I said.

As I attempted to free my hand from his, however, he held it more tightly and looked closely at me and a teasing look came into his eyes.

"I have one last question." He paused, watching me closely and I held my breath for whatever was coming. "Who let the goat out?"

For one terrible, horrifying moment I just looked at Hunter, my eyes wide in surprise and dismay. I even forgot he still held my hand. I felt the blood drain from my face. His keen eyes never wavered from mine as his hand held mine in a firm grip. He just watched me as a million thoughts were flying through my head. This could not be happening. There was no way he could possibly know. I really have no idea how long I stood there, struck dumb, my hand in his. It seemed like minutes, but surely it was only seconds. I finally had the presence of mind to pull back my hand. He did not let go. I felt the heat return to my face and finally I opened my mouth, but I could not think of one thing to say that would not incriminate me, so I closed it again. I was blushing furiously by the time he finally let go my hand. I turned my back and hurried to the kitchen, Hunter's soft chuckle following me. I picked up my empty container and covered the pie. I barely knew what I was doing. When I got to the door, I hesitated. I couldn't really leave without another word to him. I had to say something. I could no longer see him, but just before I slammed the door I hollered back into the house what, had I been innocent, I should have asked immediately.

"What goat?"

CHAPTER 18

Several nights later I awoke to the sound of bells. It took me a while to get awake. Why were bells ringing in the middle of the night? A great dread filled me. Something was terribly, terribly wrong. For just a few seconds I was too scared to move. It was not the church bells. It was a bell I had seldom heard—the town hall bell. When there were emergencies in our town, the bell on the roof of the town hall was rung—such as a fire. I jumped out of bed and ran to the window. It was raining, as it had been raining all day and nearly all week. In the darkness I could see nothing but the dim lights of the gas lamps along North Street as well as dim light in the town hall across the village green. I lit a candle and went out into the hall and met both Papa and Ray.

"Why is the bell ringing?" I asked, my heart in my throat.

"I don't see any fire," said Ray, putting on his clothes.

"Perhaps the river," said Papa soberly, concern on his face. His hair was standing on end and he stood in his pajamas.

After a rainy week, we were now hit with the rains from the hurricane that came up the Atlantic coast. It hit Connecticut and curved to the right but the rains reached us in Vermont. It had lost its punch as far as wind was concerned, but the rain was heavy.

"I'm going to see what is going on," said Ray, now donning his mackintosh. He was soon out the door and flying across the village green to the town hall.

I went out on the front porch with an afghan wrapped around me. I saw other men running toward the river, carrying lanterns. I only now became aware of a terrible roaring from the river.

"It must be the river," I said to Papa who now joined me with a bathrobe wrapped around him. "Did you ever hear it so loud?"

"I never heard it like this," said Papa, his eyes wide at the wild rumble of our otherwise placid river. It was not long before we saw Ray running back to the house.

"The river is flooding," he said, gasping for breath. "There must have been a cloudburst up on Mount Abe. Someone from up there came down and said it is over its banks in Peepers Hill and they fear that road may get washed out. The water is nearly over one small bridge that crosses the river up there already." Again he stopped for air. "I'm going back to help set up flares."

And all the water from the cloudburst would come down the river into Steeplechase. I watched as Ray, without another word, turned and ran back across the village green to join the spectators along the river.

"I want to see it, Papa. Are you coming?"

"I don't know. I may be needed here if anyone is injured. If you go, be careful. Put my mackintosh on. It will keep you dry."

"It is not raining very much anymore."

"Put it on. It may start up again. And take a lantern."

Just then I saw Peggy and the pastor coming over to us in housecoats and holding umbrellas over their tousled heads.

"The river must be flooding," they said, joining us on the porch.

"It is flooding. I am going to go over to see it. Are you coming also?" I asked Peggy.

She looked down at her housecoat and then looked at me.

"Are you going like that?"

"Maybe. It is dark and I won't be gone long. Papa said I should put his mackintosh on, and that would cover me."

Just then someone arrived on a horse. It was Hunter.

"What is happening?"

"The river is flooding."

I had not seen Hunter for a few days. Not since I ran out of his house calling 'What goat?' Now he was sitting on his horse, his eyes taking in my afghan-wrapped body, tousled hair and slippers by the light of the candles we held. I did not meet his eyes.

"Yes, and it sounds bad," said Papa. "Ray went over to help set up flares."

"Then I shall go help," said Hunter. "May I leave Ruggles here?"

"Of course," said Papa. "Just put him in the stable. Are you sure you should be out on that leg?"

"It is healing nicely and is well wrapped."

I ran in the house for Papa's big mackintosh and a lantern. I gave a fleeting glance at the clock. Twelve twenty. It would be a long night. Stepping out on the porch, I heard shouts and calls as people north of our house hurried in all sorts of night attire and umbrellas to the river.

The pastor went home for a lantern and Papa, too curious to stay home, went in for a lantern and an umbrella for a quick look at the raging river.

We then joined the stream of our neighbors and fellow villagers hurrying through the dark, wet night across the green and then down South Street to the river. There were flares set up now but they did not do well in the rain that was still falling. It was dreadfully dark and scary. The sound of the angry water was frightful. The village officials did not allow us to come all the way down to the bridge. It was too dangerous. Our dim lanterns did little to reveal what was hidden in the water although once we saw a big tree slam against the bridge. It was an awesome sight. The river was running high and wild and taking trees and vegetation with it. I was also hearing some strange sounds.

"What is that dull, knocking noise?" I asked Papa who was standing close to me.

He did not answer right away.

"It sounds impossible, but it must be the boulders knocking against each other," he said finally, awe in his voice. "I never ever thought I would hear such a sound."

It seemed impossible to think that these large boulders and rocks that stood for years in their place along the usually placid river were now being ripped from their home by the force of the wild water and were now banging against each other in the dark, turbulent river. It was an eerie sound, a frightening sound and it would change the look of the river as I knew it, forever.

We stood there perhaps twenty minutes before Papa, Peggy and the pastor went back home. I went back to Main Street thinking maybe I would see Mindy. There were other people headed out of town where there was open space by the river and where the banks were much lower. I suddenly remembered the Wolfs. They lived out there not far from the mayor, but on the same side as the river. They could be in danger.

"Amber!"

"Mindy! Isn't this terrible. I was watching the river from South Street but now I am going to see if the Wolfs are safe."

"I'm coming along. I can't believe I even recognized you in that mackintosh. Wow, it looks like the whole town is out. What is that knocking sound?"

"Papa thinks the boulders are moving and knocking against each other."

"Is it possible? That is so scary!"

We continued along Main Street and then out of town. We were not alone. There was a steady stream of people. This was an historical moment. Now we were nearly at the turn-off to the mayor's house and I was glad for my lantern. There were no gas lights out here, but all around me were the moving lights of the lanterns of the villagers. I wondered briefly where Ray and Hunter were. I saw some flares being lit up ahead of me, close to the river. The rain had nearly stopped and Papa's mackintosh felt heavy around me. But I did not dare take it off. I looked for the Wolf house. It was safe. It was a good distance from the river but the ground was pretty level here. If the river was already flooding, would they be safe?

I could see a line of moving lanterns close to the river. I wondered about their safety. As we slowly made our way through the thinly wooded area past the Wolf house, I saw a light in the house, but I found the aged couple standing on the back porch. I did not know them well, but as I passed them, I spoke.

"It sounds pretty scary, doesn't it?"

"Clarence is out there," said the woman.

"Clarence?"

"Our son."

I was embarrassed. I only knew him as Old Wolf. I had not known his name.

"He likes the river," I said. "He will find this interesting."

"He won't come in," they said in unison. "No one can get him to come in. It is dangerous out there."

I finally walked on. I thought they were overly concerned about him, and I could understand their concern. He was not quite normal. But when I got to the line of people standing a bit back from the river, I saw why they were concerned. Old Wolf was standing on a rock right along the river. The rock sloped up from our side and he was standing at the top of it. The only way I could see this was because of the lantern he held in his hand. When I got close enough, I could see him staring with wild fascination at the swirling, muddy river. He had no fear of it. The river had always been his friend. I now heard people trying to get him to come down. This was a rock he always fished from, but now the river was too high and the water could possibly wash over the rock. It would certainly be slippery and if he would trip and fall, he would be gone.

I found myself looking for Hunter and Ray. Were they around here? Every so often I would hear the sheriff's voice, urging people not to get too close. The river was clearly out of control. Anything could happen. My eyes went to the rock again. Old Wolf was probably nearly fifty. As far as I knew, he was the only child of the couple. I was just thinking of going back to his parents to tell them that he was probably too high up to get caught in the river when I heard a shout and looked up the river to see a strange sight. Not far from where we stood along the river, the ground had washed away along the bank and now, in the glare of many lanterns and torches, I could see the dark form of a tall tree moving out into the raging river. For just a moment I watched in utter amazement as the tree, standing upright began going down the river. And then its roots hit something in the river and it began to topple. I automatically stepped back a step, although it could not have hit me, but then I saw, to my horror, it was falling in the direction of Old Wolf. I saw Old Wolf looking at the tree, not realizing his own danger, and suddenly, amid horrified cries from those watching, the tree crashed, its top half coming down over the rock where Old Wolf stood.

Where he had been standing.

Those of us watching, stood frozen, barely breathing for just a moment. And then the water loosened the bottom of the tree and swung it out into the river, roots first and the rock was clear of the tree once more.

But the rock was empty.

Among those of us standing there, there was only silence—just the roaring of the deadly river. I grabbed Mindy's hand.

"He's gone!" she yelled. "Old Wolf isn't on the rock anymore."

I saw a few people go up to the rock and there was a subdued shout.

"He is here. He did not wash away."

"Go for the doctor!" came a shout.

"No," came another voice. "It is too late."

No one knelt down by the body. They did not look long at it. Horrified, I thought of his parents. I saw the sheriff step out of crowd and step up to the body. He did not look long. Then he turned and made his way slowly, thoughtfully, to the house. Mindy and I stood there for perhaps another ten or fifteen minutes. The river had turned deadly for at least one person. I wondered how late it was. Papa would be anxious. Mindy and I turned to go home. We had experienced enough this night. We would never forget what we had seen. As we got close to the Wolf house, I saw the sheriff come out. I could not comprehend the sorrow in that house.

"Mindy, I am going in to the Wolfs. You can come with me or go home without me."

She hesitated. "I'll go on home."

I did not knock. They would not have heard a knock. I simply walked in. They looked at me with faces that showed only shock. I walked up to Mrs. Wolf. She knew who I was, but I had never really spoken with her before this evening.

"I'm so sorry about Clarence," I said, feeling tears in my eyes. To cover my own tears, I put my arm around her. And suddenly she was clinging to me, crying. I do not know how long I stood there with my arms around this woman who had just lost her only son. I heard the door open and was shocked to see Hunter come in and go over to Mr. Wolf. He just stood by him, his arm on his shoulder. The man did not pull away. Neither did he weep. He just stood there in shock. When Mrs. Wolf stopped crying, she asked me my name.

"I am Amber, Dr. McDurfee's daughter. I will tell Papa to stop by here tomorrow morning," I said, knowing he would without me asking him to. She nodded.

"He loved the river," she said, speaking of Clarence. "It was his friend. But it took him."

I had no reply.

"They were going to put him in an institution," she said, "and he did not want to go. Now he won't have to go."

I was so glad that she could find something good in the tragedy.

I left then, without looking at Hunter. The old man was saying something to him and I did not wish to disturb them. As I walked away from the house, I saw most of the people had left. I had no idea what time it was, but now I wanted to get home. I suddenly felt exhausted and was glad for my lantern on the dark stretch ahead of me before the lights of town. The river, I thought, sounded deadly. And it had proven deadly.

By the time I had gotten to the road, Hunter came up behind me. He did not talk. It was not the time for pleasantries or idle talk. We walked in silence the whole way home. Just as we got to the house, he briefly laid his hand on my shoulder.

"Thanks for going to the Wolfs. Goodnight."

And then he headed for the stable for Ruggles and I slipped into the house.

CHAPTER 19

The train blew its whistle as we approached a small town. I saw a
couple little boys who were standing along the track look up and
wave furiously, big smiles on their faces. I waved back. I was sitting
with Minna on a train that seemed to be going incredibly fast as it
took us into the northeastern part of Vermont. The scenery was beautiful. The leaves were just beginning to turn and as I had never been
in this part of the country before, I was enjoying the view immensely.
Minna, however, seemed not to be enjoying the countryside as much
as I was. She had other things on her mind. Her dead husband, to be
exact. The husband she seemed to think was still alive. I could only
see this trip as a wild goose chase. I hated to spend the money for it,
but I decided I would enjoy the scenery and the festival. It was a bit
of vacation for me. I seldom got away from Steeplechase and after the
last few days, it felt good to get away.

The flood had not been very merciful to our town and community. But then, floods were not merciful. We were fortunate that there
was only one death. It could have been much worse. The main road to
Pipers Hill had been torn out and anyone wanting to get there had to
take a very roundabout route up across the mountain. Yesterday had
been the funeral for Clarence Wolf. It was a small funeral. Clarence
had few friends. There were a handful of relatives there and Papa,
knowing I had talked to Mrs. Wolf the night of the tragedy, suggested
I go with him. So I did. The service was at the church but there were
less than twenty mourners there. The coffin, such as it was, was not
opened. I had to wonder what kind of a mangled body lay in the cas-

ket. Mrs. Wolf held my hand tightly when she saw me and I was glad I had gone with Papa.

The village had some clean up to do. The tree that took Clarence's life was not the only tree that was uprooted in the flood. The river had changed its course some places. It was now much wider at places and downed trees were partly in the river, partly on its banks. Some familiar boulders along the river had moved. It was an awesome discovery how much strength was in the raging water.

"In fifteen minutes we should be there," said Minna, pulling me back to the present. "The train station is right in the middle of the village so we can walk to the inn and let our bags there before we go to the festival."

"So you will know your way around?" I asked my companion whose eyes were bright with anticipation.

"The village is no larger than Steeplechase. There will be no problem."

I was glad for nice weather. We were heading to the end of September and I did not want to be traipsing around in the rain. And it would be cool in the evening. The trees seemed to be a bit more colorful here already than in Steeplechase.

When our train screeched to a stop in the little northern village, it was immediately evident that there was a fair going on. There were many people on the street and around the train station. There was an atmosphere of fun and laughter. Children ran around shouting and holding tightly to colored balloons that were bobbing in the air above them. I heard a band playing somewhere and I could smell popcorn in the fresh air. Minna and I hurried across the street to the inn. Seeing all the people, I wondered if maybe the inn would be full and we would have to return tonight anyway.

Minna was not talking much, but her eyes were wide open, searching the faces of all we met. She led the way into the small inn. It was, in contrast to the sunny day, very dark inside. The dark wood paneling on the walls and dark blue striped wallpaper only added to the darkness. We stopped at the desk. A man of perhaps forty with a pipe in his mouth looked up at us.

"We would like a room for the night," said Minna.

The man exhaled a puff of his pipe and looked down to the book lying before him.

"You are fortunate to get a room. Someone just left. It is the only room available. Third floor."

"We'll take it," said Minna almost before he stopped speaking. She gave me a quick glance and I nodded my consent.

The inn, as I said, was not large. If there were rooms on the third floor, they were probably rooms that were generally used for the servants. There would be nothing fancy about the room. We paid and were given a key and then we made our way up the steps, each carrying our own bag. The stairs to the third floor were more narrow and even darker. At the top, we entered a narrow hallway. At one end was a small window with little light coming through. There were only perhaps four rooms here and we had no trouble finding the room assigned to us. The door was open and a maid was just finishing getting it ready for us. It was of course, very small. It looked like a double bed had been crammed into a room that was made for a single bed. We could barely get around it. But we had a room. We were glad for that. The small dormer window was toward the train station and with the train so close, I knew I would have an interrupted night.

It was nearly noon and we were hungry. It did not take us long to find our way out of the inn and up the street to the festival. We just followed the people and let the music guide us. Entering the park we passed the usual craft stands. Since this was a harvest festival, we saw displays of the largest pumpkins and wagon loads of other root vegetables. There were some home canned items for sale. There was a merry-go-round in one section of the park and tugs-of-war for children, shooting contests for men and boys, and all manner of goodies for sale scattered throughout the park.

We stopped at a stand for coca cola, a new drink they were of-fering, and later bought a sausage sandwich. At another open fire, someone was roasting potatoes. There were more and more people milling around.

Finally we found a seat where we could sit and observe. Minna had not been doing much talking. She was busy looking, her head turning constantly. But so far she had not seen the man who had re-minded her of her husband. I felt a bit sorry for her.

"You know, Minna, I heard someone say there is a dance this eve-ning. If he is here, he would probably come to that. In the meanwhile, try to enjoy what we are seeing."

"I have barely looked at anything," she admitted. "Yes, he would come to a dance."

We sat a while longer and then we got some ice cream and watched the tug-of-war that someone had organized for teenagers and then we watched the man blowing up helium balloons for the chil-dren. We bought some chocolate nut fudge and spent time looking at all the craft tables. There was a field where there was horse racing and there we talked a long time to a couple who lived in the town and they told us all about the fair. Just as we left them, Minna stopped me and turned back to them.

"I have an acquaintance by the name of Abie Stork and I think he lives in this area. Do you happen to know him?"

But they did not know him.

I was truly feeling sorry for Minna. She was so determined to find her husband, who I believed was dead. On the other hand, we were here now and this was her opportunity to look for the man who resembled him and I sincerely hoped she would see him so she could lay the whole business to rest.

Unfortunately, just when the dance was to begin that evening, it began to rain. And it was not just a little rain. There was wind and rain and there was nothing else to do but run for shelter. We ran to the inn and discovered that many others ran there, too. There was a small porch on the inn, which was crowded when we got there so we went inside. We had gotten wet. We were fortunate to have a room to go to, even if it was on the third floor. We somewhat wearily climbed up to the attic and took off our wet clothes. When the rain stopped twenty minutes later, we saw from our small dormer window that people were gathering on the parking lot of the train station. They set up lanterns. There were gas lamps along the street and at the train station, so there was some light to see by.

Soon the sound of the fiddles filled the night air, and it was not long before the young people were dancing. We stood at the attic window and watched. We could see better here than if we were down among the dancers. The window was small, so most of the time it was just Minna watching. I began to pray that God would have mercy on her and let her see the man she had thought was her husband. She was just so sure, and I feared she would never have rest until she saw that man.

"Amber," Minna said suddenly. "Come here."

I stood by the window.

"Do you see the man walking over there with the cinnamon-colored jacket? He is by himself walking around the edge of the crowd."

It took me a while but finally I saw him.

"I see him."

"Keep your eye on him." And then she was out the door.

I kept my eye on the man as good as I could.

"Lord, please let this be the man she saw the other time," I prayed. I found I could not pray that it was her husband.

I saw Minna run across the street. Then she walked slowly around the crowd. Once in a while she seemed to lose sight of the man, but then I would see her again. I could see the man. He had stopped walking and now stood, leaning his back against a gas lamp, watching the dancers. I held my breath as Minna approached him. And then he turned and looked at her and she kept right on walking. Was this the answer to my prayer? Minna continued to walk around out among the dancers and then came back, dejected.

"Was this the man you saw the other time?"

"No. When I got closer I could tell it was not him."

I could feel her disappointment. I wanted to comfort her, but did not know how. It really could have been the same man because she had not seen the other man up close either.

"Do you really think he may yet be alive?" I asked finally.

"I don't know." I saw tears in her eyes. She was hurting badly.

"Why don't we go down and have coffee and pie?" I suggested. "My treat."

We went down. It was raining once again and now the people went home. But some came in the inn. We had to wait for a free table and when we got one, it was not anywhere close to the door. In fact, we could not see the door or a good part of the room from where we sat. We ordered our coffee and apple dumplings, rather than pie, and sat in silence.

"Tell me about your parents," I said finally, wanting to talk of something else.

"My father died when I was quite small. I never knew a father. And Mama...."

Minna's voice trailed off and she gave me a strange look.

"Amber," she said breathlessly, "Abie is here. I know he is here! I feel his presence."

Looking at Minna, I began to feel creepy. Her eyes were wide and she was cautiously looking around the room. When it got too long, I spoke.

"If you are so sure he is here, walk around the room and look."

But she did not get up. Perhaps she was afraid of being disappointed once again or maybe she was feeling creepy also. Or, perhaps she suddenly did not know what she would say to him if she did see him.

"What makes you so sure he is here?" I ventured to ask, feeling my heart beat faster.

"I just know he is. I...feel it."

She almost had me convinced. She was so sure. I found it very creepy. The man was dead. They had had a funeral for him and his shoe and belt were found in the fire. There was a marker at his grave. And now she was fully convinced that he was in this inn.

"Why don't you walk around?" I asked again, perhaps a bit impatiently, I wanted her to stop the charade and get realistic.

But she just sat there, eyes wide as she cautiously looked around the inn.

It was getting late. I was tired and she would not get up and walk around to look for her dead husband.

"Minna, I would like to go to bed. You may stay down here as long as you wish, but I would like to go to bed."

"I'll come along," she said, to my relief.

We walked to the staircase and climbed the creaking steps. We walked silently to our room and with little talk, got ready for bed. When we crawled under the covers, the rain was drumming against the tin roof above them. It seemed to lower my spirit even more. Minna lay silent under the blankets.

"Minna," I said in the darkness, "do you believe in God?"

"Yes," she answered immediately.

"Have you ever prayed and told God about your doubts and concerns relating to Abie?"

She hesitated. "Not exactly."

"Would you like me to pray for you right now?"

"Yes," she said very softly.

I was surprising myself, but I wanted this whole affair to come to a peaceful ending. Barely knowing what I was going to say, I opened my mouth.

"Dear God," I began, "we need Your help. You know why we are here and You know the hurt that Minna has experienced. Now we ask for wisdom." I paused, barely knowing how to continue. "Guide our steps and thoughts so that there is a...an end to Minna's confusion." I stopped again. I did not know what words to use. I did not want to even suggest that Abie was still alive. "And God, help us to find out why she thinks she felt Abie's presence here this evening. Amen."

Minna squeezed my hand. "Thank you."

"Goodnight, Minna."

We lay in silence, but somehow sleep did not come to either of us.

"Amber," Minna said suddenly. "I just had an idea."

I was scared to ask what it was, but I did ask. "What is your idea?"

"Maybe he is not from this town. Maybe he lives far enough away that he is here overnight, too."

Oh my, I thought to myself, she has not given up yet.

"And if he is here," she continued with some triumph in her voice, "his name would be in the registry."

I held my breath. This was not the type of wisdom that I had imagined.

"How long do you think someone is at the desk?" she whispered.

"I have no idea."

"What time is it?"

And in that moment, the clock in the train station tower began striking the hour. We both lay still as we counted the strokes together. Twelve. It was midnight.

"I am going down."

"What? Now?"

"Yes."

"You must get dressed."

"I have a housecoat. Everyone is in bed."

"And you will just go to the desk and look in the book?"

"I have to, Amber. I have to check everything while I am here. Tomorrow we will be gone."

Unless you are in the jailhouse, I thought silently. What had I gotten myself into with Minna?

There was no stopping her. She was already out of bed.

"Will you stand at the top of the stairs and wait for me?"

"Oh, Minna, I'm scared. What if we get caught?"

"I am scared, too, but I must do this. You asked for guidance. Maybe God gave me this idea. Please come with me."

I got out of bed very unwillingly and put on my housecoat. She lighted a candle and led the way to the stairs. I could have also taken a candle, but I did not want more light than necessary. Who knows, we may have to hide from someone.

All was dead quiet outside the room. I followed her down the narrow hall to the second floor and stayed close behind her as she slowly made her way down the stairway. One more stairway for her to go, but I would stay at the top of the stairs on the second floor while she went to the desk. I now wished I had also brought a candle because when she left me at the top of the second stairway, I was left in complete darkness. Or almost complete. There was a dim candle in a sconce at either end of the hall.

I heard someone snoring behind a closed door. What if someone got up and came down the hall? I could not think of that. I had lost all sight and sound of Minna. Time dragged. She seemed to be gone for hours. I was so afraid I would hear a commotion and then I would know that she had been caught looking at the registry book.

Down the hall I heard another snore, then a snort as the person possibly wakened. I began to wonder if Minna got lost or if the candle fell on the registry book and she was trying to put out a fire. It was cold in the hall and I found myself trembling. At last I saw the faintest bit of light approaching the stairs. Finally, I could see the candle. She seemed to have trouble coming up the stairs. I waited anxiously, eager to return to bed. When she got to the top where I was waiting, she was trembling so badly she nearly dropped the candle. She began to whisper something to me and fearful that she would drop the candle, I took it from her and led her back to the attic and to our room. When the door was closed, I looked at her face and knew instantly that something had happened while she was down there.

"What is wrong?"

"Nothing is wrong. Abie..." she took a deep breath, "Abie is here!"

"What do you mean?"

"My husband! His name is in the registry." She was so excited she could barely talk.

"It can't be. He is dead." I found I could not believe this.

She just looked at me, trembling in shock or joy or who knows what. She did not even hear what I said.

"Maybe it is someone with the same name," I said finally. She wasn't listening.

"He is in room twenty-four."

I think the hairs on the back of my neck were standing straight up. I could not open my mouth. This man was supposed to be dead. She was so excited, but also scared. I think, in spite of her thinking or hoping he was still alive, she was now in shock. She really believed he was here. I did not want her to be disappointed and I suddenly realized that I believed her. I believed this man for some reason had not died. But it shook me somehow, and I could see that it shook Minna also.

"What are you going to do?" I asked.

"I'm going to knock on his door."

"Tomorrow?"

"Now."

"It is after midnight. He will be sleeping. You can't wake him now."

"I don't want to miss him. I know it is him. Come along down with me. You don't need to go to the door with me, but stand up the hall a few doors."

There was no time to think this through, for there was no stopping Minna. I put on my housecoat and this time I took a candle. She took one also. I did not ask what she would say. I did not say maybe he did not want to see her. Actually, I thought she must know that. If he was still alive, he had purposely let her think he was dead in the fire and he had run to freedom—away from his problems. Who would want such a man? But she seemed to love him in spite of everything.

"Are you coming?" she asked, the candle in her hand trembling as she stood by the open door.

I took my candle and once again followed Minna out into the narrow hallway and to the stairs. We took very slow, careful steps, the candles our only light. It gave almost no light. I walked with her to find the room. At this point I was also shaking. I walked away from her when we found the room and quietly walked a short way up the hall to wait and see what would happen. I could see her stand a bit uncertainly a few moments in front of the door. I could only imagine what Minna was feeling. My own heart was pounding so hard that I feared it could wake someone. Suddenly someone in the room opposite the room where she stood coughed loudly. And long. It scared her so badly that she hurried back up the hall to me until the coughing stopped.

Finally, she took a deep breath and walked back down the hall. She stopped at a door that I thought was too close. I thought she had been farther away from me. I took a step in her direction to tell her to check the number again, but she, with a firm hand had already knocked.

I drew back and held my breath. She evidently heard movement because I could see her tense up. And then the door opened. She took a step back as a fat man with gray hair standing in all directions answered the door.

"What do you want?" he asked.

"Is...is your name Abie?" It was almost a whisper.

"My name is Charlie. What is yours?"

"Oh, I am sorry, I got the wrong door," Minna stuttered.

The man looked long at her.

"Are you looking for a warm bed?" he finally asked.

Minna, without a word turned and walked very fast back up the hall to me. The man just shut the door, not watching where she went.

"You didn't go down the hall far enough," I said. "Check the number before you knock."

What I wanted to say was, let it go. Let's go back to bed and wait until morning. But I knew it was useless.

Once more, Minna made her way down the hall. I saw her check the number on the door. It was the right number this time. I held my breath when she once again knocked. And waited. After perhaps fifteen seconds, she knocked again. This time she must have heard movement, because I saw her tense up again. She stood tall as possible and held the candle high in her hand in order to see the face of the man who answered.

The door creaked open just a crack, and then wider. There was dead silence as the young man—with hair looking like a cyclone hit it—and Minna looked at each other. Then came a hoarse voice.

"Minna?" And then his candle dropped and they both bent over to get it and from what I could see in the dim light, her candle fell in the process and there was a mad scramble to pick up the candles whose lights had gone out and I could see nothing.

And then I heard the door shut and I was alone in the hall.

I stood there probably a full ten minutes before I realized that Minna was not coming back just now. I may as well go to bed. As I made my way down the hall and up to the attic room, my thoughts tumbled over and over in my head, much as a tumbleweed out in the western desert. I could not imagine what was going on downstairs. What was his reaction? Had she forced herself into the room? Would he be angry that she had found him? Or was he happy to see her? And what would be his excuse for abandoning her?

In spite of the excitement, I was now exhausted and I fell asleep almost as soon as my head touched the waiting pillow. When I woke the next morning, I was still alone in bed. I had to assume that the meeting was a joyful one.

We left the train station at ten twenty. And waving goodbye to Minna was her Abie. She would tell me the story as the train rolled southward along the tracks. I was eager to get home. The whole trip had been strenuous. My night was short, and Minna's even shorter. When she introduced us at the inn, Abie looked embarrassed. And so he should. No matter what Minna told me, it would not change my view of his cowardice.

"Thank you, thank you, thank you," she said when we settled in our seats and she could see him no more. "Thank you so much for coming with me and standing by me. You will never know how much it meant to me."

"You are welcome," I said, still doubting the sincerity of Abie. I was also glad she did not know how sure I had been that this would be a wild goose chase.

"And thank you for praying for me. I believe God gave me the idea of looking in the registry."

I had to think of my talks on prayer over the last weeks. *Was it possible that God answered my prayer?*

"Now, Minna, I want to hear the whole story—Abie's side of the story."

"I will not make excuses for him," she began, eager to talk, "but I do understand what made him leave me. We had been struggling badly financially, and when I told him I was pregnant, well, you know what I told you. And I would not get rid of the baby. The next weeks he was tight-lipped and barely talked to me. He was angry. He did not earn much and now we would have the extra expense of the baby. Otherwise, he would have been as eager for a child as I was." She paused a bit. "He began to think about leaving me, but he did not know how. He loved me, he said, but he could not see any light at the end of the tunnel. He said he should not have gotten married. He could not support us.

"And then there was the fire, and suddenly, seeing the intensity of the fire, and really nearly getting trapped in it, he saw his opportunity.

He could disappear and they would think he had died in the fire. He knew he had to leave something behind so they would think he burned, and so he threw his shoes into the fire. And, at the last minute, his belt. He saw it fell short of the flames but he had to get out of there. And so he took off. He caught a ride to Flynn Falls and hopped on the train. He had thought enough about leaving in the previous weeks and knew where he would go. He lives a bit north yet of Brighton."

She paused and her eyes had a faraway look. "He asked about the baby." She was blinking back tears.

"When I told him I lost it, he knew he was to blame and he cried."

I was glad to hear of some remorse.

"And now?" I asked. "Will he come back?"

"I don't know. He wants me to go there. He is ashamed to come back."

"And your mother?"

"I hate to leave her."

"Maybe you should talk to Pastor Thomas about the whole situation. He will listen and he will help you. Maybe he can talk to Abie. I think Abie will have to face the music sometime and the sooner he does, the better. Otherwise, he will always live in fear that someone will meet him who thinks he died. Furthermore, if he comes back, maybe you can both live with your mother for the time being until something else comes up. You have your little jobs and he will surely find work somewhere. What does he like to do? Maybe we can help him find a better paying job. I am sure something will work out."

"Oh, I know it will," said Minna. "I am so, so happy. Will you pray about it?"

I looked at her in shock. She was asking for my prayers? I, who struggled with prayers? She really believed that God led her to Abie after we prayed. I was ashamed of my own unbelief. We had indeed prayed. And God had answered.

"I'll be praying," I said.

CHAPTER 20

When we arrived at the train station in Flynn Falls we hired a carriage, which took us each to our own house. I was glad to be home and had quite the story to share. But I did not have much chance to relax. A telegram had come shortly after I left on Saturday morning. Susan wanted me to come. She had experienced some false labor pains and knew her time was very near.

I would plan to leave in the morning. Susan did not live that far away. It would take me probably a bit less than an hour to get there by train. In the meantime, I had to unpack my bag and then repack for my next adventure, which would be longer. It was a big change for me. I was seldom away from Steeplechase. I went to Laura and asked if she would fill in for me while I was gone. She said she would be glad to do so. I liked her more and more. We were fortunate to have her. Papa and Ray had not had a decent meal at noon, thinking I could cook something good for supper, and Murf, happy to have me home, wanted all my attention. I found a ham in the icebox and I fixed that with a big dish of scalloped potatoes, hoping it would last for a few meals. Vegetables they could simply heat. I had beans, peas and corn canned. I chose green beans to go with the ham.

I had no time to make pies, but I did stick a chocolate cake in the oven and since I was hungry, I talked the men into an early supper. We would eat at five.

About four o'clock, another telegram arrived. It read: Susan in labor. Stop. Come.

It nearly sent me into a spin. I had just returned from Wildcat and now, the same day would need to leave to go to Susan. Ray said there was a train at seven twenty and an answer was sent. I had had no time to think about this new baby and now it was on the way. When I called Papa and Ray for supper, I heard the knocker. Please no, not someone needing help. I let Ray answer and I went to bring the food to the table.

There was no emergency. It was Hunter's voice I heard and I was told to set another plate. I had not seen much of him lately and my heart beat a little faster when I heard his voice and I felt myself tense with pleasure.

When I brought the ham platter to the table, I looked up to our guest's intense gaze. He never gave just a glance. We locked eyes and we exchanged greetings. Once again he held my chair for me and I tried very hard to act like this happened every day.

"So you were traveling with Minna this past weekend," Hunter said to me when all the food had been passed and small talk ended.

"I was. We attended an agricultural fair close to Brighton."

"Since when are you interested in agriculture?"

"It was actually quite interesting, but that was not our main reason for being there."

"They uncovered a dead man," said Ray, taking a mouthful of potatoes.

"Excuse me?" Hunter looked at me, his eyes widening.

"Ray! You better rephrase that."

"Well, you found a man who has a grave in our cemetery."

"Minna did."

Hunter stopped eating. "Don't tell me you actually found Minna's husband?"

I nodded. For the moment I had forgotten that he knew Minna.

"She told me a bit of her story once. Seemed they never found his body."

"No, his body was very much alive and fleeing the town," said Ray.

The story came out bit by bit during the rest of the meal.

"She did not tell me not to keep it quiet," I said finally, "but maybe this should not get around town until she lets it out."

"Will he come back to Steeplechase?" asked Papa.

"That remains to be seen. I sure hope he does because her mother is here. But I think he would rather she move up there."

"If she does, you lose your housekeeper," said Ray to Hunter.

Hunter looked at me.

"I'll hire Amber."

"Oh no you won't," I said immediately.

"What? You would let me sit?"

I think he knew I was partly teasing, but he was shocked by my immediate response.

"I would let you sit. I am busy enough. You can just get married and then you have a free housekeeper."

Papa and Ray laughed out loud at my outburst. Hunter looked so startled that I had to laugh also. I almost couldn't stop and I felt myself blushing. But it felt good to have shocked him. I was feeling brave. I was leaving after supper and did not know when I would be back again. I could barely believe I had said what I did. It seemed to take Hunter a while to get his thoughts together. Finally he looked at Papa.

"I thought I knew your daughter."

"You never really know a woman," said my laughing Papa. "Get used to it."

We were finished with the main course and I needed to get my red face out of the dining room. I took some dishes with me and busied myself in the kitchen and clearing the table until my face cooled. I finally brought in the cake and a bowl of peaches. By that time they were talking about the road that was being repaired from the flood and with an eye on the clock, I ate in silence.

Just as were finishing up the dessert, there was a pounding at the door. Ray immediately went to see who was there. I could hear the man's anxious voice from the dining room.

"There was an accident and they are bringing two injured adults here."

"Take them to the office door," Ray said.

Papa was already on his feet and Ray was out of the room.

"I must leave in fifteen minutes for the train station," I said to my departing Papa. "I don't have my ticket yet."

"I'll take her," said Hunter to Papa.

"But...." My words died out. I hated being obligated to Hunter.

"No buts. I am glad to do it. It is my thanks for supper."

Papa came back and gave me a goodbye kiss, which embarrassed me in front of Hunter.

"Take good care of Susan. We will miss you."

Fifteen minutes later I was sitting next to Hunter on my way to the Flynn Falls train station. Life was proving very unpredictable. Ruggles was clopping along on the main road out of town, when Hunter turned to me.

"Could we have a bit more conversation in regards to a housekeeper?"

I had to grin but I stayed strong.

"I have said all I have to say on the subject."

He just looked at me a few seconds.

"You probably did not hear about Belshazzar's lastest mischief."

I looked at him expectantly, surprised and glad for a change in subject and then realized he had fooled me again. I quickly looked away without saying anything. Before I knew what was happening, Hunter had a finger under my chin and was turning my face to his.

"You just gave yourself away again, Miss Amber," he said quietly, his blue eyes very close to mine. "The correct question was, who is Belshazzar?"

I twisted my red face away. I was furious at myself.

"I think it is time we discuss that evening," he added, bringing the horse to a halt and then turning south to Flynn Falls. "Who let Belshazzar out?"

"How am I to know?"

"You are done, Amber. Admit it. You know how he got out."

I was done. If Hunter was guessing before, he now knew by my failure to ask who on earth Belshazzar was. There was no reason for me to try to act innocent. But I would not go down without a fight. There were things I wished to know also.

"If you want to know so much what I was doing that evening, I will tell you, on condition that you also tell me about your evening."

There was a hesitation. Not a long one—at the most several seconds—but it was a hesitation and I was secretly pleased.

"Is that a deal?" he asked.

This time I hesitated. But not long. Somehow maybe I would learn something of his time with Lucille.

"It's a deal. You first."

Hunter chuckled. "No way. I do not trust you, Amber Mc-Durfee."

"Hunter!" I said, remembering that he had a reputation for not trusting women.

"I know you too well, my little friend, and when you finish your tale, I will have it confirmed."

"Can I trust you to tell me all I want to know?"

"Hold it. Not all you want to know. I have to have some secrets. Just about that evening."

He looked at me so shocked that I burst into giggles and he chuckled along with me.

"I'm waiting," he said finally.

"Well," I said slowly, clearing my throat, and trying to think what I must tell and what I could leave out, "Mindy and I had visited Maggie, who is an aunt to Mindy, that afternoon and we saw the neighbors getting ready for the barbecue. We thought it would be fun to spy on the party. So we dressed up."

When I stopped talking, Hunter looked at me and shook his head.

"Miss Amber, there are so many holes in that story, I am surprised you are not blushing."

I did blush then, but it was dark and I hoped he could not see it. I was nearly in a sweat although the night was cool.

"What did I leave out?"

"Only you know that, but unless you tell the story again and fill in the holes, I shall not feel obligated to fulfill my part of the bargain."

He would have no mercy. I took a deep breath.

"Well," I began once more, "Mindy heard two ladies in the bakery discussing the upcoming barbecue."

"And?" he prompted when I hesitated too long.

"And the one lady said you asked her niece to go with you."

I managed a quick look at Hunter and for just a second or two, he looked straight ahead. Then he turned once more to me.

"And?"

"Well, we were so surprised that you finally were taking someone out that we decided to spy on you to see what kind of girl you would choose."

I turned just my eyes to Hunter. His head was bent to mine and he was watching me. Closely.

"Was that so important to you?"

I cringed inwardly, but tried not to show it.

"Well, we are friends and you are so quiet on that score, so we were curious."

"Who let the goat out?"

"No one. Belshazzar has a mind of his own. We couldn't find the goat when we wanted to see him, but when Maggie opened the gate to leave the pen, Belshazzar came from somewhere behind us and seeing Maggie stoop down to pick something up, he booted her from behind and she landed headfirst into the grass. And before we knew what was happening, he was through the gate, heading for the barbecue."

Hunter chuckled.

"Your turn," I said. I was afraid we would get to the train station before he told his side of the tale.

"What do you want to know?"

"About your evening."

"You mean about the girl I was with."

I did not reply and he turned and looked at me a moment in silence, a grin on his face.

I remained silent, not admitting it.

"Lucille, an old friend of mine, was here in the area for a wedding. I took her to the barbecue at the mayor's house." He paused just a bit then added, "She is a beautiful, vivacious young widow and is still a lot of fun."

I said nothing.

"Is that enough?"

"It is," I said, but I was thinking it was more than enough. Did he have to add that last sentence?

His eyes were on me. I hoped he did not see that his last words had been a punch in the stomach.

"How did you know I was at Maggie's house?"

He grinned. "You overdid the act. Mindy was bent over badly. Your hat was covering most of your face. It was not normal. Although I had no clue it was you, when I saw the couple come out of the house—I was facing that way—I thought it rather odd, so I watched in glimpses."

I was silently kicking myself.

"But when Belshazzar got out, we all heard a yell and we stopped talking and I heard what I felt sure was your voice saying the goat got out." He paused. "Where were you when I brought the goat back?"

"I'm not telling. You don't have to know everything."

He chuckled. We had arrived at the train station—to my immense relief.

"Do I hear a train whistle?"

"You do. Go get your ticket, I'll bring your bag."

I ran in. In two minutes I was out again. The train pulled in and I reached for my suitcase.

"Thanks for…"

"That is not your train, Amber," said Hunter calmly. "It is going the wrong direction. Are you safe traveling alone?"

"Oh help," I said, embarrassed at my mistake. He had me so rattled. Alone I would not have made that mistake. I hoped.

"Come sit on the bench with me. You have another ten minutes."

"You don't need to stay."

"I think I do. You just nearly took the wrong train. I probably should accompany you."

"You just had me…"

"I just had you what?"

"Rattled."

He grinned at me. "I'll take that as a compliment."

I had not meant it as such. We sat on the bench and watched the train pull out.

"How long is your ride?"

"About an hour."

"Will someone be there to pick you up?"

"I am sure Sue's husband will be there. They won't want him around the house just now anyway."

"So the baby is on its way."

"Sounds like it. Maybe it is already here."

"Are you looking forward to caring for a newborn?"

"I'm a bit scared, to tell you the truth."

"You'll have practice for caring for your own babies."

I did not reply. I was thinking of the person that I wanted to be the father of any future babies.

"How long will you be gone?"

"I don't know. Depends. Probably two weeks."

I was relieved to hear the train approaching. It was completely dark now except for the gas lamps at the station. We stood once more.

"So we say goodbye," said Hunter, his voice getting drowned out in the noise of the approaching train.

"Yes," I said. "And I do appreciate you bringing me down here to the station."

He handed me my bag. The train, steam filling the station, screeched to a stop. Hunter laid his hand on my shoulder just a moment and bent his head a bit so I could hear him.

"Don't forget to come home again."

A funny thing happened to me then. It may have been the tone of his voice or perhaps the gentle touch of his hand on my shoulder. He suddenly sounded so sincere after taking me through the mill on the way down to the station, that I suddenly choked up and could not speak. I simply nodded and blinking back the sudden moisture in my eyes, quickly turned and boarded the train.

CHAPTER 21

My brother-in-law was waiting for me at the train station. I could see him pacing back and forth on the platform from the train window. He seemed to be the only one at the station. He gave me a quick smile and although I could see that he was relieved to see me, I was well aware of the anxiety on his face.

"She's been in hard labor for a couple hours. I am afraid she will be all worn out 'til the baby finally comes," he said as we got into the carriage.

"She is a strong girl, Alan," I replied. "She'll do fine."

But I felt his fear. Sometimes both mothers and babies never made it. He drove the horse hard as we headed out of town and into the countryside. In ten minutes we were at the house.

"Just go on in," Alan said. "I'll take care of the horse and bring your bag."

I knocked and walked in the back door. No one was to be seen. It was Susan's first baby and after quietly listening a few moments, I could hear the midwife moving around upstairs. I hung my coat on a hook in the hall near the stairs but did not go up. When Alan came into the house, he ran up the stairs and knocked on the bedroom door but the midwife promptly told him he was not allowed in. I heard him tell the midwife that Susan's sister had arrived. Did Susan want to see her? I was listening at the bottom of the stairs and my sister's voice drifted down, sounding weak.

"Let her in, I want to see her."

I hurried up the stairs and walked to the bedroom door, I was almost scared to walk in. What kind of condition would she be in? However, I wanted badly to see my sister and I pushed open the door. What I saw scared me. We had barely said hello to each other when she began with another pain so I gave her a quick kiss and went back downstairs. But I was shaken. Giving birth sounded terrible. I was not sure I wanted to go through it. I saw water boiling on the stove and needing something to do, I made coffee for Alan who made me nervous. I finally told him to go do something in the barn and I promised to call him when the baby came.

It was roughly an hour later that I finally heard the welcome, hearty cry of the newborn baby. I flew out the door to the stable.

"The baby has arrived!" I shouted into the stable, tears running down my face at the pure wonder of birth.

Before I knew it, Alan was flying past me to the house and I laughed and cried as I chased after him. When I got into the house he was going up the stairs two at a time and I just stood at the bottom of the stairs. As I expected, it was ten minutes before Alan was finally allowed in the room to meet his daughter. I went in a little later and saw the wonder on his face as he held the infant. He finally put her back in her mother's arms and gave Susan a kiss.

"Thank you for my daughter," I heard him say softly, tears in his voice. "That is the greatest gift you can give me."

The baby lay in my sister's arms. She had a tiny red face, a little pug nose and her eyes were closed. My sister looked happy but terribly pale.

"Good job, Sue," I said, but her eyes were closing. She was exhausted.

The midwife shooed both Alan and me out so she could clean up. She also gave me instructions and my work at my sister's started that moment and I was kept busy 'til late that evening. My night was interrupted and my day began early. I worried a bit about Susan. She had lost a lot of blood and was too weak to do anything but nurse the baby. She just slept and I had to beg her to eat. When Alan said he was going into town, I scribbled a short note to Papa telling of the birth of little Lucinda. I barely even got that done. I had never cared for a tiny baby before. My other sisters had helped each other and I was not needed. Now I learned to bathe the baby, burp the baby, change diapers and wash the the dirty ones. I was the nurse maid, the cook and the cleaning lady. I had no time to think of home and I surely earned my keep.

Besides the work, there were visitors. Friends from church and community came by to see the baby, bringing gifts as well as food, for which I, at least, was grateful. It was less cooking for me.

Sue's recovery was not as quick as I had hoped. The two weeks went by and I found I could not think of leaving her. She was not strong enough. I wrote home, saying as much. They would just have to do without me. Until now, I had not gotten any mail from anyone. Not even Mindy. But word got out that my return was delayed and one morning I was overjoyed to get a letter from Mindy. I stuck the letter in my pocket and never thought about it again until ten o'clock that night when I went to bed. I found myself hoping that she wrote something of Hunter. I undressed and put on my night clothes and then jumped into bed and ripped open the letter.

Dear Amber,

It seems like forever since I talked to you. I hope Sue gets well fast and that you will soon be home again. I have news. I met someone that I really like. He was at church with Mr. and Mrs. Cousins and is, I believe, a nephew of theirs. He is tall and ruggedly handsome and has a teasing smile. Then on Thursday evening, there was a harvest service at church and the church looked lovely. There was also a fellowship hour afterwards with cookies and cider and that is when I talked to him. We got along really well. I have lots to tell you, but not in a letter. By the way, I saw your brother Ray ride by with a girl. Do you know anything about that? Otherwise, life goes on as usual.

The bridge is nearly repaired from the flood. I have not seen much of Hunter. He, I have heard, is putting a new porch on his house and also had the house painted. Maybe he is getting married. Or at least thinking about it. Please come home soon. I miss our chats.

Mindy

That night, when Susan got up to use the chamber pot, she stumbled over her slipper and fell. Her head hit the dresser hard and I was roused from my bed by Alan who informed me he was going for the doctor because her head was bleeding badly. By the time the doctor came, it was four o'clock in the morning and the baby was needing food and a clean diaper. By four thirty, the doctor left and Sue had three stitches on her forehead and a headache. I never got back to bed. I got up, made breakfast, washed diapers and hung them out—thanking God for a clear day. Alan shopped for me and I cooked whatever simple meals I could think up. I had no time to spend making special dishes. If I wasn't baking bread or cooking, I was tending Susan and little Lucinda. And my bed lured me every evening long before I was free to go to bed.

The next day I was surprised with another letter. This one from Laura.

Dear Amber,

Greetings from Steeplechase. We were sorry to hear about Susan's mishap and hope she recovers quickly. We miss you, but I am glad you are there to help Susan. How is your little niece? I am sure you are enjoying her—if you have the time. I am sure you have your hands full.

I have some very sad news for you. Yesterday, just as I was finishing supper for your father and brother, Peggy came flying in the kitchen door. One look at her face and we knew something terrible had happened. She was nearly beside herself and she said she needed a doctor quick. Something happened to her husband. Both Ray and your Papa went over. Pastor Thomas apparently had a heart attack and died within the hour.

I stopped reading. I was in shock. Pastor Thomas died? Poor Peggy. And what would we do without a pastor? I sat and looked into space for a long time before I continued to read.

As for other news, I have heard that Minna is indeed planning to move north. The house is for sale and her mother will move with her. Murf is growing and is missing you. He was climbing the curtains yesterday and I had to scold him. I have been coming in every day and he sticks pretty close to me. Once in a while Ray takes time to play with him, but not often enough for that busy little kitten. But you should have seen him the other day. He was sniffing around the pantry door and wanted to get in. I was curious what he wanted. He acted like it was of the utmost urgency. So I opened the door and he went in like a streak of lightning and in no time flat he had caught a mouse. It was so funny to watch. He actually caught it and ate it. And when I wanted to take it from him to throw it outside to eat, he growled at me! I laughed out loud. Such a little kitten and growling at the enemy who wanted to take his mouse! This was his mouse and no one else could touch it. He will be a good mouser. He was so proud of his feat!

I haven't seen Hunter at all since you are gone. Ray says he is doing some work on his house and also on the office. Oh, and just two days ago, Peggy told me that Waldo has sailed for Honduras. I thought you would want to know that.

God bless you and Susan and her little family.

Laura

I thought of Hunter often, but was too busy to miss him. I wondered sometimes about Lucille. When Susan finally began to do her own work, I realized my life in the last month had been restricted to Susan's house. The only time I got outside was to hang up the wash, which included many, many diapers. I would have offered to do the shopping, but we were in the country and it was really too far to walk.

"Amber," said Susan to me one day in early November, "this will be your last week here. I am strong enough to do my own work now and Alan will help at nights. You have been a Godsend to us and we owe you big time."

"I am so glad I could help you and learn to know your sweet little girl."

"Do you know what you should do before you leave?" she asked, not waiting for a response. "You should go visit Aunt Charlotte. She only lives three miles from here."

"Really? I knew she was in the general area, but did not know it was so close."

"Maybe on Saturday afternoon Alan could drop you off there for a couple hours. I know she would love to see you. She is Mama's youngest sister and now that Mama is no longer here, I think she looks more and more like Mama."

"I'd love to see her."

That afternoon I wrote Papa a note, saying I would take the evening train on Sunday and would be in Steeplechase by seven thirty. His reply came two days later.

Dear Amber,

    I shall come to pick you up. Maybe Alan can pick me up at the station. I will arrive at two forty on Sunday afternoon. We will take the six fifteen train back. I need to see my new granddaughter and Susan.

                        Love, Papa

I was pleased that Papa was coming and shared the details with Alan and Susan. They were thrilled. How I wished my mama could see this new grandchild of hers. But that was not to be. Now that my time was nearly done here, I could not believe how eager I was to go home. I'd been gone a long time and now I could not get home fast enough. However, I did wish to see my Aunt Charlotte.

On Saturday afternoon, Alan hitched up the horse and carriage and took me to my Aunt Charlotte, promising to pick me up around four thirty. It was a dreary November day—very damp and bleak with only certain trees trying to hold on to their dry, brown leaves. I really had not seen much of the colored leaves this year, only when I was out hanging up wash could I admire the two sugar maples on Susan's property and they had blazed with color. However, I did not regret being with Susan when she needed me.

Aunt Charlotte lived in a small town, possibly twice the size of Steeplechase. I had been stuck in the country so long that it was nice now to see shops and people walking on the streets. When we arrived at my aunt's house, I saw there were a couple carriages parked on the street. We had not written to say I was coming, and now I wondered if we should have let her know ahead of time. But when she came to the door, joyful surprise lit up her round face.

"Amber! Come in, come in. What a surprise!"

As I stepped inside, I heard a chattering coming from another room in the house.

"You have company," I said, worried that I interrupted something.

"It is a quilting party. We meet biweekly here. Don't worry about them. I am glad you are here. How long can you stay?"

"Just an hour or two. I've been with Susan and Alan, who recently had a baby girl."

"I heard. I just did not get over there yet, but I will go soon. Is Susan well?"

She took my coat, chattering all the time and I told her about the baby and my time with Susan. She then took me to her spare room where I found six or seven ladies, of varied ages, sitting around a quilt and chatting as they stitched. Aunt Charlotte introduced me to them as her niece from Steeplechase and explained why I was in the area. When she mentioned our town by name, a young redheaded girl looked up from her quilting, curiosity on her face.

"You are from Steeplechase?" she asked.

I nodded. She looked at me thoughtfully for a few moments and I almost thought she wanted to ask me something, but she did not. Aunt Charlotte then excused herself as she wanted to talk of family to me. So we went to her kitchen where a pot of coffee was waiting on the stove and after opening a tin of cookies, we sat in the kitchen and chatted there by the stove. She wanted to know all about life at home without Mama. And all about Papa, Ray and finally myself. I told her all I knew. The time went quickly and when the knocker sounded, I could hardly believe it was Alan already. As Aunt Charlotte went to answer the knocker, I stuck my head back in the quilting room.

"Sorry to have stolen Aunt Charlotte from you, but I am leaving now. Enjoy your quilting."

They were very friendly and wished me well. Just as I turned away, the girl with the red hair stopped me.

"Excuse me. You mentioned Steeplechase. Do you happen to know a veterinarian from that area?"

"I do," I answered, surprised at her question. "Dr. Hunter Renwick is the name of the veterinarian. Do you know him?"

She hesitated. "I knew him at one time and heard he had moved to that area." She hesitated again. "He is probably married by now?"

"Not yet," I said, purposely not letting her know that he was not even dating. I was curious who she might be. She was a bit vague about how she knew him.

I said no more, but I was very, very curious about this woman. She said no more and I admit, I walked rather reluctantly from the room. *How did she know him? Was she possibly the one who hurt him?*

She was young enough. Was she married? Alan was walking back to the carriage already when I got to my aunt.

"Aunt Charlotte, what is the name of the woman with the red hair?"

"Oh, isn't her hair beautiful? Her name is Debbie Williams."

"I have seldom seen such lovely hair," I said honestly. I was glad to talk of her hair rather than explain why I asked her name. "And it was so nice talking to you, Aunt Charlotte. You must stop in to see little Lucinda sometime."

"I shall go next week."

The next morning I attended church for the first time in a month and Papa arrived in the afternoon. He spent time with Susan, giving her tonics to help get her strength back and getting to know his little granddaughter. Papa loved babies. Alan finally took us to the station and by eight o'clock that evening, we were eating supper in the kitchen at home. Murf had indeed grown and I congratulated him on his first mouse. He purred contentedly as I held his head against my neck. When I asked where Ray was, Papa was not sure, but he suspected he was visiting some girl.

I was glad to be home and I wanted to know all about what I had missed. I kept waiting for Papa to make some mention of Hunter but he did not. I did not want to ask. I did not want to act too interested. But I did mention Waldo.

"I heard from Laura that Waldo is in Honduras again."

Papa looked at me a moment, before speaking.

"I am glad that he is there," he said slowly, "and I believe that is where God wants him. And I am glad that you are here. I believe you are also where God wants you."

CHAPTER 22

Monday dawned and we began a new week. Laura was back to three days a week and Monday was wash day. I found that I had missed her and I kept running to the basement to ask her something or to tell her something that I thought she would be interested in.

I also went over to Peggy. Pastor Thomas was already buried and I had missed the funeral. I had gone out back to check on Murf and saw Peggy moving very slowly, throwing some dirty water out on the lawn. I called to her and went over. By the time I got to her, she was in tears and we just held each other and cried. Then we went into her kitchen and had a cup of coffee together.

"I feel so lost," she said. "It is like someone took the wheels off the carriage and left me abandoned on the road. I am no longer me. I am just a half of me anymore."

I could not know what she was feeling, but I hurt with her. Mostly I just listened as she told me about her husband's death.

"And of course, I lose my home as well," she concluded. "I guess I must be glad that the legal matters are taken care of by the church, but where do I go?"

"You have children," I said softly. "Where do they live?"

"David lives close to Lake Champlain. He has a farm and little children. I think they need their whole house. I want more than a bedroom. I am not so old that I want others to care for me."

"And your daughter Mary Jean? Where is she?"

"She is not far from Flynn Falls and she has already offered me a home until I know what to do. The furniture here nearly all belongs to the church, so I will have to look for furniture also."

"How soon must you leave here?" I hated to ask, but under the circumstances, it was something she had to know.

"The new minister will not move in until December."

"Good. And I am sure the church will help you find your way also."

"They have been more than helpful. I cannot complain. Mary Jean is coming this afternoon and we will do more talking then."

When I heard a knock at the door, I returned home. She would have many visitors in the next weeks.

That afternoon Mindy stuck her head in the door.

"I can't stay, I just wanted to see that you are truly back again. I've missed you."

"Even with the new boyfriend?"

"Oh that," she said, the disappointment showing in her face. "He was more than nice, but I found out he has a girlfriend. End of romance."

Papa and Ray were busy. There were the usual number of children with colds and fevers and there were old people who were about to leave this world. Sometimes patients were brought to the office to get stitched up or to have broken bones wrapped. This morning already, it was determined that one middle-aged man had appendicitis and had to be taken to the hospital.

Papa and Ray took turns. Sometimes Ray was in the office and Papa on calls. Sometimes it was the other way around. On Tuesday, Papa came back from his rounds and had a message for me.

"I invited Hunter for supper," he said, sitting down for lunch. "I drove past his house on a sick call and realized I barely saw him since you left. He is busy working on his house in his free time but we owe him a meal for taking you to the train a month ago."

I tried not to act too excited. It was a chilly November day with a gusty, raw wind and I was hungry for sauerkraut. I hoped Hunter liked it. It was definitely a Pennsylvania Dutch meal. I also made cin-namon buns so he could fill up on them if he did not like my meal. But this chilly weather just cried out for sauerkraut, mashed potatoes and pork in my opinion.

When the knocker sounded at six thirty, Papa went to open the door and I started putting the food into the bowls. I was so eager to see Hunter again but I was never quite prepared for his direct gaze when-ever we did meet. It knocked me off kilter and I feared he knew it. I heard his deep voice and my heart beat a bit faster. When I brought the pork and sauerkraut to the table, the three men were standing by their chairs. I set the bowl down before I looked at Hunter so I would not spill it. Then I looked up. Hunter was standing, his eyes fixed on me, just a hint of a grin on his face.

"Good evening, Hunter," I said. "I hope you like sauerkraut."

"Good evening. I do like it. So you decided to come back home again."

"I went after her," said Papa as Hunter pulled my chair out for me.

I was sitting on the end to let Ray and Hunter face each other. That gave me the advantage because Hunter had to turn his head to see me but I could see him all the time.

"So what is with the house?" asked Ray after we started eating.

"It needed a new porch and I am doing some other repairs. I had some help with the porch but the rest I am doing by myself."

"Looks nice. I always admire your big shade tree at the side of the house. I remember when it was a lot smaller. Dr. Toome planted it when I was about ten. He let me help him plant it."

"I am glad for it, but I wish for a fruit tree or two. I'm thinking of an apple and a sour cherry tree."

"Sounds like you are putting down roots," said Papa.

"I plan to stay. My clients keep me busy and I love this area of Vermont. And the people."

"Where did you grow up?" asked Papa. "I think I asked you be-fore but I can't seem to recall."

"Tremont."

"Oh yes. That is, if I remember correctly, very close to where Amber was the last month. My daughter Susan married an Alan Jeffery from that area."

"I know the Jefferys. There was a Harold Jeffery in school with me."

"I think Alan has a brother with that name," said Ray, shoveling in the sauerkraut.

I had a sudden thought. I was very curious about the red head that had asked about him and this might be my opportunity to gain some knowledge.

"That would explain something," I said slowly, looking directly at Hunter. "I met an acquaintance of yours on my last day in Tremont."

I don't know if there really was a slight hesitation, or if I only imagined it.

"That could be most anyone."

"It was a young woman."

I kept my eyes on Hunter. The forkful of roast pork on its way to his mouth stopped just a few seconds while he gave me a quick look. Seeing me watching him, a mask came down over his face.

"I know quite a few young women from that area."

The fact that Hunter did not ask me her name, made me think that he suspected my answer.

"I did not ask her what her name was," I said, feeling guilty because although it was true, I did know her name. However, I did not want too much said in front of everyone.

"You should have asked her name," said Ray, "maybe it was an old girlfriend."

It was interesting to me that after just a short pause, Hunter asked Papa a medical question explaining some injury on a horse. As a result, the topic of the woman who had asked about him was pushed aside. The meal completed, the men went into the living room and I cleaned up the table, put the leftovers away and taking the pan of water that was sitting on the range, I began to wash dishes. A short time later, someone knocked at the front door and a male visitor joined them in the living room. I did not pay much attention, but just as I was finishing up the dishes, Hunter came into the kitchen. One look at him and I knew why he had come. He stood at the doorway and gave me a long, silent look and then watched me wipe down the table and anything else in sight because he made me nervous. He finally came to me, gently took the cloth from my hand and led me to the table.

"Have a seat," he said. "You just wiped the table three separate times."

Was it possible? I somehow managed to make a fool of myself every time I was with this doctor.

I sat down and he took the chair across the table from me and leaning back, put one foot on the opposite knee.

"So you enjoyed being nanny these last weeks?"

"I did, but it was hard work. Most of the time Susan was in bed. But I fell in love with little Lucinda and I shall miss her. And you? Were you busy with sick animals while I was gone?"

"I was. And with the bridge out, it was harder getting to some of the farms. I even saw Belshazzar while you were gone, but he was not the animal that needed me."

He stopped. I did not believe that he had sought me out for this conversation. I tried to think of something to say but nothing came. In the silence, Hunter put his foot back on the kitchen floor and sat up, his elbows on the table and his hands under his firm chin.

"You were a bit devious this evening." His eyes were fixed on mine, and I felt he was reading all my thoughts but I was trying to act natural, which was very hard when with Hunter.

"I was devious? How did you come to that conclusion?"

"And don't act as if you were not aware of it. Tell me about the person who asked about me."

"You are very curious."

"I think I have the right to be curious. And you don't know her name?"

"I do know her name," I said, not looking at his eyes.

"You said you did not know her name."

"No, I said I did not ask her what her name was. However, when I said goodbye to my aunt, I asked her the name of the girl with the pretty red hair."

There was a definite hesitation after I mentioned the red hair.

"Do you still want to know her name?" I asked after the silence became too long for me.

"I asked you the name."

I was having fun. This time I had Hunter on the hot seat, rather than Hunter making me uncomfortable and I was enjoying it and I am sure it showed on my face.

"I think she said um...oh, what was it? Debbie somebody or other. Perhaps Debbie Williams. Yes that was the name."

Hunter never blinked an eye. "Yes, I am acquainted with a Williams family." He paused, nailing me with his eyes. "And you really did not need to think so hard for that name."

His eyes were accusing. He knew me too well and I blushed as I smiled. But I wanted to hear more about her. I wanted proof that this was his old girlfriend. But he offered no information.

"Where did you see her?" he asked finally.

"My one outing was the day before I came home when I visited my mother's sister who lives about three miles away from Susan and Alan. There was a quilting party in progress when I got there. My aunt introduced me to the quilters. Debbie was one of them. When she heard where I was from, she instantly gave me a second glance and I thought she wanted to say something. But she did not. However, when I popped in to say goodbye to the quilters, she asked me who the veterinarian was in the area."

Hunter kept his eyes on me but he was working hard to look very casual about what I was saying.

"I told her it was a Dr. Hunter Renwick."

A silence followed. "That was all?" he asked, when I said no more. His manner was calm but his eyes were trying to read my mind.

"Not quite. Just as I was going out the door, she asked another question."

I purposely paused and Hunter just looked at me, waiting.

"She asked me if you had married."

Hunter's eyes strayed to his hands. In the silence, I heard the clock strike the hour.

Suddenly he gave me a sharp look.

"You have played with me as a cat with a mouse, Amber."

I could not hold my guilty laughter as I blushed.

"Consider yourself spanked," he added, with a crooked grin. "I am glad to see your red face at being caught at your deceitfulness."

I laughed, but I had one last question. "Was she an old girlfriend?"

It took him a long time to answer. I felt guilty for asking such a personal question until I remembered some of the personal questions he had asked me at times.

"Yes," he said finally. "And we did not part in a very friendly manner."

As he remembered with a faraway look, I had to know if she was married.

"I did not think to look for a wedding ring. Is she married?"

"Yes," he said. "Williams is her married name."

There was a long pause. There was no doubt in my mind that this was the girl who had caused him to distrust women.

"I am sorry if she hurt you," I said softly. After a hesitation I added, "Don't judge all females by her."

Hunter said nothing, but gave me a steady look. What I did not say was that she was a really stupid redhead if she thought she could do better than Hunter.

He stood up then. I heard Papa saying goodbye to someone at the door and Hunter pushed his chair back under the table.

"It is good to have you back, Amber," he said, "in spite of your wiliness. Somehow life is a bit more interesting with you around."

"Thanks," I said, glowing from his compliment, "it is good to be back."

CHAPTER 23

November continued to be chilly and at times blustery, sometimes there was sleet or flurries mixed with rain hitting the windows. I spent a lot of time doing the mending and sewing that I had not taken the time for in the summer. Thanksgiving came and went. Hunter, Ray told me, went to his parents' home for the day. Susan and family and my brother Floyd and his wife came for the day and it was so nice having at least some of the family with us.

Gone were the days that I walked to the gazebo to read or just to think. Now I spent my evenings knitting by the fire with Murf getting all tangled up in my yarn and Ray reading some medical book or debating with Papa about methods of treatment.

One gray afternoon, my cousin Sidney stopped in. I had worked for him at the inn and had seldom seen him since. Now he stopped in to chat. For once it was not raining but it was cold and cloudy. After exchanging some news, he got to the reason for his visit.

"My wife's birthday is today, Amber, and I would like you to join us for a party at the inn this evening."

"I'd love to come and see everyone again, but I don't think it will happen. I have no transportation."

He thought a bit.

"Come with me now. I know Jane and Ed Prescott, who live up North Street have been invited and I am sure you could come back with them. The only hitch is, we must leave within the next fifteen minutes because I must go to Pipers Hill yet and from there we'll just go over the mountain and hopefully be back to Flynn Falls before dark."

It was going on four o'clock. I had barely been out of the house the last couple days and a party at the inn sounded inviting. There were leftovers in the icebox that the men could fix for themselves.

"Let me go and check with Papa."

I went over to the office but Papa was in with a patient. However, I met Ray just coming back from his rounds and told him my plans.

"I'll get a ride home with the Prescotts," I said.

Fifteen minutes later, I was seated with Sidney in his carriage and heading up the mountain along the river to Pipers Hill. I realized once again how seldom I got out of my hometown. Pipers Hill was only a few miles from us, but there was no real reason for me to go up there. Now, riding alongside of Sidney, I was enjoying my ride in spite of the cold, nasty weather. The river was already freezing around the edges and the water was low. I remembered the raging floodwaters that came down this mountain and crashed through Steeplechase that terrible night, taking the life of Clarence Wolf. We loved our river, but on that night it was our enemy.

When we arrived in Pipers Hill, we passed through the small village with its cluster of houses, the church, the country store and then we went up the road just a quarter of a mile where Sidney stopped to give some information to the innkeeper at the village inn there. That done, we headed over the mountain. It was not far until we passed a whole flock of sheep in a field. The farmer was out at his mailbox, collecting his mail. He waved a friendly greeting to us as we drove by to continue our way across the mountain. It kept getting steeper and steeper and there was really no beauty at this bleak time of the year.

"I'm beginning to feel sorry for your horse," I told Sidney.

"Oh, Baxter enjoys it. It is good for him. He went over here a few times after the flood. But I am glad the bridge is repaired again. A friend of mine crossed here recently and saw a wild boar. They are very rare in Vermont and we don't want them. If we see one today, I will report it. They can do a lot of damage. And the last time I crossed here, I saw a moose. I'll show you where I saw it."

Sidney stopped a short time just to give Baxter a break. We were close to the top and then it would be downhill from there. Soon after we continued over the mountain, Sidney told me to keep my eyes open, maybe we would see the moose. I did not have much hope, but I watched.

"Now," said Sidney, "I saw the moose right around this curve to the left."

We slowly made the curve. I looked to the left.

"It is there now!" I said too loudly. The female moose had been eating grass, her face close to the earth, but hearing our carriage she turned and looked at us a moment or two, then continued eating. We watched until she slowly lumbered away. I had to wonder if this was the animal that Jonas had heard and seen when they got lost on the mountain.

"Impressive," I said, "but I think God smiled when he made the moose. She has a face only a mother could love."

Sidney laughed. "She's certainly about the homeliest female I ever laid eyes on."

And then we began going downhill and soon passed a sugar house where maple sap would be boiling in March. We passed a dwelling here and there and sometimes it was the home of someone I knew from working at the inn. But now there was a new problem. It began to sleet.

"Wow, I knew this would probably be my last trip over the mountain for this year, but I did not count on sleet," said my cousin.

The sleet was mixed with rain and I was very glad to be in a closed carriage. Fortunately, the way was easier now going downhill and since it had only begun sleeting, we would probably not encounter any real difficulty. But I think Baxter was as glad as I was when we finally pulled in at the Inn at the Falls.

The inn was big and had class. It had rooms for over fifty guests. But they needed the room. Flynn Falls was a college town and a crossroads for stagecoaches. Because it was a busy place, Sidney did well here. A beautiful Congregational Church stood across the street and the inn looked down on the village green where many activities took place during the summer.

The birthday party was scheduled for six and I had a bit of time, so I went into the kitchen and had a chance to talk to my former co-workers. I even got to help with the food for the party and it was fun to be with them again.

"So you quit the handsome Jonas," said a young girl with whom I had worked.

"I did. It wasn't going anyplace."

"Have you seen him lately?"

"Not since July."

"He is not doing well."

"Is he sick?"

"Not sick, but he has begun drinking and hanging out with the wrong crowd."

"Jonas? I can't believe it."

"Yes, Jonas. He even lost his job at the factory and his parents are quite at a loss what to do about him. He looks pretty seedy these days."

I felt bad about him. In fact the thought of him in this condition almost made me physically sick.

"Does he come in here?"

"Sometimes. He lives just across the street so it is very handy. I think he really liked you and when you quit him, it was a blow to his pride. He just seems a bit lost. It doesn't help that he would rather fish than work. He just isn't very ambitious."

I was sorry to hear this about Jonas. I knew I could never go back to him.

The party started at six and there were perhaps twenty persons attending—just the staff who were free to come and family members and friends. There were tasty dishes and french desserts. I found it fun but I did not belong here anymore and after the gifts were opened and the party was nearly over, I suddenly realized the couple that Sidney had assumed could take me home had never arrived. Most likely the sleet had kept them home. In the meantime, Sidney had disappeared—called away on some emergency—and I suddenly realized I had no way home. I looked over the dining room, hoping to see someone from Steeplechase I would know. I recognized no one. I was not in a panic because Sidney had expected this couple to come from Steeplechase and he would probably feel responsible to see that I got home. I took my coat and walked around the inn. I saw no sign of Sidney. I would wait to talk to Sidney, but in the meantime, I needed something to do. I had often stood on the bridge overlooking the falls here in Flynn Falls and it was not late yet, so I decided to run out to the falls and then I would look for Sidney. I opened the door and stepped out.

Whoa! There was ice out here! It did not seem to be raining or sleeting anymore, but I would have to be very careful. I took hold of the railing, which itself was icy, but I could get a grip and made my way down the steps very carefully and then walked on the lawn to the street. No carriages were coming. I crossed the street very cautiously and made it onto the sidewalk. Here the road sloped downhill to the bridge over the falls. I stepped very carefully on the sidewalk, but all my caution helped not at all. In a split second, I found myself sitting on my rump and sliding down the sidewalk for what seemed a very long way until I finally whirled in a complete circle and landed in the grass beside the pavement. Totally embarrassed at my long slide, I got up as fast as possible and looked around and seeing no one, decided I was the foolish one out in this weather. I looked back at the inn. It looked a long way off and I wondered how I would ever get back up there. I was a lot closer to the bridge now so I decided to continue so I could at least see the falls, since I went through all this danger to see them. I was glad for the street lamps although even they seemed to be very dim on this black night. I continued walking very carefully and finally stood at the bridge and looked down into the black water. It suddenly seemed very sinister. I could hear the roar of the falls, but there were no lights to speak of on the black water, just the dimmest of light from the upstairs window of a three-story building that stood next to the river and made a weak glimmer on the water rushing loudly over the falls.

I could not make the connection between this scene and the times in the summer when I had stood here and enjoyed the glint of the summer sun on the water below. I remembered the foam on the water beyond, where the water dropped away from the bridge. I turned to go, eager now to get back to the warm inn and away from this black, watery danger. This was not what I remembered with pleasure. As I made my way carefully along the sidewalk, I could see clouds scudding across a sky that was giving a wee bit of light from a moon hidden behind them. A carriage came slowly toward me. I did not look up. I took one careful step at a time. First the sidewalk, then, when grass was possible, I went on the grass. But now it was uphill and I had to place my foot sideways to keep from sliding back. After a slow, treacherous climb, I was finally ready to cross the road to the inn. But to do this, I had to get back on the sidewalk. I took a very careful step...and fell. I was on the grass this time, so I did not slide far. As I quickly got up, I heard the door of the inn open and voices that faded into the night. I was scared to try again, but I had to get across the road. Seeing a gas lamp just a few feet from where I stood, I walked on the grass to that spot. But I still had to get on the sidewalk, to get to the lamp, which would be something to hang on to before going out on the road.

I stood there uncertainly. The men who had come out of the inn disappeared into the night. I saw a carriage move very slowly out to the street and drive away from me. Another came down and stayed at the corner across from me for a long time. I wondered why he did not move on. And then he did, but he drove over to me, got out of the carriage and came to me. He was a big man with a kind face.

"You forgot your ice skates," he said with a kind smile.

"I am scared to move," I replied.

"Where are you headed?"

"Just to the inn."

"Will you allow me to drive you there?"

I hesitated but at the same time was confident I could trust this man. He opened his mouth to say something, but did not say it.

"I would be grateful if you would do that."

He stood between me and the carriage.

"Take my arm."

I did so. The man was powerful. He stood like the Rock of Gibraltar and let me take hold of him, rather then him taking hold of me. With little difficulty, I was in his carriage. Then he drove around the grassy square next to the inn, before stopping to let me out.

"Wait here, I will see you in."

He got out and offered me his arm and we walked without mishap up the steps to the inn. I knew I was going no place this evening anymore. I would stay here overnight. At the door I turned to thank him.

"I don't know whom to thank."

"I'm Mr. Conrad."

"And I am Miss McDurfee. I thank you for your kindness to me."

"Glad to be of help. Now have a safe evening."

I watched him go very carefully back down the icy steps and then turned to go into the lounge. There I saw Sidney.

"Amber, are you still here?"

"I think I am here for the night."

"Oh, Mr. and Mrs. Prescott never showed up, did they?"

"I did not see them. The sleet and ice probably kept them home."

"Where were you now?"

"I was foolish enough to try to see the falls, but it is sheer ice out there. I slid on my seat partway to the bridge and coming back did not know how I was going to cross the icy, slanted sidewalk. But after hanging on a street lamp for dear life, a man who was here at the inn picked me up and brought me back."

Sidney laughed heartily. He thought it was hilarious. I was embarrassed that I was so dumb to have to be helped back.

"Who helped you?"

"He said his name was Conrad. Mr. Conrad."

"Big guy?"

"Yes."

"I know who he is. I think he is single. Actually, I think he might be a minister. Maybe this is the man you have been waiting for."

I laughed. "What I need most of all right now is a room."

"So you do and you get it free."

We walked to the desk and he handed me the key. "Sleep well."

I had brought nothing for an overnight stay. I turned to the wide stairway that was just inside the front door and began going up the steps, looking down over the large lounge area as I ascended. It looked romantic in the glow of the oil lamps. It was the nicest inn around and I had been very happy to work here. Now I was seeing it as a visitor and not as my workplace.

Once upstairs in the wide hall, I walked to my room and unlocked the door. There was nothing for me to do here except go to bed. Somehow, it felt like a waste of time. I was seldom here anymore and I was not ready to go to bed. I looked out the window. There were few carriages passing the inn. I heard the wind suddenly howling in the eaves and saw some snow flurries dancing past the gas lamps. After perhaps ten minutes of this, I returned downstairs. I would go into the dining room and order a cup of hot chocolate. My stint out on the icy sidewalk had chilled me and I would sit by the fire in the dining room and enjoy my drink.

The dining room was open until eleven and it was just ten fifteen. I walked down the hall, passing a smaller room, which was the main bar. I glanced in the door and saw just a few men in there talking and having their drinks. I wondered if Jonas could possibly be one of the occupants in the room. But I did not stay to find out.

The large dining room was not at all busy at this time of night. One couple sat chatting in a corner of the room and another man sat alone in another part of the room. I found a table close to the hearth and ordered my cup of hot chocolate. Soon after the waiter brought it to me, two women came in and sat behind me. I was sitting so I could gaze into the fire, which I always enjoyed, so I could not see them. However, with the entrance of these two women, my solitude and contemplation was spoiled. Both women were quite talkative and excitedly getting reacquainted and the one had a shrill laugh that got annoying in the otherwise quiet room. They did not seem to care who could hear what they said and were lost in their own world as they talked and laughed. I could not help but follow their conversation. Indeed, all in the dining room were suddenly entertained by their chatter.

"It is so good to finally see you again, Aggie," said the one with the laugh. "It seems like ages. What have you been doing with yourself?"

"Well, I guess you know I nearly got married this past summer."

"No I did not. What happened? I don't see a ring on your finger."

"Nothing very nice. I met Neal at a social occasion in our town and we hit it off right away. He was dashingly handsome and was hilariously funny. He courted me for several months. I thought this was the man of my dreams. He was very attentive and talked of marriage. Then he met my cousin at a family reunion and she flirted so outrageously with him that he barely knew what he was doing anymore. At any rate, he decided he was more interested in her and let me drop like a hot potato."

"How dreadful! Men! They are so easily led astray."

"But you were happy, were you not, Lucy?"

"I was. Marvin was great. I could not believe it when he became so ill and there was no cure. I know some people don't want to marry again because they are afraid it won't be as good. But I think differently. I had a good marriage, and I would like it again. I am still young. I have no children and I would like children."

"But by now all the good men are married."

"Maybe, but not quite."

"You sound like you have someone in mind."

"Let's just say I have my eye on someone." She laughed coyly.

"What is he like?"

"Single!" They both laughed loudly.

"And besides that? I mean, why is he still single? I always worry a bit about that. There could be some hidden reason why no one wants him. Maybe he is unwell or has some really odd mannerisms."

"I don't think so. He is handsome, has his own business, is a true gentleman and...I am doing my best to think how I can catch him."

"How did you get to know him?"

"We were friends as children but I don't know, we just outgrew each other I guess. I think we eventually both moved away from that town."

"Where does he live?"

"Not close to me, unfortunately, which makes it hard. However, I took the opportunity to see him in—I think it was September or October—and I was impressed. I was in his area and looked him up. He even took me to a party that he had to attend. Oh, and the party was outside and next to an eccentric woman with a goat that got out and got into the yard where we were and my friend had to catch the goat and take it back to the woman. It was hilarious!"

I suddenly jerked to attention and my hand clenched the cup I held in my hand. It is a wonder that the handle of the cup did not break off. It was all I could do not to immediately turn and look at the chattering women. I had not really meant to listen. But they were the only ones talking so I had no choice. Now I had to see this woman. The other woman had called her Lucy. This had to be Lucille. The Lucille that Hunter took to the mayor's party. I tried to be discreet as I turned in my chair. I wanted to get a good look at Lucille. I think I had seen her well enough that evening to recognize her. I turned a bit in my chair and then took a quick look behind me. One of the ladies must have knocked something to the floor and stooped to pick it up. I did not see her face. The one I could see was not Lucille. This one was rather heavy and had nearly black hair. I sat there like stone, my empty cup of chocolate in my hand, somehow unable to move and ears at high alert until the two friends, still talking, got up to leave the room. On their way out of the room, I turned and looked hard at the woman, though the face was barely visible. Yes, this was the woman I remembered. Only one thought consumed me.

Hunter was being hunted.

CHAPTER 24

The invitation came by mail on a cold day in early December. I had gone to the post office myself and noticed the envelope right away. It stood out from the other mail because it was on a very nice envelope of stiff white paper. I felt sure this was special and it had my name on it. Actually, Ray's name as well as mine. I hurried home in the cold, damp air, eager to get back into the warmth of the house. I quickly sorted the mail and put Papa's in his office, then I took the letter to the living room and sat on the couch in front of the fire to open it. Murf was soon on my lap, wanting attention. The letter would not be from any of my siblings because they addressed their mail to Papa usually. I opened the envelope and looked to the bottom of the page. It was from the Coopers. Hal and Cynthia Cooper were members of our church. They were a young couple with, as of yet, no children. They lived about halfway between Steeplechase and Lake Champlain. Hal was the son of a successful businessman and was part owner of the business. He and his wife did not hurt for money, but they did hurt for lack of children. However, rather than sit and feel sorry for themselves, Cynthia volunteered for any social aspect of our church. They loved having people in and I hoped this would be an invitation to some sort of party.

I was thrilled to find it an invitation to what they called a Christmas Gathering. The party was to take place on the ninth and tenth of the month, which was the second weekend in December. That was just a week away and it was to begin on Friday evening and end on Saturday evening. An overnight party? This was getting more exciting all the time. And besides that, it was not at their home but at their camp which was, I read, some eight miles north of us.

I stopped reading for a moment to pet Murf who was chewing on the invitation. My eyes went to the window as I tried to imagine what this camp would be like. I knew they had some sort of cabin on a mountain where they sometimes entertained. I had never been there but I had heard about it and always wished that I would someday be invited. The place had started as a hunter's cabin for Hal's grandfather but Hal's father, I was told, had built on to it a couple times so now it was big enough for quite a few guests.

My eyes returned to the invitation. It stated that there would be ten guests, five ladies and five gentlemen. And one of the reasons for the invitation was to get acquainted with the new pastor and his wife who were moving into the parsonage the week before Christmas. The Coopers were putting the party on and making the food. But the real host and hostess would be Pastor Dennis Cender and his wife Gloria, and they, at the suggestion from the Coopers, were using this party as a way to learn to know some of the singles from church. A brief outline of the party was included with the invitation.

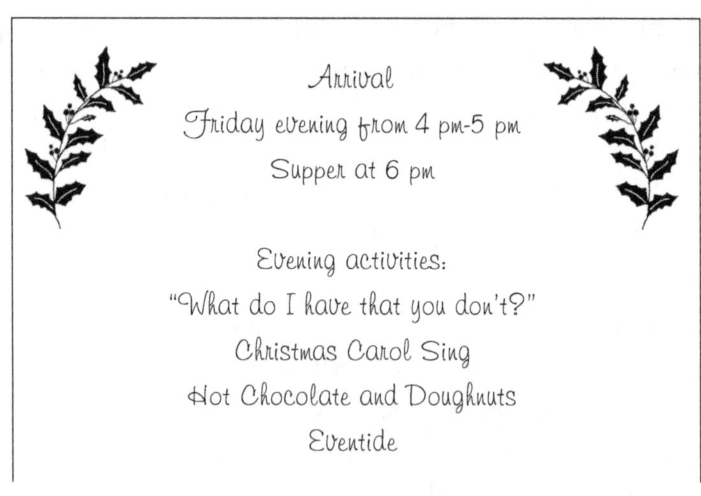

> Saturday
> Breakfast at 8
> Sleigh ride to Lake Champlain at 9:30
> Early lunch at Bluster Inn
> Back to Coopers Camp for ice skating
> Gift exchange
> Suppertime
> Home

At the end was a note that read as follows: Please bring with you a wrapped gift for someone of the opposite gender. Also, this is not a dress-up occasion. Please wear what is warm and comfortable for this weekend. Don't forget your skates and if you play a musical instrument, bring it along for the carol singing.

I just sat there on the couch, excitement building within me. I was only half aware of Murf, who now sat right on the invitation as I held it on my lap and tried eating it. I was just staring out into the falling snowflakes and wanted desperately to share my excitement with someone. Was Mindy invited? I had to know right now. I grabbed my cloak and ran out the door and up to to Main Street and then over to the bakery. She was still there but in the back room. I smiled to her mother and made my way back to the kitchen.

"Mindy!" She was scrubbing a tabletop and when she saw me she broke into a smile.

"Did you get an invitation in the mail?" she asked.

"I did! So you did, too? I am so excited. It sounds like fun. I wonder who else is invited."

"I don't know, but it must be all singles from church."

"Do you think they will invite Hunter?"

"Of course. He is the cream of the crop. You'll have to fight for his attention."

I soon ran home again, through flurries and a cold wind. December was here and the gazebo on the village green did not appeal to me. Too cold. But winter had its allurements also and this party was one of them.

As I went about my work, my mind was on the party. What would I wear and what would be my gift. That would take some thought. I would wait to see Ray and then I would write our acceptance to the invitation.

I did not see Ray until suppertime. I gave him the invitation to read at the table. He accepted the invitation immediately after consulting Papa. The rest of the meal we tried to think of what we could give as a gift.

"I do have a scarf that I knitted," I said finally. "It would suit for a man. I also have a pair of socks I knitted."

"I might have to cheat," said Ray. "I have no idea and little time to make something."

The week went by quickly. I decided on the socks. Men were always glad for home knitted socks. Ray worked evenings on a Christmas wreath of greens, pine cones and a big red ribbon. Under the ribbon he fastened two glass pill bottles in place of bells. Ray had the artistic touch in the family and I found the wreath very pretty.

By the time the weekend had arrived, we had several inches of snow on the roads and it was decided that Ray would take the sleigh and Mindy and Hunter were invited to ride with us. However, shortly before we were to leave, Hunter sent word by a messenger boy that he was tied up in Pipers Hill and we should go without him. I was dreadfully disappointed, but tried not to show it. Hunter promised to come on his own as soon as he was free.

The ride was wonderful, but cold. Ray had a thick pair of gloves made especially for holding the reins of a horse. Mindy and I were bundled up in mounds of blankets with just our faces showing. On the way, she informed me that she would not come back with us, as there was a concert in Burlington that she was attending with a cousin who would meet her there. She would just need a ride to the train station.

We arrived soon after four and were met at the end of the lane by Hal Cooper. He came out of a small shelter that was used for just such occasions as this—where he was out of the cold and wind and could wait for the guests and lead them up to the camp.

"Welcome!" he called to us. "I would like to ride up with you to show the way. There is a fork off to the left about halfway up the mountain that you do not want to take. Furthermore, this is a rough road to travel and I would like to take the reins to keep you all safe."

He then jumped into the sleigh, took the reins and gave us the ride of our lives. There was a lot more snow here on the mountain and the lane up to the camp was narrow and winding with snow piled on both sides of us. At one point we crossed a nearly frozen mountain stream on a wooden bridge with no railings. It was quite an experience just getting up the lane and we were jostled around a good deal by the time we got to the camp, laughing all the way. The sprawling log cabin stood to our right as we came up the lane. After tumbling out of the sleigh, Hal sent us inside while he took the horse and sleigh to the stable.

By this time it was getting quite dark already. There were many trees around us and some evergreens against the house whose dark boughs hung low with snow. Before we got to the door, a young man stepped out who was unknown to me. I knew this must be Pastor Dennis, whom none of us had met till now. He was a very friendly man and he welcomed us heartily and held the door for us to enter. We walked into a kind of entryway where there was room for coats to be hung and boots to be discarded. Then we entered a big room where we would be gathering for our meals as well as our social events. Here we were introduced to the minister's wife Gloria. She was not quite as vivacious as her husband, but quite friendly with a winning smile. She then led us to our sleeping quarters where we left our bags.

The original building, we were told, had been a hunter's cabin and was just a big room to sleep in with a stove to cook on. But there were changes over the years in a rather haphazard fashion and now we obediently followed the minister's wife along short, narrow halls and down a step here and up a couple steps there until we were shown a bedroom with four bunk beds. This is where the girls would sleep. After depositing our bags in the room we fixed our hair and headed to the main room where others had already gathered.

This room was surely the original cabin. It was a lovely, fairly large room and upon entering it, one's eyes went immediately to the far end where a blazing fire burned in a hearth with the stone fireplace going completely to the ceiling and nearly as wide as the room itself. It was magnificent to see. Built into the stone was the mantel and also places for books. There were upholstered chairs setting around the room with two couches facing the fire and there were various braided rag rugs at different places on the floor. A few lanterns hung from the ceiling and oil lamps stood in the wide, windowsills. The walls were mainly bare, but at the back of the room hung a large oil painting of a bear and her cubs eating blueberries in the wild.

The room, in spite of its size, was cozy warm and I now looked around to see who else had been invited. Some were familiar to me, but not all. These were, presumably all people who were affiliated with our church but not all came regularly to services. It appeared to be the older singles who probably were all over twenty.

And then the supper bell rang. It was the same kind of bell we had in school to call us in from recess. A smiling Hal Cooper rang it, his wife Cynthia standing by his side and said we would not wait for Hunter, who had been delayed. When we gathered around the table, I saw there were name cards at each place setting. We maneuvered our-selves around the table, searching for our names. When I found mine I quickly looked to see if Hunter's name was somewhere close by, and was disappointed when I failed to see it. There were places for twelve at the table. The Coopers would serve and not sit with us. Pastor Den-nis sat at one end and it was arranged that everyone sat with those of the opposite gender on either side.

Once seated, I looked around the table. A young man named Charlie sat to my right. I did not know him at all. Gloria sat across from me and Wynn, a man of perhaps twenty, who sang in the church choir, sat to my left. There were candles burning on the table and the dishes were such as one might find in a cabin—simple, flat plates of various colors and sturdy tumblers. The mountain air made me hungry and I eagerly breathed in the aroma of the food setting before us. Then the Coopers came up to the table.

"A hearty welcome to all of you," said Hal. "My wife and I will not be with your group—we will be the cooks for the two days. But I just want to formally introduce you to our new pastor, Dennis Cender and his wife, Gloria. This was their idea and I know you will enjoy getting to know them."

Pastor Dennis led in a prayer of thanksgiving for the food before us and the meal began. Once the food was passed, we began to converse with each other. Gloria got Charlie talking and he never stopped. He had curly red hair, freckles on his nose and blue-green eyes that were as merry as child's on Christmas morning. I was glad for him because I did not hear a lot of conversation around the table. We were too new to each other.

Partway through the meal, I heard the Coopers talking to someone in the entryway and in came Hunter. He looked cold and romantically handsome as he entered the room, snow flurries on his coat and pants. The Coopers took his wraps and led him to the table where he was seated between Mindy and Julie and across from Ray. I was envious of Mindy, but soon forgot my jealousy as we stuffed ourselves with meatloaf, roasted potatoes, green beans, stewed tomatoes and a carrot salad. I found Gloria a kindhearted woman who could laugh heartily with me at Charlie's jokes. Mindy and Wynn were talking a lot, but I did talk a bit with Wynn and discovered I had been in school with a sister of his. He was not a big talker but was ready to talk if I asked him something. A woman by the name of Sylvia caught my attention at the table. I did not know her at all. She was a bit chubby, and pleasant, but there was a definite look of sadness on her face. She mostly listened, but answered when spoken to. There was also Julie, whom I knew. I remembered Mindy complaining that Carl always liked to talk to Julie. I watched Julie now. She was a beautiful, blond and a flirt to boot. And she was sitting next to Hunter. Another girl I knew only vaguely was Faye. She was a petite girl who also sang in the church choir.

After eating sticky cinnamon buns made with Vermont maple syrup and coffee for dessert, we were free until seven thirty. As I stood up from the table, I glanced down at Hunter and was shocked to see Mr. Conrad, the man who had rescued me from the ice in Flynn Falls. He was talking to Hunter and when he saw me staring in surprise, he merely nodded to me and kept on talking. I somehow had missed him 'til now. He must have been sitting on the same side as me, and as there were people between us and I was busy talking to those around me I had not noticed him. I took a good look at him now. He had a deep voice and I remembered hearing the voice but not seeing him at the table.

Mindy came to me and we sat on a couch by the fire, and I hurriedly told her of my adventure on the ice and how this Mr. Conrad helped me to the inn.

"Tell me, Mindy," I said rather softly with a quick look around to see if Hunter was close by, "did Hunter say what delayed him?"

"I did not talk much to him, but I heard him tell Ray that he was first delayed in Pipers Hill and then he was just about here a half hour ago, but when he got to the little bridge we had to cross on our way up here, he found a small carriage overturned just beyond the bridge and a horse on its side with an older man trying to get it up. It was the neighbor that lives to the left of the fork. The horse was threshing around and it was difficult to get the horse back up, but they managed it. The carriage was damaged and the horse had a cut on its leg, so Hunter went with the neighbor and wrapped it and told the neighbor to let him know if he needed him again."

"So," she continued after a slight pause, "he did his good deed for the day. It sounded like a dangerous job to get the horse untangled and up on his feet."

I had a rather good imagination and could just picture Hunter and this man at this difficult task.

"Hunter is not afraid to tackle threshing horses, but he is a coward with women," I said, partly in jest, partly in earnest because I was wishing he would want to court me.

Mindy began to laugh over my remark but stopped when she looked over my shoulder.

"Uh oh."

From the look on her face, I feared I had been overheard. I turned also. Just behind me, standing near a group of men talking, stood Hunter, his sober eyes fixed on me. From his expression it was clear that he had heard what I said. I groaned out loud and put my head nearly down on my lap. I was mortified. Mindy chuckled quietly. Why had I said it? Whatever did he think? What a way to start this weekend!

I felt somehow exposed sitting there with his eyes on me. I was embarrassed and felt I had to get out of his sight for a few moments. I sat there, very uncomfortable, not knowing what was going on behind me and finally, I just got up and headed for the hall. I had to get out of there. Once in the entry room, I grabbed my coat and went out the front door. It was snowing lightly but I could see a moon trying to shine through. There was a lantern at the steps to the front door, but other than that, there was just the reflection of the lights from within shining dimly on the porch floor. I walked to the far end of the porch and just stood there a moment. I had had many and varied experiences with Hunter. This was something that I would not have wanted him to hear. He did not trust women. Maybe he had a good reason and it was his own business. And I called him a coward. Just in jest, but in truth, there was a part of me that resented the fact that he seemed to have given up on women just because of the one bad experience. I took a deep breath. Maybe he did not really hear what I said, just knew we were talking about him. I could not stay out here long, but I dreaded going back in. I did not want to see the disappointment in Hunter's eyes, knowing what

I had foolishly said. I was wishing Mindy would follow me out of the room and now when I heard the door, I was relieved. Without turning around I spoke.

"Oh, Mindy, I don't think I can go back in there. I am so embarrassed."

Curious why I got no response, I turned and caught my breath. It was not Mindy. It was Hunter himself walking slowly across the porch to me. I just held my breath as I watched him come, grateful that there was so little light. When he came close to the window where light filtered out onto the deck, I saw his face. The look on his face made me take a step back, but I was now against the rail.

Finally he stood right in front of me and just looked at me in silence as my face heated up.

"So I am a coward with women?" he asked softly, his intense blue eyes so very close to mine.

I swallowed. "I did not really mean..."

"I think you did mean it."

Was he angry? I could not tell. He seemed very sober, but I had never seen this expression on his face.

"I am sorry, I should not..."

I stopped when Hunter placed his hands on my shoulders. He just looked at me and then he slid his hands up on either side of my face. I almost forgot to breathe. And then he gently tilted my face back. My mouth went dry. His face was just inches from mine.

"In order that you never have cause to call me a coward with women again..."

I felt his breath on my face. My heart began beating furiously. He lowered his head ever so slowly until his lips touched mine, and then to my amazement, Hunter kissed me. Not a peck on the cheek. He gave me a light but lingering kiss on my lips. My world swirled. When he pulled back, his hands still on either side of my face, he looked deeply into my eyes for just a moment. His own face reflected a look of—what was it—surprise? When he let go of me, I staggered a bit.

My legs had turned to pure water. Not even pudding. Just pure water. I very nearly became a puddle on the porch floor as I leaned back for support against the wooden railing. Seeing my unsteadiness, Hunter put out a hand to steady me and then, with a very satisfied expression, he turned and without a word, slowly walked away from me. Even at the door, he did not look back.

It must have been very, very cold outside on that mountain but I was not aware of it. I made no move. I just stared at the door, not really believing what had just happened. Dr. Hunter Renwick had kissed me. He kissed me! I don't know how long I stood there. Time stood still.

And then the door opened and Mindy stuck her head out the door, trying in the dim light to see if I was there. Finally she saw me.

"Amber, come on in. The bell rang again. We are suppose to gather at the hearth. Don't worry about Hunter. He is laughing and talking to Julie."

Then she was gone.

I had to get out of the daze I was in. I finally walked across the dim porch, wondering how I would face Hunter. Finally, I opened the door and entering, hung my coat and walked into the room. I felt like everyone must know what had happened to me. But there was laughing and talking all around me and I had to assume no one had even missed me. Except Mindy. I now walked up to her.

"You look red from the cold. Don't worry about Hunter, he probably did not really hear what you said."

I did not reply, but I could have assured her that he very definitely had heard what I said.

"You look...funny," said Mindy when I made no reply.

"I feel funny," I replied.

CHAPTER 25

"If possible," said the pastor as the group took seats around the fire, "try to sit next to someone you do not know very well."

I breathed a sigh of relief. I knew Hunter too good for him to sit next to me. I sat next to Julie who was sitting on a sofa and Pastor Dennis sat on the other side of me. As I sat down, Mr. Conrad walked past.

"Good evening, Mr. Conrad," I said. "Thanks again for your good deed."

I thought he looked a bit clueless and I was a bit embarrassed. Did he think I was flirting with him? I just felt since he had rescued me in the ice storm that I should somehow acknowledge him. He simply smiled and took his seat. I must say I found it a bit strange because he had been so friendly that evening. As I had observed him chatting with Hunter, I felt they must have known each other before this meeting. I did not look around the circle but it was a bit difficult for me that I could not look easily at Pastor Dennis because he was next to me. I suddenly realized that it was very easy for Hunter to observe me for the same reason.

"We are going to play a game now that my wife made up," said the pastor. "It is just a means of getting acquainted and after I explain it to you, I'll give you a few minutes to think about it. The name of the game is 'What Do I Have That You Don't Have?' We will go around the circle and Amber will be first. She will think of something that she has that she knows the rest of us do not have and we will ask questions. Try to ask questions that will narrow it down quickly. And when we get close to it, and do not quite get it, then, Amber, just tell us. Understood? Think it over and then we'll just go around the circle. I am hoping it gives us opportunity to get to know something more about each other. And since you are all new to Gloria and me, it will help us the most."

He gave us a few minutes to think about it. I was first and I had to think fast. Murf. No one had a Murf.

And then the pastor told us to go ahead and the questions began.

"Is it something old?" asked Julie.

"No."

"Is it something you treasure?" asked Wynn.

I hesitated. "Yes."

"Is it alive?" asked the pastor.

"Yes."

"Murf?" asked Ray.

"It is."

"Okay, it probably was not quite fair having a brother here," said the pastor, "but tell us about the animal named Murf."

"I have a kitten named Murf who thinks legs are the same as tree trunks and climbs them."

"Ouch," said the pastor as the others laughed. "How old is the kitten?"

"Oh, four or five months old. I'm not sure when he was born." I automatically looked at Hunter and quickly looked away again.

"I might need a cat," said the pastor's wife. "Where did you get it?"

Why on earth did I use Murf as my thing I had that no one else had? I had not thought this far.

I hesitated just a second.

"A veterinarian gave it to me."

I did not look at Hunter. I think it would have passed, but Ray spoke up.

"Who is sitting right here."

"Oh!" said the pastor. "So Hunter gave you the kitten?"

"Yes," I said, feeling I had made another mistake by not saying so myself. Now I did not want to say he gave it as a birthday gift. My face felt hot.

"He knew I had lost my other cat."

"That is a very kind veterinarian," said Dennis. "I am guessing him to be a friend of your family."

"He is," I said, glancing again at Hunter who was observing me with a slightly amused expression. Actually, he looked like the cat that ate the canary. I breathed a sigh of relief when the next question went to Julie who sat next to me.

"Is it a thing or something alive?"

She hesitated. "I am not sure how to answer that."

"Was it ever alive?"

"Yes."

"A pet?"

"No."

"A person?"

"Yes."

"Yikes," said Charlie. "This is sounding creepy. She did not know how to answer when we asked if it was alive."

We laughed and wondered ourselves about it.

"A relative?"

"Yes and that is as close as you will get. I have a famous relative that you do not have."

"Oh? George Washington?" asked Pastor Dennis.

"No, Ethan Allen. He is a distant cousin of mine, I am told."

"Do you know how distant?"

"He was born in 1738 and, as we all learned in school, early in the Revolutionary War he captured Fort Ticonderoga."

"Distant," said the pastor and we laughed.

"Mindy, what do you have that no one else has?"

"Guess."

"Is it alive?"

"No."

"Doughnuts," I said off the top of my head.

"Oh, that was too easy. Actually, I was thinking I have lots of sweets to chose from."

"Sweets? A candy store?" asked the pastor.

"My parents own a bakery."

"Wonderful. I hope the bakery is in Steeplechase."

"It is."

"I look forward to buying from you."

After some conversation it moved on to the next person.

"Ready Charlie?" He nodded.

"Is it alive?" asked Tim.

"Yes."

Something alive always made it easier to guess as it was normally a pet. In Charlie's case, it turned out to be a talking parrot.

"What is his name?"

"It is a she and her name is Feedbag."

"Feedbag? Is that the best name you could find?" asked Ray.

"Her name was Chirp, but it became Feedbag because she seems to have a love affair with feedbags."

"Please tell us the feedbag story," said the pastor. "I am sure there is one."

"Feedbag knows where my mother has a stack of feedbags folded in a stack and when I let her out of her cage, she goes and sits on them, cuddles a bit on them and then one by one she shakes them out. When finished she pays her tax where they once stood neatly piled."

We shouted laughing.

"And who cleans up?" asked Faye.

"My mom makes me do the clean up."

"Time to move on," said the pastor, after more laughter. "It is time to question Hunter."

I finally had to look at him. I made myself small in my seat, (as if I really could) and looked in his direction. He was looking at the pastor, but me being next to the pastor, it felt like he was looking at me and I was very uncomfortable.

"Is it a pet?" asked Julie

"No." But he hesitated just a bit.

"Is it something you can carry around?" asked Wynn

"Impossible."

"Has anyone here ever seen it?" asked Cynthia who knew that some of us were acquainted.

"Yes." Hunter was not looking at me. I could relax.

"Does it have something to do with your occupation?"

"It does."

"An animal cemetery!" said Ray.

"Right."

"Ah! Yes, as a veterinarian, you would have one," said the pastor. "Who do you have in it?"

"A few dogs and cats and one pony."

"Do they have names?"

"Yes, I believe the dogs were Scrap, Cannon and Sam. The cats were Tootles and Midnight. The pony was Ginger." Hunter hesitated just a moment. "There was only one burial since I am there and that was Muggins." Hunter's eyes met mine and I looked away.

"Muggins was Amber's nasty tom cat," said Ray.

The pastor looked at me.

"He was a wonderful cat," I said, laughing. "Ray just doesn't understand cats."

Pastor Dennis laughed. "I am learning that it gets a bit more interesting having siblings here and close friends. They add to the story."

"Sylvia, how about you? Ready?"

She looked startled. "Please, I need more time. Could I be last?"

"You may."

"Wynn, what do you have that we don't?"

"Start guessing."

"Is it alive?"

"Very. Actually more than one."

"A pet?"

"No."

"A girlfriend?" asked Dennis. "Oh wait. I'll take that question back since you said whatever it is, it is more than one." We laughed.

"A relative?"

"Yes. A group of relatives that I have formed into a cousins orchestra of which I am in charge."

"Really? Tell us about it."

"I come from a musical family. My father plays a few instruments as do I. I have only one sibling, a sister who plays piano and flute. My mother plays piano as well. But it is seven cousins and I that get together weekly for the fun of it. And when asked, we give informal concerts."

"Sounds great and I hope to hear you play later this evening. Ray is on next. Let's question him."

"Is it alive?"

"Yes."

"A pet?"

"No."

"Four-legged or two?" asked Charlie.

"Two."

"Your sister?" asked Tim with a grin.

"Yes."

"The one that is here?"

"Yes."

"Ray." I said it in a warning tone and there was laughter.

"What is special about her?" asked Pastor Dennis. "Sorry, Amber, there is a lot that is special about you, but for the sake of the game... she got stitched up by a vet rather than my doctor father."

There was incredulous laughter.

"That sounds a bit unusual," said Dennis, looking at me for confirmation.

"Well, I wasn't there, but she was probably so violent that Papa sent her to an animal doctor, hoping he could handle her."

There were hoots of laughter. And questioning looks by Julie.

"That is not true at all!" I said. "You were not even home at the time."

More laughter.

"What was not true?" the pastor asked me. "No, this is your brother's story. Ray, tell us the real story now."

"Well, it seems she was in the wrong place at the wrong time and got cut up rather badly with broken glass."

"Is the story true so far, Amber?" asked Dennis.

I nodded, but I was tense as I watched my brother.

"But Amber made such a scene that Papa could not control her so he sent her to the vet."

"Not true at all!" I nearly shouted, my face red, wondering just where this was going.

"We'll give you one more chance, Ray," said Dennis, laughing hard. "I want to hear the true story. I have a feeling it is good enough without the embellishments."

"Papa had to go help a woman who was in labor and so he gave the animal doctor the job while he went to deliver a baby."

"And your sister was sent to the vet?"

"He was there already. I think he brought her home."

Dennis looked very confused and looked at me.

"The vet really sewed you up? Wait, was it Hunter who did it?" He turned to look at Hunter who silently raised a finger, indicating he had indeed given me stitches.

"Wow! Her father has great faith in you," said Dennis.

"More than his daughter," said Hunter. There was more laughter.

"I think we need more details, Ray."

"Unfortunately, I was not home. Otherwise, maybe I would have been allowed to stitch her up. That would have given me much joy. Unfortunately, I was away for some medical training."

"So you are also a doctor."

"In the process."

"All doctors are still learning. But I would like to know more about a veterinarian giving Amber stitches." He looked at Hunter.

"I might add that I am also the son of a doctor," said Hunter, "and before I decided to be a veterinarian, I helped my father. Amber was not the first human I stitched up."

"So her father actually gave you the job?"

"I saw Amber walking home and it was obvious that she had been badly hurt. I helped her get home and since I was there and Dr. McDurfee had just been called out to a woman in labor, yes, he gave me the job."

"It makes a good story," said Charlie. "Wow! Animal doctor sews up young woman. Was she really hard to handle?"

Hunter looked at me. I was trying my best to keep from shouting some threat to him, but realized that would only make the others think I really was violent. So I gave him a threatening look and he got the message.

"For the sake of my own well-being, I shall remain silent. I'll just say she was a challenge."

Once more laughter broke out, but I was nearly in a sweat and my face was hot. If the group only knew, they had not heard the half of the story.

"It is a humdinger of a story," said Ray.

"Okay, okay," said Dennis. "Maybe someday we will hear the whole story. How about it, Amber? You will tell the truth and not make it up."

"You will never hear the story from me."

I had never known if Ray knew the whole story, but I was beginning to think he knew about the brandy. I glanced once more at Hunter and was sorry. He was grinning like the Cheshire cat.

"Okay, Faye is next. Is it a person?"

"No."

"An animal?" asked Charlie.

"No."

"Is it in your house?"

"Yes."

"Is it something you treasure?" I asked.

"Yes."

"Is it something you made?"

"Yes. In fact it is a hope chest full of my crocheted items, embroidered pillowcases, and knitted things and quilts. I hope I have not done it all in vain."

We laughed at her honesty. She surprised me. She was so quiet that I thought she was shy. But I think she was just quiet. She was not the prettiest girl in the room, but I had no doubt she would make someone an energetic wife. She told us about her love of handwork and showed us the sweater she was in the process of knitting as we sat together.

"Tim, what do you have that we do not?" asked the pastor.

"Guess," said Tim.

"A lot of wool," said Hunter.

Tim laughed. "I do, but that is not what I was thinking of."

"So why do you have a lot of wool?" asked the pastor.

"I have sheep."

"Aha! We have a shepherd among us. I would like to visit you."

"You are welcome."

So Tim Conrad was a sheep farmer. I remembered now, seeing him get his mail when I drove past with Sidney. Sidney had thought he was a pastor. I had not realized it was the same man. But did he go back up to Pipers Hill that night in the sleet and ice? It did not make sense.

"So we must keep guessing," said Dennis.

"Is it alive?"

"Yes."

"A pet?"

"No."

"A person?"

"Yes."

"Ah, a twin brother," said Hunter.

"Right."

"Something tells me that Hunter and Tim know each other already," said Dennis.

They both nodded and I looked at Tim with big eyes. Was he Hunter's friend from Pipers Hill? And if he was, did Hunter know about our meeting in Flynn Falls? Tim happened to look at me and seeing my intense gaze, locked eyes just a moment. I had to think this through, but the game was going on.

"Oh, tell us about your twin. Are you identical?"

"Yes. He is a minister and has a church on the other side of Flynn Falls."

"So you both have flocks."

"Yes," said Tim, "but mine is four-legged and his is two."

There was general laughter.

A light suddenly went on in my brain.

"Wait," I said, looking at Tim. "Did you rescue me in the ice storm in Flynn Falls in November?"

"Not that I remember. And I am sure I would remember," he said now smiling.

"I wondered why you acted like you did not know me this evening."

"That would have been my brother Tom," said Tim.

"Mystery solved," I said, shaking my head, "but you are certainly identical!"

"It happens all the time," said Tim. "It gets confusing to people who only know one of us." He grinned. "Sometimes I'm not even sure who is who."

"Sylvia, I think we are back to you," said the pastor as we laughed with Tim.

I saw her take a deep breath, then look down at her folded hands in her lap. There was no laughter in her eyes.

"Pastor Dennis, if I may, I would just like to tell you what I have, rather than have you guess."

There was something in her manner that the pastor immediately gave her permission.

"What I have that none of you have, is a husband in heaven."

Sylvia paused and everything got very quiet in the room. One heard only the crackling of the fire in the hearth.

"I am ashamed to say when I heard what we were to share, I wanted to run. I automatically think first not of what I have, but what I had and lost." Sylvia paused and took another deep breath.

"Nine months after my wedding, I lost my beloved husband." She fought for control as we waited. "I knew before we got married that Phil had a weak heart, and would not live a normal life, but we were in love and married anyway. We thought we would have a few years at least. But that was not to be. I do not regret our marriage. It was wonderful and I thank God that Phil did not have to suffer. He went suddenly." She stopped once more to get control. "But this evening I want to say my broken heart is healing, and thanks to God and my church family, life is looking brighter again to me. I am now housekeeper for Tim and he is good to me. I think he must see me as one of his wounded sheep. At any rate, I am beginning to feel alive again and I am glad Tim talked me into coming and I sincerely wish for all of you long, happy years with those you love most."

All was quiet for a few moments after Sylvia spoke. I blinked back tears and I heard someone blow their nose.

"Thank you, Sylvia. That is a good note to close this part of our evening. Thank you so much for sharing that with us. Thank you Tim for encouraging her to come. This is the way the church works. We pull together through the hard places of life. God never meant for us to do it alone. God bless you Sylvia for being vulnerable and sharing openly with us. God allowed you to go through the fire, but He is making you even now a blessing to others through your experience."

"And now," said Dennis, "we have musicians with us. We invited all with instruments to bring them. If you brought one, now is the time to get it. I hope you will all join in singing Christmas carols."

Faye and Julie left the room and came back with flutes. Wynn brought a violin. We stood in a circle in front of the fire with Wynn, Faye and Julie accompanying us. The next hour was spent in singing the familiar carols "Joy to the World," "Hark the Herald Angels Sing," "Brightest and Best," and "Silent Night." As the evening drew to a close, Pastor Dennis suggested the song "O Holy Night."

"My wife has a beautiful voice and I would like her to sing the verses solo and we will join with her in the chorus." He then looked at the instrumentalists. "Can you accompany her?"

"We will try."

I got chills as the song was sung. It was a holy moment for me and I think the others felt it also.

As we sang I looked around at those gathered. Both Ray and Charlie were serious for a change. Sylvia had to stop singing and wipe her eyes. The pastor had his eyes shut for a while as he sang and Faye looked around in wonder as if she expected to see angels. My eyes strayed to Hunter and Tim. I heard their good voices blending in and I blinked back my own tears in this special moment.

By the time we were done singing it was after eleven and the Coopers were putting doughnuts and hot chocolate on the table for us to serve ourselves. We were now a tired and subdued group of people. The evening had left its mark on us. There were quiet conversations as we enjoyed the doughnuts and hot chocolate. Just before heading for bed, Pastor Dennis suggested we join hands as he prayed with us.

"Heavenly Father," he prayed softly as the fire burned low in the hearth, "thank You for those moments when we feel Your spirit among us. Thank You for this group gathered here around the fire. Continue to touch our hearts with Your love and may we in turn, offer Your love to those we meet. Now we give ourselves into Your safe keeping for the night. Amen."

"Amen," came the soft response of our circle.

We found our way to our rooms then. The girls' room had four bunk beds in it and that left one person to sleep on the upper bunk. Having never slept on the top bunk, Faye volunteered to be the person up top. There was also a small washroom for the ladies and one for the men. The additions to the original building, I was discovering, were a bit confusing and the whole place was a rambling mix of rooms and narrow hallways so that one could easily take a wrong turn. There was a lot of laughter as we made our way to and from the bedroom to the washroom. Once in the room, Julie came up to me.

"Is Hunter courting you?"

"Hunter? No, we are just friends," I stammered, wondering if she saw him kiss me.

"Do you know, is he courting anyone?"

"Not that I know of."

She seemed relieved. Julie was beautiful and a talented flute player. And a flirt. I found she made me a bit uneasy. Men, I felt, were easily lured by flirts.

Finally everyone except me was in bed. I was just ready to blow out my candle and climb into the bunk under Faye when she sat up in bed nearly hitting her head on the ceiling.

"Oh, I forgot to bring my flute back. I must go get it."

"Where is it?" I asked.

"Close to the big fireplace in the gathering room."

"Stay there, I'll get it."

"You sure?"

"It won't take a minute and you won't have to climb down again."

I slipped my housecoat and slippers back on and took my candle and went out into the passage.

All was surprisingly quiet as I made my way down the narrow, dim hall. There was only the light of my candle and being alone now everything seemed suddenly strange and I was not sure of my way. Somewhere, I heard the Coopers quietly talking. I made my way cautiously around a corner and came to a cross hallway. I made a right and hoped it would take me where I was headed. I was relieved to get to the gathering room and was glad for the light of the fire. Someone had built it up for the night and we would be glad for any heat that found its way back to our cold sleeping quarters.

I made my way to the hearth and found the flute. All was well. Now I just hoped I would make the right turns on my return to our room.

As I made my way back through the narrow passageway, I was startled by footsteps in an adjoining hall. I nearly dropped the flute, which I managed to keep in my hand, but my sudden movement to save the flute caused the candle to extinguish.

"Oh help!" I said out loud.

I was now standing in pitch darkness and I had no idea anymore where I was. And then I heard footsteps behind me and turning, saw only a candle coming in my direction. I waited, wondering if I should cough so the person would not be scared to find me. When the person got to me, I saw it was Hunter with a very surprised look on his face. I was very much aware of my housecoat and was only dimly aware that he too was dressed in a bathrobe. He held his candle up to better see my face.

I was so shocked to see him that I was, for the moment, dumbstruck.

"Were you looking for me?" he asked, trying to hide a grin and I knew he was remembering the kiss.

"Of course not!" I said, probably too quickly at his insinuation. I was glad for the darkness so he could not see my red face. "But my candle went out."

He seemed in no hurry. "May I ask what you are doing sneaking around these dark, narrow alleys at this time of the night?"

"I could ask the same of you."

"I am asking you."

"Faye forgot her flute and I offered to get it for her."

He was amused, I could tell.

"Why is it Amber, that you continually get yourself in trouble?"

"When do I get in trouble?"

"How about in Flynn Falls?"

I looked at him a moment. "You do not even know the details."

"It is enough with you going out in the bad weather and needing to rescued."

"Would you please light my candle?"

He looked at me and opened his mouth to say something, thought better of it, and then proceeded to light my candle.

"Are you sure you know the way back to your room now?"

"Of course I do." And with no further ado, I turned to leave him. However, for a split second, I was confused. The place where we were standing was a juncture of two narrow, dark halls. I could not think with Hunter looking at me. Rather than let him think I did not know my way, I just started walking down the one I was facing.

"Amber!"

I stopped but did not turn around.

"Do you really want to sleep with the men? That is where you are headed."

"Oh!" I said in disgust. "I can't think with you watching me."

"You really are not safe wandering around here alone. You should carry a compass." I heard the amusement in his voice.

I turned to go to the other hallway, glad for the lack of bright lights.

"Amber."

I stopped but did not turn around.

"Sweet dreams." I could hear the smile in his voice.

I did not answer. I walked away from him, slowly now and carefully because I did remember there was a step up or down before I got to the door. As I walked, I heard Hunter's voice drifting down what he named an alley behind me.

"And please don't walk in on the Coopers or the Cenders or they will be sending you home first thing tomorrow morning."

I found my way back to the room with no further problems and was glad to close the door behind me but I could not hide my smile and was glad the room was dark.

"Did you find my flute?" whispered Faye from the top bunk.

"I did."

"Thank you. I don't know if I could have found my way."

"Where were you so long?" Mindy whispered from another bed.

"I got lost."

"That sounds exciting. How did you find your way back?"

"Someone lit my candle."

"I'm missing something."

"Goodnight, Mindy."

Sometime I would tell her more, but this was neither the time nor the place. In fact, I needed to go over the entire evening in my head before I slept.

CHAPTER 26

I woke to the smell of bacon frying. I was instantly hungry. This cold mountain air seemed to make the food we consumed dissolve shortly after eating. I heard some movement in the other beds and someone yawned sleepily. We had one window in our room but it was frosted shut. I saw no sunshine, but this was December. What else could we expect? I enjoyed the dark of winter although some people found it difficult with so little sun. It was cold in the room and I did not want to leave my warm bed. My nose felt a bit frozen. I had two blankets and a quilt on my bed and looking around the room saw there was a quilt on each bed. It looked nice. I heard someone's feet hit the floor. It was Sylvia.

"Good morning, Sylvia," I whispered as I yawned.

"Morning to you, too. I think I'll head for the washroom."

"I am coming with you."

"Burr, it is cold in here," said Faye, jumping down from her perch.

"That is why I'm getting out of here as fast as I can to warm up in the gathering room. Isn't that fireplace gigantic? A work of art."

"Oh, do I have to get up?" asked Julie, opening one eye.

"If you want breakfast," I answered.

"Are you up already?" asked Mindy, who resembled a hibernating bear under her quilt and blankets.

"I am and you better get out, too. Do you smell that bacon? See you later."

Sylvia and I headed up the hall. It was a bit easier to find our way with more light coming in the windows. A half hour later we were all hugging the hearth, enjoying the heat.

When the breakfast bell rang, I discovered our seats were changed. Now I sat pretty much in the middle of the table, across from Julie and with Tim and Ray on either side of me.

"Why did they change the name tags?" complained Julie who was looking sadly at Hunter who now sat at the other end of the table and was talking to Charlie.

I was hoping Ray would talk to Julie, but he was talking to Sylvia who sat on the other side of him. After the bacon, sausages and pancakes were passed along with maple syrup from the Coopers' own trees, we got down to eating and chatting. I was hoping to get to know Tim a bit better. His sheep farm sounded interesting. And if he was like his twin, he would have a kind heart. However, Julie chose to talk to Tim, so I mostly listened as I drank my coffee and enjoyed my maple syrup saturated pancakes.

By nine o'clock we were dressed for a sleigh ride to Lake Champlain. A few more inches of snow had fallen during the night and the weather, although cloudy, was good. Pastor Dennis informed us that we had to walk down the lane to the main entrance from the road and that a large sleigh with a team of four horses would meet us there. So we trouped down the snowy, twisting road, across the bridge and finally, perhaps ten or fifteen minutes later arrived where we found the team of four horses, their breaths making fog around their heads and a sleigh to hold us all. We simply piled in the sleigh. I had my eye on Hunter but Julie was hanging close to him. I simply followed Mindy into the sleigh and found myself sitting next to Tim again. There were blankets to throw over us and I was more than glad for the scarf around my neck. Once the horses began moving and the bells started jingling, Tim turned to me.

"Amber, I am pleased to get to know you. My friend Hunter has talked of you—and your family—numerous times, so I feel like I know you a bit."

"Oh dear, I would rather not know what Hunter may have told you."

Tim had a deep chuckle. "You need have no fear. And as to the partial story regarding your stitches that we heard last evening, he did not tell me anything more than what we heard last evening, although, from something he said, I gathered there was more to the story. I would love to hear it."

"Not from me. I am totally embarrassed yet. Tell me about your sheep," I said, wanting to get him off the subject. "I think you must have a rather interesting life."

"I do. I love my work. I love caring for the sheep, along with my sheep dog, Wools, who does most of the work for me. And I love springtime when my flock grows and I generally need to have Hunter stop by."

As Tim talked about his sheep, I took a good look at the man. He was a real gentleman and I wondered why he had never married. He was not one to push himself forward in a group but he was a good conversationalist and was enthused about his sheep. He was slightly taller than Hunter and was a bit heavier. He looked strong, and surely he had to be strong to grab those sheep to sheer them. His hairline was receding a bit, but he had a thick, dark beard. It was not a long beard, but rather one that hugged his face and was was nicely trimmed. I would guess him to be in his early thirties.

"Do you lose lambs sometimes?"

"If you mean at birth, yes, it happens. But most of them are saved. Once in a while a mother rejects a lamb and then I need to feed it with a bottle. Sylvia gets stuck with that sometimes but loves doing it."

I looked around for Sylvia and found her talking to Ray. It seemed to me that they were together a lot this weekend.

"I would love to feed a lamb sometime," I said.

"Come up to visit in the spring. You may have your chance."

"How many lambs do you expect this spring?"

"Perhaps twenty. Maybe more if there are twins."

"I love to see the young lambs out in the field. I've seen them jump straight up with all four legs as if they are on springs. It looks so funny."

Tim laughed. "They jump for the sheer joy of living. I get many a chuckle out of them. And if I were a preacher, I think I could preach a few sermons from them, too."

"For instance?"

"People think sheep are dumb. They are not dumb. We could learn from them. Sheep follow the shepherd. Of course there is always the stray lamb who has to get lost before he learns to follow—just like people."

"And you go after the one that is lost?"

"Yes," Tim said with a smile. "Just like the Good Shepherd always goes after the one who is lost."

We talked of other things then and the time flew by and before I knew it, the horses were turning in the lane to Shelburne Farms, which was the Webb Estate on Lake Champlain. It seemed that the Coopers were friends of the Webb family and as a result we were invited to tour the place. We drove around the huge barn complex first. It was a work of art. There was a huge U-shaped building and a huge barnyard. Then we drove up to the sprawling red brick mansion, which seemed to be built on a curve. It was breathtaking with the gray sky background and the snow-covered roofs and turrets. All the buildings were spacious and beautiful and the 1,400 acres was impressive in snow even without the stunning flower beds and green lawns that I knew they had in the summertime.

The tour on the inside was exciting. I loved big houses and all that a mansion like this had to offer. I was especially intrigued by the big library and was a bit dismayed when I pulled a book off the shelf and discovered the pages were not even cut. Did they not read? What was the sense in having books if the pages were not yet cut? I almost felt sorry for the unread books!

We walked through the arched doorways and rooms rich in furnishings. There were oil lamps burning, but there was some light coming in the many windows facing Lake Champlain. We spent probably two hours there and then we were back in the sleigh and drove to the village of Shelburne where we stopped for lunch.

The Inn of Storms was a relatively small inn, but its smallness only added to the cozy atmosphere. We hung our coats on pegs by the door, slipped out of boots and were led to a room off to the side with its own fire. As we filed into the room, I suddenly found Hunter beside me and to my delight he sat next to me at the table. However, Julie, who never really let him out of her sight promptly sat across from us and chattered with him nearly the whole meal. Just once his arm brushed mine and I had to keep myself from leaning toward him for it to happen again. I was pleased to see Charlie and Faye having a good time as they ate their soup and rye bread, and was happy when Gloria and Dennis also sat close by and I could talk to them.

After leaving the inn, we headed back to the camp. The sky looked like snow and the air felt damp and chilly. After trudging back up the snowy lane, we went inside to collect our ice skates and in twenty minutes or so, we had walked out beyond the stable on a path that led to a frozen, shallow pond where we could skate. The sky was spitting snow flurries by the time we got there but it did not take long until we were skating over the ice. It was great fun. The men gathered some sticks and wood for a fire and it was soon blazing. Charlie turned out to be a great skater and some of the time we merely watched his antics on the ice. It was fascinating. I skated with all the men except Hunter. But whenever I saw him, he seemed to be skating with someone else. I wanted badly to skate with him but somehow we barely saw each other on the ice. As the hour drew to an end, I went to the fire and began removing my skates. Just as I was about to remove the second skate, Hunter skated up to me, knelt down, refastened the skate I had removed and then stood. Holding out his hand, he bowed slightly.

"May I have this dance?" He said it with just a hint of a smile and I was thrilled and I am sure he knew it by my own smile.

"You may."

He helped me to stand up and off we skated, hand in hand. It had been a strange weekend. When it had barely begun, I had gotten a kiss from this man. Since then we had had little interaction. Now, with my hand in his, I wanted to skate forever. Hunter did not talk for the first minute or so. We simply skated, and I was happy to do just that. The hour was nearly up and most of the group was gathered around the bonfire. We almost had the ice to ourselves.

"Have you enjoyed the weekend?" he finally asked.

"I did. I am glad I came. And I like Dennis and Gloria."

"So do I."

We talked a bit about the group and then I saw that they were throwing snow on the fire, and it seemed the others had already left the ice. I think Hunter saw it too. Rather than skating back, he turned so that we skated away from the fire. Then he suddenly came to a stop, though he kept my hand in his. He looked down at me and spoke softly.

"Are you needing an apology from me?"

I just looked at him a moment. There was just a glint of amusement in his eyes but at the same time I felt he was serious about asking. I knew to what it referred.

"Are you repenting?" I asked, trying to stifle my own smile.

He hesitated just a moment, watching me closely, then seeing my attempt to hide a smile, he grinned.

"No."

"Then I guess there is no sense in apologizing."

"Are you sorry?"

"For what?"

"You know what!"

I looked into those blue eyes and could not keep the smile off my face.

"No."

He just looked at me a moment and I was the one to look away first. But I would have loved to have known what he was thinking.

Then we skated back to the group. Most were starting to walk back up the trail. I could see Julie watching as Hunter helped me with my skates, and then she slowly followed the others, leaving Hunter and me to bring up the rear.

We were still about ten minutes from the house when I heard a yelp up ahead of us. Catching up to the others, we found Sylvia on her back in the snow. It seems she had slipped and fell on a snow-covered rock and hurt her ankle.

"It will be all right, just let me wait a minute," she said.

I saw Ray was there, kneeling in the snow by her side and feeling her ankle. The others kept going except for Tim who hung back.

"How can I help?" he asked. "Can you walk?"

"Let me try," she said.

But it hurt too much.

"Here," said Tim, giving his skates to Hunter to carry. "Let Ray and me support you and maybe it will work. If not, I can carry you."

Hunter and I watched as the men helped her up and then each took an arm so that she did not have to put much weight on her foot. And it worked. Once back at the house we shed our heavy clothes and before we knew it, Dennis was ringing the supper bell.

"Supper will be in about an hour, but we still have our gift exchange. So bring your gifts and gather round the fire. You can help yourself to a cup of hot chocolate or coffee and bring it with you."

Thus we found ourselves back in the circle, glad for the warmth of the fireplace. We collected our gifts and and gave them to Dennis who was placing them in two piles. Then a hat was passed around to the girls with numbered slips of paper in it. Then the same was done to the men.

"Now," said Dennis, "who of the girls has number one?"

"I do," said Mindy.

"There is a package up on the girls' pile with a one on it. Please come up, unwrap it and show it to us. If there is no name attached, guess who gave it."

Mindy went up and took a small package. Opening it, she found a lovely scented candle. "It says from Wynn. Thank you Wynn."

"You made it?" asked the pastor.

"I did, with some help from an older sister who likes making scented candles."

Number two was Julie. Her gift was from Hunter. She was thrilled. It was fudge fashioned into the face of a cow.

"Did you make the fudge?" asked Gloria.

"I made it at Tim's house with Sylvia's help. She made the cow face."

It looked delicious but Julie did not offer it to anyone. It was her gift from Hunter and she was thrilled.

Sylvia was next and because she could not walk without difficulty, Pastor Dennis brought the gift to her and when she opened it she found a very big bag of English walnuts that was from Charlie who assured her that he had gathered them himself.

After Sylvia came Faye who got the Christmas wreath that Ray made. She was quite pleased and they all laughed at his pill bottle bells.

"Amber, you are the last of the girls, but it looks like the biggest gift is yours. Come get it," said the pastor.

When I felt the package, knowing who it had to be from, I guessed what it might be and I was not disappointed. Tim had wrapped up a sheep skin.

"Oh, I love it," I said. "And Murf will too! Thank you so much!"

Tim's smile lit up his whole face, pleased that I was happy with the sheep skin. "You are welcome."

Then the men were called. Wynn got a fruit cake from Julie. Tim got a throw rug for his carriage from Sylvia. Ray got a braided rug for the floor of his carriage from Faye. Charlie got a knitted scarf from Mindy and Hunter actually got the socks I had knitted.

"Thank you," he said to me as we headed for our last meal at the cabin." I know now from whom to order socks."

"You are welcome," I said, secretly pleased that he had gotten them.

On this evening there were no name tags at our plates and I was so happy when Hunter once more sat next to me, even though Julie was on the other side of him. However, we had barely sat down to supper when there was a knock at the door. Hunter was called from the table but came back again.

"The neighbor man would like me to check his horse before I leave," he said, when Julie asked him who called for him. "It is not an emergency so I will do it right after supper."

They fed us a hearty beef stew and biscuits with apple pie and coffee for dessert. It had been a good weekend. I was sorry it was over.

"By the way," said Hunter to the whole table, "it is now snowing hard and is quite blustery."

This was followed by exclamations and the rest of the meal was eaten quickly in order to arrive home before we could no longer go home.

As soon as Hunter was finished eating he left. And soon afterward the rest of us hurried to our rooms to gather our belongings. Coming back into the gathering room to say good bye to the others, I was informed that Ray had already left with Sylvia. I knew that Mindy was suppose to be taking the train to Burlington to participate in a concert that evening and it ended up that Ray asked Hunter to see me home. In the mix-up of who was going with whom on the way home, I only knew that Julie was put out because she had to leave with Wynn and Charlie before Hunter returned and one by one everyone took their hurried leave. And then it was just the Coopers, the Cenders and me. I was just wondering if I had been forgotten when Hunter came in the door. He looked at me.

"The others are gone?"

"Yes. And Ray said he asked you...." I hated to sound like a beggar. Did he think I had put Ray up to it?

"I said I would see you home," he finished for me. "And we must leave immediately. It is getting bad out there."

Dennis, Gloria and the Coopers were also leaving. The Coopers said they would come back another day to finish cleaning up. All were eager to get off the mountain now and back to their warm homes.

Hunter took my bag, helped me into his carriage, gave me a blanket and took the reins beside me. It was cold and I wanted to lean against him for warmth.

"I am hoping it will be better once we get off the mountain," he said as we started down the hill. The road was almost impossible to see and it was already dark. We proceeded down the narrow lane very carefully and even more cautiously over the bridge and finally out to the main road. For the first ten or fifteen minutes the wind was not bad. But gradually, the gusts came more often and finally there seemed to be no letting up. For a while the Coopers and the Cenders were behind us, and there was no way to know if they had turned off on another road or not, but it seemed we were all alone on the road in this bad storm. It was dangerous. I was scared and Hunter had his eyes on the road and did not talk. When he took a turn I did not think was right, I mentioned it.

"I'm stopping at an inn for the night. This is too dangerous and too far for the horse in this weather. We should be almost there, if I have the right road."

I was relieved. I wondered how the others had made out. But Tim and also Ray had had a good half hour start on us. However, Tim was making a stop at the train station to let Mindy and Faye off.

Finally, I saw the very welcome but dim lights that heralded our arrival at a small country inn. I was greatly relieved. Hunter drove straight into the livery where he gave the horse off to the livery boy. Then he grabbed our bags and we headed to the inn, the snow flying in our faces and making our steps difficult. It was not until we were inside that I worried about us staying here overnight. This felt very strange going into an inn with Hunter. When we stepped inside the blessedly warm inn, I saw with dismay that it seemed full. We were not the only ones needing shelter. The small lounge was filled with people stranded by the storm. It was mostly men but I did see one other couple and there was a group of four teenage boys, probably out on a lark in the snow and got scared and came to the inn. I followed Hunter to the desk. This felt very strange, but I felt I should ask for my own room. I did not hear Hunter's request, but the fat-cheeked man behind the desk was shaking his head.

"We are full up. If you want to sleep in the lounge, you may. We can give you blankets and pillows."

I felt my face go pale. But before I could collect my wits, another person came up to the desk and I was both surprised and happy to see it was Tim.

"Any room?" Tim asked Hunter.

"The lounge. They will supply us with blankets and pillows."

I felt Hunter's eyes on me.

"Is it just the two of you?" asked Tim.

Hunter nodded and Tim gave me a long look. Actually, it felt better to me being with Hunter and Tim than with just Hunter.

"Let's sit down and have some coffee," said Tim. "I'm cold clear through."

"Did you get the girls to the train station?"

"I did. I don't think there will be any problem with them getting to the Burlington station, but my guess is that the concert may be canceled. But maybe not. There may be enough people in the city that will attend."

While Tim and Hunter talked, I looked around the room. Those who had rooms were disappearing from the dining area. I saw only one other woman in the room. She was with her husband but whether or not they had a room, I did not know. My eyes fell on a man alone at a table, drinking. He had a few glasses on the table and I wondered how long he'd been at it. I could not see him well from where I stood, but there was something about him that looked familiar. When I saw him look in my direction, I quickly looked away.

"Who is taking care of the sheep while you are gone?" asked Hunter of Tim.

"Johnny, my hired hand is quite good with the sheep and between him and my dog I have no reason to fear. The sheep are inside. Where is your dog?"

"At the neighbors. The boy has made good friends with Beanbags and he keeps the dog with him when I am gone." Hunter looked at me. "I wonder if Ray made it to Pipers Hill to take Sylvia home? I can't imagine it."

"Maybe she will stay at our house and have my bed tonight," I said. "At least she will have a bed."

"Sorry about this," said Hunter, probably wondering how we would sleep.

Just then the innkeeper's wife came toward our table with blankets.

"Sorry about the lack of rooms," she said. "This does not happen very often but when it does we try to make it as comfortable for you as we can." She looked at me and then at Tim and Hunter.

"Which of you two men is the husband?"

"Neither one of us," said Hunter. "I am a friend of the family and was bringing her home from a church retreat and Tim is a friend to both of us."

"Oh." She looked at me a long moment.

"I wish I could offer you even a big closet, but I can't."

"I am safe with these men," I said. "It is just awkward."

"Come with me a minute," she said.

I rose and went with her into another room.

"You can talk to me here. Are you really safe with them?"

"Yes, and thank you for your concern. The one I came with is a good friend of the family and the other man I know also and the two are good friends. We were all at a church Christmas Retreat."

"I hope you can sleep on the couch. I don't think there are any other women who have no room. As for the outhouse, the men will have to go outside, but if you wish, you can use a commode that I have in the little mudroom here. I keep it for emergencies. If you go in now, I will stay by the door."

"Thank you so much," I said, relieved that one problem was solved.

The mud room was cold, as was the commode, but at least I was out of the wind and snow. When I returned to the room, I saw both Hunter and Tim headed out the door. I hoped they would be back soon because the man drinking at the table evidently had no room either. I gave him a quick glance as I walked by his table and felt the blood drain from my face.

"All alone, Amber?"

I caught my breath and slowly turned. This could not be Jonas. He looked terrible and he had already drunk too much. I could not open my mouth.

"Come join me for a drink," he slurred. "We have the whole night."

He gave me a crooked smile. I walked away from him, shocked beyond words. This was not the Jonas I knew. I ignored him and see-ing three pillows on a heap on the floor, I went over to the pillows, threw one on the couch but when I turned around for the blanket, Jonas had stood up from his chair and was heading for me. I looked around, finding no one else in the room and stood watching him walking to me.

"I'll keep you warm tonight," he said with another wobbly smile.

"Jonas, what is the matter with you? Since when do you drink?"

"Since you quit me," he said. "I just had a few..."

He smelled terrible and I took a step back. He came closer and put a hand on my arm.

"Jonas, leave me alone," I said, looking for Tim and Hunter. I flung off his arm, but when I saw no signs of my rescuers and he made another attempt to put a hand on my arm, I turned my back on him and in desperation, I slid behind the couch.

"Bashful, are you?" laughed Jonas, trying to follow me.

Just then I heard footsteps and both Hunter and Tim came into the room. They took one look at me behind the couch and another at the grinning man.

"Sir?"

It was Hunter who spoke. His voice was cold and threatening. Jonas immediately turned and saw two men advancing on him.

"Jonas?" said Hunter, surprise and revulsion on his face.

"She's my girlfriend," said Jonas, looking from Hunter to Tim.

"I don't think so," said Hunter. "Leave the room."

Tim said nothing but his size and his steady look did wonders. It was almost funny. Neither of the men said another word. They just looked at Jonas. He turned and I saw him grab a blanket and go to the far end of the room as I slid out from behind the couch.

"Tim, help me turn this couch around," said Hunter.

I watched as he carefully moved a small table and then the two men each took an end of the couch and neatly turned it around.

"Now," said Hunter, "there is your bed. We will sleep on the floor close by." He hesitated. "Whatever happened to Jonas?"

"I have no idea. He is a different person and it makes me sick."

I took my bag, a pillow and a blanket. And then I walked behind the couch. After I was there, Hunter pushed the table nearly back to the wall, neatly blocking me in. If I got cold I could put my coat over me, but I had a feeling the men would keep the fire burning.

The innkeeper came into the room and glanced around. There were three additional men now lying on the floor of the room besides Jonas, Hunter and Tim. They would have a hard bed. I felt almost guilty on my soft couch. The innkeeper's wife came in for a last check.

"Hope you can sleep," she said to us all, turning down the gas lamps.

"We are fine," said Tim. "Don't worry about us. We are glad to be indoors."

She went out of the room. I laid down on the couch. I did not look to see where the men slept. This was a night I would never forget. In spite of the scare Jonas gave me, I felt very safe, very protected by Hunter and his friend. But what a strange night.

"Goodnight, Amber," Hunter said just a bit later.

"Goodnight, Amber," added Tim.

"Goodnight to both of you. If any of you snore, I shall throw my pillow at you."

"You'll be sorry to be without your pillow," said Hunter.

Just then, from across the room, I heard a snore. He chuckled.

"I suggest you put your head under your pillow."

The storm abated during the night. We got up early and ate just toast and coffee, we were all eager to get home. I had slept well in spite of being just several feet away from Hunter and Tim and in a room of strangers. I heard numerous snores before I slept and following Hunter's advice, I stuck my head under my pillow and slept.

We got home without incident but Hunter came along in the house to explain our absence to Papa. Papa listened without comment. I could tell he trusted Hunter and he thanked him for using common sense and not trying to get home. Hunter told him that they tried to give me some privacy in a room full of men by turning the couch around, but he did not say anything about Jonas. I would tell Papa about him later. Hunter was invited for a real breakfast and he was easily enticed. While I made scrambled eggs, fried potatoes and bacon, we drank hot coffee that warmed us on the inside. Our breakfast was consumed with gusto to say nothing of many slices of toast. Ray, Papa informed us, had made it home and did not dare try to go to Pipers Hill. So right now, they were still sleeping and Sylvia was in my bed. We let them sleep. Ray would have to take her home when they got up.

Before leaving, Hunter came to me and offered his hand.

"It will be a night to remember," he said watching me closely as he said goodbye.

"A whole weekend to remember," I said.

He smiled and squeezed my hand.

I watched him leave. There was lots to tell Papa about the weekend. But I would not tell him everything.

CHAPTER 27

The following week, our new minister and his wife moved in next door. They were no longer strangers and I was glad to have them as next-door neighbors. The church members helped them move in, but the moving was not bad since most of the furniture had remained in the parsonage, which was owned by the church. I found time to help Gloria set up her kitchen and invited them for lunch. At suppertime I took a casserole over for them.

Just as I was leaving, Pastor Dennis came laughing into the kitchen with a cardboard sign in his hand.

"Look what I found up in the attic. A 'Just Married' sign. Makes me wonder if it was from the wedding of the former minister?"

"If it is, it is in pretty good shape yet," I replied as my brain suddenly gave me ideas of what I could do with the sign. I could put it on Ray's carriage sometime and get back at him for all the teasing I had suffered at his hands.

"May I have it?" I asked.

"You planning a wedding?"

"No. A joke."

"Take it. But tell us who gets teased."

"My brother. Wait," I said suddenly thinking of Hunter. "I'm not sure. Let me think about it."

Dennis disappeared again and Gloria, guessing whom I had in mind, egged me on.

"Put it on Hunter's carriage. He is old enough to get married and he needs a push."

I gave Gloria a quick glance. Did she sense my interest in him? I laughed. I liked the idea.

"I don't know if I have the nerve to do that. Maybe if I get Mindy in on it too. But don't give us away."

I carried the sign home, took it to my room and after supper, decided to take the sign over to show Mindy. I found some newspaper that I taped over it to hide the message from inquisitive eyes and when both Papa and Ray were in the living room, I called to them that I was going over to Mindy's and went out the back door.

It was already dark, cold and a bit windy. I walked hurriedly and once on Main Street, I looked to see if Hunter was by any chance at the inn. I saw no carriage. I was glad to get out of the cold wind and when I got to the door leading to Mindy's apartment, I hurried up the many steps and knocked loudly. She was soon at the door.

"Come in. What are you up to? You seldom come to visit at night."

She looked at the package under my arm and watched as I unwrapped it.

"Just Married? Where did you get that?"

"Pastor Dennis found it in the attic of the parsonage."

"And what are you planning to do with it?" she asked, her eyes sparkling.

"I'm thinking of Hunter."

"Would you dare?"

"If you help me. I never got to tell you what happened after he heard me call him a coward. I need to get back at him."

"Something happened? With Hunter?"

I told her the story of the kiss on the porch during the Christmas Party and she was flabbergasted.

"Well, he certainly deserves this." She paused. "It sounds like he is not quite blind to women in spite of his past."

"But how will we do it? I am counting on your help. Is there any time at night that you see him here in town?"

"Well, you know he often comes to the inn for supper. Come to think of it, I saw him drop some mail in at the post office just a half hour ago."

"Well, he isn't there now. I looked for his carriage and it was not around."

"Did you look behind the inn?"

"Behind the inn? No." My heart started beating rapidly. Maybe we could do this yet tonight!

"Let's go check the back parking lot," said Mindy. She was already at the door.

"Wait, Mindy. Let's take the sign along so we don't have to come back for it if he is there. These steps nearly do me in. Do you have any tape? There are strings attached to the sign, but maybe we need tape also."

"Good idea. Let me get some tape."

While she went for the tape, my heart was pounding. This was scary business. He must never, ever know that I was behind this. Whatever would he think? But I just knew I wanted to play this trick on him. It would also get him back for all the teasing I went through about the brandy. But the problem was to fasten it on his carriage. There was a string fastened to the sign, but that did not mean that I would find a place to connect it.

"And I'm bringing a cloth to wipe it clean, if we need to use the tape," said Mindy. "Do you have string if we can tie it?"

"Yes, the string is still attached."

"We may need a light. It is dark out behind the stores."

Mindy took a lantern and we stepped out into the hall and to the top of the stairs. But now we took the thirty steps down the back way. Once down, we stepped outside and cautiously looked around. All appeared clear. There were a couple carriages behind the stores and we quietly made our way around them. When we got to the inn I saw a couple carriages there also. There was just the dimmest of lights above the livery door that stood against the back part of the parking area. It was quite dark here and I had to go close to see if any carriage belonged to Hunter. Sure enough, there was Ruggles. I could hardly believe my good fortune.

"Hi, Ruggles," I said softly, keeping an eye on the back door of the inn. The horse knew me and whinnied softly.

But time was of the essence. Hunter was already in town for a while. He would be leaving soon. Mindy was overjoyed. We needed the lantern badly, so I told Mindy to stand close enough to me to shine the light on the carriage, but at the same time to watch for any people that might walk by. Then I went to the back of the carriage and Mindy stood in such a way as to conceal me from anyone who might walk by, although the parking lot appeared quite empty and dark.

However, before I had the chance to do anything, we heard the back door of the inn opening and Hunter came hurrying out. I turned and ran toward Mindy. Then we heard a voice.

"Dr. Renwick!"

We stopped and looked between the carriages. A man had come to the door and called Hunter back. We saw him go in and the door closed behind him.

"This is so scary. Do we try it again?" I asked Mindy.

"Quick! He will be in there for at least a minute or so. Let's do it."

We went back, Mindy holding the light as I looked for a place to fasten the string. I was successful, we also cleaned a spot around the sign and taped it also, for good measure. Then we hurried back to the apartment stairs. We had not walked far before we once again heard a door. The inn door. We crept into the shadows and watched as Hunter walked to his carriage, got in and in a very short time was heading out onto North Street and home. Just as he turned north to his house, I could see, by the light of the street lamp, the sign. It looked so funny. I looked at Mindy and we bent over laughing so hard we could barely get our breath.

On my way home, I stopped at the parsonage to inform Gloria

of our success with the sign and got her solemn promise to be quiet about it, no matter if he never found out who did it.

Christmas was just ten days away. We hoped to get the whole family home, but knew that it would be nearly impossible. But we would try. We mailed letters of invitation. We did not need to order a turkey from the butcher because we always were given a twenty-pound turkey by one of Papa's patients. This would be a Christmas without Mama and it would be hard. We needed to all be together, especially for Papa's sake. I would often come into the living room and instead of reading, Papa would be staring off into space. I was sure he was missing Mama and it nearly broke my heart.

I baked cookies and made mincemeat for pies. A pumpkin pie would also be made and hickory nuts were cracked for a cake. I spent my evenings laboriously digging the nutmeat out of the tiny shells but knew I would be glad for them when the cake was baked.

Laura said she was going to her daughter's home for the holiday and would leave by train on Christmas Eve afternoon. I had not seen Hunter since the retreat, except for seeing him ride home with the "Just Married" sign on his carriage, but Ray saw him somewhere and said Hunter was leaving Christmas morning and would just be gone for the day.

A few days before Christmas, Ray told Papa and me at the supper table that someone saw Hunter's carriage with a "Just Married" sign on it. Certainly a joke, he was eager to tease Hunter about it.

I laughed and suddenly did not quite know how to react, but did not say much. Then the very next day, Hunter stopped in. I was in the kitchen and had no reason to go into the living room but I listened with both ears as he and Ray talked.

"Hey, Hunter," I heard Ray say, "what is this about you being married?"

There was a significant pause and I could imagine Hunter looking closely at Ray.

"Where did you hear that?"

"Someone saw you with a 'Just Married' sign on your carriage."

"Who told you?" Hunter was intense and quick with his question.

"A patient of ours. He lives just next to the library. He has a heart problem and does not get out much, but his wife was walking home from visiting the neighbor lady when you went past. She said there was definitely a 'Just Married' sign on the back of your carriage."

"I have no idea how it got there, but if you ever find out who is responsible, I would be much obliged if you would tell me."

"No clues as to who did it?"

"Not really. I was up in Pipers Hill that day and I stopped at the country store. When I came out a few young girls were hanging around and laughing. I did not pay any attention to them but when I got home that night I found the sign hanging on the back of the carriage. My guess it that it was those girls, although I did not recognize any of them."

"You maybe don't know the girls, but they all know you," said Ray.

On hearing that Hunter suspected someone from Pipers Hill, I got bold and walked into the living room.

"What is this about a 'Just Married' sign?" I asked. I could not help but laugh and Hunter saw it.

"Were you up on Pipers Hill on Saturday, Amber?"

"I was not, but that is so funny."

Actually, I felt free to laugh because I was off the hook. Hunter gave me a steady, scrutinizing look.

"It was probably someone wishing to be married to you," said Ray. "Someone who wants to get your attention."

Hunter looked over at me. "If it had been Amber I would make her drive around town with me with the sign on the carriage."

"Don't look at me. I was not in Pipers Hill," I said quickly and left the room before he remembered he stopped at the Carriage Inn for his supper.

CHAPTER 28

The Christmas plans were all in place. Nearly all my siblings were coming. Just Floyd and his wife would be with his in-laws and would try to come to us at a later date. I decorated my cut-out sugar cookies and made molasses candy. I had made little packages for my nieces and nephews, at least those old enough. There was no big gift exchange. Someone had given Ray a small tree and we set it up in the living room, but it needed some decorations. As for the food, it was all either prepared or in the process. My siblings would also bring food.

I woke up on the twenty-fourth of December to the sound of sleet hitting the window. I left my warm bed to look out the window into the early morning light. If I had heard sleet, it was mixed with snow. It was coming down very fine and looked like it would not be stopping any time soon. The gas lamps had tiny icicles hanging from the lamp shade. My spirits plummeted. This did not look promising for family guests. In spite of the weather, I prepared the stuffing for the turkey and made the pies and the nut cake. And all the while, I looked out the windows to a world getting whiter by the minute. What would we ever do? It was Christmas Eve day! Ray and Papa had little to do and I was glad. It was better to stay inside, because that is often when the accidents happen. Papa did visit a little boy who had a bad sore throat and cough. Later in the day Ray treated a little girl who had fallen on the sidewalk and cut her lip badly. No one wanted to be sick on Christmas and I prayed that Papa and Ray would not be called away.

Lunchtime came and went and the snow kept falling. It was getting stormier and by mid afternoon we began wondering about the evening church service. Ray offered to go over to the parsonage to ask if we would have the service. He came back, plastered with snow.

"The service will take place for those who come. I promised we would be there." He paused. "I wonder if Hunter will come. Neither he nor Laura will be able to go away."

"Well," said Papa, "if you want to invite them for the service...."

There was a knock at the back door. In came Hunter, looking like a snowman.

"Come in and get warm," said Papa.

Hunter came in, warming himself by the kitchen stove as I poured him a cup of coffee.

"We were just talking about you," said Papa. "What are you doing out in the storm?"

"Had to deliver a cat to its owner on Main Street."

"I suppose your plans have fallen flat."

"Seems so."

"I suggest you go home and take care of what needs to be done and come here for supper and the night. But come as soon as you can. The storm will only get worse. And the stable is big enough for Ruggles also."

Hunter thought a bit. "Sounds good to me."

"And stop by Laura and tell her to do the same thing. Bring her along. She will be alone as her plans will have been canceled also. There will be a Christmas Eve service at six."

"May I bring the dog?" Hunter looked at me. I was holding Murf who was batting at the strand of hair that fell over my face.

"Beanbags? He is a big dog. What is he like around cats?"

"We could find out," he said with a grin.

"Bring him. We'll manage somehow. Murf can hide upstairs."

After a cup of coffee to warm him, Hunter left again. I was excited. I was sure no siblings would make it and having Hunter and

Laura here would add to the holiday and keep us from thinking about a Christmas without Mama. Hunter could sleep with Ray and Laura would have the guest room.

I thought of the balsam tree in the living room. I had to do something about decorations for it. No one else would. My fish chowder that would be our supper would not take long to make and so I had time now for the decorating of the tree. Ray brought down the box of decorations from the attic and even helped a bit. There were even some old strings of popcorn from other years and I hung them on the tree, happy to have some of Mama's hand work on the tree.

When Hunter and Laura arrived less than an hour later, it began to feel like Christmas. We had guests and it was so different from other Christmases that I would not be feeling Mama's absence as much. Beanbags, Hunter's dog, was taken to the hearth in the living room to get warm and get rid of any snow hanging on him. I had taken Murf upstairs and locked him in my room until Beanbags was lying at Hunter's feet. Murf was not at all happy about being locked in a room when his nose told him that an enemy of his was downstairs on his turf. He yowled his disgust when I closed the door.

Some time later, when Beanbags was lying by the hearth close to Hunter, I brought Murf down the stairs into the living room. I could feel the cat get all stiff in my arms and I just kept talking to him. The cat knew Hunter, but he probably had never been near such a big dog. Beanbags, however, remained quite calm, but curious, keeping his eyes on Murf. After a short while, Hunter told me to put the cat down on the carpet. I did so. Murf immediately put his back up and spit for all he was worth. We howled laughing. Beanbags just looked at him, his tongue hanging out of his huge mouth and blinking his eyes. I went up to the dog and petted him, talking and looking at Murf. But this would take time. Murf jumped up on the wing chair and sat on the very top of it, his eyes never leaving this huge monster that somehow was allowed to come into his domain. In the meantime, Laura barely knew what to do with herself being there as a guest. I could barely keep her out of the kitchen, but she finally sat on the sofa and enjoyed the chatter of the others. Papa also sat and talked with Laura and Hunter while I watched Murf and Beanbags. I finally brought Murf over closer to the dog and set him down. Just then Beanbags opened his mouth with a loud yawn and once more Murf's back went up and he stood on his tiptoes but he did not retreat.

"Come to think of it," said Hunter, "I think the neighbor boy has a cat. So the dog is probably used to cats. I really don't think there should be a problem."

We had an early supper and left for church at quarter of six. It was not far as we just had to go out the door, past the parsonage and into the church. But we bundled up as if we were walking a mile. I had locked Murf up in the bedroom again and we set out, Ray leading the way. When we got to the church we found we were the only ones there besides the Cenders. They were very glad to see us. Just after we got there, the Fosters arrived. They were a middle-aged couple who lived a couple houses up from us on North Street and since the organist could not make it, Mrs. Foster volunteered to fill in as organist. She had only begun to play a Christmas carol when the door opened again and in came another couple, the Steiners from a few blocks away who said they just could not stay away from church on Christmas Eve. It was not Christmas without going to church and reliving the wonderful story of Jesus' birth. I felt the same way.

Every time the door opened, we felt the cold air rushing in and anyone coming in looked like a snowman. We waited ten extra minutes, in case someone else turned up but we finally were ready to begin. There were only eleven of us. It would not be a normal service. We took seats up front on the second front benches. I followed Papa in. I knew this had to be hard for him, being his first Christmas Eve service without Mama. Ray sat beside me and Laura and Hunter sat behind us. The church had some simple decorations of garlands of greens, ribbons and extra candles. The scent of the balsam greens filled the sanctuary with its fragrance and I breathed it in joyfully.

Just as Dennis stood up to begin the service, the door opened once more. I heard no voices but Dennis waited. Finally I heard someone come in and sit behind us on the bench with Hunter and Laura.

The service was very simple. Pastor Dennis read the story of Christ's birth from the book of Luke and Gloria again sang "O Holy Night." While Dennis gave some thoughts on "Making Room for Jesus" in our lives, we could hear the wind slamming against the church door. I am sure the heat was on, but I was cold just hearing that wind and knowing we had to go out in the storm again. We sang a few carols together yet before the closing prayer.

When the service ended, I turned to leave and stopped short. Hunter was talking to a woman. A woman who had come and sat next to him. And then with a sudden sinking feeling, I realized this was Lucille. Her eyes were aglow and she was smiling up into Hunter's face.

"I told my aunt," I heard her say, "that we had to come to church in the hopes I would see you here. But she was afraid we couldn't get home anymore, so my uncle walked me to church and left again. I said I would find someone else to walk me home."

It was evident to me who she expected to walk her home.

"I am here for a few days and I hope this storm does not hinder us from seeing each other."

I saw Hunter smiling at her eager face and my stomach turned sour. This woman was unashamedly after Hunter and I was sick. Why did she have to come and spoil my Christmas?

Gloria and Dennis graciously invited all of us to the parsonage after the service. It was nice of them. I think they were so new here and eager to learn to know the congregation and now so few came due to the snowstorm.

"The evening is young yet and rather than all going home, we can play games or just visit for an hour or two. And if the storm gets worse we have lots of room in the parsonage, and we welcome anyone needing a place to sleep."

The Fosters said they would go home while they could, it was not far. But the Steiners who were a bit younger, were ready for adventure, and agreed to stay for a couple hours. All Christmas plans seemed to be blown to the four winds and we would simply make the best of it.

Lucille, to my dismay, was only too happy to go to the parsonage and made her way over there, hanging on Hunter's arm. Papa, Laura, Ray and I joined the group, but I made sure I was at the opposite end of the room from Hunter and Lucille. The more relaxed she became, the more I had to hear her shrill laughter. Laura, I am sure, noticed my reaction to Lucille and she talked a lot to me. Gloria set out snacks of hot chocolate and popcorn and then we played some group games and sang some carols while Gloria played the piano. It was a nice evening except for Lucille and my—I admit it—intense jealousy. I would have loved to have been sitting by Hunter's side and sparring with him over some subject, but instead, I tried not to see nor to hear them.

Finally, I heard Lucille, who had claimed Hunter as hers the entire evening, say she really did need to return to her aunt's home for the night. She looked pleadingly at Hunter.

"I need a brave man to see me home."

He hesitated ever so slightly.

"I'll come along if you wish," said Ray. "Then you don't need to come back alone."

Lucille's face darkened immediately. "Why don't you just stay overnight with my aunt and uncle?" she asked Hunter. "They have room."

"My plans are to stay with the McDurfees," he said calmly "and my few overnight things are in their house."

She had been so insistent that he take her home that she could not say that she would stay at the parsonage now. She looked a bit deflated when Ray got dressed up and the three soon went out the door. But the storm was wild and the door banged loudly as they went out and soon after they left, a shutter came loose on the porch and made a clatter. Gloria looked at the Seiners.

"Which street do you live on?" she asked.

"On Oak Lane, about three blocks from here," they answered.

"Oh, do stay overnight. It will be more fun for all of us," said Gloria.

The Steiners looked at each other a moment,

"We were planning to go to my folks tomorrow," she said to Gloria, "but that won't happen." She looked at her husband. "Shall we stay here overnight? What do you say?"

Mr. Steiner was an easygoing man with a receding hairline, and he simply smiled and agreed. Papa said it was time for us to head home. Lucille had somehow spoiled my evening and I was disappointed in myself for letting it happen.

"Gloria, what were your plans for Christmas Day?" I asked, thinking of our twenty-pound turkey.

"Well," she admitted, "we were going to go to my folks, but that won't happen. I won't have a turkey, but I will have food for my guests. What are your plans?"

"We have already invited Laura and Hunter since neither one could do what they planned and we are not getting the guests we expected. I suggest we all eat together. You have more room so we could eat here, and I have a twenty-pound turkey, stuffing ready for the oven and lots more."

"Wonderful! I would love it! Why don't you bring the turkey over tomorrow morning early and I will make it here. I have some home canned vegetables and I made a large jelled salad that I was going to take along. And I will cook potatoes as well. What more do we need?"

"Great! How many will we be? Do you have room?"

"Of course. We will make room. My guess is that this parsonage has had big dinners many times. But I think," she counted on her fingers, "we will only be nine. We can easily do that."

"And I have pies and a cake. We'll have more than enough food," I added.

It would be a different Christmas Day, but it would be one to remember.

Papa, Laura and I made our way home through the blowing snow. I realized if I wasn't careful, I would let Lucille spoil my whole Christmas. Papa, Laura and I sat in the living room and waited for the others to come. We did not have to wait long. I breathed a sigh of relief when I heard them stomping on the porch. I did not really know how to act around Hunter, but I decided I better play it cool. Who knows what kind of a relationship he had with Lucille. I presented Hunter and Laura with the gifts of cookies and candy and Papa, Ray and I exchanged small gifts. Then, after some hot tea, we headed for bed.

Christmas morning arrived and it was still snowing, but not as stormy. By the time I got up, Ray and Hunter had shoveled paths that would probably not last very long if it continued to snow. Ray had also delivered the turkey to the parsonage where it would be roasted.

After a late breakfast, Hunter and Ray tried to make a bit of a path around Papa's office and I spent the morning in the kitchen and finally we took our prepared food over to the parsonage. Because both of the households had late breakfasts, we did not have our Christmas dinner until one thirty. We had a wonderful meal of turkey and stuffing and all the trimmings and a lot of laughter to go with it. We had fun remembering our retreat just a few weeks earlier up on the mountain and I did not look at Hunter during that conversation, remembering the kiss on the porch.

"So you are brand new to our town?" asked Papa of Dennis.

"We are. Neither or us was ever in the town until shortly before we moved."

"You are fortunate you had a nice day for moving. This is our second storm for December and you managed to move between the two storms."

"Believe me, we are grateful. Also grateful for all who helped us move. It was easier because most of the furniture was already in the parsonage. I wonder how long Pastor Thomas was here?"

"Oh, I don't rightly know," said Papa. "But he was, I think, in his late sixties when he died."

"Well, if he was that old I guess that sign that I found..."

"Stop!"

Dennis stopped in mid sentence and looked at Gloria in astonishment. His wife started laughing.

"Sorry, but you may not say what you were going to say."

Dennis looked at her a few moments, understanding finally coming to his face.

"I stand corrected," he said to us, with a crooked grin.

In the meantime, Gloria and I exchanged glances. I knew only too well what Dennis had been about to say and that would not have ended well for me.

"Ah," I said, eager for the subject to change, "here is a good example of the man being the head of the house and the woman being the neck who turns the head."

Everyone laughed and I did not dare look at Hunter, afraid he would be looking for a tell tale sign on my face. Would he possibly connect what Dennis said with the sign on his carriage? I sincerely hoped not.

"You two seem well matched," said Papa.

"I think so, too," said Dennis, "but my wife was hard to convince."

"Really?" I asked.

"She turned me down the first time I asked her out." I had to laugh at Gloria's expression. "And when I proposed, she almost turned me down again," Dennis added.

"He surprised me," said Gloria. "I did not expect him to ask me to marry him so soon."

"How soon was it?"

"Five months after he began courting me."

"Did you make him wait for an answer?"

"No, I knew I wanted him. I just had to get past the shock."

"By the way, Hunter," said Dennis, "I keep thinking I met you sometime. Do you ever think that of me?"

"No, I can't say I have."

"I think I was told at the Christmas Retreat that your father is a doctor."

"That is right."

"And you helped him sometimes?"

"I did."

"And where did you live?"

Hunter told him. Now all ears were attuned to Dennis.

"That would fit, I think," said the pastor. "Some years ago, I was visiting a cousin of mine in that town. This could be maybe seven or so years ago. My cousin, proud of his new horse and carriage, took me into town for a ride. While there he spotted some young people gathered at the train station and we stopped and visited. There was also a girl there that my cousin wanted to impress and he suggested a carriage race with a friend of his. The pastor paused. It was an open carriage and the race began on a road at the edge of town. I still don't know how it happened, but he hit a pothole and I was not holding on as I should have and I was thrown out."

"Ouch," said Hunter.

"It could have been far worse than it was. I had no broken bones, but I was hurting badly and bleeding profusely on my lower leg. So I was taken to the doctor."

Dennis stopped for a moment and looked at Hunter.

"I am pretty sure the name was Dr. Renwick. He took good care of me and I have a feeling you were there to help him. Could it be?"

"I have no recollection of it, but it is possible," said Hunter.

Dennis just looked at Hunter a moment.

"You were younger but I am pretty sure it was you. The only thing that does not fit is your personality."

Hunter looked in surprise at Dennis.

"You may have been having a bad day, but you were neither friendly nor focused. I remember wondering if you did not want to help or if you had had a spat with your father just before I came in."

Hunter looked a bit chagrined. He thought a moment.

"What year was it?"

"I believe it was in 1877 because I was just ready for my seminary studies."

"Eighteen seventy-seven was a bad summer for me," replied Hunter slowly. "My I offer a late apology?"

"No need. I am glad whatever it was, is past and hopefully healed."

"It is," answered Hunter.

The pastor then got talking to the Steiners and the meal went on happily. But I wondered about Hunter's rough spot in his past. Was this his Debbie problem?

After the meal there was a lot of clean up in the kitchen for us women while the men sat in the living room. It must have been three or after when I dried the last pan. I was eager to join the others in the living room. And then I heard the knocker. I first thought of an emergency for Papa, who had left a note on the door saying where he could be found. However, I soon heard a voice I was beginning to despise. Lucille. I could not believe it. She was invited in and it sounded like she was planning to stay and visit. I did not want to see her hanging onto Hunter.

"Hunter, I walked all the way to your house and you were not home," she said. "So I thought just maybe you might be here."

I looked out the window. The snow was almost over. I wanted to leave.

"Gloria," I said, trying not to show my annoyance, "I think I shall take my leftovers to the house right away. I probably will not be back. Thank you so much for making the turkey and supplying the room."

"Who came?"

"It sounds like Lucille." I said no more, but I think Gloria understood.

"You sure you want to leave?"

"I am. I guess there is no path from the back door?"

"Unfortunately not."

It sounded like someone had started a game in the living room. Hopefully they would be busy enough not to pay much attention to me going out the door. Loaded with a roasting pan of my share of the leftovers, I headed quickly into the hall. Just as Gloria opened the door for me, Papa called to me.

"Amber?"

"Yes."

"You going home?"

"Yes. I am taking some food back and I think I will not return."

"I need a nap. I shall come with you."

"Fine," I said, not looking at Hunter who was sitting with Ray and Lucille, playing a game.

"Laura? Maybe you would like a nap, too?" asked Papa.

"I would. I see it is no longer snowing, Maybe I can get home yet today."

"You probably can."

As they put on their wraps and boots, I stayed in the hall, but I was in view of the occupants of the room. I acted like I had not seen Lucille whose back was to me. Hunter was facing me but I refused to look at him. I was glad when Papa and Laura were ready to go.

"Merry Christmas, everyone," I called as I went out the door, but my own Christmas was no longer so merry.

Once home, Papa disappeared.

"Laura, make yourself comfortable in the living room. I'll join you soon. If you want to nap, you can go to the guest room."

"I think I will just rest here," she said, "if you don't mind."

When I joined her in the living room, she was already dozing. I picked up a book and tried to read, but my thoughts were at the parsonage. How did that woman dare to come over to the parsonage? She was here for one reason only. She wanted Hunter. That I knew from fact.

Somewhere around six a little girl was brought to the house. She had fallen and had a big goose egg on her forehead and the mother wanted the doctor to see her. While he was in the office, Ray arrived. Hunter had walked Lucille home. I bit back my irritation. This was Christmas. It was not unreasonable to expect that he would most likely stay a while there. I tried my best to be cheerful. However, in about fifteen minutes, Hunter arrived to pick up his bag.

"Hey, Hunter, I saw some pie in the kitchen," said Ray. "Want some?"

Hunter looked at me.

"You are welcome," I said. "It is nearly seven and it's been a while since we ate. Let me put out some turkey meat for sandwiches and I'll make coffee for your pie."

Just then Papa came into the room.

"Good. I'm hungry, but I am not sure why."

So the five of us had supper together. I played it a bit cool, but I was happy to have Hunter back in my house without Lucille. I felt his eyes on me, but I did not look at him too much. I had no claim on him, but I was hurt.

Finally around eight o'clock, Hunter and Laura headed home in the sleigh and Ruggles, I am sure was glad to be out of the stable and in the cold night air. I had to laugh to see Beanbags sitting beside Laura in the sleigh. I know Murf, whose feelings were also hurt, was glad to see him go.

CHAPTER 29

Lucille put a damper on my whole Christmas. I felt guilty about it. Jesus, the Prince of Peace had come and I was disjointed about Lucille. Somehow I had to realize that I had no more claim on Hunter than Lucille had. He was gallant, handsome, intriguingly silent at times and very much the prince charming as far as I was concerned. But what had he ever said to me to give me hope? We had some serious talks, some sharing of our lives, and yes, that kiss on the mountain. But what was that all about? Proof that he was not a coward around women?

A few days later I was feeling blue. The winter stretched out ahead of me. The weather was mostly miserable. No nice snow. Just fog, rain, sleet and sometimes a mix with a few sorry snowflakes. I stopped in one day to talk to Mindy and she was in no better shape than I was. She could not forget Carl. And it was winter and there was no going to the park or any events where she could even see him. And no, Hunter never said anything more about the sign. It seemed to be forgotten.

I in turn, grumbled about Lucille who I knew wanted Hunter, who I had not seen since Christmas. For all I knew he could be courting her. Maybe she never even went home again. Ray had seen Hunter once up on Pipers Hill and made the comment that Hunter was working on his house during the evenings.

We were about ten days into January when I got the wedding invitation. It was from a girl that both Mindy and I had been friends with for some time although we had not gotten together recently.

She had, at some time, lived in Steeplechase and had attended our church although her parents did not attend. She was a bit of a loner with few friends, but she was so funny that Mindy and I enjoyed her and sort of took her under our wing and did things with her. Her family owned the Pipers Inn on Pipers Hill and it was well known that the sheriff kept a close watch on that place. I think maybe that was why she did not have many friends.

Now, years later, I found that both Mindy and I were invited to the wedding. Well, not quite. The wedding would be just family in the bride's home, but both Mindy and I were invited to a reception to be held at the Pipers Inn. I had never been inside this inn, but I knew where it was. It was smaller than ours in Steeplechase and so I knew it would not be a very big party. What was important was that it was a social event to attend in the middle of these winter doldrums. I looked forward to it even though I would probably not know many of those attending. I was tired of thinking about Lucille and what progress she might be making in the game of lassoing Hunter as a husband. Yes, I was ready for a wedding invitation.

I hoped the weather would improve. Because of the freezing fog and rain the roads as well as sidewalks were icy, which meant, as all doctors know, broken bones. Papa and Ray were out in the weather day in and day out, slipping, sliding, and hoping they themselves would not break a bone. But many bones did get broken and Papa and Ray were kept busy.

The wedding was in mid January. The Saturday evening reception would take place at six o'clock. It was not a good time to be going up the mountain to Pipers Hill and who knew how long the reception would last. Papa told Ray to take us and we should just stay at the inn overnight. Then no one had to be out on the bad roads. Mindy's father agreed and said he would pick us up the next morning.

We arrived in Pipers Hill shortly before six. The evening was dark and dismal as most of January had been so far. The village of Pipers Hill was not much more than a scattering of houses, a small country store where one could buy anything from a sandwich to a hunter's gun. In hunting season the villagers would bring their mounted animals from former years and they were proudly displayed around the quaint store. These could include beaver, deer heads, a fisher cat or even the head of a bobcat. Now, as we left the little village behind, I was surprised how far back the winding, gloomy road we had to travel before we arrived at the inn. I found myself hoping there were lots of people at the reception to make up for the inn's isolation.

Ray stopped in front of the inn then left, probably to visit Sylvia for the evening. In the meanwhile, Mindy and I made our way to the door of the inn. The building was built of dark, stained wood but the windows were lit up with oil lamps and candles and the warm glow drew us quickly up the winding walkway to the door. There we were met by the bride's father who welcomed us and after showing us where to hang our wraps, he led us through the bar and dining room to a larger room where the reception was taking place. I took a quick look around and guessed there were perhaps twenty to thirty people present. Not a big group but big enough for this small inn.

"Do you think we should secure a room now, in the case that others will also stay the night?" asked Mindy.

"That sounds like a good idea. I'd hate to be told there is no room," I replied, remembering my recent stay at the inn where I slept in the lounge. So after a brief look around, we went back to the reception desk. There a handsome young man stood waiting.

"We would like to have a room for the night," I said.

"Are you here for the reception?"

"Yes. Are others staying?"

"A few. I expect we will fill up this evening."

He then smiled charmingly and offered us a double bed in Room Twenty-two. As we signed the book and gave our money, a big black cat lying in a basket on a shelf behind the desk, observed us with his green eyes reflecting the light from the candles.

"Oh, what is the name of your cat?" I asked. "He is beautiful."

"Boo."

"How appropriate," laughed Mindy.

"I will see you to your room," the young man said, his eyes sliding down my dress.

We followed him to the stairs, which was an enclosed, dark stairway. He had a candle and there were only a couple dim wall sconces in the upstairs hall. He took us to the room and opened the door for us. Then he gave us the key and left us.

We placed our overnight bags on the floor. The room was cold and was therefore not very inviting although there was a pretty quilt on the bed. After locking the door we returned to the reception room where we met the bride and her husband Bill.

"Thank you so much for coming," said Miranda. "We haven't seen much of each other lately, but for old times sake I wanted you here."

"We are glad to be here and celebrate with you," I replied as we presented our gifts to her.

"And this is my husband Bill," she said, nodding to the man at her side.

I knew Bill vaguely from Flynn Falls. He seemed to be quite taken with Miranda and I wished them well.

We were then told to find our places at the table and without glancing around much at who was there, we looked for our names and were relieved to see we were seated next to each other. Next to me was a stout woman whom I did not know at all and there were two seats still empty next to Mindy. There was a lot of talking and laughing around us and just when the host called for attention, I noticed a couple slip in next to Mindy. I felt her stiffen and a small gasp escaped her lips. I looked up to see Carl, her old boyfriend, taking the seat next to Mindy. A girl I did not know had come with him. I reached over and squeezed Mindy's hand and then I turned my attention to the father of the bride who was making a speech after which the couple were toasted and the meal was served. There was some Italian blood on the groom's side so the meal was spaghetti and meatballs with green beans and a salad. The girl Carl was with was a rather loud chatterbox, talking not only to Carl but to everyone around her and she took his full attention. It was when the waitress came around serving coffee that Carl suddenly realized who was sitting next to him. He could not cover his surprise.

"Mindy!"

"Hi Carl." Mindy sounded very nervous.

"I did not see you until now. How are you?"

"Good."

Carl's date was shouting to someone down at the other end of the table.

"Hi, Amber," Carl greeted me.

As I responded, Carl's date turned to him and seeing him talking to us, she introduced herself.

"Hi," she said. "I'm Erma. Miranda is my cousin. Isn't she beautiful? I never thought she could look this good." Erma snickered behind her hand. "Well, she wasn't the most popular girl."

I felt that Carl was nearly as tense as Mindy. I wondered how long he had known this girl Erma and how he could possibly be attracted to her.

Sometime during the meal the woman sitting to my left turned her attention to me. Her husband was chatting with the man across from him and she wanted to talk.

"Hello," she said. "I am Isabel, an aunt to Bill. How do you know Miranda?"

"Oh, Mindy and I were friends with her some years back and we were surprised to get an invitation to the wedding," I replied.

"She never had many friends. Her father owns this inn and he wanted her here as housekeeper. So she has been rather isolated, but I think this is where she met her husband Bill. She is leaving here now and I am happy for her. They will live, I believe in Flynn Falls or thereabouts. Her mother died several years ago and I think Miranda was really used hard here." She leaned a bit closer to me. "I never liked her father much," she whispered. "And his son is not much better."

The woman paused to take a drink from her goblet before turning again to me.

"This place doesn't have the best reputation, you know."

I just looked at her but said nothing. This did not deter her from talking.

"Oh, you were maybe too young when it all started, but, well, for that matter, it already had a bad name when the old man had it. Always rumors of women and then when Al took over, that is Miranda's father, it did not change much. Actually, the inn was not doing well and suddenly it began doing much better without the help of new guests. After a year or two, the sheriff caught him in a smuggling ring of some sort, but they needed more proof than they had to prosecute, so he got away with it. I think he must still be involved in something because if you take notice, this inn looks very nice but I never hear much of guests."

There was a pause. I had not added any fuel to the conversation and it petered out. I thought it was best to change the subject.

"I was admiring the beautiful quilt on our bed. I wonder if all the beds have quilts on them?"

"Oh dear, are you staying the night? Just you two girls? Better see that the door is locked. We are staying too, but my husband is with me. Yes, there is a quilt on our bed also. Besides the nice quilts, there is quite nice furniture and, I must say, delicious food. My husband and I have been here for numerous occasions and we always get excellent food. But when I see the big rings on Al's fingers and his expensive clothes, I wonder...."

She was interrupted by the serving of the cake, which the bride and groom brought around to each person. We chatted a bit with Miranda as we received our cake and when the bride and groom moved on, Isabel continued.

"Then two years ago, or was it longer than that, there was a dead man found out back of the inn."

Isabel, seeing my startled look, was pleased to have gotten my attention again.

"It was a hushed-up affair, but he must have been dead for a few days because an animal had started eating him. Al told the sheriff he never saw him before and the sheriff took his word for it. But there are some things that have happened up here in the outback of Vermont that make me uneasy. I still say...."

The woman's story gave me the shivers. I saw the innkeeper talking to his son, the young man who was at the desk when we had first arrived. I remembered him being very well dressed for a country inn. And very handsome.

When the meal came to an end, a young man stood up and made some rather course jokes about the bride and groom and eventually the tables were cleared, set to the side and the dancing began.

Mindy and I sat on chairs along the perimeter of the dance floor and watched the proceedings. There was a slightly raised platform in one corner of the room where the musicians sat. Two had violins, one an accordion and one a mandolin. They played while the bride and groom danced alone for the first dance. Then the bride danced with her father and the groom with his mother. And then anyone who wanted to dance was welcome. Mindy had gotten very quiet and I knew she was thinking about Carl and watching him dance. Seeing him here had given her a jolt.

"You still like him, don't you?" I whispered.

"I do. I think he is the handsomest man here tonight. I just can't figure out what he is doing with Erma. I somehow feel he does not know her very well."

"I don't know, but she sure has him dancing. Would you dance with him?"

Mindy looked around the room. It was now folk dancing with lots of movement and clapping and because of the small space, bumping into each other.

"No," she answered, "but I would like to talk to him."

In the meantime, I was not too excited by what I was seeing. Between each dance, the dancers went to the punch bowl, which was certainly spiked. This was a drinking crowd. The young man from the desk was now drinking and more than once I saw him eyeing me up. I tried to shrink back into my chair. I had thought him nice looking when we came, but the more I saw of him, and the more I heard about the inn, the less I found to admire. I watched the bride. She seemed to be having fun. Her husband did not seem to be drinking. At least he was not showing any signs of drunkenness.

I saw a young man cut in on Carl and Erma. Carl stood back and glanced at our table. Then he slowly came back and sat down.

"It is a bit wild on the dance floor," he said to Mindy.

"Looks like it."

There followed a bit of silence. I sensed that they wanted to talk, but did not know how to begin.

"Carl, your date will be dancing all night. I hope you have the energy," I teased.

There, I had given him a reason to explain Erma. And he did.

He laughed a bit. "She is a cousin to the bride and I know the groom. I was asked to be her date this evening. I don't really know her."

I saw him give Mindy another look. I stood.

"Mindy, I need to stretch my legs. I'll be back shortly."

I left them to themselves. I would walk around a bit. They needed to find their way. Before I left the room, I glanced back in time to see Carl lean a bit closer to Mindy. But I did not hear what he had to say, but at least they were talking.

I did not know where I was going to go, but I needed to give them a bit of privacy. I really did not know anyone else that was here. Some guests I knew from seeing them in town, but not to talk to. And there really was no room to walk around. The space was filled. I decided to go to our room for a few minutes. There I would have room to relax before I returned to Mindy. I climbed up the dim, narrow stairs and was heading down the hall when a woman of perhaps forty, who had sat just down from us at the table, rushed up behind me. I realized she needed to get by me quickly by the way she ran up the hall but before I could make room for her, she bumped me to the side and then threw up, right in front of the door to our room before rushing on up the hall. I stood in shock, not quite believing what I was seeing. And what I was seeing, considering the spaghetti we had been served, was not a pretty sight.

I turned around and went to the desk, hoping to find the owner of the inn. No one was there, but suddenly his son stood not far from me. He leered at me as I approached him. However, when I told him about the clean up that was needed in the hall, he muttered some curse word and left me. When I looked over to Mindy, she was alone and in the melee of the dancers, I saw Carl was once more with Erma. I hurried over to my friend.

"Mindy," I said, taking my seat next to her, "how did you make out?"

"I think there might be hope," she said. "He said he misses me and he seemed...interested. But I could not think of anything to say, and neither could he, evidently. And then Erma came for him again. Where were you?"

"This is not going to be a very pretty story," I began. "I was heading for our room where I thought I would relax for a few moments to give you and Carl some privacy. The halls were full. But when I got upstairs a woman rushed past me and threw up right in front of our door."

"Ugh. I could almost throw up just imagining it," said Mindy looking a bit pale. "Did anyone clean it up?"

"I told Miranda's brother about it. He was not happy."

"I hope they clean it up quickly." She glanced around the room. "I am feeling the need of fresh air. Do you think we could make a trip to the outhouse?"

"Well, we surely can't go to our room just now, so let's go."

We pushed ourselves through the crowd of people and finally got to our coats. Our next step was to find the back door. It took us a while, but we found it. When we opened the door, we were dismayed to see only blackness and mist. After our eyes adjusted to the lack of light, we, by the dim light of a partially hidden moon, could see the outhouse. We made our way carefully along a beaten path and were happy to find it empty. Mindy went in first and I waited. As I waited I looked around me. It was gloomy here, no doubt about it. I wished for the gas lamps we had in town. I heard a sound to my left and when I looked I saw the thick tail of a fox disappear around a rock. Then the back door of the inn opened and I heard and saw Miranda's brother come out with another young man. They were laughing and talking and seemed to be looking for someone. Then they saw me. The brother said something and laughed as they headed in our direction.

"Mindy, hurry, we're getting company," I hissed through the door.

The door opened and Mindy and I exchanged places. "Wait for me," I said.

I was not in long. When I came out, the two boys were closer to us. Waiting. Seeing us hesitate to head toward them on the narrow pathway, they began walking toward us again, and the gap between us was narrowing. I looked around. There was little light out here and there were some bushes and rocks around us. Not easy to get around if we had to. But maybe I was imagining things.

"Hi beautiful," the brother said, coming ever closer, his eyes on me. "How about we get better acquainted?"

Just then the back door opened and more people came out. The boys turned to see who it was and in that moment I grabbed Mindy's hand.

"Let's run!"

We took off where there was no trail. I ran into a bush and had to stop and find my way around it, but we kept running and finally arrived at the front of the inn. I did not stop to see if we were being followed. We just ran across the soggy lawn until we got to the front entrance. Then I swung open the door and we burst into the inn. We stood a few moments, just glad to be back inside. Then we put our coats back on the pegs on the wall and walked back into the room with the wedding guests. I only then felt safe.

It was clear to me that the reception had become a lot more interesting to Mindy since her few words with Carl. But his date kept him dancing. We sat and watched. Both Mindy and I were offered dances, but we remained where we were. Later on, when Erma was dancing with someone else, Carl found his way back to his seat beside Mindy. But few words were exchanged before Erma spied him. I think she must have gotten a bit worried to find him with Mindy again and after that she kept him with her the entire evening. The music seemed louder and the shouting and mood of the guests did not pull me to the dance floor.

"Let's see if the hall is cleaned up," said Mindy a couple hours later.

We went up the stairs. The hall was cleaned and we hurried into our room. We were surprised to find it unlocked.

"Do you have the key?" I asked Mindy.

"Yes, and I am sure I locked it."

"This is getting creepy. Let's make sure it is locked now."

She fumbled quite a while with the key. Finally she gave up.

"See if you can lock it. I don't think this is the right key."

I tried, but it would not lock. It turned so that one thought it was locked, but it was not.

"This key says twenty-two. It matches the room number."

"Well, I am not staying in a room here tonight that does not lock," said Mindy. "Not with this gang. And since when does the person at the desk take us to our rooms?"

"It is a small inn," I said in the young man's defense. I looked around the room. "We'll put this chair under the doorknob."

"Does that really work?"

"I don't know. I never tried it before, but we will find out."

"If it doesn't work, it will be too late."

However, when I tried it, the back of the chair was too low for the doorknob. There was nothing else available to use.

"What time is it?"

"A bit after ten. Too early for bed. Why did Papa say we should stay here?"

"He did not know what kind of crowd would be here," said Mindy. "What do we do? It is too noisy to sleep."

What we did was sit on the bed and talk. It had been a long time since we had really talked and the time flew by. Once we were interrupted by loud stamping and running past our door and suddenly our door popped open and a young man I did not know looked in the room.

"Is the bride in here?"

"No, she is not and close that door," Mindy answered.

"They are stealing the bride, I presume," I said.

"Preserve me from ever being stolen by such a gang," said Mindy. "And he walked right in. I feel like I am sleeping in a brothel."

I shuddered. Finally we got into our nightclothes and crawled into bed. It had gotten quiet. However, we were barely in bed when we heard low voices out in the hall. I thought I recognized the voice of the young man at the desk.

"Mindy, I am not going to be able to sleep. Let's drag the bed in front of the door."

"Really? Do you think we can?"

"It is worth a try. It is that or stay awake all night."

We should have done it earlier when there was so much noise downstairs. The bed moved unwillingly and with strange creaks and groans. We got the giggles after an especially loud groan and had to bury our faces in the bed clothes to stifle them. Finally, with the headboard of the bed against the door, I blew out the candle and with a quick look out the window at the clouds sailing past the moon, I crawled into bed.

"We are safe, but if there is a fire, we have to jump out the window," said Mindy.

"I'll take the chance," I replied. "And if I hear anyone trying to get in, let's pound on the door to wake everyone."

"Fine with me. I think this place is slowly giving me the heebie jeebies."

The inn had quieted. I heard some noise now and then, but finally sleep overtook me. I do not know how long I had slept when I again awoke. I was not sure what had awakened me. I could not hear anything. Or did I? I lay quite still for a moment or two and then I heard the doorknob just above our heads move ever so slightly. Was I just imagining it? I waited and heard it again. I could only think of Miranda's brother and knowing I was safe, I got angry. I poked Mindy and together we got on our knees and then we pounded as hard as we could on the door. It made quite a din. We soon heard voices in the hall.

"What's going on?" one irate man called.

"Don't know," answered another. "I heard a couple people running down the stairs."

It seemed everyone was out in the hall except us. Finally someone knocked on our door.

"Yes?"

"Are you all right?"

"Yes. Someone was trying to get into our room and we did the pounding to scare them off."

"Well, you scared them all right. Back to bed, everybody," the man called to the others.

I was trembling when we again got under the colorful quilt. I prayed a silent prayer to God, thanking Him for giving us the idea of moving the bed.

"I am never, ever coming to this inn again," whispered Mindy. "Not as long as this man owns it."

I felt sure the danger was past and eventually we fell asleep again. Morning could not come too soon.

CHAPTER 30

Papa was not happy when I told him the story of our night at the Pipers Inn and said he would never advise anyone to go to that inn again. But the whole experience at least had given me something to add some spice to the long, dreary winter. However, our winter was about to make its mark in another way. Before the week was up, I got sick. It began with a sick stomach and I was soon throwing up. According to Papa and Ray, there was a lot of sickness going around and I did not know if I got it from the lady at the inn or from someone else. It had been a middle-aged woman who got sick at the wedding reception, and the hour was not late enough for her to have gotten drunk, so it was quite possible that she spread the sickness to others. Now I was feeling feverish, and had a sore throat.

It was a Thursday and there was no Laura, but I finally told Papa I was sick and I crawled into bed. He came to me between patients and gave me medicine and orders to stay in bed. There was illness everywhere it seemed. Papa and Ray were already overworked and on Friday, when Laura found out that I was sick, she offered to come every day. Hunter had found another girl to help him one day a week and so Laura, who was helping him out, no longer worked for him.

Being sick was not fun. I had a fever, was coughing and sneezing and feeling rotten. Day after day dragged by. Maybe I should not say it dragged. I slept most of the time but my sleep was interrupted with my coughing and my stuffy nose and I was very tired. Murf came regularly to my bed, batted at my face a few times with his soft paw, and seeing I was not responding, would curl up close to me and sleep for a time. I had no appetite and my cough got worse. Finally, Papa ordered Laura to make a mustard and onion plaster for me. I hated it. I was also scared Laura would get sick and then where would we be? I was just so miserable and the only time I smiled was when a curious Murf would come and peer into my face, his whiskers tickling my face.

After a week of being sick, I was determined to be over being sick. If I told myself I was well, maybe I would get over it faster. I pushed myself to go downstairs and try to make breakfast and to act like I was well. Instead, I had a relapse and barely knew what was going on in the world for another two weeks. In the meantime, Laura got sick. Poor Papa. He did not know what to do. He told Laura she could not go home to an empty house. Instead she was put in the guest room so Papa could care for us both right at home. After three days, without me knowing it, Papa sent a wire to my oldest sister to see if she could possibly help out. Ruby lived about ten miles away and she and her husband lived on one side of a farmhouse and her husband's parents lived on the other side. Her husband worked the farm for his father. Their children were old enough to have their mother go away, especially since the grandparents were right there to cook for them. Ruby arrived the next day by train in Flynn Falls and took the stagecoach to Steeplechase.

I was not informed that Ruby was coming and could hardly believe my eyes when she showed up at my bed. She was so like Mama. She was a fast worker and efficient. Papa's relief was evident, but he still had more to do than he was able. He sometimes needed Ruby in the office, or to run errands and she was pulled in all directions. Ruby barely had time to cook, but she made simple soups and tried to keep the house clean. When Gloria heard of our plight, she came over to do the laundry, God bless her.

But things were about to get worse.

Two nights after Ruby arrived, Mindy stopped over to see me. She had been sick also, but had no relapse and so was feeling good again and came to cheer me up. She sat by my bed and she told me all the news from the bakery and town. I asked if she saw Hunter but he just did not seem to be around town much either. One time she saw him going to the bank and another to the post office. I was hoping for more news of him so I was disappointed.

While we were visiting, we heard the knocker and then a frantic voice.

"Mindy, go downstairs and see what is going on. Just try to stay out of sight of the visitor. I am so bored here I need to hear whatever news there is to hear."

Mindy did as I said. About five minutes later she returned.

"I had to go all the way down the stairs to hear anything and was seen by Ray," she said when she returned. "A man broke his leg while ice fishing and I think Ray is going to bring him here."

Before she could tell me anything more, we heard Ray's voice.

"Mindy?"

"Yes?"

She ran down the stairs and in a few minutes all was quiet. I waited for her return but it stayed quiet. I could not understand what was happening. Where was Mindy? She seemed to have gone home without a word to me. That was strange. I wanted to go downstairs but felt too bad. Papa was out on a call and I did not know where Ruby was.

Finally I heard a door and Ruby's footsteps.

"Ruby?"

"Coming." I heard her running up the stairs.

"Where is everybody? Mindy was here visiting me and she disappeared when Ray called for her."

"I just fetched a loaf of bread that Gloria baked for us and coming back I saw Mindy and Ray ride off together. I have no idea why she went with him."

"Are you sure it was Mindy? He was going to a man who somehow broke his leg ice fishing."

"I am sure it was Mindy. Guess we will have to wait and find out."

I had a sudden fit of coughing and the discussion ended. Ice fishing. How had the man broken his leg ice fishing? Had the ice given way? Now I worried about the ice. Was it thick enough? I had visions of Ray trying to help the man and then falling through the ice himself. I had heard a horror story of fishermen and their hut disappearing through the ice on Lake Champlain one time. I was remembering that some years earlier, I had gone ice fishing with Ray and our Cousin Sidney. They had access to a hut and I don't remember how they ever chopped a hole in the ice, but the three of us spent the day fishing from that hole. I remember it being amazingly warm in the hut. We even caught a fish or two. Mama had packed a lunch for us, and we ate every crumb of it. Our appetites were hearty. It had been a fun experience and at that time I had no fear of the ice breaking. In spite of my worries, I finally drifted off to sleep.

I do not know how much later it was that, my bedroom door being left open, I awoke to some activity downstairs. Some exclamations from Papa and Ruby and hurried steps. *What had happened now? Had the ice given way? Was Ray safe?* I got out of bed and put on my housecoat. I had to know what was going on. I was wobbly on my feet and I stood leaning against my dresser a bit before I slowly made my way to the stairs, and being greeted once again with just silence, determinedly and carefully, made my way down the stairs with a firm grip on the railing. I found no one around again. That seemed strange. No Papa, no Ruby, no Ray, no Mindy. I was not going back upstairs until I found out what was going on. I went to the couch in the living room, threw an old quilt over me and curled up and waited. And prayed.

A fit of coughing woke me when I dozed off and I finally I heard someone in the kitchen.

"What is going on?" I called. Ruby came in.

"What are you doing down here?"

"I had to know what was going on. Everyone disappeared for the second time tonight."

Ruby sighed. "You won't believe it. Ray stepped into a hole in the field and wrenched his foot badly. Papa says a small bone broke in his foot."

"Not Ray too!" I wailed and promptly began to cough.

"Papa says this is becoming the Steeplechase Hospital. I must go back over to the office in a few minutes to take a pair of crutches that Papa has in the kitchen closet."

"What about the man with the broken leg?"

"Guess who it was?"

"How should I know? Oh, not Jonas?"

"Jonas. I did not hear how it happened, but it was broken so badly they were going to take him to the hospital. Ray says Jonas will need surgery. Ray and this other man who came for Ray, I think he called him Jim, were trying to move him when Ray got his foot in a hole along the pond. Because he was helping to carry Jonas, he did not want to drop him and so with the foot stuck in the hole, it got twisted. Then, of course, he could no longer carry Jonas. They were trying to figure out what to do when a carriage came by and this Jim ran out in the road and waved them down. I guess they were desperate. So they sent Jonas to the hospital with that carriage driver and Jim brought Ray and Mindy home."

"Why did Mindy go along?"

"This Jim was fishing there, too. Alone. Besides him it was just Jonas and a girlfriend. And the girlfriend was frantic. She had never been ice fishing and now Jonas was badly hurt and there was only this one other man there and it was dark and cold. I don't blame her for freaking out. And she had to stay there alone with Jonas while the man came here for help. And I am sure Jonas was in bad pain. Jim wanted someone to calm her down, so Mindy went along. I think the girlfriend went along with the other driver to the hospital with Jonas. And Mindy went home again. She said she was frozen and thought you were sleeping by now."

"What a night," I said between coughs. "What are we going to do? Papa needs Ray so badly."

"Ray is not sick and the hurting will lessen. It is a small bone that is broken and he will probably feel better tomorrow already. But he must stay off his foot. He will have to somehow do the office visits and Papa must go out on the road. I will have to help Ray and I don't know how much I will get done here in the house. I wish we could get more help, but our other sisters have small children. They can't come."

She left me then and I crept back up to bed. Poor Papa. How could he hold out?

We somehow managed. Ray was hurting but it was possible for him to do the office calls. Ruby was the one who was chased from one chore to another. In the middle of the second week in February, Ruby went back home. She needed to get back to her family and she surely needed a rest after her hectic days with us. Laura was not getting well very fast but my cough was better. At night it always got worse and it left me very tired. The weather was milder but we did get six inches of snow one day and three days later another four inches. But it was beginning to melt where the sun hit it.

Gradually, oh, so gradually, I was regaining my strength. I was beginning to enjoy food again. Not too much of it, but what I could eat tasted good. The problem was, I was too tired to cook and so our meals were wanting. Gloria brought food sometimes, and sometimes Papa ate at the inn. Ray even went with Papa to the inn once. In the carriage, no less, even though we lived so close.

February fourteenth dawned bright and sunny. It did me good to see the sun. I had gotten really lazy during my sickness and usually slept till eight. By then Murf was tickling my face with his whiskers. I suddenly realized it was Valentine's Day. It would be a very busy day for Mindy. Every year the bakery made some special confection for those seeking a gift for their special friend. The last few years they even had the option for someone to give this confection without a name attached. The bakery would deliver it. It was always great fun because there were always those who chose this way of giving a valentine that they would have been too shy to give otherwise.

I got out of bed and tried to make myself a bit presentable. I did not feel too bad. I had not been in a dress for so long but when I thought of the energy I needed to put one on, I chose to stay in my nightgown and housecoat. I would be taking naps and I would be more comfortable in my nightgown. I would save my energy for other things. Maybe I could cook a little today. When I went to check on Laura, she was coughing and was very weak, but I thought she looked a wee bit brighter.

"I feel so guilty lying here in your guest room and making you care for me when you feel so lousy yourself," she said.

"I no longer feel lousy. I am mostly just tired. In spite of the sleep I get, I get tired quickly. No, Laura, you cared for me for two weeks until you got sick. There is no reason for guilty feelings. Furthermore, this way Papa does not have to run to your house and we do not need to worry about you being there alone. I am glad you are here. Papa calls this the Steeplechase Hospital. Of course Ray is up and about again with his crutches and does the office visits but poor Papa runs all over the place taking care of the sick. Was there ever such a lot of sickness in January and February? It did not get as cold in January and maybe that is why everyone got sick. Now, Laura, I will go get my coffee. Do you want coffee?"

"No. Maybe tea."

"How about pussy soup?"

She had to smile. "You know, that finally sounds good. Yes, you can make me some."

I went down into the kitchen. I did not move very fast, but it felt good to be doing something normal again. I put some bread over the stove to toast for Laura and for me—all in slow motion and with Murf at my heels. I heated milk, then buttered the toast, put it in a soup bowl and added the hot milk and finally salt. Then I gave some warm milk to Murf. I even salted it a wee bit and put a dab of butter in it. After a sip of my coffee and a bite of toast I took the pussy soup to Laura. I watched as she ate it all.

"Strange how this tastes so good when one is sick. Other times I never eat it." She sighed. "And now I am sleepy again."

"Sleep," I said. "Sleep is healing."

I returned to the kitchen and fried an egg for me. As I was eating, Papa came in.

"You up? How are you?"

"Not bad. Just tired. Will I ever get my energy back?"

"Don't push yourself. We don't want another relapse. How is Laura?"

"She just had breakfast and a little later I will try to get her to wash herself a bit and get her in a fresh nightgown and clean sheets."

I hoped Papa did not mind seeing Laura in Mama's nightgowns, but I couldn't let her lie naked under the covers, especially with Papa being her doctor.

I turned as I heard someone coming slowly down the stairs. Ray.

"How are you?" I asked as Papa looked on.

"Not bad. Slept pretty good, too."

"Those crutches won't help you if you carry them," said Papa.

"I am tired of them already."

Just then Gloria knocked at the door and walked in.

"How are the sick?" she asked me. "I was gone for a few days. My mother was ill and my father wanted my help."

"I am moving and eating," I replied.

"That is an improvement. I need to see more life around here again. Murf was so lonely I had to comfort him whenever I came over. And Laura?"

"I think she is a bit improved and she ate some breakfast."

"Well, I just wanted to see if it is a good day to do your sheets and laundry."

"It is," I replied. "You are an angel in disguise."

"Tell that to my husband. I burned his toast this morning. I will come back later and pick the laundry up. It is a nice day. I can hang the wash out. The snow is melting and I am getting the first urges of spring fever."

"I promise to make this up to you some day, Gloria," I said as she turned to go.

"I'm glad to help."

It was mid morning when the knocker on the front door sounded. I just hoped it was not some emergency. We needed some calm for a change. Gloria had just picked up the laundry and I had stayed downstairs, and was lying on the couch. I just did not want to go back to my bedroom. I needed to see something other than my four walls. I was the only one there to answer the door, so I wrapped my housecoat around me, and opening the door found it to be a delivery boy. My heart beat a bit faster as I remembered what day it was. Was I getting a valentine?

"Good morning," I said with a smile.

The young man looked a bit shyly at me.

"Is this where Laura Harper lives?"

"No, but she is staying here just now."

"Oh. Well, this is for her."

I took the small box and closed the door. So much for that. It was Laura who got the valentine!

Who on earth was sending Laura a valentine? I was, in that moment, envious. However, it would be fun to present her with the small box. I hoped she was not sleeping. But how did they know to bring the valentine here? But of course, Mindy knew she was here.

I trudged up the stairs a bit wearily. I had gone these steps a few times already today and they got longer each time. I also felt like I could sleep again. When I peeked into Laura's room she had her eyes closed, but I could tell she was not sleeping.

"Laura?"

She opened her eyes.

"Surprise. You have a valentine."

"A what?" Her eyes opened wide.

"A delivery boy just left this off for you. You have been holding out on us. Who is your sweetheart?"

Laura huffed. "You know as well as I do there is no sweetheart. They got the wrong name. It is surely for you."

"I wish it were, but it is not." I handed her the small white box. She took it with a strange look on her face. She was clearly clueless.

On the box was her name, but written in the hand of Mindy or her mother. And, as I had suspected, there was no name as to who was the sender.

"That should get you well in a hurry," I teased.

"Oh," she said, "I am too tired to think. It must be a mistake."

I laughed. "Then go to sleep. But I bet you won't sleep right away."

The morning slipped by. Papa did not show up at lunch and Ray relaxed on the couch at noon rather than sit at the table. He was weary. He had somehow bumped his foot and it was hurting and he was wanting a nap. By two-thirty he was back in the office.

It must have been around three o'clock that the knocker sounded again. Papa had eaten a late lunch and left again. I went to the door and was surprised to see the same delivery boy from the bakery. My hopes were raised.

"Are you Amber McDurfee?" he asked.

"I am," I answered and could not keep the smile from my face. I was handed the box without any further ado and I quickly closed the door.

"Please God, let there be a name and let the name be Hunter," I prayed. But I knew that it would not be. I quickly looked inside. There was the beautiful, yummy looking confection with red cherries. The same as Laura's. But there was no name on mine either. I wanted a name. A certain name. It could not be Jonas and of course it could not be Waldo who probably did not know it was Valentine's Day, and who else? Ray would not be so mean as to do it as a joke, would he? I thought of Bentley. If he were younger, I could have thought he might have done it. He was always so admiring of me. But at his age? No. I could not fathom it. He was certainly past such jokes. I remembered the kiss. Could it possibly be Hunter? Please God, let it be him.

I just knew I was too tired to think right now. It was time for a nap. I curled up on the sofa by the fire in the living room and was soon asleep.

Sometime later, I awoke to the sound of voices coming from the kitchen. One voice belonged to my brother Ray and he came into the living room, using his crutches.

"Oh, there you are. Hunter brought two chickens."

I sat up quickly and there stood Hunter behind Ray, his eyes fixed on my tousled hair and sleepy eyes.

"May we come in?" asked Ray belatedly.

"Yes," I said. "Excuse the way I look. Getting dressed takes too much energy and I spend most of the day lying around anyway." This of course was directed at Hunter, who was a sight for sore eyes. He came toward me a bit hesitantly.

"Don't worry about it," he said. "How are you, Amber? You have been sick a long time."

"I have been. I am much better but I am tired all the time. My energy is sadly lacking."

"I should not have come, perhaps," said Hunter. "But a client paid me with two big chickens and I did not know what to do with them."

"Chickens?" I said. I just looked at him. Somehow a real meal was sounding very good to me.

"Chickens are not hard to roast," I said slowly. "Just put them in a pan and stick them in the oven. But with my low energy it sounds like a lot of work."

"I could try to help you after four," said Ray. "Roast chicken sounds very good after all the beans Papa and I have eaten."

I found myself looking at Hunter. I had not seen him for so long I could not stop admiring him.

"Amber," said Hunter. "If you let me go home and put a sign on the office door, saying where I am, I would help you. You can tell me what to do and I will do it."

"Really?" I am sure my face brightened. "You really would?"

"I would," he said, suppressing a smile. "If I am invited for supper."

"It's a deal."

A half hour later Hunter was back. I was feeling more alive than I had since Christmas. I did not know if there was anything going on between Hunter and Lucille, but he was here now and offering to make supper.

"So, where do we start?" asked my would-be cook.

"Wash your hands and put on an apron. You will be glad for it. There are a couple hanging by the sink."

I smothered a smile as he obediently washed his hands and put on one of Mama's old aprons that I often wore. In the meantime, I made myself comfortable on the fainting couch in the kitchen.

Then I proceeded to tell him where to find the big roasting pan. It was all done in rather slow motion. The kitchen was not his place of ease. I had to smile as he awkwardly proceeded to put the spices I asked for on the two chickens.

"This will be a lot of chicken," I said, "but once it is cooked, you can make soup from a bit of it and eat from the rest of it. The leftovers will all go home with you."

"I have a feeling there will be lots of chicken for us all," replied Hunter. "Now what?"

"Now you must peel potatoes."

Hunter looked at me with undisguised shock in his eyes. He had not thought of potatoes.

"That sounds nearly impossible."

"Well, on the other hand, wash them good. Mama has a scrubber she used. It is in the drawer over by the counter. We'll just put them in with the chickens, skin and all. And you will have to wash at least one carrot for each of us and throw in a couple whole onions. Just be glad you don't need to chop them. You would be in tears." I grinned as he gave me one of his "looks."

I continued to give out orders. At first Hunter did not say too much. He was too engrossed in his first cooking lesson. However, partway through he stopped and looked at me.

"You are enjoying this, aren't you?"

"I am," I admitted, not able to hide my smile. "You take orders rather well. I did not expect that from you."

"What is that suppose to mean?"

"Well, you...always seem in charge."

"Is that bad?"

"No, I guess not, but I would think that would make it harder for you to take orders from others. Especially a woman."

Hunter shook his head and smiled. "Ah, how little you know me."

Just then Papa came into the kitchen. I had been giving Hunter his orders from the fainting couch, which was always in the kitchen. It came in handy there because somehow the kitchen became the center for much of our family life. And now here I was, still in my nightgown and housecoat, half lying on the couch and Hunter was washing potatoes.

"Hello," said Papa, stepping into the kitchen and then coming to a dead halt. "What have we here?" He looked around in astonishment. He clearly did not know quite what to make of it. "Hunter, who got you into an apron?" asked my amazed Papa now with an amused look on his face.

"It will save his clothes," I said quickly. "And will keep whatever was on his clothes from any animal, off the food."

Papa smiled but still looked back and forth from Hunter to me. So I explained to Papa about the chickens given to Hunter and how he offered to help cook.

"Wonderful. It seems like a long time since a good meal was cooked here. So you brought the chickens to us?"

"Well, I could not very well use them since I am not a cook. I thought maybe if I brought them here, I would get invited to help eat them."

"You are always a welcome guest here, Hunter. You do not need an invitation. Amber, how are you?" Papa turned his medical eyes to me.

"I had a nap and now I am enjoying bossing Hunter."

There was a chuckle from Papa as he and Hunter exchanged looks.

"And you are taking orders from her?" he asked Hunter

"Sometimes one has no choice. I'd like some roast chicken."

"I understand the dilemma. Where is Ray?"

"In the office," I said. "There seems to be a steady stream of patients today. He rested a bit at noon. He bumped his foot and it was hurting and it makes him tired."

"And how is Laura?"

She ate pussy soup for breakfast and more toast at noon.

"Pussy soup?" said Hunter with the strangest expression in his eyes and dropping the potato in his hand on the floor. "You gave her Murf's food?"

I laughed and explained the toast, butter and milk. "We always call it pussy soup. I guess because cats like it. It tastes good when you are ill and not hungry for ordinary food."

"I shall go check on Laura," said Papa, leaving Hunter shaking his head over the pussy soup.

"Ask her about her valentine," I called after Papa.

"Her valentine?" Papa stopped short. "Is someone trying to steal our housekeeper?"

I laughed. "It was unsigned. From the bakery. A nice cherry and whipped cream concoction. I think she has been holding out on us."

Papa left the room and I soon heard him going up the stairs.

I hoped Hunter would ask if I got a valentine, but he said nothing.

When the chickens and vegetables were finally in the biggest roasting pan Mama had, Hunter took a kitchen chair and set it close to me. Then he sat down, his arms resting on his knees and leaned toward me.

"So Laura got a valentine?"

"She did. I have no clue and neither does she. Actually, I think it is hilarious. What old man is setting his cap for her? How old could she be?"

Hunter gave me long look.

"You sure she has no clue?"

I looked at him in surprise. "Of course. Do you have a clue?"

He took his time and I thought he looked at me as if contemplating whether or not to answer.

"Actually, I do," he said finally.

"You think you know who sent her the unsigned valentine?"

He just looked at me a long moment then nodded.

"Who?" I asked, completely puzzled. His eyes held mine and I almost thought he would not answer.

"How about your Papa?"

I looked at him blankly. He just looked back at me.

"What? Of course not!"

Hunter could see my dismay and immediately held up both hands. "Sorry, I did not mean to upset you."

"What makes you even think that?" My words were a bit sharp.

"I just have observed a few things and...found them interesting."

"He wouldn't." I was amazed at the nasty thoughts spinning in my brain. "He wouldn't do that to Mama. Never."

Hunter leaned a bit more in my direction, his elbows on his knees again.

"Amber," he said softly, "no one will ever replace your mother. Hang on to the memories and thank God for them. But life goes on. You will eventually marry, as will Ray. Your father is lonelier than you think. The other half of him is gone, and she is not coming back. He needs a companion. Can you think of anyone better than Laura? She is already part of the family." He hesitated as I tried to comprehend what he was saying. "Amber, just think about it as a possibility. That is all."

"What do you know about loneliness?" I asked with a bit of a bite. "You claim Papa is lonely yet you do quite well apparently."

He hesitated, ignoring my question.

"What you probably do not know is that I lost my mother when I was twelve."

"Oh!" I was instantly sorry for the bite in my tone.

"The mother I have now is my step-mother. She is a good companion to my father and a good substitute mother to us boys. We'd have rather had my real mother, but she was gone."

"I'm so sorry," I said, and somehow my emotions were weak from being sick and I blinked back sudden tears.

"It was a rough time for all of us for awhile because we boys were young yet. We did not want a strange woman acting like she was our mother. But she was kind and patient with us and eventually we were happy to call her mother."

"Amber!" yelled Papa, coming down the stairs. "When is supper?"

"Six thirty," I said and promptly yawned.

"I suggest you take a nap. Your eyes look tired. Do you have a fever?"

"No, I am sure I do not. I feel good. Just weary."

But he came to me anyway and laid his hand on my forehead to make sure.

"The stove needs more wood," I said.

"I'll do it. Anything else to be done?"

"There is applesauce in the ice box and I think that will do it for supper."

Two hours later I woke from my nap in the living room. Someone was at the door. I saw it was Mindy. Her eyes widened when I opened the door clad in housecoat and slippers.

"Amber? Are you still sick?"

"I don't think I am sick, just very, very tired. Come in."

"It smells wonderful in here. Who is cooking? You don't look like you are up to it."

"Hunter is cooking."

"Hunter is cooking supper for you?"

I had to laugh at Mindy's face. "Well, he got it ready for the oven according to my instructions, and then went home again 'til supper-time. Papa will help get the chicken cut up and food on the table."

"Ah, and who makes the gravy?"

"Oh, I forgot the gravy! None of them can do it. Maybe..."

"I'll do it now if the chicken is done."

God bless Mindy. She surely saved us from lumpy gravy. It took her a while to get the birds and the vegetables out of the roasting pan so she could pour the juices in another pan, but she managed.

While she stirred the gravy, I washed my face, fixed my hair and checked on Laura. I even invited Mindy for supper, but after a short visit, she left again. I looked at the staircase and wondered if I had the strength to climb them once more and change to a dress. But I could not face the many steps. My housecoat would stay on. It covered me well and Hunter had already seen me in it. I was too tired to care.

When the men arrived, Ray sat at the table while Papa and Hunter very awkwardly put the food in bowls and on the table. I enjoyed watching. I did not join them at the table. I decided I would rather sit on the fainting couch to eat. It would be too wearisome to sit so long at the table.

The meal was delicious and I gave praise to Hunter. I think he was quite proud of himself although he said I was really responsible for it. Partway through the meal, Gloria came over with the finished laundry.

"Whoa, this looks like an improvement! Who was the cook?"

"Our benefactor Hunter. He cooked here under Amber's supervision," said Papa.

"Wow! I'm impressed. How is Laura?"

"A bit better. I will take her some chicken, potatoes and gravy later. She was sleeping when I last looked," said Papa.

"She got a valentine today," I told Gloria, with a furtive glance at Papa. "Unsigned."

"Laura got a valentine? One of those yummy concoctions from the bakery?" asked Gloria.

I nodded, wanting to look at Hunter, but refrained.

"How interesting. I would expect you could get one, but Laura?"

"Maybe someone wants to steal my housekeeper," said Papa.

"And Hunter? I hope you delivered a valentine yourself."

There was a hesitation of a few seconds.

"I did, actually."

"The chickens?"

Oops. Gloria made a mistake, implying that Hunter gave me the chickens as a valentine. I winced, but Hunter seemed to ignore it.

"No, a valentine. Signed."

I sat in stunned silence, and my heart landed somewhere under the fainting couch. So Hunter had actually delivered a valentine to someone. Was Lucille at her aunt and uncle's? I felt as if I could faint. It had to be Lucille.

"And Amber? Did you get one?"

Neither Papa nor Ray knew of the valentine I had gotten. They both looked at me. I hoped I would not cry.

"I did, sometime this afternoon. But it was probably Bentley. He is my only admirer at the time."

"I doubt very much it was Bentley," said Gloria laughing. "If it was unsigned I would say it was just someone who was too cowardly to sign his name."

"I hope Dennis gave you one," said Hunter to Gloria.

"He did. He came home with one red rose from the flower shop. He, of course, is the best valentine I could have."

"Did you ever give Mama a valentine?" I asked Papa, still wondering if Hunter was right about Papa and Laura.

Papa got quiet and studied the tumbler he was holding in his hand with a faraway look. "I proposed on Valentine's Day," he said softly.

"Oh Papa, how romantic. I never knew you were so romantic."

"Ah," said Papa, coming back from his memories, "you just think I am an old man and was never young. And from whom do you think you inherited all your romantic notions?"

We all joined in the laughter. Gloria left again and the room now seemed rather quiet. I could not forget the valentine Hunter had delivered. Who had gotten a valentine from him? And no one speculated on the one I got. I wished Gloria had never asked Hunter. It spoiled my evening. Now I had to act cheerful and my heart was bleeding.

Somehow Ray remembered that there was a partial apple pie somewhere and Papa got up and found it and the men finished it up. Then Ray and Hunter did the clean up with one whole chicken going back to Hunter. He would have chicken for days. I was told to stay put on the fainting couch and I told them what to do with the leftovers. While they were doing the dishes, I just listened to them talk. The energy I had run on since Hunter's arrival had dwindled to nothing. In fact, I was fighting tears. Hunter had delivered a signed valentine and it was not to me. I felt like someone had crushed me into the earth with a heavy boot.

When Murf arrived, demanding some chicken, Ray got it for him and set it by the couch.

"By the way, Hunter," said Ray, going back to scrubbing the roasting pan, "thanks for making the delivery for me. I knew I could not get up to Pipers Hill today and when you said you were heading that way it seemed the right thing to do. What did she say?"

"She beamed."

My eyes flew open. I looked at Hunter at just the moment he gave me a quick glance. Did he see my relief? He evidently had delivered Ray's valentine to Sylvia. Maybe he had not even given any valentine. My spirits were once more buoyed. I felt like a ton of bricks had fallen off my back. I tried to tell myself that he still could have delivered a valentine to someone else, but I could not deny the hope that came into my heart. I said nothing, but my mood changed completely.

The clean up finished, Hunter prepared to leave. I stayed on the couch and watched him collect his chicken and put on his coat. Ray, who was going over to the office went out the door first. But when Ray had gone, Hunter turned to me, the leftover chicken in his hands.

"Thanks for the cooking lesson and the good supper."

"Anytime. You did quite well." I tried to smile but did not quite make it.

Hunter just stood and looked at me a few moments as if undecided regarding something. Then he put the chicken back on the table and slowly walked over to me. I watched him curiously as he approached and I looked up in surprise as he took my hand in his and leaned down close to my face.

"Enjoy your valentine confection."

His voice was low and his eyes held mine for a long moment, my hand in his. It was as if he was waiting for me to understand something. Suddenly my eyes opened wide and he grinned and with his forefinger, ran it down the side of my face. And then he turned and once more picked up the chicken and went to the door. Just before he closed the door he looked once more in my direction and found me starry-eyed and beaming.

I watched as the door closed behind him. I stared at the door a long time after he left.

And then I put my hand to my face and very gently placed it on my cheek where Hunter's finger had so recently touched me.

CHAPTER 31

March arrived with a thaw but by the end of the first week, it got cold and stayed below freezing for two whole weeks. I knew from Ray that the lambing had already begun for Tim. I felt sorry for lambs born in this cold weather, but also knew that Tim would take good care of them. I hoped to sometime get up there to see them, but I knew it would be stretched out over several weeks so I would wait for warmer weather.

After a week of the cold, cold weather, the shallow pond in the field where we saw the fireworks in July froze over and there was ice skating. This was a bonus. Ice skating should have been over by now. I ran over to the bakery and asked Mindy if she would go skating with me that evening. She promised to go with me.

When we got to the pond that evening, it was full of skaters. Teenagers, children and adults were all weaving around on the ice. Who knows how many days we could skate yet? We all took advantage of it. Mindy and I quickly put on our skates. I kept hoping I would see Hunter, but I was not seeing him. Maybe he would come later. We were soon skimming over the ice, breathing in the cold air and sometimes chatting with other skaters.

"Keep your eyes open for Hunter," I said after a while. "I don't think he is here, but maybe I just missed him."

"Oh," said Mindy. "I don't know how much truth is in it, but just to warn you, evidently Lucille is here again. Or maybe she is just coming today. I am not sure. But her aunt was talking to my mother and said she is hoping for a June wedding."

My heart plummeted. In fact it felt like it went right under the ice. Something really must be going on for her to talk about a wedding. Was I wrong about the valentine confection? I remembered how Hunter had leaned over me, and just looked at me a while after telling me about enjoying it. Would he say that if he knew it came from someone else? Of course not! But in spite of what I told myself, I found myself doubting. The aunt was talking of a wedding? I wanted to throw up. It seemed every time I thought he really did like me, then something like this turned up. I felt like I was in a carriage on a very bumpy road and just when I felt like I was flying through the air over a nice hump in the road, I would come down hard again with my heart being thrown under the wheels and ground into the dust

As a result of this bit of news, my thoughts were occupied and I was not watching where I was going. As a result, we collided with another skater and we all three fell. Before I could get up, the young man we skated into was up and helping Mindy to get on her feet. He did so much apologizing and so did Mindy that I was left to pick myself up. In fact, I don't know if he even knew I was involved. He seemed to have eyes only for Mindy. He asked her to skate and I was left standing. Or skating. When Mindy finally joined me again, she laughed. When the young man discovered she was two years older then he was, he soon found someone else to skate with him.

Mindy had not yet heard from Carl, but I sincerely hoped when the orchestra started practicing that they would get back together. As for Hunter, I never did see him that evening.

———

"Amber!" Ray called to me the next morning. "I need someone to deliver a book to Hunter."

Ray was spending all his spare moments with his head in medical books.

"And who did you have in mind?"

"You, of course. He wants to read this book and I promised it to him a couple days ago and I really don't want to take the time now. Papa is out on calls and I expect someone here in the office within minutes."

"And if Hunter is not home?"

"Just put it in his house. It is always open."

I had not seen Hunter to really talk to since Valentine's Day. The winter had been long and lonely and my hopes had soared after his words to me that day. But now there was silence again. Thoughts of Lucille kept invading my thoughts of Hunter. What was happening with him and Lucille? Why did she keep coming to Steeplechase? But of course, I knew why. I had heard her talking of him at the inn. Was he giving her hope? Maybe the aunt was not exaggerating.

In spite of my doubts, I could not suppress a bit of excitement in me now as I agreed to deliver the book. I could not help myself. I wanted to see him again.

It was cold and I dressed warmly. There was a bit of a breeze from the north and I pulled my cloak tightly around me. Halfway there, I stopped at the library and dropped off a book and warmed up a bit as I chatted with the librarian. Then I was once more on my way. As I turned in the lane I heard the ring of an ax. So he was home. My heart beat faster. I walked toward the sound of the ax and found Hunter next to his stable. He was swinging his ax with terrible force and the wood was flying. I stopped and watched just a bit. He almost looked like he was frowning and he was so involved he never saw me. Finally I got close enough that some movement caught his eye. He looked up and I saw the surprise on his face. And the slightest of smiles.

"Amber."

"Wow," I said, ignoring my thumping heart and trying to act as if he were just the newspaper boy. "I'd hate to be the object of your frustration the way you are attacking that wood."

Hunter looked soberly at me for a moment before replying, and my heart told me he was certainly not the newspaper boy.

"You are the object."

I was so stunned by his words, I felt the blood leave my face. But surely he was joking.

"Are you telling me that I am the reason you are hitting that wood like you are killing a dragon?"

He merely nodded without a smile, his look keen.

"Am I allowed to ask why?"

He did not answer. He just continued to look at me as if I were a creature he was seeing for the first time. But I told myself he could not be angry without cause. That was not Hunter.

"What did I do?"

"What did you do? You intruded into my life."

"All I did was bring you this book from Ray," I said, a bit shrilly. I could not believe this conversation. All I could think of was Lucille. Was he falling for her? Was I an obstacle? I felt his sober scrutiny as I faced him. I was hurt and angry and close to tears. My emotions could not take this continual up and down. Before the tears would be seen, I had to get out of there. This was a big let down after being excited about seeing him again. I swallowed hard.

"Here is Ray's book you wanted to read," I said, throwing it on his jacket that he had thrown on the ground. "Chop your wood." And with this childish reaction, I turned away.

"Amber!"

I ignored him, walking as fast as I could. It felt good ignoring him. I was somehow getting him back. I wanted him to come after me and apologize, but he did not. That made me feel worse yet. I blinked back tears. I had really messed things up now. I was mentally kicking myself all the way out the lane. I had to forget this man. Forget the kiss on the mountain and the cherry confection on Valentine's Day. I would prove to myself that I could forget.

"Did you take the book to Hunter?" Ray asked at the supper table.

"Yes," I answered. I said no more.

"Was he at home?"

"Yes."

"He was probably surprised I finally got it to him," said Ray between bites of his supper.

I made no comment. Both Papa and Ray looked at me. I realized that my answers were too short.

"He was busy chopping wood," I said, trying to fill in the emptiness of my short answers.

"Hunter must be thinking of getting married with all his house renovations," Ray observed.

It scared me stiff. Ray also said that he and Sylvia were going skating after supper. I was happy for them. They made a cute couple. She needed his sense of humor and he needed her seriousness to even things out. He was now much more serious and he was enjoying his work with patients and did a lot of personal studying. When he asked if I was going skating, I hedged. I was not in an ice skating mood. But on the other hand, it was quite possibly the last night of skating for the winter. It would be better to get out on the ice and in the cold night air than to sit here in the house and brood about Hunter.

About an hour later, still in shock about my talk with Hunter, I headed for the ice, my skates over my shoulder. My steps were slow and I felt that I had not a friend in the world. I had not talked to Mindy but now I would simply look for her. She would probably be there.

By the light of a bonfire along the pond I saw there were a good many skaters. I saw Mindy flying around the ice with someone that could have been Carl. It was really too dark to see very well. I sat down on a log by the fire and slowly put on my skates, wondering if Hunter would be there. What would I do if he attempted to talk to me? I was really not ready to see him after this morning's meeting. I was hoping I would have some time to skate with Mindy, but I could not count on it. Not if it was Carl she was skating with.

It took me forever to get my skates on but I was finally ready to skate. I stood and was just ready to step on the ice when a couple skated past me. I stopped breathing. The man was definitely Hunter. I would know him anywhere. But who was he with? Definitely a female but with all the warm clothes and scarves, it was hard to recognize anyone. Also, the only light was from the bonfire and a few torches around the pond.

I walked away from the fire into the shadows and waited for Hunter to come around again. The pond was not that big and if I waited long enough, I was sure to see them. The girl's face had been turned from me, possibly because she was talking to Hunter. I watched with bated breath, hoping no one would interrupt my spying and silently waited. Finally, my waiting was rewarded and my heart hit the ground.

Lucille.

She was even laughing her shrill laugh as they passed me. I would know that laugh anywhere. As they passed, however, Hunter looked over to the fire and then in my direction and I had the strangest feeling he saw me in spite of the shadows. I was not certain. But I was sick. He really was with Lucille again! Was that the reason for Hunter's wild wood splitting? He was blaming me for his frustrations. Did he know I was in love with him and he was reluctant to tell me about Lucille? I felt tears near the surface and quickly went back to the fire, took off my skates and without another look at the ice or the skaters, headed back the way I had come. I could not skate where Hunter and Lucille were skating. I found my legs felt shaky. I walked into the cold air, past the gas lamps and the lantern lit houses but saw nothing. The wind whipped through the bare branches of the trees above me and the cold wind stung my face. I felt terribly, frightfully alone. Was this serious between Hunter and Lucille? She admitted she was out to get him. I had no reason to feel betrayed, but I did. So he was getting the house fixed up for her. I had tears streaming down my face and I bent my face into my scarf and walked as quickly as I could. I was glad for the dark. I was glad Ray was not home. But I had to get myself in shape before I saw Papa. Now I welcomed the cold air and I took deep breaths of it. My legs ached from walking so fast, but finally I could turn off and follow a path through the park. At the end of the park I wiped my eyes, crossed the avenue in front of our house and stepped in the door. Papa sat in his chair reading. He looked up in surprise. I did not give him more than a quick glance.

"You done skating already?"

"I changed my mind. It is cold out there."

"The cold never seemed to bother you before."

I walked into the hall, put my clothes in the closet and my skates in the back porch.

"I'm going to bed early."

"Amber." I walked back to the door of the living room. "Is everything all right?" asked Papa.

Papa was so perceptive. He knew something was wrong in my world. I could not fool him.

"No, Papa," I replied, my voice trembling ever so slightly. "Nothing is right. But I don't want to talk about it."

He was still looking at me as I abruptly turned and headed up the stairs.

Papa was still up when Ray got home. It was late, but Papa did not mind snoozing on his chair.

"That you Ray?"

"Yep. Why are you still up?"

"Were you skating?"

"Yes. I thought Amber was coming."

"She was there and left. Was Hunter there?"

"Hunter? Actually, yes, I did see him. He was with that Lucille again. She comes to visit rather often, if you ask me."

"That answers my question," said Papa with a sigh.

Ray looked at Papa in silence a moment. "I thought for sure something was happening between Hunter and Amber."

Papa made no comment.

"I saw him just before I left," continued Ray. "He was alone then. I told him to come for supper tomorrow night for my birthday. I also asked Sylvia. Is that okay?"

"I hope it is. Let's invite Laura, too. It might help Amber."

<hr>

I had mixed emotions when I heard at breakfast that Hunter was invited to the birthday supper. A part of me was happy to know I would be seeing him again. On the other hand, if he was seeing Lucille, I had no wish to see him. I decided that I had to let him know he could not brazenly kiss me at the Christmas Party, give me a valentine, and then let Lucille turn his head when she turned up. Had he known she was coming to the Christmas Eve service? I doubted it. She did not live around here. I was sure she was making excuses to come to see her aunt. It was very clear to me that she was after Hunter. And he was letting her pull him around. That is what made me angry. How could he be so weak? He never gave me any indication of a weak character before. I was angry and just wanted to cry. And this evening he was to be here and I had to know how I was going to treat him. I stewed about it as I cooked. It was Laura's day to work so she helped me cook the birthday supper. I finally decided I would just treat him like I would anyone else. I would imagine he was a brother-in-law. That would be hard. I wanted to look into his eyes. I wanted to enjoy watching him as he talked to others at the table. But I would try to look elsewhere. I would not be attentive to him. Not at all.

Laura must have wondered about my mood, because I was distracted and talked little. But she said nothing. I planned ahead of time where everyone would sit. I would have Papa at the head of the table with Hunter on one side of him and Ray on the other. I would sit at the other end with Laura to one side and Sylvia on the other. Safe from Hunter.

So I planned. That evening when Hunter arrived, I stayed in the kitchen as long as possible and when I got into the dining room, they were all standing at the table. Papa had Laura on one side of him and an empty chair on the other side for me. Ray was at the other end with Hunter on one side and Sylvia on the other. Why had I stayed in the kitchen so long? I should have put name cards by the plates. To my dismay, I had to sit between Papa and Hunter. Seeing this I stopped, with I'm afraid, my mouth open. But I caught myself and I smiled and greeted both Hunter and Sylvia in one breath. As soon as I got to the table, Papa helped Laura, Ray helped Sylvia and Hunter held my chair for me.

"Wow. We have a table full of gentlemen this evening," I said breezily, not letting my eyes linger on Hunter.

"Hunter taught us well," said Papa as he took his seat.

"Oh, this food smells wonderful," said Sylvia, after Papa said the blessing.

"My favorite meal," said Ray, who was now twenty-three. I observed the two of them and was amazed at how at ease they were with each other. I suddenly realized there would probably be a wedding sometime in the future. I had hardly been aware of their courtship. I had been so involved with my own life.

When Hunter passed the potatoes to me, our fingers touched. I tried to tell myself it was the same as touching Ray's, but it was not. I felt my face was red ever since I came in the room and this did not help. I had to think of someone else.

"Sylvia, how is life on the sheep farm? How many days do you work?" I asked.

"Five. My most fun is when I get to feed a lamb."

"Oh, are the lambs coming already?" I already knew they were, but said it for the sake of conversation.

"They are. They are born late winter or early spring. Hunter," she said, turning to him, "did I see you there yesterday?"

"Yes, you did. Tim expected trouble with one of the ewes and asked me to stop by."

"And?"

"It was good I came when I did. There were complications." Hunter turned to me. "You need to go up there soon to see the lambs. You would love them."

"I'm sure I would," I said, barely looking at him. "Would someone please pass the gravy?"

I was aware of a searching look from Papa. I was not fooling him. And what was all the talking between Papa and Laura? She even looked a bit red in the face. Could something possibly be happening there? I felt tears in my throat and quickly set my sights on the piece of beef roast on my plate, cutting with a kind of violence. Soon Sylvia and Ray were laughing about something and Papa was telling Laura some story about Ray when Hunter turned to me.

"Did I see you at the bonfire last evening or was it my imagination?"

Why did it seem to me like everyone at the table stopped talking?

"You may have," I said, looking at my food. There was a part of me that loved sitting next to Hunter. I wanted to lean against him and feel his strength. But I forced myself to stay cool. And to lean a bit in the opposite direction.

"But I never saw you on the ice."

I wanted to reply that I was surprised that he saw me at all with Lucille's hand in his.

"I changed my mind. It was cold and I...decided that I just didn't really feel like skating."

There was complete silence for a few moments.

"Can I bring anyone more water?"

"We're fine," said Papa with a knowing look in my direction.

I concentrated on my food as Sylvia, Hunter and Ray got talking about Tim and his sheep again. I felt so left out, but it was my own fault. I just did not know how to act and it was making me nearly weepy.

"Oh, Amber," said Laura softly. "I almost forgot to tell you. I saw Minna and Abe Stork the other day. They were at the bakery and were getting the stage to the train station. Minna said to give you greetings and to tell you things were going well for them."

"I am so glad to hear it. I still have problems believing he is alive."

In a quieter voice, Laura leaned toward me and added, "And she said to tell you that there is a little one on the way."

"I am so happy for her."

"She also asked about you, Hunter," said Laura in a louder tone. "She asked whether you found a replacement for her or if you got married."

I froze.

I had no reason to freeze. Even if he were planning to marry Lucille, he would not announce it here. As it was, Hunter said not a thing and I could not take the stress.

"I think I shall get the dessert before there is a call for help and our doctors leave the table," I said, getting up immediately.

There was a general murmur as plates were stacked and I took things to the kitchen. Laura began to stand up, but I quickly told her I could handle it. I needed a bit of solitude in the kitchen. As I was clearing the table, I overheard Ray asking Hunter about his house renovations.

"I put running water in the house and also an indoor toilet," I heard him say. "Also some living room renovations."

"Soon the outhouse will be outdated," said Ray.

"I think it will take a while yet, but I am glad to have the indoor toilet. You have had it for a year already, I believe."

"True. I don't want to live without it anymore."

When I brought in the birthday cake with the lighted candles, we sang for Ray. I had given him his sweater at breakfast already. He needed it badly. The conversation turned to Ray and I calmed a bit. The birthday celebration did not last long after supper. Laura needed to go home and Papa said he'd walk her home. Said he needed the exercise after that meal. Ray would soon take Sylvia back to Pipers Hill and I was sure Hunter would be gone soon, too. As I set a stack of dishes on the counter, I heard footsteps behind me. I tensed up when I saw it was Hunter with a load of dishes. He put them on the table. I gave him a quick glance and busied myself with the clean up.

"Thanks," I said. "But that was not necessary."

I did not look at him but he did not leave.

"I beg to disagree. It was necessary," he countered.

When he made no move to leave, I looked at him. He gave me a long, sober look. For some reason, I caught myself blinking back tears and I looked away and again busied myself with my dishes.

"I want to know why you did not skate last evening."

I hoped he was sorry I left. I finally looked at him. We were standing across the table from each other and suddenly the words just slipped out.

"I came home to chop wood."

I saw the understanding on his face.

"Thanks for the good meal," he said quietly, not smiling, and left the kitchen. I did not see him again. When I was sure I was the only one home anymore, I no longer blinked back the tears. Instead I let them drip into the dish water. It was not fun being cool to the man I most admired.

The senior Dr. McDurfee was just ending his office hours the next day when to his surprise he saw one last patient had slipped in.

"Well, Hunter, I hope your case is not serious."

"It is. It is very serious, but I think not deadly."

The Dr. chuckled and locked the outside door.

"Can I see you here in the waiting room?"

"Please. Believe it or not, I do not like going to the doctor," he said with a very slight smile.

Dr. McDurfee took a seat close to Hunter and waited while his last patient collected his thoughts.

"It is Amber," he said finally, wanting some sort of response from her Papa.

"I sensed her coolness at the birthday party."

"It was more like frostbite," said Hunter, dryly.

Dr. McDurfee chuckled and waited.

"I am in trouble with your daughter," Hunter said slowly. And then he was suddenly standing and began pacing across the room. "I believe it is a misunderstanding and some poor action on my part."

The doctor said nothing. He could be very patient.

"I intend to try to fix things up. But I do not know when it will be or how I will do it."

The doctor waited with just a hint of amusement in his eyes as he observed the struggling Dr. Renwick. The silence grew long.

"And?" coached the doctor.

"If I get the problem solved, I...I'd like your permission to..." Hunter stopped pacing and faced the doctor. "I want to marry Amber and I would like your blessing."

Dr. McDurfee smiled. A big smile.

"Glad to hear it, Hunter." Now the doctor stood also. "I had you picked out for Amber the first time you came for supper."

"I am humbly grateful. I do not know when it will happen, but if we ever get our lives untangled, I wanted to be sure I have your blessing before I ask her."

"You have my blessing, Hunter, but walk carefully. Amber is more like a snowman than a teddy bear just now."

Hunter finally smiled as the doctor offered his hand. At least he had her Papa's blessing. Now to face the snowman.

CHAPTER 32

The day after Ray's birthday party, I got a letter from my brother Floyd. He was just next to me in age and worked in a hospital in Burlington. In the letter he said his wife Alice broke her wrist and wondered if I would come and help out for a week or so. He added that the winter had been long for her and she tended to get depressed easily, so the company would be good. I showed the letter to Papa and after he conferred with both Ray and Laura, it was decided. I was free to go until Easter, which fell in mid April this year.

The following day, I took the mid-morning stagecoach from the Carriage Inn. Mud season was beginning and I was not eager for the trip during this time of the year. It would be hazardous. I first thought I would be the only one on the coach, but then Bentley Queens got on at the last moment. He looked at me with surprise and then his big grin took over his whole face.

"Well, look who I get to ride with," he beamed.

"I am glad to ride with you too, Bentley. How have you been this winter?"

"Not bad," he said his eyes twinkling as he made himself comfortable beside me. "I just had to have your Papa over one time. He said his house was a virtual hospital. Said you were sick, too."

"Don't remind me. It was bad. I don't even want to think about it. Where are you headed?"

"To my daughter, so I will be getting off again at the next stop. And you?"

"I am going to Burlington."

"Ah, I would like to see Burlington again. The city, according to the newspaper, keeps growing."

"So my brother tells me."

"And how long are you staying?"

"Hopefully not too long. But I think I shall enjoy it. I am tired of winter. I need to see something new. My sister-in-law broke her wrist and needs help. But I am hoping for time to see the shops there."

"I hope you brought lots of money," said Bentley with his signature grin.

The carriage came to a halt in a small village and it was time for Bentley to get off already. For several miles I rode alone. I had time to look at the scenery and was appalled by the conditions of the road. They would get worse, but they were bad enough already. Sometimes we could swerve to the other side of the road. Other times we plowed through the mud. About three miles later we picked up two young men and a married couple. There was a lot of talk between the two young men and I mostly just listened to them while I feasted my eyes on villages we passed through and the fields, which were showing bits of green.

The stage arrived without incident in Burlington about an hour later. I discovered the streets here were just as muddy as everywhere else. Maybe more so due to the amount of traffic on the streets. But I was busy taking in the relatively young city. I had been in Burlington only once or twice before and it was a bustling lumber and manufacturing center. I gazed with awe at the fine architecture. Also, just ten or so years earlier the waterfront was extended by the construction of the Pine Street Canal. I exited the carriage at a large inn on the main street in Burlington. From there I hired a carriage to take me directly to my brother's house. Floyd and Alice lived within sight of Lake Champlain and my heart was already lifted from my winter doldrums. Here I would forget about Hunter and enjoy myself. There were no babies to tend, I just needed to help Alice with the housework and mending and laundry and cooking. And I would have time to explore the city.

I knocked on the door and Alice answered. She was looking somewhat pale and had her wrist in a sling. I was glad I had come to help.

"Oh, Amber, it is so good to see you! Come in! I feel like such a baby asking for your help but my wrist hurts badly if I try to move it and I can't even dress myself."

"I am glad to be here. It has been so long since we visited. And it will be good for me. The winter has been difficult. I am looking forward to our time together."

She suggested tea by the fire and I told her I would get it. She showed me a small room where I could sleep and then I went into her kitchen and made myself at home there. It was not long before we were sitting close to the fire and drinking our steaming tea.

"You must tell me everything about Steeplechase. I hear once in a while from my mother, but she does not like to write, so it does not happen often," began Alice. "And now I can't write either."

So I told Alice all the news, carefully sifting through all my stories to not give away my heartache. When I was done, I asked about Burlington.

"Floyd is working at the hospital and loves it. He sometimes wonders if he should have become a doctor like his father, and I will support him if that is what he wishes. As to the city, there is always something going on here and I hope we can go shopping one day. Here you see the latest fashions, can attend good concerts, and you can even go fishing in Lake Champlain with Floyd if you wish."

I laughed. "I don't think we will be fishing in this weather. But in the summertime a picnic along the lake would be inviting."

By the time my brother Floyd came home from work, I had a chicken and noodle casserole in the oven and the evening was spent pleasantly around the fire. Floyd, unlike Ray, was a serious person much like Papa. He thought before he spoke. He mulled topics over in his mind before he gave his opinion. He was just older than I and we had been close when he was at home.

The following days felt like a vacation for me in spite of the fact that I did a lot of the work. As the days passed, Alice felt better, but she was hampered by the wrapped-up wrist. But we found time on sunny days to walk around the university and to stroll past the shops. There was so much more to offer in the way of clothes that I never tired of just window shopping.

On a sunny day in early April, the three of us took the ferry across the lake to Port Kent. There we hired a carriage to take us the three to four miles to Ausable Chasm, a sandstone gorge, where we walked along the river with the high walls of the chasm on both sides of us. It was damp but exciting. There was a lot of water flowing through the chasm and one had to be careful where one stepped. But it was not good weather and after a while we were too cold and we headed home again. However, I promised myself I would come back in the summertime and take the small boat through the chasm when it was not so cold.

By the time Good Friday arrived, it was time to travel back home. There was a Good Friday service at the church Floyd and Alice attended and I joined them for the service. In the afternoon, I headed for home. Truly, winter had melted into spring and the roads were so bad I did not want to take the stage. Instead I took the train to Flynn Falls. There were many stories of carriages stuck in the oozing mud and I would have enough of that from Flynn Falls home. It was a longer journey this way, but safer.

Suppertime was spent telling Papa and Ray all about my life in the city. They had many questions and I asked all about home. I was hoping for some word of Hunter, but got not one word and was too proud to ask about him. Or scared. Saturday I dyed a few eggs and prepared food for an Easter meal. I was informed that Sylvia was coming as well as Laura. Papa said Laura worked hard for them the last two weeks and deserved to eat a meal she had not prepared. When Papa told Ray he should invite Hunter, I held my breath. But Ray said that Hunter was going to his parents for the day. That was all. I wanted to hear much more, but at least there was no talk of Lucille.

Easter morning the sun was shining and the air mild. What a

blessing. I welcomed spring with outstretched arms this year. I was sorry I would not see Hunter at church, but was eager to see Gloria and Mindy again. We had a glorious service. I got my thoughts off of myself and my misery, and I joined my voice with the church in singing glad hymns of the Resurrection of Jesus. I praised the Lord and gave thanks and it cheered me considerably.

After the service, I turned to go out the aisle and stopped short. Three benches behind me was Hunter. Why was he here? He was going to his parents for Easter. And then, right before my eyes and before I had a chance to meet Hunter's eyes, a woman from the other side of the church walked across the aisle and greeted him with a big smile and gushing words. Lucille. I just could not believe it. Why had he told Ray he was going to his parents? Or was he taking her along? My heart froze and I somehow got out of church without another glance in their direction and went home without talking to anyone else on this wonderful Easter day.

I was just miserable. Actually, I was angry. Not only had this woman spoiled part of my Christmas, here she was to put a damper on my Easter. I was nearly sick with all that my imagination offered me on the subject of Hunter and Lucille. Finally, during our Easter dinner, Ray informed Papa that Hunter broke a carriage wheel in the mud and could not go to his folks. By the time Ray had invited Hunter for dinner, he had already been invited to Lucille's uncle and aunt. And had accepted.

There was, however, something good that happened at the Easter dinner. Papa suggested a family reunion. He suggested that we meet for a one-year anniversary of Mama's death. It gave me something to think about. Something to plan and get my thoughts off the illusive bachelor. And the anniversary of Mama's death was only two weeks away.

I was happy for every sign of spring—every snowdrop, any greening blade of grass, any new bird song that had not been heard all winter. The past months had been so difficult. The long sickness. The ups and downs of my relationship with Hunter. The scepter of Lucille that still hung over my head. Now my thoughts were on the family reunion. I would see Ruby again. What a blessing she had been when we were all sick. And Connie. She lived not far from Flynn Falls and was a farmer's wife who was up to her neck with work and caring for four children. And when had I seen Joe last? He was busy working his own small farm and milked cows and never got away. I hoped that by the beginning of May it might be a bit warmer and I needed warmth in my inner being as well. I caught Papa looking at me sometimes with a worried look. I was sad. I was trying to be happy, but deep down, I was sad. The reunion would be good for me. It would blow Hunter out of my thoughts. We could remember Mama and tell stories about her. Just talking about her would bring her into our midst once again. And so it was planned. The whole family was informed and all responded with a yes. I know we all looked forward to it.

One morning when Papa and I were discussing the reunion, Gloria dropped by, needing to borrow a cup of sugar for a cake she was baking.

"You are having a family reunion? Wonderful! You missed each other at Christmas. I love family reunions and know it will be a lot of work. Let me help with it. I could bake a ham and then you can have potato salad, and that sort of thing to go with it."

"Gloria, you are the best neighbor yet! If you bake the ham you and Dennis may consider yourselves part of the family and join us," I assured her.

The reunion would take place on a Sunday afternoon. The day preceding the reunion I was kept busy all morning preparing food and getting ready for a family invasion in the house. By mid afternoon the salads were made and the house, thanks to Laura's special cleaning on

Friday, was in order. I flopped down on the couch just as Ray came into the room.

"Amber, I am heading up to Pipers Hill to see a patient. I can drop you off at Tim's sheep farm if you want to come along. You really need to see the lambs. You missed most of the smaller ones although I think some are still being born. They are growing so fast they will be big mamas themselves if you wait much longer."

It sounded good to me. I had supper planned and all was ready for the reunion.

"I would love to. Let me get my shawl."

The day was mild and skating on the pond was a distant memory. Spring was in full bloom. The snowdrops were already past and the daffodils and forsythia and even a few tulips were blooming. The sun warmed my face as I eagerly took my place beside Ray in his carriage. Mud season was over and the ride up to the farm was enjoyable. Soon all would be green and warm. The river was running high with the melted snow off the higher mountains. I was enjoying the day except for the heaviness in my heart when I thought of Hunter. Just a few hours earlier I had come back from the butcher to see Hunter ride by. It was actually the only time I had seen him since Easter morning. He was headed out of town and when he saw me, he merely nodded. He could have waved and smiled. But of course, I did not smile either. I did not know what was going on in his life and did not want to act too happy to see him if he was secretly courting Lucille.

I could see the lambs already as we approached the farm. They were enjoying the sunshine and running over the green meadows. Ray dropped me off at the end of the lane and said he would be back in a half hour or so. I knew he would not leave without a quick visit with Sylvia when he returned, so I did not hurry.

Tim saw me as I approached the barn. I had seldom seen him since the Christmas Party. Now he was in his work clothes, obviously enjoying his work with the sheep.

"So you finally made it to my farm," he greeted me.

"Ray dropped me off on his way to see a patient. Oh, look at those lambs frolicking out on the meadow."

"They love the sunshine."

We stood a moment and looked out over the field. Every so often one would jump straight up in the air with all four legs.

"They must have springs in their feet," I said, laughing over their antics.

"You would think so," he answered, grinning. "I love watching them." He paused, turning to me. "And how are you?" He looked at me closely and I felt it was not just a casual, polite question.

"I'm...okay. The winter was long and I am glad for springtime."

"We all are. Come into the barn. I have a lamb that needs some extra loving care and Sylvia is going to feed it in a few minutes. Or better yet, why don't you run in and maybe Sylvia will give you the honor of feeding it."

I went to the house and knocked. Sylvia was surprised to see me and, of course, happy to hear that Ray would be dropping in. We soon went out to the barn where the lamb was in a pen. I fell in love with it immediately. She put it in my arms and I did not want to let it down again. I loved holding it and wanted to take it home with me. But the lamb was hungry. Sylvia showed me how to feed it and then let me do the honors. The lamb was very small. It was the smaller one of twins and would not have made it without the regular feeding with the bottle. But it was getting stronger. I put the lamb down and I held the bottle and it drank very willingly. It was so much fun.

The time went quickly and before I knew it, Ray was back and seeing us at the barn, came over to us.

I saw the look he and Sylvia gave each other and I was envious.

"Ray, do you have time for a cup of coffee?" she asked.

"Always."

"How about you, Amber?"

"Actually, I'd rather be out here with the lambs."

Of course, I would have been glad for the coffee, but I was thinking they would rather be alone. I wandered around and then just stood in the barn and enjoyed the scene before me. A mother sheep who was still waiting to give birth looked very fat. There was a pen where several lambs were frolicking about. One lamb came over to me and let me pet it and I was soon talking to it. As I talked, I heard Tim coming through the barn behind me and as he got closer to me I turned, smiling.

"I just love..."

I instantly sobered. This was not Tim. It was Hunter. I stood transfixed, not moving, remembering not to smile and to play it cool.

He continued walking slowly, but determinedly toward me, speaking not a word, and not stopping until he was right in front of me, his blue eyes searching my own brown ones.

"How are you Amber?"

"I am fine," I said, which of course was an untruth.

Hunter just stood and looked at me, clearly not believing what I just told him.

"I don't think you are," he said slowly, and I could have cried. It felt so good that he was concerned about me. But I had to remember Lucille. I did not know how to respond to his comment and stood a bit dumbly before him, while his blue eyes searched mine.

"Why do I get the feeling that I have somehow fallen from grace in your eyes and have been shoved off your friends' list?"

Hunter's look was such a mix of curiosity mixed with sadness that it instantly brought tears to my eyes. It was not my fault that we were not very friendly anymore. Or maybe it was. I blinked my eyes, no words possible.

"I would like to come to see you this evening," he said softly, never taking his eyes from mine and saying it in such a way that I had no choice in the matter.

I did not expect this. What did he have to say to me? I could still see him chopping wood and how the pieces were flying and remembered he said it was because of me. I was scared to hear why he wanted to talk to me. I was scared he would confirm that he was involved with Lucille, although why he would have to tell me, I did not know. But as I looked into his eyes, I also saw kindness, openness and caring. My emotions were very near the surface and I found myself blinking back tears lest they slip down my cheeks.

"I don't think we have anything to talk…" I looked beyond him and out the door to the blue sky as a tear rolled down my face.

"I think we do," he replied softly. "I used to feel a warm glow when I talked to you. Now I get an icy chill." He paused. "This evening at seven o'clock I am coming to pick you up."

"Why do we need to talk?"

I was scared of this talk. All I could see was Lucille. I did not want to hear what he had to say.

He put his hand against my face and brushed the tear from my cheek.

"Because of this."

My resolve to stay cool wanted to melt when I felt his hand on my face.

"Are you hearing me?"

I swallowed at the tone of voice.

"Yes."

He stood a moment longer, his eyes fixed on my face, trying to read my thoughts.

"Till then."

He turned then and walked away from me. I feasted my eyes on his broad back until he left the barn. I was happy and sad at the same time. He melted my heart, but I had to be strong. I had to brace myself and remain cool. Valentine's Day was far behind us and maybe I misunderstood him. But Easter morning proved that there was a connection yet between him and Lucille and it scared me to even think about it.

We ate supper at six. Ray was called away to a patient and Papa and I were soon done. When Papa saw me looking at the clock, he asked me what my plans were for the evening.

"I saw Hunter today and he wants to talk tonight. "

"Ahh," said Papa after a moment or two. "So you will be gone this evening."

"I don't know. Maybe we will talk here," I said scrubbing the dishes.

Papa looked at the clock. "When is he coming?"

"Seven."

"You better go get ready."

"I think it will just be a quick thing and I am not treating it as anything special. Rumor has it that he is getting serious about Lucille."

There was a bit of a pause as Papa thought about what I told him.

"So you will meet him in your everyday dress?"

"It is a good dress."

"Go put on your blue dress."

"My blue dress? Whatever for? We are just talking."

"Do it for me. I like that blue dress. You like Hunter, don't you?"

I was surprised at Papa. He was not letting this go.

"Yes, Papa. I like him, but he has never actually asked me out and has never given me any reason to build my hopes on him. And now it seems he is finally interested in Lucille."

I heard the tears in my voice and suddenly I was a little girl again, telling Papa my woes. And then Papa did a strange thing. He got up from his chair and came and put his arms around me. It shocked the tears right out of me. But I knew if no one else loved me, Papa did.

"Will you wear the blue dress?"

"For you, Papa. Only for you."

I heard the knocker promptly at seven. Papa had disappeared and Ray was not back yet. I answered the door with mixed feelings. I was convinced Hunter knew I was in love with him and now he was coming to tell me about Lucille and I did not want to hear it. He could marry whomever he pleased. I would, I hoped, eventually get over it.

But when I opened the door and looked into those intense blue eyes I could not imagine ever forgetting him. Not that he ever was "mine" except in my daydreams.

"Good evening," I said, giving him a fleeting look and trying to act like I was saying hello to a brother-in-law.

"Good evening, Amber."

I wished he had not said my name. It just made things harder. It sounded more intimate. Dear God, help me through this. I saw the admiration in his eyes as he took in the blue dress. He opened his mouth as if to comment, but closed his mouth again without speaking.

Murf came and wound his body around Hunter's legs. I wanted to tell Murf not to be so friendly. I did not know if Hunter was friend or enemy at this point. I also knew that Hunter was studying me and I was nervous. Neither of us seemed to have anything to say.

"Are we going away?" I asked. "We could talk here."

"We will go somewhere else to talk."

He seemed to have it all planned. His look was sober and he did not say where he was taking me. It seemed we were doing little talking and our words seemed stilted. I went for my shawl and tried not to think how handsome this man was as he helped me put it over my shoulders. And then, without a word, we went out the door and to his carriage.

I was curious where we were going. Would he take me to an inn to talk? Although the day was mild, it would be too cool to sit out. He drove the carriage along Park Avenue and turned left toward town. At North Street, he turned left again, past our house and up past the library. All without either of us speaking. As we passed Laura's house I was shocked to see Papa at her door. What was he doing at Laura's house this evening? He had said nothing of going there. But I had no time to think that through because now we were out of town and driving into Hunter's lane. Ruggles must have thought his master was losing his mind, to be home so soon. Only when he stopped the carriage, did Hunter look at me.

"I don't think your Papa would approve of this, but I want to be undisturbed when we talk."

I did not know what to say, so I said nothing. Yes, I supposed, Papa would disapprove of us being here alone.

Hunter led the horse back into his stall and walked me to his house. He even walked me to the front door. I laughed a bit then. Not a real laugh.

"I even get to come in the front door this time."

"You are my guest," he said simply. There was no banter.

He opened the door and the glow from the hearth gave a welcoming light as we entered. He first began lighting lamps and then came and took my shawl.

"You look nice in that dress," he said softly.

"Thanks," I replied, but even as I answered him, I told myself not to listen to his compliments. This man is merely being nice. He is good at being nice I reminded myself.

As Hunter placed my shawl on a chair, I casually looked around the room. And then I saw the staircase. It looked different. It looked brand new. I had been in this room when Hunter was laid up with a bad leg. I did not remember the railing being so elegant. It gleamed in the light of the lamps. The balustrades were certainly fashioned by a craftsman.

"Wow," I said, not able to hide my appreciation for the fine work. "Did you do this?"

Hunter stood by me. "I did all but the craft work on the balustrades. The old railing was in bad shape. Do you like it?"

"I do."

"I'm happy with it, too. I bought the house from Dr. Toome's son who inherited it but did not want to live here. He was already established in New York City and did not want to leave. So he gave me a good deal, and left most of the furniture. Now that I am comfortable with my work clientele in Steeplechase, I am working at improving the place. The railing was wobbly and shabby."

I was silent. As I looked around, I thought of things I would do to the house. Things to make it homey and bright. A colorful afghan, a nice pillow, a plant or two on the deep windowsills. A brighter picture on the wall. And then I caught myself and quit dreaming.

"Should I never marry, I shall rent the house out and add on to the office. I don't need a lot of space."

His comment hit me. I had him nearly married to Lucille and now he was suggesting that he might never marry.

"What a waste." I said it softly, turning a bit from him.

"What do you mean? Someone would be enjoying the house."

"I did not mean the house," I said under my breath, and barely audible, but I did not look at him. I said no more. He had not brought me here to see his house. He wanted to talk. I would not help him with small talk this evening.

"Would you like a cup of coffee?"

I wanted to say no, but thought maybe I would be glad to be doing something with my hands. They seemed to be dangling uselessly at my sides.

"Yes, please."

"And you take sugar and cream."

"I do."

"Take a seat while I get it."

I took a seat, my heart pounding. I did not want to cry, but I felt close to it already. He was getting me a cup of coffee in his own house. A new thing. I loved being here with him. But I did not dare let myself go. This was, I was sure, about Lucille. Why did we have to talk? He never courted me. If he wanted Lucille, let him have her. I steeled myself for the coming discussion and soon Hunter was back with two steaming cups of coffee.

The coffee was too hot to drink, so I set it down on a small table and sat back on the sofa. Hunter stood by the hearth and fed the fire. Finally, he turned to me, his back to the fire.

"So, Amber, we have not had a very serious talk lately and I am remembering something you told me some weeks ago."

"What was that?"

"You said that you were chopping wood."

"Oh, that." His blue eyes watched me closely. I did not expect this introduction. I smiled a wee bit. Again, not a real smile. "It was a figure of speech." I looked into the fire, ill at ease.

"Who were you chopping up?"

The question was asked softly. I hesitated and looked at my cup rather than at him.

"You," I whispered and then quickly sipped my coffee.

"So I assumed. You say that without apology."

"You made no apology the day you were chopping me up."

"No, Amber. Never would I chop you up even figuratively."

"Your memory seems to be failing," I responded, remembering my shock at his words.

"I have a good memory, but you misunderstood my comment. You were the cause of my frustration, but it was myself I was chopping up."

I had to think about that a bit.

"You also said I was intruding by bringing the book to you."

"No, Amber, it had nothing to do with your coming that day. What I meant was that you intruded in my life plans in general."

"That does not sound like a compliment but you have my apology for intruding."

Anything to get this over with, but I heard the tears in my voice. Hunter must have heard them, too, because he came and sat beside me. I felt myself stiffen. I had to keep cool and I was blinking back tears. I cleared my throat and took a deep breath.

"Hunter, we do not need to talk. You have your life. I have mine. You can marry whomever you please." I almost choked on my own words. Who was talking about marriage? That was not what I meant to say. To save myself, I added, "I heard that you may be getting married to Lucille and that is your business."

Hunter took my hand and I knew I should yank it out of his hand, but it was so warm and big and comforting. No way could I pull my hand from his.

"Where did you hear that gossip?"

I did not answer. I was thinking how nice it was with my hand in his and did not want to make Mindy the gossip.

"We do need to talk, Amber. I need to tell you about Lucille."

"I don't need to know about her," I said, fighting to keep my voice steady even as I allowed him to hold my hand.

"Yes, Amber, you must know."

Suddenly there were footsteps running up on the porch and the knocker sounded. Hunter quickly got up and went to the door. It was an anxious farmer and our talk was over. Being a doctor's daughter, I was used to interruptions but this was the wrong time for an interruption. Or maybe I was spared a bit more time.

Hunter closed the door and turned to me, apologetically.

"It is okay, Hunter. I'll walk home."

"I shall take you home. Or do you want to come along?"

I was surprised he asked but when his eyes swept my blue dress, I shook my head.

"No. Not tonight. Just go."

"No," he said decisively, "I shall take you home."

I don't remember what, if anything, was said on the way home. I just know that when we got to my house, he apologized once more.

"I am very sorry, Amber."

I gave him a sad smile. "That is life, Hunter."

And then he was off.

I was home before Papa. I went up to my room, glad I did not have to face anyone. However, shortly thereafter I heard the door downstairs and I went into the hallway.

"Is that you, Papa?"

"Yes. What are you doing home already?" He came and stood at the bottom of the stairs. He looked very concerned.

"Hunter had to go tend to a sick cow."

There was a grunt from Papa. "Did you get everything straightened out?"

"What do you mean?"

"You know what I mean."

I did not want to answer but Papa stood firmly at the bottom of the stairs, waiting for my answer.

"No. No time." Silence. "I saw you at Laura's house."

I thought Papa looked at me in surprise. He hesitated just a moment.

"I thought since she spent so much time helping to make things nice for tomorrow, she should come, too."

"I am glad you invited her," I said. And I was.

CHAPTER 33

By the time our family and varied guests were ready to eat on Sunday, our family reunion also included Laura, Sylvia, Dennis, Gloria and Hunter. The last guest was a surprise because Papa just invited Hunter at church. The picnic was at one o'clock and although May can be cool and rainy, God blessed our gathering with a surprisingly mild day with plenty of sunshine and a full family gathering.

At one o'clock the last of the family arrived and we were all starving. Gloria brought the hot ham out in a roasting pan full of savory slices of meat. We set everything up on the village green, just across from the house. We had tables of salads, relishes and extra tables for desserts. We put blankets on the ground and set up as many chairs as possible. I was so busy with food and family that I really did not have time to think about Hunter, although to say I was unaware of him would be a lie. I was always aware of where he was, but other than a half smile in his direction, I did not speak to him. When my farmer brothers learned he was a vet, there was no shortage of conversation between them.

It was so much fun having all my siblings together. The last time we were all together was such a sad time. We were all in shock yet over Mama's death. This time there was a new baby and announcements of other babies on the way. The little children had so much fun running in the park, and even Murf joined us but he often had to run for his life from children who held him too tightly. The chatter of the family and the good food made for a very pleasant afternoon.

It was just as we were having dessert, that Bentley Queens came by. I had not seen him since our carriage ride together and it was nice to observe his big grin as he approached the party. He was immediately offered some apple pie by my sister Ruby, who knew him well. He took it gratefully. In the meantime, I was sitting with Susan and hearing all her baby stories and at the same time keeping Hunter, who was ever in my thoughts, in my line of vision. Our discussion had been brought to a quick end the evening before. I wondered if and when it would resume. He wanted to tell me about Lucille, he had said. Just what did he want to tell me about her?

"This Hunter," Susan said, suddenly looking at him mingling with the men, "he seems like a nice person."

"He is," I said a bit wistfully.

"I do not see a wife."

"There is no wife."

"Then why are you not flirting with him?"

I had to laugh at her brashness. "It is a long story and I am not about to go into it with the man within sight."

"So there is some history with him?"

"One could say so."

As I said this, I looked at Hunter who was now chatting with Bentley. The old man was grinning one of his famous grins while Hunter was leaning a bit in his direction, trying to understand what he was saying. Bentley had a soft voice and with all the children running around shouting and everyone chatting, I could understand his need to listen carefully. Suddenly Murf raced past me with a child chasing him and my attention was diverted from Hunter. However, when I looked at him again, he and Bentley were both staring at me. Bentley was smiling from ear to ear and Hunter was just looking wide-eyed at me as if seeing me for the very first time. It made me nervous. Bentley was always teasing me about a boyfriend and who knows what he may have said to Hunter. I sure hoped he was not telling Hunter he should be courting me. I doubted that Hunter would want any push in that direction from anyone. He was very capable of getting his own girlfriend and he did not seem to want to commit. I looked away, but my curiosity would not let me look elsewhere for long. When I again looked at Hunter and Bentley, Hunter slowly began walking across the lawn toward me, his eyes never leaving my face. And I found it impossible to look away. It reminded me of the time he came to me on the cabin porch on the mountain and kissed me. But I was sure that was not his intention now.

When Hunter reached my chair, he simply stood for a few moments and looked down at me. His face was a mixture of sternness and merriment. I could not think what was going on, but his intense look brought the heat to my face. He finally spoke, leaning down so his face was not far from mine.

"So it was you that hung the sign on my carriage."

I was so shocked I simply looked at him a moment, eyes wide. This was so out of the blue, it took me a moment or two to regain my composure. Finally, I realized I had to defend myself.

"I was nowhere near Pipers Hill that day!"

"That, my dear," said Hunter, his eyes never leaving my face, "is not what I said."

I finally pulled my eyes away and looked at Bentley who was still standing at the same spot, grinning at us. I could not figure this out. What did Bentley know of the sign?

"What makes you say this?"

"Because after acting like you were so innocent of the whole deal, I would like to hear you speak the truth this time."

Hunter's face was a study. There was a very pleased look on his face, but his words were spoken very seriously. As for me, I was nearly squirming with guilt and there was no way I could escape his questions.

"I admit to nothing," I said, knowing that somehow the jig was up, but not ready to admit it. "You have no reason to think I would do such a thing."

"Stand up, Amber."

I looked at him just a moment, wondering where this was going.

There was something about the tone of his voice and the look in his eyes that I knew I had no choice. I stood, with his help.

"Now we shall walk to my carriage."

I caught my breath. What was going on? I looked at him to protest, but his hand was on the small of my back as he propelled me in the direction of his carriage. I did not look at Susan or anyone else. I am sure she was not believing her ears or eyes. To my dismay, I could tell that others of the family were taking note of what was happening. I caught another glimpse of Bentley, who was still standing where he had been and was grinning from ear to ear. And then we were at the carriage.

"Now, Miss McDurfee, you will step up into the carriage."

I was suddenly remembering something he had once said about what he would do if he caught the person who hung the sign.

"I am not doing this, Hunter."

"Oh, yes you are," he said. And with that he put his hands on my waist and in a moment I was in his carriage. As I sat down, he reached into the back of the carriage and pulled out the "Just Married" sign. Then he walked toward the back of the carriage.

"Hunter! You can't..."

I stood up and attempted to step off the carriage. But with two strides, Hunter was back at the carriage, his hand on my arm.

"Oh, yes I can, Amber. This is payday. I have waited a long time and I should have suspected you from the beginning. I was just so sure it happened on Pipers Hill. And," he continued with a very satisfied smile, and a firm tone in his voice, "I am warning you that any attempt to get away will result in me bringing you back to the carriage. Even if I have to carry you."

And with that he turned once more and fastened the sign. I was scared to move. By the time he had hung the sign we had an audience. Pastor Dennis, who knew about the sign, began hooting with laughter. Others joined in. I looked at no one. My face burned. Then Hunter jumped into the carriage, and with a triumphant look at me, flicked the reins.

I was so thoroughly confused with my emotions. A part of me wanted to have fun. Another side of me was totally embarrassed, especially since the Lucille thing. I wanted to laugh and cry at the same time. Hunter was making me pay big time. I hid my head in my hands, trying to collect my wits.

"Amber," said my determined driver, "you are making it look like we are having our first fight. You better raise your head or we shall have to kiss and make up."

That brought my head up.

By now we had passed the church and rounded the curve to the stop sign at Main Street. If he turned left we would be going toward all the stores.

"Please, not Main Street," I begged.

I do not know if I changed his mind or not. Perhaps he had not planned to turn left. Maybe he himself did not want to drive on Main Street. After all, this concerned him also and the gossips would be busy. At any rate, Hunter wordlessly turned right, away from town and went to the first street and turned right again. Here and there I heard some whistles or a shout from someone seeing the sign. But at least there were less people on this side street. We drove several blocks, which took us to the north edge of town. There he turned right to North Street. I hoped we would now return to the park, but instead, he turned left and in a short time we were driving in his lane. All this time Hunter said nothing, but every so often he would turn and look at me, a very pleased expression on his handsome face. I looked straight ahead. I did not know how to act. I did not know where I stood with Hunter. His friend Lucille stood solidly between us. I was still trying to figure out how he knew I had hung the sign and what Bentley had to do with it. For surely it was Bentley who told him.

"What makes you think it was me?"

Hunter looked at me and shook his head.

"Amber, Amber. You will not admit it, will you? You know where Bentley lives. His bedroom window faces the back of the inn. He can see over the low roof of the inn's livery that borders his property. He says he always looks out the window to the inn before getting into bed." Hunter paused. "Need I say more?"

"It is dark back there."

"You should know. That is why Mindy held the lantern for you. Or at least I presume it was Mindy."

I let out a groan. That is all the admitting of guilt he would get from me. I said nothing as we drove past his office, then turned on a path past the animal cemetery where my poor Muggins was buried, on out a short lane to a strand of sugar maples. Here he stopped, tethered Ruggles to a tree and reached for my hand.

"Are you very angry with me?" he asked softly as he helped me out of the carriage.

"Let's say I am totally embarrassed."

He gave me a long look and putting his hand on my back, guided me to a little brook that flowed beyond the trees. It was a nice view. The Champlain Valley was bathed in sunshine. Trees were budding and birds were singing and building nests. After a few moments of silence, Hunter spoke.

"I would like to continue our conversation from last evening." He waited for a response but I said nothing. I steeled myself for his words. "I see it is important for me to tell you about Lucille," he continued.

I did not look at him, but instead I allowed my eyes to sweep the broad Champlain Valley. There was an old wooden bench under one of the trees and Hunter guided me to it. But he did not sit down with me.

"Lucille and I met on the first day of school in third grade. We lived in the same village although she had just moved there and was a total stranger to me. She was walking just ahead of me as we approached the school. It was raining and it began to rain harder just as we got on the school property and she ran, slipped and fell in the mud. She looked bad. Especially for the first day in a new school. She got up and looked like she was going to cry. On the porch of the school there were a few boys who burst out laughing at her. I realized there was no way she could go into the schoolroom with that muddy dress. I told her I would walk home with her so she could change her dress. She looked so relieved that I knew I had done the right thing. When we got back to school, she explained why she was late and so did I. She was excused. I was not. I had to stay after school a half hour. But we were friends ever since. We did not spend much time together in school, but she lived close by and we went fishing together, to church, played hide and seek with others from the village and somehow got into trouble on a regular basis. Then we hit eighth grade and somehow we got timid around each other and we drifted apart. Soon after that, her family moved away. I had no clue what happened to her.

"However, on the evening before the barbecue at the mayor's house, she stopped in at my place. She was in the area for a wedding and heard my name mentioned and found out I was the local veterinarian. She stopped in to see if we could get together the next evening—her last before leaving for home. Since I was already invited to the barbecue, and it was our only chance to see each other, I invited her to come along." He paused, and since I made no comment, he then continued. "Then at Christmas, as you know, she came to her aunt and uncle for the holiday and we met again. And then, in March she was in the area once more and you saw us skating on the pond."

He stopped talking for a moment. I remained silent.

"When Lucille came the first time, we renewed our acquaintance. When she came the second time, I knew she came for Christmas with her relatives. However, when she came the third time, I realized she came not to see her aunt and uncle, but she came to see me."

He stopped and I could hear the gurgle of the brook.

"You do not need to tell me this. You don't need my permission to court her," I said, but to my dismay, my voice trembled just a bit. I kept looking out across the valley, but I was seeing Lucille. I was hearing her talking to her friend that night at the inn. She was going to get Hunter.

"Look at me, Amber."

I blinked back the tears and saw the kindness in his eyes and knew that I loved this man deeply and could not bear the thought of losing him.

"Realizing now that she came to see me, I told her about you."

"About me?" I could barely hear my own voice.

"About you," he said softly. "I told her I would be her friend, but it would never be anything more." He paused. "I told her my heart belonged to someone else."

I quit breathing and blinked back tears. I just looked at him, and I am sure my heart was in my eyes.

"I was not very smart about the relationship with Lucille. We always had fun together, but when I saw you standing by the bonfire and looking out on the ice, I sensed your pain. I wanted to skate with you but I felt obligated to skate with her since she did not know any-one else. However, when you told me you went home and chopped wood, I knew I was wrong in what I did."

My mind was spinning. What was he telling me? I remembered his own literal chopping wood again. I needed time to think.

"Why were you angry with me when you were chopping wood?"

"I was not angry with you. But you were a big part of my frustra-tion. I had no intention of falling in love again. I had a bad experience some years before and I was convinced girls were not to be trust-ed. When Lucille suddenly came on the scene I spent time with her, knowing I would not want to marry her. In the meantime, you got sick. When I was given the chickens, I decided this was my chance to see you. I enjoyed that afternoon. Then you went to Burlington. So I buried myself in my work here at the house. I wanted to visit you, but you had been giving me the cold shoulder and I told myself I would just live alone and not marry. That would be less problematic. I made myself remember my experience with Debbie."

In the pause that followed, I spoke.

"Tell me about Debbie."

Hunter took a step away from me, looking at the ground first and then out across the valley.

"There is really not much to tell. I thought I was in love with her and she with me. We spent a lot of time together. Her affections must have cooled and I was slow to notice. It was my brother who clued me in that she was seeing someone else on the side. So one night I did some spying in the town park and discovered that what he said was true. I let her know I saw her, then I...." He paused, grinned a bit and continued. "I did something Jesus told His disciples to do if those they preached to rejected them. I made sure she saw me, then I took off my shoe and blew the dust off of it. Then I walked away and never saw her again." He paused. "And as I walked out of that park, I told myself I would never trust a woman again."

A blue jay flew over us, screeching. I watched a bee bury itself in a yellow buttercup. My thoughts were tumbling over each other, not making any sense.

"During this winter I spent a lot of time alone. And discovered that I was lonesome. So I kept myself busy. However, I finally admitted to myself that I did want to get married, and I knew whom I wanted to marry. And then Lucille showed up and we went skating and you saw us and went home again. On top of that, I was invited to your brother's birthday party."

He looked away from the valley, his blue eyes nailing me.

"And at the supper table, you very neatly placed an iceberg between us."

My own eyes strayed to the sunlit valley. So he had felt it. I was secretly pleased.

"I suspected that you were hurting. I was hurting also," he said.

"But Lucille came again," I said, remembering my sad Easter, "and you went to her aunt and uncle for Easter dinner."

"It was not my choice, but my plans had changed and when she invited me, I had no excuse not to go. She knew where my feelings lay but, I admit, she did not give up easily."

I said nothing. I was trying to comprehend what was happening.

Suddenly Hunter was down on one knee and he took my hand in his.

"I am willing to trust again, Amber. I know I love you and do not want to live without you. I want you to be my wife, the mother of my children, my other half. I want to marry you. Will you have me?"

I threw my arms around him, tears of happiness streaming down my face.

"I will be all that for you. You have my whole heart," I said, trying to stifle my tears.

He somehow got to his feet and took me in his arms and kissed me. It was not the same kind of kiss he had given me on the mountain. There was a lot more emotion in this kiss. A lot more promise.

After a few minutes, he just looked down in my face.

"I wanted to propose last evening. You looked so lovely in your blue dress. I'd never seen you so beautiful."

"I did not wear it for you," I said sheepishly. "I wore it for Papa."

"For Papa?"

"He wanted me to dress up for last evening. I was not going to. Mindy heard Lucille's aunt tell a woman in the bakery that she hoped for a June wedding. I was sure you were going to tell me that you and Lucille were getting married and I did not want to dress up for that. Strange, now that I think back, it is almost as if Papa knew what the evening would hold."

"He had a good idea."

"What do you mean?"

"I hoped we could clear things up. So I asked his permission perhaps a month ago already, to marry you."

"That long ago?" I wailed. "And I went through all this misery since then?"

He had to smile. "You were not the only one miserable. By the way, your Papa said he picked me out for you the first time I came for supper."

"He is the best Papa in the world," I said. "He never said a word to me, but no wonder he kept inviting you for supper."

Hunter smiled down at me with eyes that turned my insides to jelly.

"Was the valentine really from you?"

"Of course."

"I thought so, after you told me to enjoy it, but..."

"And then you doubted."

"I think I had reason to doubt."

"Do you still doubt me?"

"No."

He kissed me again. "And now I better get you home."

"Do we have to?"

He laughed his wonderful deep chuckle. "You seldom see your family. But first, let me do something to this sign."

Fifteen minutes later we drove the carriage back to Park Avenue and stopped close to the gathered family. They all turned eagerly to us as we got out of the carriage.

"It took you a long time to get back here," said Ray. "Where were you? Is the sign still on?"

"Good things take time," said Hunter, as he watched Ray go back to check the sign.

I said nothing, as I walked up to Susan but I kept my eyes on Ray. I saw his eyes grow bigger.

"Look!" he shouted to anyone within hearing. "Check out this sign!"

Some of the family went to see what Ray was talking about.

"It says 'Just Engaged!'" shouted my brother.

They all just stopped walking and looked at us, wondering if this was another trick. But when Hunter walked up to me and slid his arm around me, the hooting and hollering began. The next fifteen minutes I must have been hugged by everyone present, including Bentley.

"Aren't you glad I told on you?" he asked, blue eyes twinkling and his face beaming.

My siblings were mostly floored. Susan scolded me soundly for not telling her more when she asked.

"Really, I am only engaged since we went on our ride," I said to her. "We were not even courting."

"I want to do the wedding," said Dennis after Gloria was done crowing over the two of us. "I can hardly wait. I've been watching you two skirt around each other for a long time."

Papa finally got to us.

"Well, Hunter," he said, as he gave him a couple thumps on his back, "welcome to the family. It seems you still needed a month to melt the snowman."

"Snowman?" I asked.

Hunter just looked down at me and grinned.

EPILOGUE

*H*unter and I got married on October first. It was autumn in Vermont and the mountains were dressed in their finest colors. The sugar maples were brilliant in their red and golden leaves. Other trees displayed yellow, rust, even some green which added to the color spectrum. It was a wonderful time of the year. The old was passing with a blaze of color, but there would be new leaves in the spring. The old was passing for me also, but the new for me would begin today. Within the hour I would be Hunter's bride. Mrs. Hunter Renwick. I loved the sound of it. I had been ready for a long time. My only regret was that Mama was missing my wedding.

The air was crisp that morning but now, shortly before two o'clock, the sun warmed the air as Mindy, Susan, Papa and I stepped out the front door to walk to the church. Mindy and Susan went on ahead, and Papa and I followed. My family, as well as Hunter's parents and brothers were all at the church. Only Papa stayed back with me. He wanted to walk me to the ceremony that would make Hunter and me a married couple.

I could barely wait to see Hunter. I had not see him since the night before when we had taken a load of my things over to his house. Our house. My heart was full. Papa, it seemed, was in no hurry to get to the church and I matched my steps to his and cherished this walk with him.

"So you approve of Hunter?" I asked as we walked past the parsonage.

"I said many a prayer for you," Papa said, shaking his head. "I think I expected you to eventually wake up and see through Jonas, but you had me worried with Waldo. He just was too eager. He was not thinking of you—just that you would make a good partner in Honduras. But when I saw Hunter the first time, I thought this is someone I could approve of. He would fit in our family. The more I saw of him, the more I liked him. I liked the way he treated you. I could see you were impressed with him. It took a bit of time until you finally got together, but I drew a deep breath when he asked for your hand in marriage."

"Oh, Papa. And I had only thoughts of Hunter and missed seeing you fall in love with Laura. That valentine was from you and Hunter was the one who caught on first."

Papa chuckled. He and Laura had been married on a hot day in August and I was happy for them. Now he would not be alone when Ray left. I expected there would be another wedding sometime within the next year.

I heard some clapping and looked over to the village green. Some strangers strolling through the park had caught sight of us. I smiled and waved to them and now, as we turned in at the church the bell began to ring. My heart beat faster and I already got misty eyed. This was it. Dr. Hunter Renwick was in this church waiting for me, his bride.

We stepped into the church where Mindy and my sister Susan, who were my attendants, waited eagerly. It was cool in the church and a bit dark in the entry. I took a deep breath as the organ music changed and with a quick glance at me, Susan headed up the aisle. Mindy followed just seconds later. And then I took a firm grip on Papa's arm and we stepped into the sanctuary. My legs felt wobbly as I looked over the people to the front of the church. And then I saw him, standing tall and just about as handsome as I had ever seen him. His eyes were fixed on me. He did not smile. It was our last chance to change our minds. What was he thinking when he saw me? Was he regretting this? I only knew I would not change my mind. The closer I got to Hunter, the more I saw in his expression. There was kindness and love in his eyes. By his side stood his two brothers. I had met them just last evening. Fun-loving younger brothers, although both were already married. And now, I was at the alter. With a squeeze of my hand Papa stepped back, and Hunter took his place by my side.

Pastor Dennis, his Bible in his hands was looking very pleased but solemn. And then the ceremony began. In my nervousness, my arm somehow brushed against Hunter's arm and I was glad for the solid feel of this person beside me, as my legs still felt wobbly. Pastor Dennis read the love chapter from the Bible and had words of wisdom for us in a short meditation. And then it was time to pledge our lives to each other. Shall I ever forget the feel of my hand in Hunter's strong hand as he promised to love and care for me? And when I looked into his eyes as I pledged myself to him, my throat caught and I had to blink my eyes to see him clearly. He smiled—just a hint of a smile— but it was there, all wrapped up in love.

And then, with a few simple words from the pastor, we were pronounce husband and wife. What a thrill. I could not comprehend it at all.

The reception was held on the village green. There were tables loaded with food. Mindy had baked the wedding cake and Hunter and I sliced it for everyone. There was so much joy around and in me that I felt like I might burst. Mindy was with Carl again and she had stars in her eyes. Ray and Sylvia stood happily, side by side on the green, content in each other's company. And Papa and Laura? They sat on a park bench holding hands! It was a good day to be alive. It seemed the whole world was celebrating with us. I thanked God for this day and for my husband.

When Hunter finally sought me out to leave for our week-long honeymoon, it was late afternoon. Ray brought Hunter's carriage to the front of the house and loaded our baggage on the carriage. We were headed to the Coopers' cabin on the mountain where Hunter had first kissed me. It would be a wonderful place in autumn. Family and friends stood by as we came out to the carriage. Ray was busy behind the carriage and Hunter and I walked to see what he was up to. Sure enough, there was a new "Just Married" sign hanging there.

Hunter, giving me a significant look, helped me into the carriage. Then before stepping into the carriage himself, he turned to Papa who stood close by. In typical princely fashion, Hunter solemnly took Papa's hand in his. Theirs was a good understanding.

"Thank you for your daughter," I heard Hunter say quietly to Papa.

"Take good care of her," replied Papa, equally as serious, his voice a bit husky.

"Always."

And then Hunter took his place by my side and amid the voices of our friends and family wishing us well, he flicked the reins and Ruggles stepped forward. As we pulled out onto North Street, and headed toward the cabin on the mountain, Hunter's arm slid around me. There were no words needed. His eyes said it all.

THE END

ABOUT *the* AUTHOR

*L*OIS KULP was born in eastern Pennsylvania. At the age of twenty-five, she sailed on the S.S. United States for a two-year term under Rosedale Missions in Espelkamp, Germany, which was one of Hitler's ammunition centers during World War II. Eventually she spent twelve years in Germany, sixteen months of that time in the walled-in city of Berlin. She later moved to Vermont, spending fourteen years there. This book takes place in one of the towns she lived in, although she changed the name for the book. She now resides in eastern Pennsylvania, where she has her roots.